Lisa Kleypas is the au ⬛D0863404⬛ and contemporary romance ⸱ ⸱hed in fourteen languages. In 1985, she was named Miss Massachusetts and competed in the Miss America pageant in Atlantic City. After graduating from Wellesley College with a political science degree, she published her first novel at age twenty-one. Her books have appeared on the *New York Times* bestseller lists. Lisa is married and has two children.

Visit Lisa Kleypas online:

www.lisakleypas.com
www.facebook.com/LisaKleypas
@LisaKleypas

Praise for Lisa Kleypas:

'A funny and charming story that will delight
readers from the first page to the last'
Kirkus Reviews

'Flawlessly written ... Kleypas brings together
richly nuanced characters, an emotionally riveting
plot, and a subtle touch of the paranormal to create an
unforgettable romance that is pure reading magic'
Booklist

'Magical'
RT Book Reviews

By Lisa Kleypas

The Ravenels Series:
Cold-Hearted Rake
Marrying Winterborne
Devil in Spring
Hello Stranger
Devil's Daughter

Friday Harbour Series:
Christmas Eve at Friday Harbour
Rainshadow Road
Dream Lake
Crystal Cove

Travis Series:
Sugar Daddy
Blue-Eyed Devil
Smooth Talking Stranger
Brown-Eyed Girl

Wallflower Series:
Secrets of a Summer Night
It Happened One Autumn
The Devil in Winter
Scandal in Spring

Hathaway Series:
Mine Till Midnight
Seduce Me at Sunrise
Tempt Me at Twilight
Married by Morning
Love in the Afternoon

Bow Street Series:
Someone to Watch Over Me
Lady Sophia's Lover
Worth Any Price

Available from Piatkus Entice:
Again the Magic
A Wallflower Christmas

LISA KLEYPAS

Devil's Daughter

The Ravenels meet
The Wallflowers

piatkus

PIATKUS

First published in the United States in 2019 by Avon Books,
an imprint of HarperCollins publishers
First published in Great Britain in 2019 by Piatkus

3 5 7 9 10 8 6 4 2

A CIP catalogue record for this book
is available from the British Library.

ISBN 978-0-349-40768-5

Printed and bound in Great Britain by
Clays Ltd, Elcograf S.p.A.

Papers used by Piatkus are from well-managed forests
and other responsible sources.

MIX
Paper from
responsible sources
FSC® C104740

Piatkus
An imprint of
Little, Brown Book Group
Carmelite House
50 Victoria Embankment
London EC4Y 0DZ

An Hachette UK Company
www.hachette.co.uk

www.littlebrown.co.uk

To our beloved friends *Amy* and *Scott*,
who left us too early

"*My* candle burns at both ends,
It will not last the night;
But ah, my foes and oh, my friends—
It gives a lovely light."
—EDNA ST. VINCENT MILLAY

Chapter 1

$\mathcal{P}$HOEBE HAD NEVER MET West Ravenel, but she knew one thing for certain: He was a mean, rotten bully. She had known it since the age of eight, when her best friend, Henry, had started writing to her from boarding school.

West Ravenel had been a frequent subject of Henry's letters. He was a heartless, hardened case of a boy, but his constant misbehavior had been overlooked, as it would have been in nearly any boarding school. It was seen as inevitable that older boys would dominate and browbeat younger boys, and anyone who tattled would be severely punished.

Dear Phoebe,
*   I thought it would be fun to go to bording school but it's not. There's a boy named West who always takes my brekfast roll and he's already the size of an elefant.*

Dear Phoebe,
*   Yesterday it was my job to change the candlestiks. West sneaked trick candles into*

*my basket and last night one of them went off
like a rocket and singed Mr. Farthing's brows.
I got my hand caned for it. Mr. Farthing
should have known I wouldn't have done
something so obvyus. West isn't a bit sorry. He
said he can't help it if the teacher is an idyut.*

*Dear Phoebe,
I drew this picture of West for you, so if you
ever see him, you will know to run away. I'm
bad at drawing, which is why he looks like a
pirate clown. He also acts like one.*

For four years, West Ravenel had annoyed and
plagued poor Henry, Lord Clare, a small and weedy
boy with a delicate constitution. Eventually Henry's
family had withdrawn him from school and brought
him to Heron's Point, not far from where Phoebe
lived. The mild, healthful climate of the coastal resort
town, and its famed seawater bathing, had helped to
restore Henry's health and good spirits. To Phoebe's
delight, Henry had visited her home often, and had
even studied with her brothers and their tutor. His intelligence, wit, and endearing eccentricities had made
him a favorite with the Challon family.

There had never been a specific moment when
Phoebe's childhood affection for Henry had turned into
something new. It had happened gradually, twining all
through her like delicate silver vines, blossoming into a
jeweled garden until one day she looked at him and felt
a thrill of love.

She had needed a husband who could also be a friend, and Henry had always been her best friend in the world. He understood everything about her, just as she did him. They were a perfect match.

Phoebe had been the first one to broach the subject of marriage. She'd been stunned and hurt when Henry had gently tried to dissuade her.

"You know I can't be with you forever," he'd said, wrapping his lean arms around her, twining his fingers in the loose curls of her red hair. "Someday I'll fall too ill to be a proper husband or father. To be of any use at all. That wouldn't be fair to you or the children. Or even to me."

"Why are you so resigned?" Phoebe had demanded, frightened by his quiet, fatalistic acceptance of his mysterious ailment. "We'll find new doctors. We'll find out whatever it is that's making you ill, and we'll find a cure. Why are you giving up the fight before it's even started?"

"Phoebe," Henry had said softly, "the fight started long ago. I've been tired for most of my life. No matter how much I rest, I scarcely have enough stamina to last through the day."

"I have stamina for both of us." Phoebe had rested her head on his shoulder, trembling with the force of her emotions. "I love you, Henry. Let me take care of you. Let me be with you for however long we'll have together."

"You deserve more."

"Do you love me, Henry?"

His large, soft brown eyes had glistened. "As much as any man has ever loved a woman."

"Then what more is there?"

They had married, the two of them a pair of giggling virgins discovering the mysteries of love with affectionate awkwardness. Their first child, Justin, was a dark-haired and robustly healthy boy who was now four years old.

Henry had gone into his final decline a year ago, just before the birth of their second son, Stephen.

In the months of grief and despair that had followed, Phoebe had gone to live with her family, finding a measure of solace in the loving home of her childhood. But now that the mourning period was over, it was time to start a new life as a young single mother of two boys. A life without Henry. How strange that seemed. Soon she would move back to the Clare estate in Essex—which Justin would inherit when he came of age—and she would try to raise her sons the way their beloved father would have wished.

But first, she had to attend her brother Gabriel's wedding.

Knots of dread tightened in Phoebe's stomach as the carriage rolled toward the ancient estate of Eversby Priory. This was the first event outside of her family's home that she would take part in since Henry's death. Even knowing she would be among friends and relations, she was nervous. But there was another reason she was so thoroughly unsettled.

The bride's last name was Ravenel.

Gabriel was betrothed to a lovely and unique girl, Lady Pandora Ravenel, who seemed to adore him every bit as much as he did her. It was easy to like Pandora, who was outspoken and funny, and imaginative in a way that reminded her a little of Henry. Phoebe had also found herself liking the other Ravenels she'd met when they'd come to visit her family's seaside home. There was Pandora's twin sister, Cassandra, and their distant cousin Devon Ravenel, who had recently inherited the earldom and was now styled Lord Trenear. His wife, Kathleen, Lady Trenear, was friendly and charming. Had the family stopped there, all would have been well.

But Fate had turned out to have a malicious sense of humor: Devon's younger brother was none other than West Ravenel.

Phoebe was finally going to have to meet the man who'd made Henry's years at school so wretched. There was no way to avoid it.

West lived on the estate, no doubt puttering about and pretending to be busy while sponging off his older brother's inheritance. Recalling Henry's descriptions of the big, lazy sloth, Phoebe envisioned Ravenel drinking and lying about like a seal on the beach, and leering at the housemaids as they cleaned up after him.

It didn't seem fair that someone as good and kind as Henry should have been given so few years, whereas a cretin like Ravenel would probably live to be a hundred.

"Mama, why are you cross?" her son Justin asked innocently from the opposite carriage seat. The elderly nanny beside him had leaned back to doze in the corner.

Phoebe cleared her expression instantly. "I'm not cross, darling."

"Your brows were pointed down and your lips were pinched up like a trout," he said. "You only do that when you're cross or when Stephen's diaper is wet."

Looking down at the baby in her lap, who had been lulled by the repetitive motion of the carriage, she murmured, "Stephen is quite dry, and I'm not at all out of humor. I'm . . . well, you know I haven't kept company with new people for a long time. I feel a bit shy about jumping back into the swim of things."

"When Gramps taught me how to swim in cold water, he told me not to jump in all at once. He said go in up to your waist first, so your body knows what's coming. This will be good practice for you, Mama."

Considering her son's point, Phoebe regarded him with fond pride. He took after his father, she thought. Even at a young age, Henry had been empathetic and clever. "I'll try to go in gradually," she said. "What a wise boy you are. You do a good job of listening to people."

"I don't listen to *all* people," Justin told her in a matter-of-fact tone. "Only the ones I like." Kneeling up on the carriage seat, the child stared at the ancient Jacobean mansion in the near distance. Once the fortified home of a dozen monks, the huge, highly ornamented structure bristled with rows of slender chimneys. It was earthbound, stocky, but it also reached for the sky.

"It's big," the child said in awe. "The roof is big, the trees are big, the gardens are big, the hedges are big . . . what if I get lost?" He didn't sound worried, however, only intrigued.

"Stay where you are and shout until I find you," Phoebe said. "I'll always find you. But there'll be no need for that, darling. When I'm not with you, you'll have Nanny . . . she won't let you stray far."

Justin's skeptical gaze went to the dozing elderly woman, and his lips curled in an impish grin as he looked back at Phoebe.

Nanny Bracegirdle had been Henry's beloved primary caretaker when he was young, and it had been at his suggestion that she oversaw his own children's nursery. She was a calm and comfortable woman, her figure stout in a way that made her lap the perfect place for children to sit while she read to them, her shoulders just right for crying babies who needed soothing. Her hair was a crisp white meringue swirled beneath the cambric pouf of her cap. The physical rigors of her occupation, such as chasing after rambunctious children or lifting chubby infants from the bath, were now largely left to a young nursemaid. Nanny's mind was still sharp, however, and aside from needing an extra nap here and there, she was as capable as she had always been.

The caravan of fine carriages progressed along the drive, conveying the entourage of Challons and their servants, as well as a mountain of leather-bound bags and trunks. The estate grounds, like the surrounding farmland, were beautifully maintained, with deep mature hedges and old stone walls covered with climbing roses and soft, fluttery bursts of purple wisteria. Jasmine and honeysuckle perfumed the air where the carriages came to a slow halt in front of the portico.

Nanny awoke from her light snooze with a start and began to gather odds and ends into her carpetbag. She took Stephen from Phoebe, who followed Justin as he bounded out.

"Justin . . ." Phoebe said uneasily, watching him dart through the mass of servants and family members like a hummingbird, chirping little hellos. She saw the familiar figures of Devon and Kathleen Ravenel—Lord and Lady Trenear—welcoming the arriving guests. There were her parents, and her younger sister Seraphina, her brother Ivo, and Pandora and Cassandra, and dozens of people she didn't recognize. Everyone was laughing and talking, animated by excitement over the wedding. A shrinking feeling came over Phoebe at the thought of meeting strangers and making conversation. Sparkling repartee wasn't even a possibility. If only she were still dressed in protective mourning, with a veil concealing her face.

In the periphery of her vision, she saw Justin trotting up the front steps unaccompanied. Aware of Nanny starting forward, Phoebe touched her arm lightly. "I'll run after him," she murmured.

"Yes, milady," Nanny said, relieved.

Phoebe was actually glad Justin had wandered inside the house—it gave her an excuse to avoid the gauntlet of guests being received.

The entrance hall was busy, but it was calmer and quieter than outside. A man directed the tumult of activity, giving instructions to passing servants. His hair, a shade of brown so dark it could easily have been mistaken for black, gleamed like liquid as the light moved over it. The man listened closely to the housekeeper as she explained something about the arrangement of guest bedrooms. Simultaneously he tossed a key to an approaching under-butler, who caught it with a raised hand and dashed off on some errand. A hall boy carrying a tower of hatboxes stumbled, and the dark-haired man reached out to steady him. After adjusting the stack of boxes, he sent the boy on his way.

The man radiated a crisp masculine vitality that seized Phoebe's attention. He was easily over six feet tall, with the athletic brawn and the sun-bronzed complexion of a man who spent a great deal of time outdoors. But he wore a well-tailored suit of clothes. How curious. Perhaps he was an estate manager?

Her thoughts were interrupted as she noticed her son had gone to investigate the elaborate wood carving on one side of the grand double staircase. She followed him quickly. "Justin, you mustn't wander off without telling me or Nanny."

"Look, Mama."

Her gaze followed the direction of his small forefinger. She saw a carving of a little nest of mice at the base of the balustrades. It was a playful and unexpected touch amid the grandeur of the staircase. A smile spread across her face. "I like that."

"Me too."

As Justin crouched to stare at the carving more closely, a glass marble dropped out of his pocket and hit the inlaid parquet floor. Dismayed, Phoebe and Justin watched the little sphere roll away rapidly.

But its momentum was brought to an abrupt halt as the dark-haired man pinned it with the tip of his shoe in a display of perfect timing. As he finished his conversation, he bent to pick up the marble. The housekeeper bustled away, and the man turned his attention to Phoebe and Justin.

His eyes were shockingly blue in that suntanned face, his brief smile a dazzling flash of white. He was *very* handsome, his features strong and even, with faint, pale whisks of laugh lines radiating from the outer corners of his eyes. He seemed like someone who would be irreverent and amusing, but there was also something shrewd about him, something a bit flinty. As if he'd had his share of experience in the world, and had few illusions left. Somehow that made him even more attractive.

He came to them without haste. A pleasant outdoors scent clung to him: sun and air, a dusty, sedge-like sweetness and a hint of smoke, as if he'd been standing near a peat fire. His eyes were the darkest blue she'd ever seen, the irises rimmed with black. It had been a long time since a man had looked at Phoebe like this, direct and interested, and the slightest bit flirty. The strangest feeling came over her, something that reminded her a little of the early days of her marriage to Henry . . . that shaky, embarrassing, inexplicable desire to press her body intimately against someone else's. Until now, she'd never felt it for anyone but her husband, and never anything like this fire-and-ice jolt of awareness.

Feeling guilty and confused, Phoebe backed away a step, trying to pull Justin with her.

But Justin resisted, evidently feeling it had fallen to him to begin the introductions. "I'm Justin, Lord Clare," he announced. "This is Mama. Papa isn't here with us because he's dead."

Phoebe was aware of a brilliant pink flush racing from her scalp down to her toes.

The man didn't seem a bit flustered, only sank to his haunches to bring his face level with Justin's. His low-pitched voice made Phoebe feel as if she were stretching across a deep feather mattress.

"I lost my father when I wasn't much older than you," he said to Justin.

"Oh, I didn't *lose* mine," came the child's earnest reply. "I know exactly where he is. Heaven."

The stranger smiled. "A pleasure to meet you, Lord Clare." The two shook hands ceremoniously. He held the marble up to the light, viewing the tiny porcelain figure of a sheep embedded into the clear glass marble. "A fine piece," he remarked, and handed it to Justin before standing up. "Do you play Ring Taw?"

"Oh, yes," the boy replied. It was a common game in which players tried to knock each other's marbles out of a circle.

"Double Castle?"

Looking intrigued, Justin shook his head. "I don't know that one."

"We'll play a game or two during your visit, if Mama doesn't object." The man gave Phoebe a questioning glance.

Phoebe was mortified by her inability to speak. Her heartbeat was stampeding out of control.

"Mama isn't used to talking to grown-ups," Justin said. "She likes children better."

"I'm very childlike," the man said promptly. "Ask anyone around here."

Phoebe found herself smiling up at him. "You're the estate manager?" she asked.

"Most of the time. But there's no job at this estate, scullery maid included, that I haven't tried at least once, to gain at least some small understanding of it."

Phoebe's smile faded as a strange, terrible suspicion flickered through her mind.

"How long have you been employed here?" she asked cautiously.

"Since my brother inherited the title." The stranger bowed before continuing. "Weston Ravenel . . . at your service."

Chapter 2

WEST COULDN'T STOP STARING at Lady Clare. He had the feeling if he reached out to touch her, he would come away with his fingers scorched. That hair, blazing from beneath a simple gray traveling bonnet . . . he'd never seen anything like it. Bird-of-paradise red, with glimmers of crimson dancing amid the pinned-up locks. Her skin was flawless ivory except for a tender spray of freckles sprinkled across her nose, like a finishing spice on some luxurious dessert.

She had the look of someone who had been nurtured: educated and well dressed. Someone who had always been lovingly sheltered. But there was a shadow in her gaze . . . the knowledge that there were some things no human being could be protected from.

God, those eyes . . . light gray, with striations like the rays of tiny stars.

When she smiled, West had felt a hot tug deep inside his chest. But immediately after he'd introduced himself, her winsome smile had faded, as if she'd just woken from a lovely dream into a far less pleasant reality.

Turning to her son, Lady Clare gently smoothed

a cowlick at the crown of his dark head. "Justin, we have to rejoin the rest of the family."

"But I'm going to play marbles with Mr. Ravenel," the boy protested.

"Not with all the guests arriving," she countered. "This poor gentleman has much to do. We're going to settle in our rooms."

Justin frowned. "Do I have to stay in the nursery? With the babies?"

"Darling, you're four years old—"

"Almost five!"

Her lips quirked. There was a wealth of interest and empathy in the gaze she bent on her small son. "You may stay in my room, if you like," she offered.

The child was appalled by the suggestion. "I can't sleep in your room," he said indignantly.

"Why not?"

"People might think we were married!"

West concentrated on a distant spot on the floor, struggling to hold back a laugh. When he was able, he took a steadying breath and risked a glance at Lady Clare. To his secret delight, she appeared to be considering the point as if it were entirely valid.

"I hadn't thought of that," she said. "I suppose it will have to be the nursery, then. Shall we go look for Nanny and Stephen?"

The boy heaved a sigh and reached up for her hand. Looking up at West, he explained, "Stephen is my baby brother. He can't talk, and he smells like rotten turtles."

"Not all the time," Lady Clare protested.

Justin only shook his head, as if the point weren't worth debating.

Charmed by the easy communication between the two, West couldn't help comparing it to the stilted exchanges he'd had with his own mother, who had always seemed to regard her offspring as if they were someone else's children who were bothering her.

"There are far worse smells than a baby brother," West told the boy. "Sometime during your visit, I'll show you the foulest-smelling thing on the estate home farm."

"What is it?" Justin demanded in excitement.

West grinned at him. "You'll have to wait to find out."

Looking troubled, Lady Clare said, "You're very kind, Mr. Ravenel, but we won't hold you to that promise. I'm sure you'll be quite busy. We wouldn't wish to impose."

More surprised than offended by the refusal, West replied slowly, "As you wish, my lady."

Seeming relieved, she curtsied gracefully and whisked her son away as if they were escaping something.

Baffled, West stared after her. This wasn't the first time a highly respectable woman had given him the cold shoulder. But it was the first time it had ever stung.

Lady Clare must know about his reputation. His past had been rife with more episodes of debauchery and drunkenness than most men under the age of thirty could ever hope to claim. He could hardly blame Lady Clare for wanting to keep her impressionable child away from him. God knew he would never want to be responsible for ruining a fledgling human being.

Sighing inwardly, West resigned himself to keeping his mouth shut and avoiding Challons during the next few days. Which wouldn't be easy, since the house was bloody full of them. After the newly wedded couple's departure, the bridegroom's family would stay on for at least three or four more days. The duke and duchess intended to take advantage of the opportunity to spend time with some old friends and acquaintances in Hampshire. There would be luncheons, dinners, excursions, parties, picnics, and long nights of parlor entertainments and conversation.

Naturally all this would have to take place at the beginning of summer, when the estate farms were in a ferment of activity. At least the work gave West a justifiable reason to spend most of his time away from the house. And as far from Lady Clare as possible.

"Why are you standing here dumbfloundering?" a female voice demanded.

Torn from his thoughts, West glanced down at his pretty dark-haired cousin, Lady Pandora Ravenel.

Pandora was an unconventional girl: impulsive, intelligent, and usually filled with more energy than she seemed able to manage. Of all three Ravenel sisters, she had been the least likely to marry the most eligible bachelor in England. However, it spoke well of Gabriel, Lord St. Vincent, that he was able to appreciate her. In fact, from all accounts, St. Vincent had gone head over heels for her.

"Is there something you'd like me to do?" West asked Pandora blandly.

"Yes, I want to introduce you to my fiancé, so you can tell me what you think of him."

"Sweetheart, St. Vincent is the heir to a dukedom, with a large fortune at his disposal. I already find him wildly enchanting."

"I saw you talking to his sister, Lady Clare, just now. She's a widow. You should court her before someone else snaps her up."

West's mouth curled in a humorless smile at the suggestion. He might have an illustrious family name, but he had neither fortune nor lands of his own. Moreover, the shadow of his former life was inescapable. Here in Hampshire, he'd made a new start among people who didn't give a rag for London society gossip. But to the Challons, he was a man of ruined character. A ne'er-do-well.

And Lady Clare was the ultimate prize: young, wealthy, beautiful, the widowed mother of an heir to a viscountcy and a landed estate. Every eligible man in England would pursue her.

"I don't think so," he said. "Courting sometimes has the unpleasant side effect of marriage."

"But you've said before that you'd like to see the house filled with children."

"Yes, other people's children. Since my brother and his wife are ably supplying the world with more Ravenels, I'm off the hook."

"Still, I think you should at least become acquainted with Phoebe."

"Is that her name?" West asked with reluctant interest.

"Yes, after a cheerful little songbird that lives in the Americas."

"The woman I just met," West said, "is not a cheerful little songbird."

"Lord St. Vincent says Phoebe is affectionate and even a bit flirtiddly by nature, but she still feels the loss of her husband very deeply."

West tried his best to maintain an indifferent silence. In a moment, however, he couldn't resist asking, "What did he die of?"

"A kind of wasting disease. The doctors could never agree on a diagnosis." Pandora paused as she saw arriving guests funneling into the entrance hall. She tugged West toward the space beneath the grand staircase, her voice lowering as she continued. "Lord Clare was ill since the day he was born. He suffered dreadful stomach pains, fatigue, headaches, heart palpitations . . . he was intolerant to most kinds of food and could hardly keep anything down. They tried every possible treatment, but nothing helped."

"Why would a duke's daughter marry a lifelong invalid?" West asked, puzzled.

"It was a love match. Lord Clare and Phoebe were childhood sweethearts. At first he was reluctant to marry her, because he didn't want to be a burden, but she persuaded him to make the most of the time they had. Isn't that terribly romantic?"

"It makes no sense," West said. "Are we certain she didn't have to marry in haste?"

Pandora looked perplexed. "Do you mean . . ." She paused, trying to think of a polite phrase. ". . . they may have anticipated their vows?"

"That," West said, "or her first child was sired by another man, who wasn't available to wed."

Pandora frowned. "Are you *really* that cynical?"

West grinned at her. "No, I'm much worse than this. You know that."

Pandora moved her hand in a pretend swat near his chin, as if administering a well-deserved reprimand. Deftly he caught her wrist, kissed the back of her hand, and released it.

So many guests had crowded into the entrance hall by then that West began to wonder if Eversby Priory could accommodate them all. The manor had more than one hundred bedrooms, not including servants' quarters, but after decades of neglect, large sections were now either closed off or in the process of restoration.

"Who are all these people?" he asked. "They seem to be multiplying. I thought we'd limited the guest list to relations and close friends."

"The Challons have many close friends," Pandora said, a touch apologetically. "I'm sorry, I know you don't like crowds."

The remark surprised West, who was about to protest that he did like crowds, when it occurred to him that Pandora knew him only as he was now. In his former life, he'd enjoyed the company of strangers, and had lurched from one social event to another in search of constant entertainment. He'd loved the gossip, the flirtations, the endless flow of wine and noise that had kept his attention firmly fixed outward. But since he'd come to Eversby Priory, he'd become a stranger to that life.

Seeing a group of people entering the house, Pandora bounced a little on her heels. "Look, there are the Challons." A mixture of wonder and unease colored her voice as she added, "My future in-laws."

Sebastian, the Duke of Kingston, radiated the cool confidence of a man who had been born to privilege. Unlike most British peers, who were disappointingly average, Kingston was dashing and ungodly handsome, with the taut, slim physique of a man half his age. Known for his shrewd mind and caustic wit, he oversaw a labyrinthine financial empire that included, of all things, a gentlemen's gaming club. If his fellow noblemen expressed private distaste for the vulgarity of owning such an enterprise, none dared criticize him publicly. He was the holder of too many debts, the possessor of too many ruinous secrets. With a few words or strokes of a pen, Kingston could have reduced nearly any proud aristocratic scion to beggary.

Unexpectedly, rather sweetly, the duke seemed more than a little enamored of his own wife. One of his hands lingered idly at the small of her back, his enjoyment in touching her covert but unmistakable. One could hardly blame him. Evangeline, the duchess, was a spectacularly voluptuous woman with apricot-red hair, and merry blue eyes set in a lightly freckled complexion. She looked warm and radiant, as if she'd been steeped in a long autumn sunset.

"What do you think of Lord St. Vincent?" Pandora asked eagerly.

West's gaze moved to a man who appeared to be a younger version of his sire, with bronze-gold hair that gleamed like new-minted coins. Princely handsome. A cross between Adonis and the Royal Coronation Coach.

With deliberate casualness, West said, "He's not as tall as I expected."

Pandora looked affronted. "He's every bit as tall as you!"

"I'll eat my hat if he's an inch over four foot seven." West clicked his tongue in a few disapproving *tsk-tsk*s. "And still in short trousers."

Half annoyed, half amused, Pandora gave him a little shove. "That's his younger brother Ivo, who is eleven. The one *next* to him is my fiancé."

"Aah. Well, I can see why you'd want to marry that one."

Folding her arms across her chest, Pandora let out a long sigh. "Yes. But why does he want to marry *me*?"

West took her by the shoulders and turned her to face him. "Why wouldn't he?" he asked, his voice gentling with concern.

"Because I'm not the sort of girl everyone expected him to marry."

"You're what he wants, or he wouldn't be here. What is there to fret about?"

Pandora shrugged uneasily. "I don't really deserve him," she confessed.

"How splendid for you."

"Why is that splendid?"

"There's nothing better than having something you don't deserve. Just say to yourself, 'Hooray for me, I'm so very lucky. Not only do I have the biggest piece of cake, it's a corner piece with a sugar-paste flower on top, and everyone else is sick with envy.'"

A slow grin spread across Pandora's face. After a moment, she said in an experimental undertone, "Hooray for me."

Glancing over her head, West saw someone approach—someone he had *not* expected to see on this occasion—and a breath of annoyed disbelief escaped him. "I'm afraid I'm going to have to start off your wedding festivities with a small murder, Pandora. Don't worry, it will be over quickly, and then we'll go back to celebrating."

Chapter 3

"WHO ARE YOU GOING to do away with?" Pandora sounded more interested than alarmed.

"Tom Severin," West said grimly.

She turned to follow his gaze, as the lean, dark figure approached. "But you're one of his close friends, aren't you?"

"None of Severin's friends are what I would call close. Generally, we all try to keep out of stabbing distance."

It would be difficult to find a man still on the early side of his thirties who had acquired wealth and power at the speed that Tom Severin had. He'd started as a mechanical engineer designing engines, then progressed to railway bridges, and had eventually built his own railway line, all with the apparent ease of a boy playing leapfrog. Severin could be generous and considerate, but his better qualities were unanchored by anything resembling a conscience.

Severin bowed as he reached them.

Pandora curtsied in return.

West leveled a cold stare at him.

Severin wasn't handsome in comparison to the

Challons—of course, what man would be?—nor was he handsome by strictly conventional standards. But there was something about him that women seemed to like. West was damned if he knew what it was. Severin's face was lean and angular, his build lanky and almost rawboned, his complexion librarian pale. His eyes were an unevenly distributed mixture of blue and green, so that in strong lighting they appeared to be two entirely different colors.

"London was boring," Severin said, as if that explained his presence.

"I feel quite sure you're not on the guest list," West said acidly.

"Oh, I never need invitations," came Severin's matter-of-fact reply. "I go wherever I want. I'm owed favors by so many people, no one would dare ask me to leave."

"I would dare," West said. "In fact, I can tell you exactly where to go."

Before West could continue, Severin turned quickly to Pandora. "You're the bride-to-be. I can tell by the sparkle in your eyes. An honor to be here, delighted, felicitations, et cetera. What would you like for a wedding present?"

Despite Lady Berwick's rigorous instruction in etiquette, the question caused Pandora's propriety to collapse like a pricked balloon. "How much are you going to spend?" she asked.

Severin laughed, delighting in the innocently crass question. "Ask for something big," he said. "I'm very rich."

"She needs nothing," West said curtly. "Especially from you." Glancing down at Pandora, he added, "Mr. Severin's gifts always come with strings. And the strings are attached to rabid badgers."

Leaning closer to Pandora, Severin said in a conspiratorial aside, "Everyone likes my presents. I'll surprise you with something later."

She smiled. "I don't need any gifts, Mr. Severin, but you're welcome to stay for my wedding." Seeing West's reaction, she protested, "He's come all the way from London."

"Where are we going to put him?" West asked. "Eversby Priory is packed full. Every room that's slightly more comfortable than a cell in Newgate has been taken."

"Oh, I wouldn't stay here," Severin assured him. "You know how I am about these ancient houses. Eversby Priory is charming, of course, but I prefer the modern conveniences. I'll be staying in my private train carriage, at the quarry railway halt on your property."

"How appropriate," West remarked sourly, "in light of the fact that you tried to steal the mineral rights to that quarry, even knowing it would leave the Ravenels financially destitute."

"Are you still miffed about that? It wasn't personal. It was business."

Hardly anything was personal to Severin. Which begged the question of why the man was really here. It was possible he wanted to become acquainted with the well-heeled Challon family with future business dealings in mind. Or he could be trolling for a wife.

Despite Severin's staggering fortune and the fact that he owned majority shares in the London Ironstone railway company, he wasn't welcome in upper-class circles. Most commoners weren't, but Severin *especially* wasn't. So far, he hadn't found an aristocratic family that was sufficiently desperate to yield one of their wellborn daughters in matrimonial sacrifice. However, it was only a matter of time.

West scanned the gathering in the entrance hall, wondering what his older brother, Devon, made of Severin's presence. As their gazes met, Devon sent him a grimly resigned smile. *Might as well let the bastard stay*, was his unspoken message. West responded with a short nod. Although he would have enjoyed throwing Severin out on his arse, no good would come of making a scene.

"I'll need only the slightest excuse," West told Severin, his expression deceptively pleasant, "to send you back to London in a turnip crate."

The other man grinned. "Understood. Now if you'll pardon me, I see our old friend Winterborne."

After the railroad magnate had sauntered away, Pandora took West's arm. "Let me introduce you to the Challons."

West didn't budge. "Later."

Pandora gave him an imploring glance. "Oh, *please* don't be stubborn, it will look odd if you don't go to greet them."

"Why? I'm not the host of this event, and Eversby Priory isn't mine."

"It's partly yours."

West smiled wryly. "Sweetheart, not one speck of dust in this place belongs to me. I'm a glorified estate manager, which I assure you the Challons will not find compelling."

Pandora frowned. "Even so, you're a Ravenel, and you have to meet them now because it will be awkward if you're obliged to introduce yourself later while passing one of them in the hallway."

She was right. West cursed beneath his breath and went with her, feeling ill at ease.

Breathlessly Pandora introduced him to the duke and duchess; their teenage daughter, Seraphina; their youngest son, Ivo; and Lord St. Vincent. "You've already met Lady Clare and Justin, of course," she finished.

West glanced at Phoebe, who had turned away on a pretext of brushing invisible lint from the back of her son's jacket.

"We have one more brother, Raphael, who's traveling in America on business," Seraphina said. She had reddish-blond curls and the sweet-faced prettiness usually depicted on boxes of scented soap. "But he couldn't return in time for the wedding."

"That means I can have his cake," said the handsome boy with deep red hair.

Seraphina shook her head and said drolly, "Ivo, Raphael would be *so* glad to know you're managing to carry on in his absence."

"Someone has to eat it," Ivo pointed out.

Lord St. Vincent came forward to shake West's hand. "Finally," he said, "we meet the least seen and most often discussed Ravenel."

"Has my reputation preceded me?" West asked. "That's never good."

St. Vincent smiled. "I'm afraid your family takes every opportunity to praise you behind your back."

"I can't fathom what they find to praise. I assure you, it's all in their imagination."

The Duke of Kingston, the groom's father, spoke in a voice that sounded like expensive dry liquor. "Nearly doubling the estate's annual yields is no figment of the imagination. According to your brother, you've made great strides in modernizing Eversby Priory."

"When one starts at a medieval level, Your Grace, even a small improvement seems impressive."

"Perhaps in a day or two, you might give me a tour of the estate farms and show me some of the new machinery and methods you're using."

Before West could reply, Justin broke in. "He's going to take *me* on a tour, Gramps, to show me the smelliest thing on the farm."

A glow of errant tenderness softened the duke's diamond-blue eyes as he looked at the boy. "How intriguing. I insist on coming along, then."

Justin went to the duchess, locking his arms around her hips with the familiarity of a well-loved grandchild. "You can come too, Granny," he said generously, hanging onto the complex draperies of her blue silk dress.

Her gentle hand, adorned only with a simple gold

wedding band, smoothed his dark, ruffled hair. "Thank you, darling boy, but I would rather spend time with my old friends. In fact"—the duchess sent a quick, vibrant glance to her husband—"the Westcliffs have just arrived, and I haven't seen Lillian for ages. Do you mind if I—"

"Go," the duke said. "I know better than to stand between the two of you. Tell Westcliff I'll be along in a moment."

"I'll take Ivo and Justin to the receiving room for lemonade," Seraphina volunteered, and sent West a shy smile. "We're parched after the journey from London."

"So am I," Phoebe murmured, beginning to follow her younger sister and the boys.

She stopped, however, her back straightening as she heard Lord St. Vincent remark to West, "My sister Phoebe will want to go on the farm tour. It's fallen to her to maintain the Clare lands until Justin comes of age, and she has much to learn."

Phoebe turned to St. Vincent with mingled surprise and annoyance. "As you're well aware, brother, the Clare lands are already being managed by Edward Larson. I wouldn't dream of insulting his expertise by interfering."

"Sister," St. Vincent replied dryly, "I've been to your estate. Larson's a pleasant fellow, but his knowledge of farming hardly counts as 'expertise.'"

West was fascinated to see a tidy spot of unruly pink sweep up Phoebe's chest and throat. It was like watching a cameo come to life.

The brother and sister exchanged a hard stare, engaging in a wordless argument.

"Mr. Larson is my late husband's cousin," Phoebe said, still glaring at her brother, "and a great friend to me. He is managing the estate lands and tenants in the traditional manner, exactly as Lord Clare asked him to do. The tried-and-true methods have always served us well."

"The problem with that—" West began, before he thought better of it. He broke off as Phoebe turned to give him an alert glance.

It felt like a collision, the way their gazes met.

"Yes?" Phoebe prompted.

Wishing he'd kept his mouth shut, West summoned a bland smile. "Nothing."

"What were you going to say?" she persisted.

"I don't want to overstep."

"It's not overstepping if I'm asking." She was irritated and defensive now, her face turning even pinker. With that red hair, it was a riveting sight. "Do go on."

"The problem with traditional farming," West said, "is that it won't work anymore."

"It's worked for two hundred years," Phoebe pointed out, not incorrectly. "My husband was opposed to experimentation that might put the estate at risk, and so is Mr. Larson."

"Farmers are experimental by nature. They've always looked for new ways to get the most they can from their fields."

"Mr. Ravenel, with respect, what qualifications do you have to speak on the subject with such authority?

Did you have farming experience before you came to Eversby Priory?"

"God, no," West said without hesitation. "Before my brother inherited this estate, I'd never set so much as a foot on a farm. But when I started talking to the tenants, and learning about their situations, something quickly became clear. No matter how hard these people worked, they were going to be left behind. It's a matter of simple mathematics. They can't compete with cheap imported grain, especially now that international freight prices have dropped. On top of that, there are no young people left to do the back-breaking labor—they're all heading north in search of factory jobs. The only solution is to modernize, or in five years—ten at most—the tenants will be gone, your country manor will have turned into a big white elephant, and you'll be auctioning its contents to pay your tax bill."

A frown knitted Phoebe's forehead. "Edward Larson has a different view of the future."

"While trying to live in the past?" West's mouth twisted derisively. "I have yet to meet a man who can simultaneously look over his shoulder and see straight ahead."

"You're impertinent, Mr. Ravenel," she said quietly.

"I beg your pardon. In any case, your tenants have been the lifeblood of the Clare estate for generations. You should at least learn enough about their situation to provide some oversight."

"It's not my place to supervise Mr. Larson."

"Not your place?" West repeated incredulously.

"Whose stakes are higher in all of this—his or yours? It's your son's inheritance, by God. If I were you, I'd have a hand in making the decisions."

In the weighted silence that followed, West realized how presumptuous he'd been to lecture her in such a fashion. Looking away from her, he let out a taut sigh. "I warned you I'd overstep," he muttered. "I apologize."

"No," Phoebe said curtly, surprising him. "I wanted your opinion. You've made some points worth considering."

West's head lifted, and he looked at her with unconcealed surprise. He'd fully expected her to give him a sharp set-down, or simply turn on her heel and walk off. Instead, Phoebe had set aside her pride long enough to listen to him, which few women of her rank would have done.

"Although next time you might try a gentler manner," she said. "It usually helps criticism go down easier."

Staring into her silver eyes was like drowning in moonlight. West found himself at a complete loss for words.

They were within arms' reach of each other. How had that happened? Had he moved closer, or had she?

His voice was a husk of sound as he managed a reply. "Yes. I . . . I'll be gentle next time." That hadn't sounded right. "Gentler. With you. Or . . . anyone." None of that sounded right, either. "It wasn't criticism," he added. "Just helpful hints." *Christ.* His thoughts were in a heap.

She was breathtaking up close, her skin reflecting light like the silk of butterfly wings. The lines of her throat and jaw were a precise framework for a mouth as full and rich as flowers in deep summer. Her fragrance was subtle and dry and alluring. She smelled like a clean, soft bed he would love to sink into. The thought made his pulse thump insistently . . . *want* . . . *want* . . . *want* . . . God, yes, he'd love to show her all his gentleness, browsing over that slender body with his hands and mouth until she was quivering and lifting to his touch—

Stop this, you sodding idiot.

He'd gone without a woman for too long. When was the last time? Possibly a year ago. Yes, in London. Good God, how could so much time have passed? After the summer haymaking, he would go to town for at least a fortnight. He would visit his club, have dinner with friends, see a decent play or two, and spend a few evenings in the arms of a willing woman who would make him forget all about red-haired young widows named after songbirds.

"You see, I have to keep my promises to my husband," Phoebe said, sounding nearly as distracted as he felt. "I owe it to him."

That rankled far more than it should have, jolting West out of the momentary trance. "You owe the benefit of your judgment to the people who depend on you," he said in a low voice. "Your greater obligation is to the living, isn't it?"

Phoebe's brows rushed down.

She had taken that as a jab against Henry, and West couldn't say for certain that he hadn't meant it that way. It was absurd to insist the work of farming be done exactly as it had always been, without regard to what might happen in the future.

"Thank you for your helpful hints, Mr. Ravenel," she said coolly, before turning to her brother. "My lord, I would like a word with you." Her expression didn't bode well for St. Vincent.

"Of course," her brother replied, seeming not at all concerned about his imminent demise. "Pandora, love, if you don't mind . . . ?"

"I'm fine," Pandora told him airily. As soon as the pair departed, however, her smile vanished. "Is she going to hurt him?" she asked the duke. "He can't have a black eye for the wedding."

Kingston smiled. "I wouldn't worry. Despite years of provocation from all three brothers, Phoebe has yet to resort to physical violence."

"Why did Gabriel volunteer her for the farm tour in the first place?" Pandora asked. "Even for him, that was a bit high-handed."

"It pertains to an ongoing quarrel," the duke said dryly. "After Henry's death, Phoebe was content to leave all the decisions to Edward Larson. Lately, however, Gabriel has been urging her to take a stronger hand in the management of the Clare lands—just as Mr. Ravenel advised a minute ago."

"But she doesn't want to?" Pandora asked sympathetically. "Because farming is so boring?"

West gave her a sardonic look. "How do you know if it's boring? You've never done it."

"I can tell by the books you read." Turning to Kingston, Pandora explained, "They're all about things like scientific butter making, or pig keeping, or smut. Now, who could possibly find smut interesting?"

"Not that kind of smut," West said hastily, as he saw the duke's brows lift.

"You're referring to the multicellular fungi that afflicts grain crops, of course," Kingston said blandly.

"There are all different kinds of smut," Pandora said, warming to the subject. "Smut balls, loose smut, stinking smut—"

"Pandora," West interrupted in an undertone, "for the love of mercy, stop saying that word in public."

"Is it unladylike?" She heaved a sigh. "It must be. All the interesting words are."

With a rueful smile, West returned his attention to the duke. "We were talking about Lady Clare's lack of interest in estate farming."

"I don't believe the problem stems from a lack of interest," Kingston said. "The issue is one of loyalty, not only to her husband, but also to Edward Larson, who offered support and solace at a difficult time. He gradually assumed responsibility for the estate as Henry's illness worsened, and now . . . my daughter is reluctant to question his decisions." After a reflective pause, he continued with a slight frown, "It was an oversight on my part not to anticipate she would need such skills."

"Skills can be learned," West said pragmatically. "I myself was prepared for a meaningless life of indolence and gluttony—which I was thoroughly enjoying, by the way—before my brother put me to work."

Kingston's eyes glinted with amusement. "I was told you were a bit of a hellion."

West slid him a wary glance. "I suppose that came from my brother?"

"No," the duke said idly. "Other sources."

Damn. West recalled what Devon had said about the gaming club, Jenner's, started by the duchess's father and eventually landing in Kingston's possession. Of all the clubs in London, Jenner's had the deepest bank and the most select membership, which included royalty, nobility, members of Parliament, and men of fortune. An endless flow of gossip and information was passed upward from the croupiers, tellers, waiters, and night porters. Kingston had access to the private information of England's most powerful individuals—their credit, their financial assets, their scandals, and even their health issues.

My God, the things he must know, West thought glumly. "Whatever unflattering rumors you've heard about me are probably true," he said. "Except for the really vile and disgraceful ones: those are definitely true."

The duke seemed amused. "Every man has his past indiscretions, Ravenel. It gives us all something interesting to discuss over port." He offered Pandora his arm. "Come, both of you. I want to introduce you to some of my acquaintances."

"Thank you, sir," West said with a negative shake of his head, "but I'm—"

"You're delighted by my invitation," Kingston informed him gently, "as well as grateful for the honor of my interest. Come along, Ravenel, don't be a hairpin."

Reluctantly West closed his mouth and fell into step behind them.

Chapter 4

FUMING, PHOEBE HAULED HER brother by the arm along a small hallway until she found an unoccupied room. It was sparsely furnished with no specific purpose, the kind of room one often found in very large, old houses. After dragging Gabriel inside, she closed the door and whirled to face him.

"What do you mean by volunteering me for a farm tour, you lunkhead?"

"I was helping you," Gabriel said reasonably. "You need to learn about estate farming."

Of all her siblings, Gabriel was the one to whom Phoebe had always felt closest. In his company, she could make petty or sarcastic remarks, or confess her foolish mistakes, knowing he would never judge her harshly. They knew each other's faults and kept each other's secrets.

Many people, if not most, would have been flabbergasted to learn that Gabriel had any faults at all. All they saw was the remarkable male beauty and cool self-control of a man so elegantly mannered that it never would have occurred to anyone to call him a lunkhead. However, Gabriel could sometimes be arrogant and manipulative. Beneath his charming exterior, there was a steely core that made him ideally suited to oversee the array of Challon properties and businesses. Once he decided what was best for someone, he took every opportunity to push and goad until he had his way.

Therefore, Phoebe occasionally found it necessary to push back. After all, it was an older sister's responsibility to keep her younger brother from behaving like a domineering ass.

"You'd help more by minding your own business," she told him curtly. "If I decide to learn more about farming, it certainly won't be from *him*, of all people."

Gabriel looked perplexed. "What do you mean, 'him of all people'? You've never met Ravenel."

"Good heavens," Phoebe exclaimed, wrapping her arms tightly across her chest, "don't you know who he is? You don't remember? He's *the bully*. Henry's bully!"

Gabriel shook his head, giving her a mystified glance.

"At boarding school. The one who tormented him for almost two years." As he continued to look blank, Phoebe said impatiently, "The one who put trick candles in his basket."

"*Oh.*" Gabriel's brow cleared. "I'd forgotten about that. He's that one?"

"Yes." She began to pace in a tight back-and-forth pattern. "The one who turned Henry's childhood into a nightmare."

"'Nightmare' might be putting it a bit strongly," Gabriel commented, watching her.

"He called Henry names. He stole his food."

"Henry couldn't have eaten it anyway."

"Don't be facetious, Gabriel—this is very upsetting to me." Phoebe's feet wouldn't stay still. "I read Henry's letters to you. You know what he went through."

"I know it better than you," Gabriel said. "I went to boarding school. Not the same one as Henry's, but every last one of them has its share of bullies and petty tyrants. It's the reason our parents didn't send me, or Raphael, until we were mature enough to handle ourselves." He paused with an exasperated shake of his head. "Phoebe, stop ricocheting about like a billiard ball, and listen to me. I blame Henry's parents for sending him away to boarding school when he was so obviously unsuited for it. He was a sensitive, physically frail boy with a fanciful nature. I can't conceive of a worse place for him."

"Henry's father thought it would toughen him," Phoebe said. "And his mother has all the kindness of a baited badger, which is why she agreed to send him back for a second year of hell. But the blame isn't all theirs. West Ravenel is a brute who was never held to account for his actions."

"What I'm trying to explain is that a boarding-school environment is Darwinian. Everyone bullies or is bullied, until the hierarchy is sorted out."

"Did *you* bully anyone when you were at Harrow?" she asked pointedly.

"Of course not. But my situation was different. I was raised in a loving family. We lived in a house by the sea with our own private sand beach. We each had our own pony, for God's sake. It was an embarrassingly perfect childhood, especially in contrast to the Ravenel brothers, who were the poor relations of their family. They were orphaned at a young age and sent to boarding school because no one wanted them."

"Because they were mean little ruffians?" she suggested darkly.

"They had no parents, no family, no home, no money or possessions . . . what would you expect of boys in their situation?"

"I don't care what caused Mr. Ravenel's behavior. All that matters is that he hurt Henry."

Gabriel frowned thoughtfully. "Unless there's something I missed in those letters, Ravenel did nothing particularly vicious. Never bloodied Henry's nose or thrashed him. It was more pranks and name-calling than anything else, wasn't it?"

"Fear and humiliation can inflict far worse damage than fists." Phoebe's eyes stung, and a hard lump formed in her throat. "Why are you standing up for Mr. Ravenel and not my husband?"

"Redbird," Gabriel said, his tone gentling. It was the pet name only he and their father used for her. "You know I loved Henry. Come here."

She went to him, sniffling, and his arms closed around her in a comforting embrace.

In their youth, Henry, Gabriel, Raphael, and their friends had spent many a sunny afternoon at the Challon estate in Heron's Point, sailing little skiffs in the private cove or rambling through the nearby woodland. No one had ever dared bully or tease Henry, knowing the Challon brothers would thrash them for it.

At the end of Henry's life, when he'd been too weak to go anywhere on his own, Gabriel had taken him fishing one last time, carrying him to the bank of his favorite trout stream and setting him on a triangular camp stool. With endless patience, Gabriel had baited the pitches and helped Henry reel the line in, until they had returned with a creel full of trout. That had been Henry's last day outside.

Gabriel patted her back and briefly laid his cheek against her hair. "This situation must be damned difficult for you. Why didn't you mention it before? At least half the Ravenel family stayed with us at Heron's Point for a week, and you didn't say a word."

"I didn't want to cause trouble while you and Pandora were trying to decide if you liked each other well enough to marry. And also . . . well, most of the time I feel like a rain cloud, glooming up the atmosphere everywhere I go. I'm trying not to do that anymore." Stepping back, Phoebe wiped the wet corners of her eyes with her fingertips. "It's not right for me to dredge up past grievances that no one else remembers, especially at such a happy time. I'm sorry I mentioned it at all. But the prospect of being in Mr. Ravenel's company fills me with dread."

"Are you going to say something to him about it? Or would you like me to?"

"No, please don't. It would serve no purpose. I

don't think he even remembers it. Promise you'll say nothing."

"I promise," Gabriel said reluctantly. "Although it seems only fair to give him a chance to apologize."

"It's too late for apologies," she muttered. "And I doubt he would anyway."

"Don't be too hard on him. He seems to have grown up into a decent fellow."

Phoebe gave him a dour look. "Oh? Did you come to that conclusion before or after he lectured me as if I were some feudal overlord who'd just been trampling the peasants?"

Gabriel fought to suppress a grin. "You handled that well," he said. "You took it with good grace when you could have sliced him to ribbons with a few words."

"I was tempted," she admitted. "But I couldn't help remembering something Mother once said."

It had been on a long-ago morning in her childhood, when she and Gabriel had still needed books stacked on their chairs whenever they sat at the breakfast table. Their father had been reading a freshly ironed newspaper, while their mother, Evangeline, or Evie, as family and friends called her, fed spoonfuls of sweetened porridge to baby Raphael in his high chair.

After Phoebe had recounted some injustice done to her by a playmate, saying she wouldn't accept the girl's apology, her mother had persuaded her to reconsider for the sake of kindness.

"But she's a bad, selfish girl," Phoebe had said indignantly.

Evie's reply was gentle but matter-of-fact. "Kindness counts the most when it's given to people who don't deserve it."

"Does Gabriel have to be kind to everyone too?" Phoebe had demanded.

"Yes, darling."

"Does Father?"

"No, Redbird," her father had replied, his mouth twitching at the corners. "That's why I married your mother—she's kind enough for two people."

"Mother," Gabriel had asked hopefully, "could you be kind enough for *three* people?"

At that, their father had taken a sudden intense interest in his newspaper, lifting it in front of his face. A quiet wheeze emerged from behind it.

"I'm afraid not, dear," Evie had said gently, her eyes sparkling. "But I'm sure you and your sister can find a great deal of kindness in your own hearts."

Returning her thoughts to the present, Phoebe said, "Mother told us to be kind even to people who don't deserve it. Which includes Mr. Ravenel, although I suspect he would have liked to deliver a dressing-down to me right there in the entrance hall."

Gabriel's tone was cinder dry. "I suspect his thoughts had less to do with dressing-down than *un*dressing."

Phoebe's eyes widened. "*What?*"

"Oh, come," her brother chided, amused. "You had to notice the way his eyes were waving about on stalks like a lobster about to be boiled. Has it been so long that you can't tell when a man is attracted to you?"

Gooseflesh rose on her arms. One of her hands crept up to her midriff, trying to calm a storm of butterflies.

As a matter of fact, it *had* been that long. She could read the signs of other people's attractions, but not, apparently, when any of it applied to her. This was unknown territory. Her relationship with Henry had always been safely tempered by a sense of the familiar.

This was the first time Phoebe had ever felt so drawn to a stranger, and for it to be a man who was all brawn and boorishness was a cruel joke. There couldn't be a greater contrast to Henry. But as Mr. Ravenel had stood there, radiating virility, his gaze shocking her with its directness, she had felt her knees wilt and her blood race. It was mortifying.

Even worse, she felt as if she were betraying Edward Larson, with whom she had an understanding of sorts. He hadn't proposed yet, but they both knew he would someday, and she would probably accept.

"If Mr. Ravenel has any interest in me," Phoebe said shortly, "it's because he's a fortune hunter. Most second sons are."

Gabriel's eyes twinkled with affectionate mockery. "Thank God you know what labels to affix to people. It would be so inconvenient to have to judge them individually."

"As always, 'annoying lunkhead' is perfect for you."

"I think you secretly liked the way Ravenel talked to you," Gabriel said. "People are always telling us what they think we want to hear. Raw honesty is a refreshing change, isn't it?"

"Refreshing for you, perhaps," Phoebe said with a reluctant smile. "Well, you'll certainly get that from Pandora. She's incapable of being awed by anyone."

"It's one of the reasons I love her," her brother admitted. "I also love her wit, her zest for life, and the fact that she needs me to keep her from walking in circles."

"I'm glad you found each other," Phoebe said sincerely. "Pandora's a dear girl, and you both deserve to be happy."

"So do you."

"I don't expect ever to find the kind of happiness I had with Henry."

"Why not?"

"A love like that can only happen once in a lifetime."

Gabriel pondered that. "I certainly don't understand everything about love," he said almost humbly. "But I don't think it works like that."

Phoebe shrugged and tried to sound brisk. "There's no point in worrying over my future—it will happen as it wants to. All I can do is try to carry on in a way that will honor my husband's memory. What I know for certain is that as much as Henry hated Mr. Ravenel, he wouldn't have wanted me to be spiteful or vindictive."

Her brother's warm gaze searched every nuance of her expression. "Don't be afraid," he surprised her by saying.

"Of Mr. Ravenel? Never."

"I meant don't be afraid of liking him."

That startled a laugh from Phoebe. "There's no danger of that. But even if there were, I would never betray Henry by making friends with his enemy."

"Don't betray yourself, either."

"In what way—how do you think I—Gabriel, wait!" But he had gone to the door and opened it.

"Time to go back, Redbird. You'll sort it all out eventually."

Chapter 5

To PHOEBE'S RELIEF, MR. RAVENEL was nowhere in sight when they returned to the entrance hall. Guests milled about and chatted as old friends were reacquainted and new ones were introduced. A battalion of footmen and maids carried trunks, traveling cases, hatboxes and all manner of luggage toward the back stairs.

"Phoebe," came a light, sweet voice, and she turned to find Devon's wife at her side. Kathleen, Lady Trenear, was a petite woman with red hair, tip-tilted eyes and high cheekbones. Phoebe had come to like her very much during the week the Ravenels had stayed at Heron's Point. Kathleen was cheerful and engaging, albeit a bit horse mad, since both her parents had been in the business of breeding and training Arabians. Phoebe liked horses, but she didn't know nearly enough about them to carry on a detailed conversation. Fortunately, Kathleen was the mother of an infant son who was close to Stephen's age, and that had provided ample ground for conversation.

"I'm so delighted to have you here," Kathleen said, taking Phoebe's hands in her small ones. "How was the journey?"

"Splendid," Phoebe said. "Justin found the train ride very exciting, and the baby seemed to enjoy the swaying."

"If you like, I'll show your nanny and the children up to the nursery. Perhaps you'll want to have a look?"

"Yes, but must you leave all your guests? We could have a housemaid show us the way."

"They can do without me for a few minutes. I'll explain the layout of the house as we go. It's a labyrinth. Everyone gets lost the first day or two. We have to send out search expeditions every few hours to collect the stragglers."

In most grand households, children, nursemaids and nannies were usually relegated to the servants' stairs in the back, but Kathleen insisted they use the central staircase during their stay. "The nursery is much easier to reach this way," she said as they ascended.

Phoebe carried Stephen, while Justin held Nanny's hand and pulled her along like a small, determined tugboat towing a freighter. At each landing, Phoebe caught glimpses of rooms through wide-open doorways, some with fireplaces large enough to stand in.

For all its size, the house had a friendly, cozy feeling. The walls were covered with antique French and Italian tapestry hangings, and oil paintings in heavy gilded frames. She saw signs of the manor's venerable age: exposed joists sagging a little here or there, scarred places on the oak floors, thin patches on the Aubusson carpeting. But there were notes of luxury everywhere: jewel-toned Venetian-glass lampshades,

Chinese porcelain vases and tea jars, sideboards holding heavy silver trays of liquor in glittering decanters. The air smelled like old books, fresh flowers, and the agreeable whiff of furniture polish.

When they reached the nursery, Phoebe saw that a footman had already conveyed her children's carriage box of clothes and supplies upstairs. The spacious room was filled with charming child-sized furniture, including a table and chairs and an upholstered settee. Two children napped on small cots, while Kathleen's son, Matthew, slept soundly in his crib. A pair of white-aproned nursemaids came forward to meet Nanny Bracegirdle, smiling and whispering as they introduced themselves.

Kathleen showed Phoebe to an empty crib lined with soft embroidered bedding. "This is for Stephen," she whispered.

"It's perfect. If I were just a bit smaller, I might try to curl up in there myself."

Kathleen smiled. "Why don't I show you to your room, and you can nap in a proper bed?"

"That sounds like heaven." Phoebe kissed and nuzzled Stephen's warm, silky head before giving him to the nanny. She went to Justin, who was investigating a set of shelves filled with toys and books. He had taken interest in a toy theater with changeable backdrops and a box of painted cutout characters. "Will you like staying here, darling?" she asked softly, kneeling beside him.

"Oh, yes."

"Nanny will be here with you. Tell her or one of the nursemaids if you want me, and I'll come."

"Yes, Mama." Since he didn't like giving kisses in front of strangers, Justin surreptitiously pressed his lips to the tip of his forefinger and held it out. Phoebe did the same and touched her fingertip to his. They exchanged a smile after the secret ritual. For an instant, the crescent shapes of his eyes and the little crinkle of his nose reminded her of Henry. But the wisp of memory didn't come with the expected twinge of pain, only a trace of wistful fondness.

Phoebe left the nursery with Kathleen, and they went back down to the second floor.

"I remember how it felt to come out of mourning after losing my first husband," Kathleen said. "For me, it was like leaving a dark room and going into the glare of daylight. Everything seemed too loud and fast."

"Yes, that's exactly how it feels."

"Do whatever you like here, just as you would at home. You mustn't feel obliged to take part in any activities that don't appeal to you. We want very much for you to be comfortable and happy."

"I'm sure I will be."

They went down a second-floor hallway and reached a bedroom where Ernestine, her lady's maid, was in the process of unpacking her trunks and boxes.

"I hope this room will do," Katherine said. "It's small, but it has its own dressing room and washroom, and a view of the formal gardens."

"It's lovely." Phoebe looked over the room with pleasure. The walls were covered in French paper featuring a delicate vine pattern, with a fresh coat of white paint covering the trim and panel work.

"I'll leave you, then, while you settle things to your liking. At six o'clock, we meet in the drawing room for sherry. Dinner is at eight. Formal dress, but after the newlyweds leave tomorrow, we'll be easy and casual."

After Kathleen had left, Phoebe watched Ernestine unearthing stacks of carefully folded linens and neat little parcels from an open trunk. Every pair of shoes had its own little plain-woven drawstring bag, and every pair of gloves had been tucked into a narrow pasteboard box.

"Ernestine," she said, "you're a marvel of organization."

"Thank you, milady. It's been so long since we've gone away from Heron's Point, I'd almost forgotten how to pack." Still kneeling by the trunk, the slim, dark-haired young woman looked up at her with a box of trimmings in hand, which had been removed from hats and caps to prevent them from being crushed. "Shall I air out your ecru dress while you nap?"

"Ecru?" Phoebe echoed with a slight frown.

"The silk one with flower trim."

"Gracious, did you bring that one?" Phoebe had only a vague memory of the formal gown, which she'd had made and fitted in London before Henry had gone into his final decline. "I think I would feel more comfortable in my silver gray. I'm not quite ready for colors yet."

"Ma'am, it's ecru. No one would call that a color."

"But the trimmings . . . aren't they too bright?"

For answer, Ernestine pulled a garland of silk flowers from the box of trimmings and held them up for display. The silk peony and rose blossoms were tinted in delicate pastel shades.

"I suppose that will be all right, then," Phoebe said, amused by the lady's maid's sardonic expression. Ernestine had made no secret of her wish for her mistress to be done with the subdued grays and lavenders of half mourning.

"It has been two years, milady," the young woman pointed out. "All the books say that's long enough."

Phoebe removed her hat and set it on the nearby satinwood vanity table. "Do help me out of this travel dress, Ernestine. If I'm to make it through tonight without collapsing, I'll need to lie down for a few minutes."

"Aren't you looking forward to the dinner?" the young woman dared to ask as she took Phoebe's traveling jacket. "Many of your old friends will be there."

"Yes and no. I want to see them, but I'm nervous. I'm afraid they'll expect me to be the person I was."

Ernestine paused in the midst of unfastening the buttons on the back of her dress. "Pardon, ma'am . . . but aren't you still the same person?"

"I'm afraid not. My old self is gone." A humorless smile tugged at her lips. "And the new one hasn't turned up yet."

SIX O'CLOCK.

Time to go down to the drawing room. A glass of sherry would be a welcome start to the evening, Phoebe thought, fiddling with the artfully draped folds of her dress. She needed something to steady her nerves.

"You look beautiful, ma'am," Ernestine said, delighted with the results of her work. She had drawn Phoebe's hair up into a coil of neatly pinned rolls and curls, winding a velvet ribbon around the base. A few loose curls had been allowed to dangle down the back of her head, which felt a bit strange: she wasn't accustomed to leaving any loose pieces in her usual hairstyles. Ernestine had finished the arrangement by pinning a small, fresh pink rose on the right side of the coil.

The new coiffure was very flattering, but the formal gown had turned out to be far less inconspicuous than Phoebe had expected. It was the pale beige of unbleached linen or natural wool, but the silk had been infused with exceptionally fine metallic threads of gold and silver, giving the fabric a pearly luster. A garland of peonies, roses, and delicate green silk leaves trimmed the deeply scooped neckline, while another flower garland caught up the gossamer-thin silk and tulle layers of the skirts at one side.

Frowning at her pale, glimmering reflection in the long oval mirror, Phoebe experimentally covered her eyes with one hand, lifted it away, and repeated the motion a couple of times. "Oh, God," she murmured aloud. She was fairly certain that a quick glance at the dress gave a brief, startling impression of near-nudity, except for the flowers. "I have to change dresses, Ernestine. Fetch the silver gray."

"But . . . but I haven't aired or pressed it," the lady's maid said in bewilderment. "And this one is so pretty on you."

"I didn't remember the fabric shimmered like this. I can't go downstairs looking like a Christmas tree ornament."

"It's not *that* shiny," the girl protested. "Other ladies will be wearing dresses with beading and spangles, and their best diamond sets." Seeing Phoebe's expression, she heaved a sigh. "If you want the silver gray, ma'am, I'll do my best to have it ready soon, but you'll still go down late."

Phoebe groaned at the thought. "Did you pack a shawl?"

"A black one. But you'll roast if you try to cover yourself in that. And it would look odd—you would earn more attention that way than by going as you are."

Before Phoebe could reply, there came a knock at the door. "Oh, galoshes," she muttered. It was hardly a curse worthy of the situation, but she'd fallen into the habit of saying it when she was around her children, which was most of the time. She sped to the corner behind the door, while Ernestine went to see who it was.

After a brief murmured exchange, the lady's maid opened the door a bit wider, and Phoebe's brother Ivo stuck his head inside.

"Hullo, sis," he said casually. "You look very nice in that gold dress."

"It's ecru." At his perplexed look, she repeated, "*Ecru.*"

"God bless you," Ivo said, and gave her a cheeky grin as he entered the room.

Phoebe lifted her gaze heavenward. "Why are you here, Ivo?"

"I'm going to escort you downstairs, so you don't have to go alone."

Phoebe was so moved, she couldn't speak. She could only stare at the eleven-year-old boy, who was volunteering to take the place her husband would have assumed.

"It was Father's idea," Ivo continued, a touch bashfully. "I'm sorry I'm not as tall as the other ladies' escorts, or even as tall as you. I'm really only half an escort. But that's still better than nothing, isn't it?" His expression turned uncertain as he saw that her eyes were watering.

After clearing her throat, Phoebe managed an unsteady reply. "At this moment, my gallant Ivo, you tower above every other gentleman here. I'm so very honored."

He grinned and offered her his arm in a gesture she had seen him practice in the past with their father. "The honor is mine, sis."

In that moment, Phoebe had the briefest intimation of what Ivo would be like as a full-grown man, confident and irresistibly charming.

"Wait," she said. "I have to decide what to do about my dress."

"Why do you have to do something about it?"

"It's too . . . flagrant."

Her brother cocked his head, his gaze traveling over the dress. "Is that one of Pandora's words?"

"No, it's a dictionary word. It means standing out like a sore thumb."

"Sis. You and I are *always* flagrant." Ivo pointed to his red hair. "When you have *this*, you have no choice but to be noticed. Go on and wear that dress. I like it, and Gabriel will like it that you look pretty for his wedding-eve dinner."

A commanding speech, coming from a boy not yet twelve. Phoebe studied him with fond pride. "Very well, you've talked me into it," she said reluctantly.

"Goodness me," Ernestine exclaimed, sounding relieved.

Phoebe smiled at her. "Don't wait up here for me, Ernestine—take some time for yourself, and have dinner in the servants' hall with the others."

"Thank you, ma'am."

Phoebe took Ivo's arm and let him escort her from the room. As they proceeded to the grand central staircase, she glanced at his formal Eton suit, made with black serge trousers, a white waistcoat, and a black satin bow tie. "You've graduated to long trousers," she exclaimed.

"A year early," Ivo boasted.

"How did you talk Mother into it?"

"I told her a fellow has his pride, and as far as I was concerned, wearing short trousers is like going about with your pants at half-mast. Mother laughed so hard, she had to set down her teacup, and the next day the tailor came to measure me for a suit. Now the Hunt twins can't make fun of my knees anymore." The fourteen-year-old boys, Ashton and Augustus, were the youngest offspring of Mr. and Mrs. Simon Hunt, who had been close friends to the Challons since before Phoebe had been born.

"The twins made fun of you?" Phoebe asked in surprised concern. "But you've always been great friends with them."

"Yes, that's what fellows do. We call our friends names like 'Spoony' or 'Knobby-knees.' The better the friend, the worse the insult."

"But why not be nice?"

"Because we're boys." Ivo shrugged as he saw her bewilderment. "You know how our brothers are. The telegram Raphael sent to Gabriel yesterday said, 'Dear Brother, congratulations on your wedding. I'm sorry I won't be there to warn your bride about what a useless arse-wedge you are. All my love, Raphael.'"

Phoebe couldn't help laughing. "That sounds like him. Yes, I know how they like to taunt each other, though I've never understood why. I suppose my two boys will be the same. But I'm glad Henry wasn't. I never heard him mock or tease anyone."

"He was a nice man," Ivo said reflectively. "Different. I miss him."

Her hand tightened on his arm in an affectionate squeeze.

To Phoebe's relief, the gathering in the drawing room turned out to be far less intimidating than she'd expected. Her parents and Seraphina were there to keep her company, as were Lord and Lady Westcliff, whom she and her siblings had always called "Uncle Marcus" and "Aunt Lillian."

Lord Westcliff's hunting estate, Stony Cross Park, was located in Hampshire, not far from Eversby Priory. The earl and his wife, who had originally been an American heiress from New York, had raised three sons and three daughters. Although Aunt Lillian had teasingly invited Phoebe to have her pick of any of her robust and handsome sons, Phoebe had answered— quite truthfully—that such a union would have felt positively incestuous. The Marsdens and the Challons had spent too many family holidays together and had known each other for too long for any romantic sparks to fly between their offspring.

The Marsdens' oldest daughter, Merritt, was one of Phoebe's closest friends. She had gone to Essex on several occasions to help when Henry was especially ill, caring for him with skill and good humor. In fact, Phoebe had trusted her more than she had Henry's mother, Georgiana, whose nerves had rarely been up to the task of nursing an invalid.

"Darling Phoebe," Merritt said, taking both of her hands, "how ravishing you are."

Phoebe leaned close to kiss her cheek. "I feel ridiculous in this dress," she murmured. "I can't think why I ever had it made in this fabric."

"Because I told you to," Merritt said. "I helped you order your trousseau at the dressmaker's, remember?

You objected to the fabric at first, but I told you, 'No woman should be afraid to sparkle.'"

Phoebe chuckled ruefully. "No one will ever sparkle as fearlessly as you, Merritt."

Lady Merritt Sterling was a vibrantly attractive woman with large, dark eyes, a wealth of lustrous sable hair, and a flawless porcelain complexion. Unlike her two sisters, she had inherited the shorter, stockier frame of the Marsden side instead of the slender build of her mother. Similarly, she had her father's square-shaped face and determined jaw instead of her mother's delicate oval one. However, Merritt possessed a charm so compelling that she eclipsed every other woman in the vicinity, no matter how beautiful.

Merritt focused on whomever she was talking to with a wealth of sincere interest, as if she or he were the only person in the world. She asked questions and listened without ever seeming to wait for her turn to talk. She was the guest everyone invited when they needed to blend a group of disparate personalities, just as a roux would bind soup or sauce into velvety smoothness.

It was no exaggeration to say that every man who met Merritt fell at least a little in love with her. When she had entered society, countless suitors had pursued her before she'd finally consented to marry Joshua Sterling, an American-born shipping magnate who had taken up residence in London.

Drawing a little apart from their families, Phoebe and Merritt stole a few minutes to speak privately. Eagerly Phoebe told her friend about the encounter with West Ravenel, the proposed farm tour, and the presumptuous comments he'd made.

"Poor Phoebe," Merritt soothed. "Men do love to explain things."

"It wasn't explaining, it was a lecture."

"How bothersome. But one must allow new people room for error. It's often a clumsy business, this making of friends."

"I don't want to become friends with him, I want to avoid him."

Merritt hesitated before replying. "No one could blame you, of course."

"But you think it's a mistake?"

"Darling, opinions are tiresome, especially mine."

"Then you do think it's a mistake."

Merritt looked sympathetic. "Since your families are now aligned, you'll cross paths with him in the future. It would be easier for all concerned, especially you, to keep things civil. Would it be so difficult for you to give Mr. Ravenel a second chance?"

Phoebe frowned and averted her gaze. "It would be," she said. "For reasons I'd rather not explain."

She hadn't reminded Merritt that West Ravenel was the childhood bully Henry had hated. Somehow it didn't seem right to smear a man's reputation for things he'd done as a boy—it wouldn't help anyone now.

But Merritt stunned her by asking, "Because of what happened at boarding school?"

Phoebe's eyes widened. "You remember?"

"Yes, it was important to Henry. Even in adulthood, the memory of Mr. Ravenel was always a thorn in his side." Merritt paused reflectively. "I think such events loom larger in our minds over time. I wonder if it was perhaps easier for Henry to focus on a human adversary instead of a disease." She looked beyond Phoebe's shoulder. "Don't turn around," she said, "but there's a gentleman who keeps stealing glances at you from across the room. I've never seen him before. I wonder if he's your Mr. Ravenel?"

"Good heavens, please don't call him *my* Mr. Ravenel. What does he look like?"

"Dark haired, clean-shaven and quite sun-browned. Tall, with shoulders as broad as a plowman's. At the moment he's talking with a group of gentlemen, and—oh, *my*. He has a smile like a hot summer day."

"That would be Mr. Ravenel," Phoebe muttered.

"*Well.* I recall Henry describing him as pale and stout." Merritt's brows lifted slightly as she peeked over Phoebe's shoulder once more. "Someone had a growth spurt."

"Looks are irrelevant. It's the inner man that counts."

Laughter threaded through Merritt's voice. "I suppose you're right. But the inner Mr. Ravenel happens to be quite beautifully packaged."

Phoebe bit back a grin. "And you, a married lady," she whispered in mock scolding.

"Married ladies have eyes," came Merritt's demure reply, her face alive with mischief.

Chapter 6

As usual, the guests entered the dining room in order of precedence. Regardless of personal age or fortune, the first people in line were those whose title, or patent of nobility, was the oldest. That made Lord and Lady Westcliff the couple of highest rank, even though Phoebe's father held a dukedom.

Accordingly, Devon, Lord Trenear, escorted Lady Westcliff, while Lord Westcliff escorted Kathleen. The rest of the guests followed in prearranged pairs. Phoebe was relieved to discover she would be accompanied by Westcliff's oldest son, Lord Foxhall, whom she had known her entire life. He was a big, boldly handsome man in his twenties, an avid sportsman like his father. As the earl's heir, he had been accorded a viscountcy, but he and Phoebe were far too familiar to stand on ceremony.

"Fox," she exclaimed, a wide smile crossing her face.

"Cousin Phoebe." He leaned down to kiss her cheek, his dark eyes snapping with lively humor. "It seems I'm your escort. Bad luck for you."

"To me it's very good luck—how could it be otherwise?"

"With all the eligible men present, you should be with one who doesn't remember you as a little girl in pigtails, sliding down one of the banisters at Stony Cross Manor."

Phoebe's smile lingered even as she sighed wistfully and shook her head. "Oh, Fox. Those days are long gone, aren't they?"

"You still have most of it ahead of you," he said gently.

"None of us knows how much time we have."

Foxhall offered his arm. "Then let's eat, drink and be merry while we're able."

They made their way to the dining room, where the air was blossom-scented and gilded with candlelight. The mammoth Jacobean table, with its legs and support rails carved like twisted rope, had been covered with pristine white linen. A row of broad silver baskets filled with billows of June roses rested on a long runner of frothy green maidenhair ferns. The walls had been lined with lush arrangements of palms, hydrangeas, azaleas and peonies, turning the room into an evening garden. Each place at the table had been set with glittering Irish crystal, Sèvres porcelain, and no fewer than twenty-four pieces of antique Georgian silver flatware per guest.

Long rows of footmen stood back at both sides of the room while the gentlemen seated the ladies. Lord Foxhall pulled out Phoebe's chair, and she moved toward the table. But she froze as she saw the man who had just seated the lady to his right.

On the place card beside hers, a name had been written in elaborate calligraphy: *Mr. Weston Ravenel.*

Her stomach plummeted.

Mr. Ravenel turned toward her and hesitated, appearing no less surprised than she. He cut an impressive figure in formal evening clothes. The white shirt and necktie contrasted sharply with the amber glow of his skin, while the tailored black coat emphasized the stunning breadth of his shoulders.

The way he stared at her was too focused, too . . . *something.* She couldn't decide what to do, only looked back at him helplessly, her insides strung with hot twinges and pangs.

Mr. Ravenel's gaze flicked down to the place cards and back to her face. "I had nothing to do with the seating arrangements."

"Obviously," Phoebe replied crisply, her thoughts in turmoil. According to etiquette, a gentleman usually directed the majority of his attention and conversation to the lady on his left. She was going to have to talk to him for the entire meal.

As she cast a distracted glance around the room, she caught sight of Gabriel.

Seeing her dilemma, her brother began to mouth the words, *Do you want me to—*

Phoebe gave a quick little shake of her head. No, she would not make a scene the night before her brother's wedding, even if she had to sit next to Lucifer himself—a seating arrangement she would have preferred to this one.

"Is something amiss?" came Lord Foxhall's quiet voice near her left ear. She realized he was still waiting to seat her.

Gathering her wits, Phoebe replied with a forced smile, "No, Fox, everything is splendid." She occupied the chair, arranging her skirts deftly.

Mr. Ravenel remained motionless, a frown tugging at the smooth space between his dark brows. "I'll find someone to change places with me," he said quietly.

"For heaven's sake, just *sit*," Phoebe whispered.

He occupied the chair cautiously, as if it might collapse beneath him at any moment. His wary gaze met hers. "I'm sorry for the way I behaved earlier."

"It's forgotten," she said. "I'm sure we can manage to tolerate each other's company for one meal."

"I won't say anything about farming. We can discuss other subjects. I have a vast and complex array of interests."

"Such as?"

Mr. Ravenel considered that. "Never mind, I don't have a vast array of interests. But I feel like the kind of man who does."

Amused despite herself, Phoebe smiled reluctantly. "Aside from my children, I have no interests."

"Thank God. I hate stimulating conversation. My mind isn't deep enough to float a straw."

Phoebe did enjoy a man with a sense of humor. Perhaps this dinner wouldn't be as dreadful as she'd thought. "You'll be glad to hear, then, that I haven't read a book in months."

"I haven't gone to a classical music concert in years," he said. "Too many moments of 'clap here, not there.' It makes me nervous."

"I'm afraid we can't discuss art, either. I find symbolism exhausting."

"Then I assume you don't like poetry."

"No . . . unless it rhymes."

"I happen to write poetry," Ravenel said gravely.

Heaven help me, Phoebe thought, the momentary fun vanishing. Years ago, when she'd first entered society, it had seemed as if every young man she met at a ball or dinner was an amateur poet. They had insisted on quoting their own poems, filled with bombast about starlight and dewdrops and lost love, in the hopes of impressing her with how sensitive they were. Apparently, the fad had not ended yet.

"Do you?" she asked without enthusiasm, praying silently that he wouldn't offer to recite any of it.

"Yes. Shall I recite a line or two?"

Repressing a sigh, Phoebe shaped her mouth into a polite curve. "By all means."

"It's from an unfinished work." Looking solemn, Mr. Ravenel began, "There once was a young man named Bruce . . . whose trousers were always too loose."

Phoebe willed herself not to encourage him by laughing. She heard a quiet cough of amusement behind her and deduced that one of the footmen had overheard.

"Mr. Ravenel," she asked, "have you forgotten this is a formal dinner?"

His eyes glinted with mischief. "Help me with the next line."

"Absolutely not."

"I dare you."

Phoebe ignored him, meticulously spreading her napkin over her lap.

"I double dare you," he persisted.

"Really, you are the most . . . oh, very well." Phoebe took a sip of water while mulling over words. After setting down the glass, she said, "One day he bent over, while picking a clover."

Ravenel absently fingered the stem of an empty crystal goblet. After a moment, he said triumphantly, ". . . and a bee stung him on the caboose."

Phoebe almost choked on a laugh. "Could we at least pretend to be dignified?" she begged.

"But it's going to be such a long dinner."

She looked up to find him smiling at her, easy and warm, and it sent a curious shiver through her, the kind that sometimes happened after she woke from a long sleep and stretched until her muscles trembled.

"Tell me about your children," he said.

"What would you like to know?"

"Anything. How did you decide on their names?"

"Justin was named after my husband's favorite uncle—a dear old bachelor who always brought him books when he was ill. My younger son, Stephen, was named after a character in an adventure novel Lord Clare and I read when we were children."

"What was the title?"

"I can't tell you; you'll think it's silly. It *is* silly. But we both loved it. We read it dozens of times. I had to send Henry my copy, after—"

After you stole his.

In Henry's view, the worst of West Ravenel's offenses had been stealing his copy of *Stephen Armstrong: Treasure Hunter* from a box of possessions beneath his bed at school. Although there had never been proof of the thief's identity, Henry had remembered that Ravenel had previously mocked him when he'd seen him reading it. *"I know he's the one,"* Henry had written. *"He's probably done something awful with it. Dropped it down the privy. I'd be surprised if the nincompoop can even read."*

"Someday when we're big," Phoebe had written in response, full of righteous vengeance, *"we'll go thrash him together and take it back from him."*

But now she was sitting next to him at dinner.

"—after he lost his copy," she finished awkwardly. She watched as a footman poured wine into one of her glasses.

"How did he—" Mr. Ravenel began, and stopped with a frown. He moved in the chair, seeming uneasy, and began again. "When I was a boy, there was a book—" Another pause, and he tried to angle his body more toward hers.

"Mr. Ravenel," Phoebe asked, puzzled, "are you quite all right?"

"Yes. It's only—there's a problem." He scowled down at his trousers.

"A problem involving your lap?" she asked dryly.

He replied in an exasperated whisper, "As a matter of fact, yes."

"Really." Phoebe wasn't certain whether to be amused or alarmed. "What is it?"

"The woman on my other side keeps putting her hand on my leg."

Stealthily Phoebe leaned forward to peek around him at the culprit. "Isn't that Lady Colwick?" she whispered. "The one whose mother, Lady Berwick, taught etiquette to Pandora and Cassandra?"

"Yes," he said curtly. "It appears she neglected to teach it to her daughter."

From what Phoebe understood, Dolly, Lady Colwick, had recently married a wealthy older man but was reportedly having affairs behind his back with her former suitors. In fact, it had been Dolly's scandalous carryings-on that had resulted in an accidental meeting between Pandora and Gabriel in the first place.

Mr. Ravenel flinched irritably and reached beneath the table to push away the unseen, exploring hand.

Phoebe understood his dilemma. If a gentleman called attention to such outrageous behavior, he would be blamed for embarrassing the lady. Moreover, the lady could easily deny it, and people would be far more inclined to believe her.

All along the table, footmen filled glasses with water, wine, and iced champagne. Deciding to take advantage of the stir of activity, Phoebe said to Mr. Ravenel, "Lean forward, please."

His brows lifted slightly, but he obeyed.

Reaching across the broad expanse of his back, Phoebe prodded Lady Colwick's bare upper arm with her forefinger. The young woman gave her a mildly startled glance. She was very pretty, her dark hair pinned up in an ornate mass of shiny ringlets interwoven with ribbons and pearls. The brows over her heavy-lashed eyes had been carefully plucked into a pair of perfect thin crescents, like a china doll's. A thick rope of pearls, weighted with diamond drops the size of Bristol cherries, glittered around her neck.

"My dear," Phoebe said pleasantly, "I can't help but notice that you keep trying to borrow Mr. Ravenel's napkin. Do take this one." She extended her own napkin to the young woman, who began to reach for it reflexively.

In the next instant, however, Lady Colwick snatched her hand back. "I haven't the faintest idea what you're talking about."

Phoebe wasn't deceived. A guilty blush had infused the young woman's cheeks, and the set of her rosebud lips had turned distinctly sullen. "Must I explain?" she asked very softly. "This gentleman does not enjoy being poked and pried like an oyster at Billingsgate Market while he tries to have his dinner. Kindly keep your hands to yourself."

Lady Colwick's eyes narrowed balefully. "We could have shared him," she pointed out, and turned back to her plate with a disdainful sniff.

A muffled snort of laughter came from the row of footmen behind them.

Mr. Ravenel leaned back in his chair. Without turning, he gestured over his shoulder and murmured, "Jerome."

One of the footmen approached and leaned down to him. "Sir?"

"Any more snickering," Mr. Ravenel warned softly, "and tomorrow you'll be demoted to hall boy."

"Yes, sir."

After the footman had withdrawn, Mr. Ravenel returned his attention to Phoebe. The little whisks of laugh-lines at the outer corners of his eyes had deepened. "Thank you for not sharing me."

Her shoulders lifted in a slight shrug. "She was interfering with a perfectly unstimulating conversation. Someone had to stop her."

His mouth curved in a slow grin.

Phoebe had never been so wholly aware of anyone as she was in that moment. Every nerve had come alive in response to his nearness. She was riveted by those eyes, the unrelieved blue of indigo ink. She was fascinated by the heavy beard grain visible beneath his clean-shaven skin, and the snug fit of the crisp white collar over his muscled neck. Although one couldn't excuse Lady Colwick's behavior, it was certainly understandable. What must his leg have felt like? Probably very hard. Rock solid. The thought caused her to fidget on the chair.

What's the matter with me?

Tearing her gaze from him, she focused on the tiny engraved menu card between their place settings. "Beef consommé or purée of spring vegetables," she read aloud. "I suppose I'll have the consommé."

"You'd choose weak broth over spring vegetables?"

"I never have much appetite."

"No, just listen: the cook sends for a basket of ripe vegetables from the kitchen gardens—leeks, carrots, young potatoes, vegetable marrow, tomatoes—and simmers them with fresh herbs. When it's all soft, she purées the mixture until it's like silk, and finishes it with heavy cream. It's brought to the table in an earthenware dish and ladled over croutons fried in butter. You can taste the entire garden in every spoonful."

Phoebe couldn't help but enjoy his enthusiasm. "How do you know so much about the preparation?"

"I've spent a fair amount of time in the kitchen," he admitted. "I like to know about the staff's responsibilities and working conditions. And as far as I'm concerned, the most important work at Eversby Priory is keeping everyone on the estate healthy and well-fed. No one can work well on an empty belly."

"Does the cook mind having her territory invaded?"

"Not as long as I keep out of the way and don't stick my fingers into bowls."

She smiled. "You like food, don't you?"

"No, I *love* food. Of all earthly pleasures, it's my second favorite."

"What's your first favorite?"

"That's not a subject fit for dinner." After a pause, he offered innocently, "But I could tell you later."

The rascal. This was flirtation at its stealthiest, a seemingly bland comment weighted with innuendo. Phoebe chose to ignore it, gluing her gaze to the menu card until the jumble of letters sorted themselves into words. "I see there's a choice for the fish course: turbot with lobster sauce, or sole à la Normandie." She paused. "I'm not familiar with the latter."

Mr. Ravenel answered readily, "White sole filets marinated in cider, sautéed in butter, and covered with crème fraîche. It's light, with a tang of apples."

It had been a long time since Phoebe had thought of a meal as anything other than a perfunctory ritual. She had not only lost her appetite after Henry died, she'd also lost her sense of taste. Only a few things still had flavor. Strong tea, lemon, cinnamon.

"My husband never—" The urge to let down her guard with him was almost overpowering, even though it felt like a betrayal of Henry.

Mr. Ravenel regarded her patiently, his head slightly tilted.

"He couldn't tolerate milk or cream, or red meat," Phoebe continued haltingly. "We ate only the plainest dishes, everything boiled and unseasoned. Even then, he suffered terribly. He was so sweet and good-natured, he didn't want me to forgo things I enjoyed just because he couldn't have them. But how could I eat a pudding or drink a glass of wine in front of him? After living that way for years . . . with food as the adversary . . . I'm afraid I'll never be able to eat for pleasure again."

Immediately Phoebe realized how out of place such a confession was at a formal dinner. She lowered her gaze to the gleaming row of flatware in front of her, so embarrassed that she was briefly tempted to stab herself with a salad fork. "Forgive me," she said. "I've been out of society for so long, I've forgotten how to make polite small talk."

"Polite small talk is wasted on me. I spend most of my time around farm animals." Mr. Ravenel waited for her brief smile to fade before continuing. "Your husband must have been a man of great inner strength. If I'd been in his place, I wouldn't have been sweet or good-natured. In fact, I'm not that way even when things are going well."

The praise of Henry caused some of her buried animosity to melt. It was far easier to hate a person when he was a distant figure, a concept, than when he was a living, breathing reality.

Thinking over his last comment, Phoebe asked, "Do you have a temper, Mr. Ravenel?"

"Good God, haven't you heard? Ravenels are powder kegs with quick-match fuses. It's why there are so few males left in the family line: constant drinking and brawling don't usually lend themselves to happy old age."

"Is that what you do? Constantly drink and brawl?"

"I used to," he admitted.

"Why did you stop?"

"Too much of anything is tiresome," he said, and grinned at her. "Even pleasure-seeking."

Chapter 7

As it turned out, the purée of spring vegetables exceeded Mr. Ravenel's description. The soft reddish-orange emulsion really did taste like a garden. It was a bold, creamy harmony of astringent tomato, sweet carrots, potatoes, and greens, bound together in a lively snap of springtime. As Phoebe bit into a half-crisp, half-sodden crouton, she closed her eyes to savor it. God, it had been so long since she'd really *tasted* anything.

"I told you," Mr. Ravenel said in satisfaction.

"Do you think your cook would share the recipe?"

"She would if I asked her to."

"Will you?"

"What will you do for me in return?" he parried.

That surprised a laugh out of her. "How ungallant. What about chivalry? What about largesse?"

"I'm a farmer, not a knight. Around here, it's quid pro quo."

The way he spoke to her had none of the deference and sympathy people usually accorded to widows. It felt like . . . flirtation. But she couldn't be sure. It had been so long since anyone had flirted with her. Of course, he was the last man she would ever welcome that kind of attention from, except . . . it flustered her in an oddly pleasant way.

An endless round of toasts began, to the happiness and prosperity of the bride and groom, the well-being of the families about to be joined, the queen, the host and hostess, the clergyman, the ladies, and so forth. Glasses were repeatedly replenished with fine old wines, the empty soup bowls were withdrawn, and tiny plates of chilled ripe melon slices were set out.

Each course was more delectable than the last. Phoebe would have thought nothing could have surpassed the efforts of the French cook at Heron's Point, but this was some of the most delicious fare she'd ever had. Her bread plate was frequently replenished with piping-hot milk rolls and doughy slivers of stottie cake, served with thick curls of salted butter. The footmen brought out perfectly broiled game hens, the skin crisp and delicately heat-blistered . . . fried veal cutlets puddled in cognac sauce . . . slices of vegetable terrine studded with tiny boiled quail eggs. Brilliantly colorful salads were topped with dried flakes of smoked ham or paper-thin slices of pungent black truffle. Roasted joints of beef and lamb were presented and carved beside the table, the tender meat sliced thinly and served with drippings thickened into gravy.

As Phoebe sampled one offering after another, in the company of her husband's lifelong enemy, she enjoyed herself immensely. West Ravenel was worldly and wickedly funny, making audacious comments that managed to stay just within the margins of respectability. His relaxed interest seemed to wrap gently around her. The conversation was easy, pleasurable, like an unfurling bolt of velvet. She couldn't remember the last time she had talked like this, her tongue going on like a mill-clapper. Nor could she remember consuming this much food in one sitting in years.

"What courses are left?" she asked as palate-clearing sorbet was brought out in miniature crystal cups.

"Just cheese, and then dessert."

"I can't even manage this sorbet."

Mr. Ravenel shook his head slowly, regarding her with somber disappointment. "What a featherweight. You're going to let this dinner defeat you?"

She sputtered with a helpless laugh. "It's not a sporting event."

"Some meals are a fight to the finish. You're so close to victory—for God's sake, don't give up."

"I'll try," she said doubtfully. "I do hate to waste food."

"Nothing will be wasted. The leftover scraps will go either to the compost heap or the pigs' trough."

"How many pigs do you keep?"

"Two dozen. A few of the tenant families also keep pigs. I've been trying to convince our smallholders—especially those with less productive land—to farm more livestock instead of corn. But they're reluctant. They consider raising stock—especially pigs—a step down from growing crops."

"I don't see why—" Phoebe began, but she was interrupted by Pandora's cheerful voice.

"Cousin West, are you talking about pigs? Have you told Lady Clare about Hamlet?"

Obligingly Mr. Ravenel launched into an anecdote of the time he'd visited a tenant farmer and rescued a runt piglet from being culled. Soon the attention of the entire table turned to him.

He was a gifted storyteller, drolly casting the piglet as a waif from a Dickens novel. After having rescued the newborn creature, he related, it had occurred to him that someone had to take care of it. Accordingly, he had brought it back to Eversby Priory and given it to Pandora and Cassandra. Over the objections of the rest of the family and the servants, the twins had adopted the piglet as a household pet.

As the creature grew older and considerably larger, Mr. Ravenel had been blamed for the multitude of problems it had caused.

"To make matters worse," Pandora added, "we weren't aware until it was too late that the pig should have been 'altered' while still in infancy. Sadly, he became too smelloquent to live inside."

"Lady Trenear threatened to kill me every time she saw the pig trotting through the house with the dogs," Mr. Ravenel said. "I didn't dare turn my back to her for months."

"I did try to push him down the stairs once or twice," Kathleen admitted with a perfectly straight face, "but he was too large for me to gain sufficient leverage."

"You also made colorful threats involving the fireplace poker," Mr. Ravenel reminded her.

"No," Kathleen retorted, "that was the housekeeper."

The story continued its descent into farce as Mr. Winterborne volunteered that he'd stayed at Eversby Priory while recovering from eye injuries and hadn't been told about the pig. "I heard it from my sickbed, and assumed it was another dog."

"A dog?" Lord Trenear repeated from the head of the table, staring at his friend quizzically. "Did it *sound* like a dog to you?"

"Aye, with breathing problems."

The group dissolved in hilarity.

Smiling, Phoebe glanced at Mr. Ravenel and found his gaze on her. A curious and inexplicable spell of intimacy seemed to have settled over them. Swiftly he turned his attention to an unused fruit knife near his plate, picking it up in one hand, scraping his thumb across the blade to test its sharpness.

Phoebe's breath caught with concern. "No, don't," she said softly.

He smiled crookedly and set aside the knife. "A force of habit. Forgive my manners."

"It wasn't that. I was afraid you might cut yourself."

"You needn't worry. My hands are as tough as whitleather. When I first came to Eversby Priory—" He paused. "No. I said I wouldn't talk about farming."

"Oh, do go on. When you first came here . . . ?"

"I had to start visiting the tenants, which scared the wits out of me."

"I should think they would have been more scared of you."

A breath of amusement escaped him. "There are many things that scare farmers, but a pot-bellied, half-drunk buffoon from London isn't one of them."

Phoebe listened with a faint frown. She'd rarely, if ever, heard a man speak so unsparingly about himself.

"The first day," Mr. Ravenel continued, "I was somewhat the worse for wear, having decided to stop living like a swill-tub. Sobriety didn't agree with me. My head ached, I had all the balance of a toy sailboat, and I was in the devil's own mood. The farmer, George Strickland, was willing to answer my questions about his farm as long as he could do it while working. He had to cut oats and bring them in before it rained. We went out to the field, where some men were scything and others were gathering and binding the cut stalks. A few were singing to keep everyone in rhythm. The oats were as high as my shoulder, and the smell was so good—sweet and clean. It was all so . . ." He shook his head, unable to find the right word, his gaze distant.

"Strickland showed me how to bind the stalks into sheaves," he continued after a moment, "and I worked along the row while we talked. By the time I reached the end of the row, my entire life had changed. It was the first useful thing I'd ever done with my hands." He smiled crookedly. "I had a gentleman's hands, back then. Soft and manicured. They're not nearly so pretty now."

"Let me see them," Phoebe said. The request sounded more intimate than she had intended. Heat crept up her throat and cheeks as he complied slowly, extending them a bit lower than the tabletop, palms down.

The noise all around them, the fastidious clatter of flatware against china, the shimmers of laughter and light conversation, receded until it seemed as if they were the only two people in the room. She looked down at his hands, sturdy and long-fingered, the nails filed until only the thinnest white crescents were visible at the fingertips. They were immaculately clean, but the tanned skin was a bit dry and roughened at the knuckles. There were a few small scars left from nicks and scrapes, and the last vestige of a dark bruise lingering beneath one thumbnail. As Phoebe tried to picture those capable hands being soft and manicured, she found it impossible.

No, they weren't pretty. But they were beautiful.

She shocked herself by imagining how his hand might feel on her skin, rough-textured and gentle, with wicked knowledge in his fingertips. *No, don't think of it—*

"An estate manager doesn't usually have to work alongside the tenants, does he?" she managed to ask.

"He does if he wants to talk to them. These men and their wives don't have time to set aside their labors for a leisurely cup of tea at midmorning. But they're willing to have a conversation while I help repair a broken fence or take part in brickmaking. It's easier for them to trust a man with a bit of sweat on his brow and calluses on his hands. Work is a kind of language—we understand each other better afterward."

Phoebe listened carefully, perceiving that not only did he respect the estate tenants, he sincerely liked them. He was so very different from what she'd expected. No matter what he had once been, the cruel and unhappy boy seemed to have made himself into someone capable of empathy and understanding. Not a brute. Not a bad man at all.

Henry, she thought ruefully, *our enemy is turning out to be awfully difficult to hate.*

Chapter 8

$\mathcal{U}$SUALLY WEST AWAKENED FEELING refreshed and ready to begin the day. This morning, however, the rooster's crowing seemed to scrape his nerves raw. He'd slept badly from too much food and wine, and too much stimulation in the form of Phoebe, Lady Clare. His broken sleep had been filled with dreams of her, in his bed, involved in a variety of sexual acts he was willing to bet she'd never consent to. Now he was frustrated, surly, and as randy as a roebuck.

West had always congratulated himself on being too clever to desire a woman he couldn't have. But Phoebe was as rare as a year with two blue moons. All through dinner, he'd marveled at how beautiful she was, the candlelight striking gleams from her hair and skin like rubies and pearls. She was clever, perceptive, quick as a whip. There had been hints of an absolutely lacerating wit, which he loved, but there were also touches of shyness and melancholy that went straight to his heart. She was a woman who badly needed to enjoy herself, and he wanted to indulge her in some thoroughly adult fun.

But Phoebe, Lady Clare, wasn't meant for him. He

was a former wastrel with no property, no title, and no wealth. She was a highborn widow with two young sons. She needed a proper, well-heeled husband, not a scandalous affair.

That didn't stop West from imagining it, however. That red hair, loose and flowing across the pillow. Her mouth, kiss-swollen and open under his. Naked skin, all ivory and pink. The warm hollows of her elbows, the smooth, cool curves of her breasts. A little triangle of fiery curls for him to play with . . .

With a faint groan, West rolled to his stomach and buried his face in his pillow. He was suffused with an excited but wretched hot-and-cold feeling. He thought he might be feverish. Maybe it had something to do with his prolonged period of abstinence. Going without physical release was said to be bad for a man's health. It must be that he was suffering from a dangerous buildup of male essence.

With a muffled curse, he left the bed and went to wash in cold water.

As he dressed in his everyday clothes, West could hear the bustle of busy servants trying not to wake the guests. Doors opened and closed, voices murmured quietly. Unidentifiable clinkings and clankings littered the air. He could hear horses and vehicles outside on the gravel drive, having come with deliveries from the florist, the baker, the confectioner, the wine merchant.

The wedding would take place in approximately five hours, followed by an extravagant breakfast attended not only by the guests from last night, but also the local gentry, townspeople, and Eversby Priory tenants. The crowd would overflow from the house to the gardens, where rented folding tables and camp chairs had been set up. Musicians had been hired for the ceremony and breakfast, and an incredible amount of champagne had been ordered. The event had cost a bloody fortune. Thankfully that was Devon's concern, not his.

After brushing his teeth and combing back his damp hair, West went downstairs. Later, with the assistance of Devon's valet, Sutton, he would shave and put on his wedding attire and morning coat. For now, he had to make certain everything was proceeding as planned.

Devon was the only person in the morning room, sitting at one of the round tables with a page or two of notes and a cup of coffee. Ironically, even though he didn't usually arise at this hour, he looked fresh and rested, whereas West felt tired and irritable.

His older brother looked up from his notes and smiled. "Good morning."

"What are you so bloody pleased about?" West went to the sideboard and helped himself to coffee from a steaming silver urn.

"After today, Cassandra will be the only unmarried sister left."

Not long ago, without warning, Devon had inherited a wreck of an estate with its finances in shambles, as well as the responsibility for two hundred tenants, an aging staff of fifty servants, and three young, unworldly

Ravenel sisters. He could have easily sold everything that wasn't entailed and razed the manor house to the ground. He could have told everyone who lived at Eversby Priory—including the Ravenel sisters—to fend for themselves.

However, for reasons West would never entirely understand, Devon had taken on the overwhelming burden. With hard work and some luck, he had managed to stop the estate's downward spiral. Now the manor house was in the process of restoration, their balance sheet was in order, and the farm yields would actually turn a small profit this year. Helen, the oldest sister, had married Rhys Winterborne, who owned a department-store empire, and Pandora was, improbably, about to marry the heir to a dukedom.

"You've worried over those girls for two years, haven't you?" West asked. "A damn sight more than their own father and brother ever did. You've done well by them, Devon."

"As have you."

West responded with a snort of amusement. "I'm the one who told you to wash your hands of the entire mess and walk away."

"But you agreed to help anyway. You took on more grueling work than anyone else, including me. I could argue that you've done the greater part of saving the estate."

"Good God. Let's not make too much of some half-competent land management."

"The land *is* the estate. Without it, the family name

and the earldom are meaningless. Because of you, we may turn a profit for the first time in a decade. And by some miracle you've managed to drag some of the tenants into the era of modern agriculture."

"Kicking and screaming the entire way," West added dryly. He sat beside his brother and glanced at the notes. "The broken pew in the chapel has been repaired—you can cross that off the list. The keg of caviar arrived yesterday. It's in the icehouse. I don't know whether the extra camp chairs are here yet. I'll ask the butler." He paused to drink half his coffee in one swallow. "Where's Kathleen? Still abed?"

"Are you joking? She's been awake for hours. At the moment she's with the housekeeper, showing deliverymen where to set the flower arrangements." A fond smile crossed Devon's lips as he rolled the pencil against the tabletop with the flat of his hand. "You know my wife—every detail has to be perfect."

"It's like staging a production at St. James's Music Hall. Without, sadly, the chorus girls in pink tights." West drained the rest of his coffee. "My God, will this day never end?"

"It's only six o'clock in the morning," Devon pointed out.

They both sighed.

"I've never thanked you properly for marrying Kathleen at the registrar's office," West commented. "I want you to know how much I enjoyed it."

"You weren't there."

"That's why I enjoyed it."

Devon's lips twitched. "I was glad not to have to wait," he said. "But had there been more time, I wouldn't have minded going through a more elaborate ceremony for Kathleen's sake."

"Please. Shovel that manure in someone else's direction."

Devon grinned and pushed back from the table, taking his cup to the sideboard for more coffee. "I thought last night went well," he remarked over his shoulder. "You and Lady Clare appeared to hit it off."

"How did you arrive at that conclusion?" West asked, trying his best to sound indifferent.

"For most of the dinner, you stared at her as if she were the dessert course."

Making his face expressionless, West leaned back in his chair and regarded his empty cup. He could barely wedge one fingertip through the ornate loop. "Why are the handles on these teacups so small? Were they made for babies?"

"It's French porcelain. Kathleen says we're supposed to pinch the handle between the thumb and forefinger."

"What's wrong with adult-sized cups?"

Unfortunately, the diversionary tactic didn't budge Devon from his original subject. "I wasn't the only one to notice the attraction between you and Lady Clare."

"At the moment," West said, "I'd be attracted to any available woman under the age of ninety. The spring breeding season hasn't yet finished, and every creature on this estate has been happily fornicating for weeks. Except me. Do you know how long I've been celibate? Every morning I wake up in a state of medical crisis."

"I should think an attractive young widow would be able to help with that," Devon said, resuming his seat.

"You must still be half crocked from all the wine last night. There's no possibility a woman like Lady Clare would take a serious interest in me. Nor would I want her to."

Devon gave him an astute glance. "You think her too far above you?"

Fiddling with the teacup handle, West accidentally caught a fingertip in it. "I don't *think* it. She *is* too far above me—morally, financially, socially, and any other 'ly' you can think of. Besides, as I've said many times before, I'm not the marrying kind."

"If you're trying to hang on to your carefree bachelor's existence," Devon said, "it died approximately two years ago. You might as well accept that and settle down."

"I would show you the appropriate finger," West muttered, "if it weren't stuck in this baby handle." He tugged at his imprisoned middle digit, trying to free it without snapping the teacup's porcelain loop.

"If a woman like Lady Clare has even the slightest interest in you, you don't slink away. You fall to your knees in gratitude."

"For the first half of our lives," West retorted, "you and I were at everyone's mercy. Pushed, pulled, and manipulated by relations who made our lives pure misery. We were puppets on strings. I won't live like that again."

He would never forget those years of being desperately poor and powerless. He and Devon had been outsiders at boarding school, where the other boys had all seemed to know each other. They had all been to the right places, and made jokes he hadn't understood, and he'd envied their ease with themselves and each other. He'd hated feeling different, always out of place. Devon had quickly learned how to adjust to his circumstances. West, on the other hand, had been angry, awkward, and chubby. His only defense had been to turn into a crass, sneering bully.

In time, West's resentment had eased, and he'd learned to mask his rough edges with humor. After he'd come of age, a small but tidy annuity from a trust left by his parents had enabled him, finally, to live well, dress well. But the sense of not quite belonging was never far from the surface. In a way, it had helped him learn to navigate between the worlds of aristocrats, poor tenant farmers, servants, tradesmen, bankers, cobblers, and herdsmen. As an outsider, he could see their problems and needs more clearly. Belonging nowhere was almost like belonging everywhere. It had its limitations, however, especially when it came to women like Phoebe, Lady Clare.

"Taking a rich wife . . . a duke's daughter . . . there would be strings. Golden chains. It would all have to be her way. Her decision would always be the last."

West tugged irritably at his trapped finger. "I'll be damned if I dance to her tune, or her father's."

"We all have to dance to someone's tune. The best you can hope for is to like the music."

West scowled. "You never sound like more of an idiot than when you try to say something wise and pithy."

"I'm not the one with his finger stuck in a teacup," Devon pointed out. "Is there any other reason you won't pursue her, besides the money? Because that one rings hollow."

It wasn't just the money. But West was too tired and surly to try to make his brother understand. "Just because you've given up all masculine pride," he muttered, "doesn't mean I have to do the same."

"Do you know what kind of men are able to keep their masculine pride?" Devon asked. "Celibate ones. The rest of us don't mind doing a little begging and appeasing, if it means not having to sleep alone."

"If you're finished—" West began, with an irritated gesture of his hand.

At that moment, the teacup came unstuck, flung itself off his finger, and went soaring through an open window. Both brothers stared blankly after the path of its flight. A few seconds later, they heard a crash of porcelain on a graveled pathway.

In the silence, West shot a narrow-eyed glance at his brother, who was trying so hard not to laugh that his facial muscles were twitching.

Finally, Devon managed to regain control of himself. "So glad your right hand is free again," he said in a conversational tone. "Especially since it seems that for the foreseeable future, you'll be making frequent use of it."

THE SURPRISE OF Pandora and Lord St. Vincent's wedding day was that there were no surprises. Thanks to the meticulous planning done by Kathleen and the housekeeper, Mrs. Church, and the skill of the household staff, the ceremony and breakfast were impeccable. Even the weather had cooperated; the morning was dry and clear beneath a crystalline blue sky.

Pandora, who walked down the aisle of the estate chapel on Devon's arm, was radiantly beautiful in a dress of white silk, the billowing skirts so intricately gathered and draped that no lace or ornamental trim had been necessary. She wore a coronet of fresh daisies and a veil of sheer tulle and carried a small bouquet of roses and daisies.

If West had any remaining doubts about St. Vincent's true feelings for his bride, they were forever banished as he saw the man's expression. St. Vincent stared at Pandora as if she were a miracle, his cool composure disrupted by a faint flush of emotion. When Pandora reached him and the veil was pushed back, St. Vincent broke with etiquette by leaning down to press a tender kiss on her forehead.

"That part isn't 'til later," Pandora whispered to him, but it was loud enough that the people around them overheard, and a rustle of laughter swept through the crowd.

As the pastor began to speak, West glanced discreetly at the pew across the aisle, where the Challons were seated in a row. The duke whispered something in his wife's ear that made her smile, before he brought her hand up to kiss the backs of her fingers.

Phoebe sat on the duchess's other side, with Justin on her lap. The boy leaned back against the soft curves of his mother's bosom, while he played with a small toy elephant made of leather. The elephant trotted up one of Phoebe's arms. Gently she pushed the toy back down and tried to direct Justin's attention to the ceremony. In a moment, however, the elephant crept stealthily up her arm again, past her elbow, up to her shoulder.

West watched with covert interest, expecting Phoebe to reprimand the child. Instead, she waited until the elephant had almost reached the joint of her neck. Turning her head, she bit it playfully, her white teeth closing on the little trunk. Justin snatched the elephant away with a giggle and subsided in her lap.

West was struck by how natural and affectionate their interaction was. Clearly this was not the usual upper-class arrangement in which a child was raised by the servants and seldom seen or heard by his mother. Phoebe's sons meant everything to her. Any candidate for her next husband would have to be ideal father material: wholesome, respectable, and wise.

God knew that left him out of the running.

That life—of being Phoebe's husband, father to her children—was ready-made for someone else. A man who deserved the right to live with her in intimacy and watch her nightly feminine rituals of bathing, slipping on a nightgown, brushing out her hair. He alone would take her to bed, make love to her, and hold her while she slept. Someone out there was destined for all of that.

Whoever he was, West hated the bastard.

Chapter 9

THE MORNING AFTER THE wedding, Phoebe waited with her father and son in the front receiving room. Despite her reluctance, she had decided to go on the farm tour after all. There were few other options: it was still quite early, and the houseguests would all be sleeping for hours yet. She had tried to stay abed, but her brain was too restless, and it took more effort to keep her eyes closed than open.

The bed was comfortable but different from the one at home, the mattress stuffing a bit softer than she preferred.

Home . . . the word summoned thoughts of her family's wide, airy, low-slung house by the sea, with arbors of pink roses over the courtyard entrance, and the holloway in the back leading down to the sandy beach. But soon she would have to start thinking of the Clare estate as home, even though when she returned, she would feel nearly as much of a stranger as she'd been on the day Henry had brought her there as his bride.

She was uneasy about the condition of the land and farms. According to Edward, who sent her quarterly reports on estate business, rental income and crop yields had gone down for the second straight year. And grain prices had fallen. He'd told her that even though the estate had hit a rough patch, everything would eventually go back to the way it had always been. These things were cyclical, he'd said.

But what if he was wrong?

Justin charged across the room on his wooden hobbyhorse, made of a wooden stick with a carved horse head on one end and a little set of wheels on the other. "Gramps," he asked, prancing and trotting around Phoebe's father, Sebastian, who sat at a small table reading correspondence, "are you very graceful?"

The duke looked up from the letter in his hand. "Why do you ask, child?"

The wooden horse reared and turned in a tight circle. "Because everyone always talks about your grace. But why?"

Sebastian exchanged a laughing glance with Phoebe. "I believe you're referring to the honorific," he told Justin. "People call a nonroyal duke or duchess 'Your Grace' as a term of respect, not as a reference to personal qualities." A reflective pause. "Although I do happen to be quite graceful."

The child continued to dash about on the hobbyhorse.

Hearing the metal wheels knock against a table leg, Phoebe winced and said, "Justin, dear, do be careful."

"It wasn't me," her son protested. "It was Splinter. He has too much energy. He's hard to control."

"Tell him if he doesn't behave, you'll have to stable him in a broom closet."

"I can't," Justin said regretfully. "There are no holes in his ears for the words to go in."

As Phoebe watched her son romp out of the room into the entrance hall, she said, "I hope Splinter doesn't knock over a housemaid or overturn a vase."

"Ravenel should be here soon."

Phoebe nodded, picking restlessly at a bit of frayed upholstery on the arm of her chair.

Sebastian's voice was soft and interested. "What's troubling you, Redbird?"

"Oh . . ." Phoebe shrugged and smoothed the upholstery threads repeatedly. "For two years, I've given Edward Larson free rein in managing the Clare estate. Now I regret not having taken more of a hand in it. I have to start thinking like a businesswoman—which is about as natural to me as singing opera. I hope I'll prove equal to the job."

"Of course you will. You're my daughter."

She smiled at him, feeling reassured.

West Ravenel entered the room, dressed in a sack coat, well-worn trousers, and a collarless shirt. The leather boots on his feet were scuffed and scarred to a condition that no amount of polish could ever restore. The sight of him, big and handsome in the rough casual attire, caused a breath to stick in Phoebe's throat.

That long, luxurious, strangely intimate dinner now seemed like a dream. She'd been so animated, so chatty—it must have been the wine. She remembered behaving foolishly. Laughing too much. She recalled telling Mr. Ravenel that she no longer took pleasure in eating, after which she'd proceeded to devour a twelve-course meal like a starving London cab horse. God, why hadn't she behaved with her usual restraint? Why hadn't she guarded her tongue?

Her face turned hot, the skin of her cheeks smarting.

"My lady," he murmured, and bowed. He turned to her father. "Kingston."

"Have you been working already?" Sebastian asked.

"No, I rode out to the east side to have a look at the quarry. We're mining a rare deposit of hematite ore, and—" Mr. Ravenel paused as he caught sight of Justin ducking behind a settee with the hobbyhorse. Resting most of his weight on one leg in a relaxed stance, he said with feigned regret, "Someone's let a horse into the house. What a nuisance. Once they're inside, it's impossible to get rid of them. I'll have to tell the housekeeper to set out some traps and bait them with carrots."

The wooden horse peeked out from behind the top edge of the settee and shook his head.

"Not carrots?" Mr. Ravenel asked, advancing stealthily toward the settee. "What about apples?"

Another shake.

"A lump of sugar?"

"Plum cakes," came a small, muffled voice.

"Plum cakes," Mr. Ravenel repeated in villainous satisfaction. "A horse's greatest weakness. Soon he'll be caught in my trap . . . and then . . ." He dove behind the settee, pouncing on Phoebe's unseen son.

A shriek tore through the air, followed by a rush of boyish giggles and the sounds of rough-and-tumble play.

Uneasily Phoebe began to move forward to intervene. Justin wasn't accustomed to interacting with adult males except for her father and brothers. But her father stopped her with a light touch on her arm, a slight smile on his face.

Mr. Ravenel rose from behind the settee, disheveled and rumpled. "Pardon," he said with an air of mild concern, "but do I have something on my coat?" He twisted and turned to look over his shoulder, revealing Justin, who clung to his back like a monkey, short legs clamped around his lean waist.

Phoebe was both puzzled and disarmed to see her son playing so easily with a virtual stranger. She couldn't help but compare it to his interactions with Edward Larson, who was not the kind to indulge in spontaneous romping.

"Shall we be off?" Mr. Ravenel asked her father.

"I'm coming too," Phoebe said. "If you have no objections."

Mr. Ravenel's expression was unfathomable. "It would be a pleasure, my lady."

"Justin," Sebastian said, "come walk with me. We'll let Mr. Ravenel escort Mama."

Phoebe shot a vexed glance at her father, who pretended not to notice.

Mr. Ravenel crouched low for Justin to wriggle down from his back and came to Phoebe.

She was vaguely aware of her father saying something about taking Justin outside.

Mr. Ravenel's quiet voice cut through the kettledrum clamor of her heartbeat. "I hope you haven't been coerced into this."

"No . . . I want to come."

A husky laugh rustled across her senses. "Said with all the enthusiasm of a sheep in the middle of its first shearing."

Seeing that his expression was friendly rather than mocking, Phoebe relaxed slightly. "I'm embarrassed for you to discover how little I know about any of this," she admitted. "You'll think badly of me. You'll think it was willful ignorance."

Mr. Ravenel was silent for a moment. When he replied, his tone was very gentle.

She blinked in surprise as she felt him touch her chin, angling her face upward. His fingers were dry and warm, textured like sandpaper and silk. The sensation carried and throbbed all through her. Two of his knuckles rested against the front of her throat with gossamer-light pressure. She stared up into his dark blue eyes, while a mysterious awareness brooded between them.

"You had an invalid husband and a young son to raise," he said gently. "You had your hands full. Did you think I wouldn't understand that?"

Phoebe was sure he could feel the movement of her swallow before his touch was slowly withdrawn. "Thank you," she managed to say.

"For what?" He offered his arm, and she took it, her fingers curling over the sleeve of his unlined linen coat.

"For not criticizing, after I just gave you the perfect opportunity."

"A man with my history? I may be a scoundrel, but I'm not a hypocrite."

"You're very hard on yourself. What did you do in the past that was so unforgivable?"

They left the house and began on a wide gravel path that led behind the manor. "Nothing stands out in particular," he replied. "Only years of common-run debauchery."

"But you've changed your ways, haven't you?"

A sardonic smile crossed his face. "On the surface."

The day was warming fast, the air weighted with the sweetness of clover and grass and pasture scents. A dunnock fluted notes from its perch in an ancient hedge, while robins called from the treetops.

Her father and Justin had already gone far ahead, veering off the path to investigate the row of four glasshouses beyond the formal gardens. In the distance, a set of farm buildings loomed over rows of stockyards and sheds.

Phoebe tried to think of what a businesswoman might ask. "Your approach to land management . . . the modern methods, the machinery . . . Edward Larson told me it was called 'high farming.' He says it stands for high expenses and high risk, and some of the landowners who've tried it have been ruined."

"Many have been," Mr. Ravenel surprised her by admitting. "Mostly because they took foolish risks or made improvements that didn't need to be made. But that's not what high farming is about. It's about scientific methods and common sense."

"Mr. Larson says the tried-and-true traditions are all a gentleman farmer needs to know. He says science should be kept apart from nature."

Mr. Ravenel stopped in his tracks, obliging Phoebe to turn and face him. His lips parted as if he were about to say something blistering, then closed, and opened again. Eventually he asked, "May I speak plainly, or do I have to be polite?"

"I prefer politeness."

"All right. Your estate is being managed by a damned idiot."

"That's the polite version?" Phoebe asked, mildly startled.

"To begin with, science isn't something separate from nature. Science is how nature works. Second, a 'gentleman farmer' isn't a farmer. If you have to preface your occupation with 'gentleman,' it's a hobby. Third—"

"You know nothing about Edward," Phoebe protested.

"I know his kind. He'd rather choose extinction than keep pace with progress. He'll drag your estate into ruin, just so he doesn't have to learn new ways of doing things."

"Newer isn't always better."

"Neither is older. If doing things the primitive way is so bloody marvelous, why allow the tenants to use a horse-drawn plow? Let's have them scatter the seeds across the field by hand."

"Edward Larson isn't against progress. He only questions whether a mechanical reaper polluting the fields is better than the wholesome work done by good, strong men with scythes."

"Do you know who would ask that question? A man who's never gone out to a cornfield with a scythe."

"No doubt you have," Phoebe said tartly.

"As a matter of fact, I have. It's brutal work. A scythe is weighted to create extra momentum as it cuts through the thicker stalks. You have to twist your torso in a constant motion that makes your sides burn. Every thirty yards, you have to stop to hammer nicks out of the blade and hone it sharp again. I went out with the men one morning, and I lasted less than a day. By noon, every muscle was on fire, and my hands were too blistered and bloody to grip the handle." Mr. Ravenel paused, looking irate. "The best scythe-man can cut one acre of corn in a day. A mechanical reaper will cut twelve acres in the same amount of time. Did Larson happen to mention that while rhapsodizing about field labor?"

"He did not," Phoebe admitted, feeling simultaneously annoyed with herself, Edward, and the man in front of her.

From a distance, she heard her father's lazy voice: "Arguing already? We haven't even reached the barn."

"No, Father," Phoebe called back. "It's only that Mr. Ravenel is rather passionate on the subject of scything."

"Mama," Justin exclaimed, "come see what we found!"

"One moment, darling." Phoebe stared up at Mr. Ravenel with narrowed eyes. He was standing too close to her, his head and shoulders blocking the sunlight. "You should know that looming over me like that doesn't intimidate me," she said curtly. "I grew up with two very large brothers."

He relaxed his posture instantly, hooking his thumbs in his trouser pockets. "I'm not trying to intimidate you. I'm taller. I can't help that."

Hogwash, Phoebe thought. He knew quite well he'd been standing over her. But she was secretly amused by the sight of him trying so hard not to appear overbearing. "Don't think I couldn't cut you down to size," she warned.

He gave her an innocent glance. "Just as long as you do it by hand."

The smart-aleck remark surprised a laugh from her. *Insolent rascal.*

West Ravenel smiled slightly, his gaze holding hers, and for a moment her throat tingled sweetly at the back, as if she'd just swallowed a spoonful of cool honey.

By tacit agreement, they resumed walking. They caught up to Sebastian and Justin, who had stopped to watch a young cat wandering along the side of the path.

Justin's small form was very still with excitement, his attention riveted on the black feline. "Look, Mama!"

Phoebe glanced at Mr. Ravenel. "Is she feral?"

"No, but she's undomesticated. We keep a few barn cats to reduce the rodent and insect population."

"Can I pet her?" Justin asked.

"You could try," Mr. Ravenel said, "but she won't come close enough. Barn cats prefer to keep their distance from people." His brows lifted as the small black cat made her way to Sebastian and curled around his leg, arching and purring. "With the apparent exception of dukes. My God, she's a snob."

Sebastian lowered to his haunches. "Come here, Justin," he murmured, gently kneading the cat along its spine to the base of its tail.

The child approached with his small hand outstretched.

"Softly," Sebastian cautioned. "Smooth her fur the same way it grows."

Justin stroked the cat carefully, his eyes growing round as her purring grew even louder. "How does she make that sound?"

"No one has yet found a satisfactory explanation," Sebastian replied. "Personally, I hope they never do."

"Why, Gramps?"

Sebastian smiled into the small face so close to his. "Sometimes the mystery is more delightful than the answer."

As the group continued to the farm buildings, the cat followed.

The mixed odors of the stockyards hung thick in the air, the sweetness of straw, stored grain and sawdust mingling with the smells of animals, manure, sweat, and lather. There was the acrid bite of carbolic soap, whiffs of fresh paint and turpentine, the dusty richness of a granary, the earthy mustiness of a root house. Instead of the usual haphazard scattering of farm structures, the barns and sheds had been laid out in the shape of an E.

As Mr. Ravenel led them past barns, workshops, and sheds, a group of workers and stockmen approached him freely. The men snatched off their caps respectfully as they greeted him, but even so, their manner was more familiar than it would have been with the master of the estate. They conferred with him easily, grins appearing as they joked back and forth. Phoebe was close enough to hear a comment about the wedding, followed by an impudent question about whether Mr. Ravenel had found a lady willing to "buckle to" him.

"Do you think I'd find the makings of a good farm wife in *that* crowd?" Mr. Ravenel retorted, causing a round of chuckles.

"My daughter Agatha's a big, strong-docked girl," a huge man wearing a leather apron volunteered.

"She'd be a prize for any man," Mr. Ravenel replied. "But you're a blacksmith, Stub. I couldn't have you as a father-in-law."

"Too grand for me, are you?" the blacksmith asked good-naturedly.

"No, it's only that you're twice my size. The first time she ran home to you, you'd come after me with hammer and tongs." Hearty laughter rumbled through the group. "Lads," Mr. Ravenel continued, "we're in fine company today. This gentleman is His Grace, the Duke of Kingston. He's accompanied by his daughter, Lady Clare, and his grandson, Master Justin." Turning to Sebastian, he said, "Your Grace, we go by nicknames here. Allow me to introduce Neddy, Brick-end, Rollaboy, Stub, Slippy, and Chummy."

Sebastian bowed, the morning light striking glitters of gold and silver in his hair. Although his manner was relaxed and amiable, his presence was formidable nonetheless. Thunderstruck by the presence of a duke in the barnyard, the group mumbled greetings, bobbed a few bows, and gripped their caps more tightly. At a nudge from his grandfather, Justin lifted his cap and bowed to the cluster of men. Taking the boy with him, Sebastian went to speak to each man.

After years of experience running the club on St. James, Sebastian could talk easily with anyone from royalty down to the most hardened street criminal. Soon he had the men smiling and volunteering information about their work at Eversby Priory.

"Your father has a common touch," came Mr. Ravenel's quiet voice near her ear. He watched Sebastian with a mix of interest and admiration. "One doesn't usually see that in a man of his position."

"He's always mocked the notion that vice runs more rampant among commoners than nobility," Phoebe said. "In fact, he says the opposite is usually true."

Mr. Ravenel looked amused. "He could be right. Although I've seen a fair share of vice among both."

In a moment, Mr. Ravenel drew Phoebe, Sebastian, and Justin with him to the engine barn, which had been divided into a series of machine rooms. It was cool and dank inside, with narrow spills of sun coming from high windows. There were scents of dry stoker coal, wood shavings, and new pine boards, and the sharp notes of machine oil, tallow grease, and metal polish.

Complex machines filled the quiet space, all massive gears and wheels, with innards of tanks and cylinders. Phoebe craned her neck to look up at a contraption equipped with extensions that reached two stories in height.

Mr. Ravenel laughed quietly at her apprehensive expression. "This is a steam-powered thresher," he said. "It would take a dozen men and women an entire day to do what this machine does in one hour. Come closer—it won't bite."

Phoebe obeyed cautiously, coming to stand next to him. She felt a brief pressure on her lower back, the reassuring touch of his hand, and her heartbeat quickened in response.

Justin had crept closer as well, staring at the enormous thresher with awe. Mr. Ravenel smiled, reached down, and hoisted Justin high enough to see. To Phoebe's surprise, her son instantly curved a small arm around the man's neck. "They load the sheaves in there," Mr. Ravenel explained, walking to the rear of the machine and pointing to a huge horizontal cylinder. "Inside, a set of beaters separates grain from straw. Then the straw is carried up that conveyor and delivered onto a cart or stack. The corn falls through a series of screens and blowers and pours out from there"—he pointed to a spout—"all ready for market."

Still holding Justin, Mr. Ravenel walked to a machine next to the thresher, a large engine with a boiler, smokebox and cylinders, all affixed to a carriage foundation on wheels. "This traction engine tows the thresher and gives it power."

Sebastian came to examine the traction engine more closely, running a thumb lightly over the riveted seams of the metal shell around the boiler. "Consolidated Locomotive," he murmured, reading the manufacturer's mark. "I happen to be acquainted with the owner."

"It's a well-made engine," Mr. Ravenel said, "but you might tell him that his siphon lubricators are rubbish. We keep having to replace them."

"You could tell him yourself. He's one of your wedding guests."

Mr. Ravenel grinned at him. "I know. But I'm damned if I'll insult one of Simon Hunt's traction engines to his face. It would ruin any chance of getting a discount in the future."

Sebastian laughed—one of the full, unguarded laughs he permitted himself when in the company of family or the closest of friends. There was no doubt about it—he liked the audacious young man, who clearly didn't fear him in the least.

Phoebe frowned at the use of a curse word in front of Justin, but she held her tongue.

"How does the engine know where to go?" Justin was asking Mr. Ravenel.

"A man sits up there on that seat board and pushes the steering post."

"The long stick with the handle?"

"Yes, that one."

They squatted to look at the gearing leading to the wheels, their two dark heads close together. Justin seemed fascinated by the machine, but even more so by the man who was explaining it to him.

Reluctantly Phoebe acknowledged that Justin needed a father, not merely the extra time his grandfather and uncles could spare. It grieved her that neither of her sons had any memories of Henry. She'd had fantasies of him walking through a blooming spring garden with his two boys, stopping to examine a bird's nest or a butterfly drying its wings. It was disconcerting to contrast those hazy romantic images with the sight of West Ravenel showing Justin the gears and levers of a traction engine in a machine shop.

She watched apprehensively as Mr. Ravenel began to lift her son to the seat board of the traction engine. "Wait," she said. He paused, glancing at her over his shoulder. "Do you mean for him to climb up there?" she asked. "On that machine?"

"Mama," Justin protested, "I just want to sit on it."

"Can't you see enough of it from the ground?" she asked.

Her son gave her an aggrieved glance. "That's not the same as sitting on it."

Sebastian grinned. "It's all right, Redbird. I'll go up there with him."

Mr. Ravenel glanced at the workman standing nearby. "Neddy," he asked, "will you distract Lady Clare while I proceed to endanger her father and son?"

The man ventured forward, a bit apprehensively, as if he thought Phoebe might rebuke him. "Milady . . . shall I show you the piggery?" He seemed relieved by her sudden laugh.

"Thank you," she said. "I would appreciate that."

Chapter 10

$\mathscr{P}$HOEBE WENT WITH THE workman to a partially covered pen where a newly farrowed sow reclined with her piglets. "How long have you worked on the estate home farm, Neddy?"

"Since I be a lad, milady."

"What do you make of all this 'high farming' business?"

"Couldn't say. But I trust Mr. Ravenel. Solid as a brick, he be. When he first came pokin' about Eversby Priory, none of us wanted nothin' to do with a fine-feathered city toff."

"What changed your mind about him?"

The old man shrugged, his narrow rectangular face creasing with a faint, reminiscent smile. "Mr. Ravenel has a way about him. A good, honest man, he be, for all his cleverness. Give him a halter, and he'll find a horse." His smile broadened as he added, "He be a sprack 'un."

"Sprack?" Phoebe repeated, unfamiliar with the word.

"A lively lad, quick in mind and body. Up early and late. Sprack." He snapped his lean fingers smartly as he said the word. "Mr. Ravenel knows how to make it all go together—the new ways and the old. Has a touch for it. Put the land in good heart, he has."

"It seems I should take his advice, then," Phoebe mused aloud. "About my own farms."

Neddy looked at her alertly. "*Your* farms, milady?"

"They're my son's," she admitted. "I'm looking after them until he comes of age."

He looked sympathetic and interested. "You be a widder, milady?"

"Yes."

"You should buckle to Mr. Ravenel," he suggested. "A fine husband he'd make. You'd get some great rammin' bairns off that one, certain sure."

Phoebe smiled uncomfortably, having forgotten how frank country folk could be in discussing highly personal matters.

They were soon joined by Mr. Ravenel, Sebastian, and Justin. Her son was bright-eyed with enthusiasm. "Mama, I pretend-steered the engine! Mr. Ravenel says I can drive it for real when I'm bigger!"

Before the tour resumed, Mr. Ravenel ceremoniously escorted Justin to a shed containing cisterns of pig manure, claiming it was the worst-smelling thing on the farm. After stopping at the shed's threshold and sniffing the rank air, Justin made a revolted face and hurried back, exclaiming in happy disgust. They proceeded to a barn with an attached dairy, a feed house, and a shed of box stalls. Red-and-white cows meandered in a nearby paddock, while the rest of the herd grazed in the pasture beyond.

"This is stock rearing on a larger scale than I expected," Sebastian commented, his assessing gaze moving to the rich land on the other side of the timber rail fence. "Your cattle are pasture-raised?"

Mr. Ravenel nodded.

"There would be less expense involved in stall-raising them on corn," Sebastian pressed. "They would fatten more quickly, would they not?"

"Correct."

"Why let them out to pasture, then?"

Mr. Ravenel looked somewhat chagrined as he replied. "I can't confine them in stalls for their entire lives."

"Can't or won't?"

Phoebe glanced at her father quizzically, wondering why he found the subject so absorbing, when he'd never shown any interest in cattle before.

"Mama," Justin said, tugging at her elbow-length sleeve. She looked down to discover the black cat brushing against the hem of her skirts. Purring, the creature wound around Justin's legs.

Phoebe smiled and returned her attention to Mr. Ravenel.

". . . would be a better business decision to keep them in stalls," he was admitting to her father. "But there's more to consider than profit. I can't bring myself to treat these animals as mere commodities. It seems only decent . . . respectful . . . to allow them to lead healthy, natural lives for as long as possible." He grinned as he noticed the expression of a nearby workman. "My head cowman, Brick-end, disagrees."

The cowman, a heavyset mountain of a man with piercing gimlet eyes, said flatly, "Stall-fattened beef brings a higher price at the London markets. Soft, corn-fed meat's what they want."

Mr. Ravenel's reply was conciliatory; clearly it was an issue they'd discussed before, without a mutually satisfactory resolution. "We're crossing our stock to a new shorthorn line. It will give us cows that fatten more easily on pasture grass."

"Fifty guineas to hire a prize bull from Northampton for the season," Brick-end grumbled. "It would be cheaper to—" He broke off abruptly, his sharp eyes focusing on the cow paddock.

Phoebe followed his gaze, and a shock of horror gripped her as she saw that Justin had wandered away and climbed through the paddock's timber fence rails. He appeared to have followed the cat, which had scampered inside the enclosure to bat playfully at a butterfly. But the paddock contained more than cows. A huge brindle bull had separated from the herd. It stood in an aggressive broadside display, shoulders hunched and back arched.

The bull was no more than twenty feet away from her son.

Chapter 11

"JUSTIN," PHOEBE HEARD HERSELF say calmly, "I want you to walk backward to me, very slowly. Right now." It took twice as much breath to produce the usual amount of sound.

Her son's small head lifted. A visible start went through him at the sight of the bull. Fear made him clumsy, and he tripped backward, falling on his rump. The massive animal swung to face him in a lightning-swift change of balance, hooves churning the ground.

Mr. Ravenel had already vaulted the fence, his hand touching the top of a post, his feet passing over the top rail without even touching it. As soon as he landed, he ran to interpose his body between Justin and the bull. Giving a hoarse shout and waving his arms, he distracted the animal from its intended target.

Phoebe scrambled forward, but her father was already easing through the rails in a supple movement. "Stay," he said curtly.

She clung to one of the rails and waited, quivering from head to toe, as she watched her father stride swiftly to Justin, scoop him up, and carry him back. A sob of relief escaped her as he handed her child to her through the fence. She sank to her knees with her arms around Justin. Every breath was a prayer of gratitude.

"I'm sorry . . . I'm sorry . . ." Justin was gasping.

"Shhh . . . you're safe . . . it's all right," Phoebe said, her heartbeat tumbling over on itself. Realizing Sebastian hadn't climbed out yet, she said unsteadily, "Father—"

"Ravenel, what can I do?" he asked calmly.

"With respect, sir"—Mr. Ravenel was double-dodging and darting, trying to anticipate the bull's movements—"get the hell out of here."

Sebastian complied readily, slipping back through the rails.

"That goes for you too, Brick," Mr. Ravenel snapped, as the head cowman climbed the fence to straddle the top. "I don't need you in here."

"Keep him circling," Brick-end shouted. "He can't move forward if he can't swing his hindquarters around."

"Right," Mr. Ravenel said briskly, orbiting the enraged bull.

"Can you try to step a bit more lively?"

"No, Brick," Mr. Ravenel retorted, running at an angle and sharply reversing direction. "I'm fairly sure this is as fast as I can move."

More workmen had come running to the fence, all shouting and throwing hats in the air to draw the bull's attention, but it was firmly fixed on the man in the paddock. The one-ton animal was astonishingly lithe, its glossy loose-skinned bulk stopping dead, shifting to one side and the other, then pinwheeling in pursuit of his adversary. Mr. Ravenel never took his gaze from the creature, instinctively countering every movement. It was like some macabre dance in which one misplaced step would be fatal.

Dodging to the right, Mr. Ravenel tricked the bull into a half-twist. Doubling back, he ran full-bore to the fence and dove between the rails. The bull pivoted and thundered after him, but stopped short, snorting in fury, as Mr. Ravenel's legs slithered through the barrier.

Cheers of relief and excitement went up from the assembled workmen.

"Thank God," Phoebe murmured, pressing her cheek against Justin's damp, dark hair. *What if . . . what if . . .* God, she'd barely managed to survive losing Henry. If anything had happened to Justin . . .

Her father's hand patted her back gently. "Ravenel's been hurt."

"*What?*" Phoebe's head jerked up. All she could see was a cluster of workmen gathered around a form on the ground. But she'd seen Mr. Ravenel dive cleanly between the fence rails. How could he be hurt? Frowning in worry, she eased Justin out of her lap. "Father, if you would take Justin—"

Sebastian took the boy without a word, and Phoebe leaped to her feet. Gathering up her skirts, she rushed to the group of workmen and pushed her way through.

Mr. Ravenel was half sitting, half reclining with his back propped against a fence post. His shirt hem had been tugged free of his trousers. Beneath the loose fabric, he clasped a hand to his side, just above the hip.

He was breathing hard and sweating, his eyes gleaming with the half-mad exhilaration of a man who'd just survived a life-threatening experience. A crooked grin emerged as he saw her. "Just a scratch."

Relief began to creep through her. "Neddy was right," she said. "You *are* a sprack 'un." The men around them chuckled. Drawing closer, she asked, "Did the bull's horns catch you?"

Mr. Ravenel shook his head. "A nail on the fence."

Phoebe frowned in concern. "It must be cleaned right away. You'll be fortunate if you don't end up with lockjaw."

"Nothing could lock that jaw," Brick-end said slyly, and the group erupted with guffaws.

"Let me have a look," Phoebe said, kneeling by Mr. Ravenel's side.

"You can't."

"Why not?"

He sent her a vaguely exasperated glance. "It's . . . not in a proper location."

"For heaven's sake, I was a married woman." Undeterred, Phoebe reached for the hem of the shirt.

"Wait." Mr. Ravenel's tanned complexion had turned the color of rosewood. He scowled at the workmen, who were observing the proceedings with great interest. "Can a man have a bit of privacy?"

Brick-end proceeded to shoo the small crowd away, saying brusquely, "Back to work, lads. Don't stand there a-garpin'."

Mumbling, the workmen retreated.

Phoebe pulled up Mr. Ravenel's shirt. The top three buttons of his trousers had been unfastened, the waistband sagging to reveal a lean torso wrought with layers of muscle. One strong hand clamped a sooty, greasy-looking cloth a few inches above his left hip.

"Why are you holding a filthy rag against an open wound?" Phoebe demanded.

"It was the only thing we could find."

Phoebe took three clean, crisp handkerchiefs from her pocket, and folded them to make a pad.

Mr. Ravenel's brows lifted as he watched her. "Do you always carry so many handkerchiefs?"

She had to smile at that. "I have children." Leaning over him, she carefully peeled away the dirty cloth. Blood welled from the three-inch wound on his side. It was a nasty scratch, undoubtedly deep enough to require stitches.

As Phoebe pressed the pad of handkerchiefs over the injury, Mr. Ravenel winced and leaned back against the post to avoid physical contact with her. "My lady . . . I can do that . . ." He paused to take an agitated breath, his hand fumbling to replace hers. His color was still high, the blue of his eyes like the flickering core of a heartwood fire.

"I'm sorry," she said. "But we have to apply pressure to slow the bleeding."

"I don't need your help," he said testily. "Let me have it."

Taken aback, Phoebe let go of the folded pad. Mr. Ravenel refused to meet her gaze, his thick dark brows knitting together as he held the cloth against the wound.

She couldn't help stealing a covert glance at the exposed part of his torso, the flesh so firm and tanned it appeared to have been cast in bronze. Lower down near his hip, the satiny brown skin merged into a line of ivory. The sight was so intriguing—and intimate—that she felt her stomach tighten pleasurably. Leaning over him as she was, she couldn't help breathing in the dusty, sweaty, sun-heated scent of him. A stunning urge seized her, to touch that brown-and-white borderline with her fingertip, trace a path across his body.

"I'll have your men fetch a horse and cart to convey you back to the estate," she managed to say.

"There's no need for a cart. I can walk."

"You'll worsen the bleeding if you exert yourself."

"It's a scratch."

"A deep one," she persisted. "You may need stitches."

"All I need is salve and a bandage."

"We'll let a doctor decide. In the meanwhile, you must ride in the cart."

His voice was low and surly. "Are you planning to use bodily force? Because that's the only way you'll load me into the damn thing."

He seemed every bit as riled and menacing as the bull had a few minutes ago. But Phoebe wasn't about to let him make his injury worse out of pure male stubbornness.

"Forgive me if I'm being tyrannical," she said in

her most soothing tone. "I tend to do that when I'm concerned about someone. It's your decision, naturally. But I wish you would indulge me in this, if only to spare me from worrying over you every step of the way home."

The mulish set of his jaw eased. "I manage other people," he informed her. "People don't manage me."

"I'm not managing you."

"You're trying," he said darkly.

An irrepressible grin spread across her face. "Is it working?"

Slowly Mr. Ravenel's head lifted. He didn't reply, only gave her a strange, long look that spurred her heartbeat until she was light-headed from the force of its pounding. No man had ever stared at her like this. Not even her husband, for whom she'd always been close and attainable, her presence woven securely into the fabric of his days. Since childhood, she'd always been Henry's safe harbor.

But whatever it was this man wanted from her, it wasn't safety.

"You should humor my daughter's wishes, Ravenel," Sebastian advised from behind her. "The last time I tried to refuse her something, she launched into a screaming fit that lasted at least an hour."

The comment broke the trance. "Father," Phoebe protested with a laugh, twisting to glance at him over her shoulder, "I was two years old!"

"It made a lasting impression."

Phoebe's gaze fell to Justin, who stood half hidden behind Sebastian. His small face was tearstained and woebegone. "Darling," she said softly, wanting to comfort him, "come here."

Her son shook his head and retreated farther behind his grandfather.

"Justin," she heard Mr. Ravenel say in a gruff tone, "I want to talk to you."

Phoebe shot him a wary, wondering glance. Was he planning to scold her son? A few harsh words from him would devastate Justin.

Sebastian nudged the child forward.

Justin trudged reluctantly to Mr. Ravenel's side, his lower lip trembling, his eyes glassy.

As the man surveyed the crestfallen boy, his face gentled in a way that reassured Phoebe there was no need for her to intervene.

"Listen to me, Justin," Mr. Ravenel said quietly. "This was *my* fault. Not yours. You can't be expected to follow the rules if I haven't told them to you. I should have made certain you understood not to go inside one of the enclosures or pens by yourself. Never, for any reason."

"But the cat . . ." Justin faltered.

"She can take care of herself. She's over there, with at least eight lives left—you see?" Mr. Ravenel gestured to a nearby timber post, where the cat was grooming the side of her face delicately. The outer corners of his eyes tipped upward as he saw the boy's relief. "Regardless, if an animal is hurt or in danger, don't go near it. Ask an adult for help next time. An

14Lisa Kleypas

animal is replaceable. A boy is not. Do you understand?"

Justin nodded vigorously. "Yes, sir." The grace of forgiveness, when he'd expected harsh judgment, left him glowing with relief.

"Ravenel," she heard her father say, "I'm in your debt."

Mr. Ravenel shook his head immediately. "I deserve no credit, sir. It was all pure idiot reflex. I jumped in with no plan or forethought."

"Yes," Sebastian said reflectively, "that's what I liked about it."

By the time Mr. Ravenel had made it to his feet, the horse and cart had been brought around. The combination of pain and fading excitement had left him too weary to quarrel. After a testy comment or two, he climbed slowly into the vehicle. To Justin's delight, Mr. Ravenel invited him to ride in the cart as well. They settled on a stack of folded blankets, with Justin tucked against the man's good side. As the cart began to roll toward the manor house, the black cat leaped into the vehicle's open back.

Walking back with her father, Phoebe smiled ruefully at the sight of her son's beaming face in the distance. "Justin worships him now."

Her father arched a quizzical brow at her tone. "Is that a problem?"

"No, but . . . to a young boy, Mr. Ravenel must seem like a fantasy of a father. His own personal hero. Poor Edward Larson has little chance of competing."

Although her father remained relaxed, she sensed his sharp interest. "I wasn't aware Larson was in the running for such a role."

"Edward and I are fond of each other," Phoebe said. "And he's fond of the boys, too. He's known both of them since they were born. The last time he came to visit Heron's Point, he made it clear that he would be willing to assume Henry's place."

"Willing to assume Henry's place," Sebastian repeated with slow emphasis, his face darkening. "Is that how he declared himself?"

"It wasn't a marriage proposal, it was a prelude to a deeper conversation. Edward isn't one to rush things. He's a gentleman of courtesy and delicacy."

"Indeed. He doesn't lack for delicacy." Suddenly her father's voice was caustic enough to dissolve granite.

"Why do you say it like that?" Phoebe asked in surprise. "What do you have against Edward?"

"I can't help but question how my spirited daughter could fix her choice, once again, on a tepid Larson male. Is your blood really so thin that it calls for such milk-warm companionship?"

Phoebe stopped in her tracks, while outrage raced through her like wildfire. "Henry was not *tepid*!"

"No," her father allowed, stopping to face her. "Henry did have one passion, and that was you. It's why I eventually consented to the marriage, despite knowing the burden you would have to shoulder. Edward Larson, however, has yet to evince any such depth of feeling."

"Well, he wouldn't in front of you," she said hotly. "He's private. And it was never a burden to take care of Henry."

"Darling child," he said softly, "the burden is what you're facing now."

Chapter 12

$\mathcal{B}$Y THE TIME PHOEBE and her father had entered
the house, servants were running along the hallways
with toweling and cans of cold and hot water, and the
housekeeper was directing a footman to carry her
medicine case up to Mr. Ravenel's room.

"I'm going to speak to Lord and Lady Trenear," Sebastian murmured, and headed for the stairs.

Nanny Bracegirdle stood in the entrance hall with
Justin, who held the black cat against his chest. The
half-wild feline should have shredded him by now, but
she rested passively in his grasp, gazing around in bewildered curiosity at her strange new surroundings.

"Nanny," Phoebe exclaimed, hurrying over to them.
"Have you heard what happened?"

The older woman nodded. "Master Justin told me,
and so did the cart driver. The household's all in a
tither."

"Did you see Mr. Ravenel when he came in?"

"No, milady. They said he was a bit gray faced, but
steady on his feet. They sent for a doctor even though
he said not to."

Justin looked up at her with a grimace. "His scratch

wouldn't stop bleeding. The handkerchiefs you gave him are all ruined, Mama."

"That doesn't matter," she said. "Poor Mr. Ravenel—he'll definitely have to be stitched up."

"Will he have to stay in bed? I'll bring my cat to visit him."

Phoebe frowned regretfully. "Justin, I'm afraid you can't keep her."

"Oh, I already knew that."

"Good. Well, then—"

"—but you see, Mama, she wants to keep *me*."

"I'm sure she does, darling, but—"

"She wants to come live in Essex with us."

Phoebe's heart sank as she looked into his hopeful face. "But this is where she does her job."

"She wants to work for us now," her son informed her. "There are mice in Essex. Big, fat ones."

"Justin, she's not a house cat. She won't want to live with a family. She'll run off if we try to make her stay with us."

His brows lowered in a determined expression that was pure Challon. "No, she won't."

"It's time for a wash and a nap," Nanny intervened.

Phoebe seized gratefully on the pronouncement. "You're right as usual, Nanny. If you'll take Justin and the cat up to the nursery—"

"The cat can't come to the nursery." The nanny's face was dumpling soft, but her tone was unyielding.

"Even temporarily?" Phoebe asked weakly.

Nanny didn't even dignify that with an answer, only prodded Justin to hand the cat over.

Justin gave Phoebe an imploring glance. "Mama, *please* don't lose my cat—I want to see her after my nap."

"I'll look after her while you rest," Phoebe said reluctantly, reaching out for the bedraggled creature. The cat mewled in protest and scrabbled for purchase, anxious not to be dropped. "Galoshes," Phoebe swore beneath her breath, fumbling with the squirmy parcel of fur and bones.

Justin twisted to look back at Phoebe skeptically as Nanny towed him away.

"I have her," Phoebe assured him brightly, while the cat tried to use its back feet to climb the ridges of her corset like a ladder. She clamped the furry, skinny body against her shoulder, holding it firmly. After a moment, the cat surrendered and conformed against her, claws still needling into her bodice.

Phoebe carried the cat upstairs, struggling to manage it with one arm while holding up her skirts with her free hand. Finally, she reached her room.

Ernestine, who was sitting by the window with some mending, set aside her sewing basket and came to her immediately. "What's this?"

"An undomesticated barn cat," Phoebe said. "Justin acquired her during our farm tour."

"I *love* cats! May I take her?"

"You can try." But as Phoebe tried to lift the cat away, it hissed and dug its claws into the bodice of the dress. The harder she tried to pry away the cat, the more tenacious it became, growling and clinging desperately. Giving up the battle, Phoebe sat on the floor near one of the windows. "Ernestine, would you run down to the kitchen and fetch something to tempt her? A boiled egg, or a sardine—"

"Right away, my lady." The lady's maid dashed out.

Left in silence with the stubborn cat, Phoebe stroked her back and sides. She could feel the grooves between her tiny ribs. "Would you mind retracting your claws?" she asked. "I feel like a pincushion." In a moment, the little needles withdrew, and Phoebe sighed in relief. "Thank you." She continued to pet the silky dark fur and encountered a little knot beneath one of her arms. "If this is a tick, I'm going to start screaming like a lunatic."

Fortunately, further investigation revealed that the knot was a clump of some resinous matter, like pine-sap. It would have to be cut out. Slowly the cat's body relaxed, and a resonant purring began. She clambered up to the sunny windowsill behind Phoebe's shoulder and reclined on her side. Surveying the room with a bored, queenly air, the cat began to lick one paw.

Phoebe stood and tried to straighten her clothes, discovering the front of her gray dress was hopelessly frayed.

Soon Ernestine returned with a plate of shredded boiled chicken and set it near the window. Although the cat flattened its ears and viewed the lady's maid with slitted eyes, the chicken was too compelling to resist. After jumping to the floor, the feline slunk to the plate and devoured it ravenously.

"She's not such a wildling as the usual barn cat,"

Ernestine commented. "Most of them never purr or want to be held."

"This one seems at least half tame," Phoebe agreed.

"She's trying to rise above her station," the lady's maid suggested with a laugh. "A barn cat with dreams of being a house cat."

Phoebe frowned. "I wish you hadn't put it like that. Now when I take her back to the barn, I'll feel terribly guilty about it. But we can't keep her."

A FEW MINUTES LATER, dressed in blue summer serge with a white silk bodice, Phoebe made her way to the wing of the house where the Ravenel family members resided. After asking directions from a maid who was sweeping the hallway carpet, she approached a long, narrow passageway. At the far end of the passageway, she saw three men conferring at the threshold of a private suite: Lord Trenear, her father, and a man holding a doctor's bag.

Phoebe's heart quickened as she caught a glimpse of West Ravenel, wearing a dark green dressing robe and trousers, just inside the threshold. The group talked companionably for a minute, before Mr. Ravenel reached out to shake hands with the doctor.

As the men departed, Phoebe backed away and went into a small parlor, staying out of view. She waited until the group had passed and the sound of voices had faded. When the coast was clear, she headed to Mr. Ravenel's room.

It wasn't at all proper for her to visit him unaccompanied. The appropriate thing would be to send a note expressing her concern and good wishes. But she had to thank him privately for what he'd done. Also, she needed to see with her own eyes that he was all right.

The door had been left ajar. Bashfully she knocked on the jamb and heard his deep voice.

"Come in."

Phoebe entered the room and stopped with a head-to-toe quiver, like an arrow striking a target, at the sight of a half-naked West Ravenel. He was facing away from her, standing barefoot at an old-fashioned washstand as he blotted his neck and chest with a length of toweling. The robe had been tossed to a chair, leaving him dressed only in a pair of trousers that rode dangerously low on his hips.

Henry had always seemed so much smaller without his clothes, vulnerable without the protection of civilized layers. But this man, all rippling muscle and bronzed skin and coiled energy, appeared twice as large. The room scarcely seemed able to contain him. He was big-boned and lean, his back flexing as he lifted a goblet of water and drank thirstily. Phoebe's helpless gaze followed the long groove of his spine down to his hips. The loose edge of a pair of fawn-colored trousers, untethered by braces, dipped low enough to reveal a shocking absence of undergarments. How could a gentleman go without wearing drawers? It was the most indecent thing she'd ever seen. The inside of her head was scalded by her own thoughts.

"Hand me a clean shirt from that stack on the

dresser, will you?" he asked brusquely. "I'll need help putting it on; these damned stitches are pulling."

Phoebe moved to comply, while a thousand butterflies swirled and danced inside her. She fumbled to retrieve the shirt without overturning the stack. It was a pullover style with a half-placket, made of beautiful fine linen that smelled like laundry soap and outside air. Hesitantly she moved forward and dampened her lips nervously, trying to think of what to say.

Setting down the water goblet, Mr. Ravenel turned with an exasperated sigh. "Good God, Sutton, if you're going to be that slow—" He broke off as he saw her, his expression turning blank.

The atmosphere in the room became still and charged, as if lightning were about to strike.

"You're not the valet," Mr. Ravenel managed to say.

Phoebe held out the shirt clumsily. To her mortification, she was staring at him openly, ogling, and she couldn't seem to stop. If the back view of West Ravenel was fascinating, the front was absolutely mesmerizing. He was *much* hairier than her husband had been, his chest covered with dark fur that narrowed to a V at his midriff, and there was more hair on his forearms, and even a little trail below the navel. His shoulders and arms were so powerfully developed, one had to wonder why he hadn't simply wrestled the bull into submission.

Slowly he came forward to take the shirt from her nerveless hands. Bunching the garment awkwardly, he pushed his hands into the sleeves and began to lift it over his head.

"Wait," Phoebe said in a suffocated voice, "let me help."

"You don't have to—"

"The placket is still buttoned." She moved to unfasten the short row of buttons while he stood there with his hands caught in the gathered sleeves.

His head bent over hers; she could feel the rush of his unsettled exhalations. The hairs on his chest were not flat and straight, but softly curling. She wanted to brush her nose and lips across them. He smelled of soap, male skin, clean earth and meadow grass, and every breath of him made her feel warm in places that hadn't been warm in years.

When the placket was finally unfastened, Mr. Ravenel raised his arms and let the shirt settle over his head, wincing as the neat row of stitches at his side was strained. Phoebe reached up to tug at the hem of the garment. Her knuckles inadvertently grazed the dark fleece on his chest, and her stomach did an odd little flip. From the surface of her skin down to the marrow of her bones, her entire body was alive with sensation.

"Forgive me for intruding," she said, her gaze lifting to his face. "I wanted to find out how you were."

Amusement flickered in his eyes. "I'm well. Thank you."

With the short, dark layers of his hair all disheveled, he looked so attractive, somehow both cuddly and uncivilized. Hesitantly Phoebe reached for one of his wrists and began to button his cuff, and he went very still. How long it had been since she'd done this for a man. She hadn't realized how she missed the small, intimate task. "Mr. Ravenel," she said without looking at him, "what you did for my son . . . I'm so grateful, I don't know what to say."

"You don't have to be grateful. It's a host's responsibility not to let a dairy bull gore the houseguests."

"I wish I could do something for you in return. I wish . . ." Phoebe flushed as it occurred to her that appearing uninvited in a man's room and making such a statement while he was half dressed could easily be misinterpreted.

But he was being a gentleman about it. There were no mocking or teasing comments as he watched her fasten his other shirt cuff. "What I'd like more than anything," he said quietly, "is for you to listen to an apology."

"You have nothing to apologize for."

"I'm afraid I do." He let out a measured breath. "But first, I have something to give you."

He went to a cabinet in a corner of the room and rummaged through its contents. Finding the object he sought . . . a small book . . . he brought it to her.

Phoebe blinked in wonder as she read the gold and black lettering on the battered cloth cover. The title was worn and faded, but still legible.

STEPHEN ARMSTRONG: TREASURE HUNTER

Opening the book with unsteady fingers, she found the words written on the inside cover in her own childish hand, long ago.

Dear Henry, whenever you feel alone, look for the kisses I left for you on my favorite pages.

Blinded by a hot, stinging blur, Phoebe closed the book. Even without looking, she knew there were tiny x's in the margins of several chapters.

Mr. Ravenel's voice was hushed and gravelly. "You wrote that."

Unable to speak, she nodded and bent her head, a tear splashing on her wrist.

"After we talked at dinner," he said, "I realized your Henry was the one I knew at boarding school."

"Henry was sure you were the one who took this book," she managed to say. "He thought you'd destroyed it."

He sounded utterly humble. "I'm so sorry."

"I can't believe you kept it all these years." She tugged a handkerchief from the bodice of her dress and pressed it hard over her eyes, willing the tears to stop. "I cry too easily," she said in vexation. "I always have. I hate it."

"Why?"

"It shows weakness."

"It shows strength," he said. "Stoic people are the weak ones."

Phoebe blew her nose and looked up at him. "Do you really think so?"

"No, but I thought saying that might make you feel better."

A laugh trembled in her throat, and her eyes stopped watering.

"You sat down to dinner with me," Mr. Ravenel said, "knowing what a brute I was to Henry, and you said nothing. Why?"

"I thought it would be kinder to keep silent."

Something relaxed in his expression. "Phoebe," he said softly. The way he said her name, like an endearment, made her insides feel pleasantly weighted. "I don't deserve such kindness. I was born wicked, and I only grew worse after that."

"No one is born wicked," she said. "There were reasons why you fell into mischief. Had your parents lived, they would have loved you and taught you right from wrong—"

"Sweetheart . . . no." His smile was edged with bitterness. "My father was usually too far in the drink to remember he had children. My mother was half mad and had fewer morals than the barn cat we brought back today. Since none of our relations wanted custody of a pair of impoverished brats, Devon and I were sent to boarding school. We stayed there most holidays. I became a bully. I hated everyone. Henry was especially irritating—skinny, odd, fussy about his food. Always reading. I stole that book from the box under his bed because it seemed to be his favorite."

Pausing uncomfortably, Mr. Ravenel raked a hand through his disordered hair, and it promptly fell back into the same gleaming, untidy layers. "I didn't plan to keep it. I was going to embarrass him by reading parts of it aloud in front of him. And when I saw what you'd written on the inside cover, I could hardly wait to torture him about it. But then I read the first page."

"In which Stephen Armstrong is sinking in a pit of quicksand," Phoebe said with a tremulous smile.

"Exactly. I had to find out what happened next."

"After escaping the quicksand, he has to save his true love, Catriona, from the crocodiles."

A husky sound of amusement. "You marked *x*'s all over those pages."

"I secretly longed for a hero to rescue me from crocodiles someday."

"I secretly longed to be a hero. Despite having far more in common with the crocodiles." Mr. Ravenel's gaze focused inward as he sorted through long-ago memories. "I didn't know reading could be like that," he eventually said. "A ride on a magic carpet. I stopped bullying Henry after that. I couldn't jeer at him for loving that book. In fact, I wished I could talk to him about it."

"He would have adored that. Why didn't you?"

"I was embarrassed that I'd stolen it. And I wanted to keep it just a little longer. I'd never had a book of my own." He paused, still remembering. "I loved finding the marks you put on your favorite scenes. Forty-seven kisses, all totaled. I pretended they were for me."

It had never occurred to Phoebe that the book might have meant just as much to West Ravenel—more, even—than it had to her and Henry. Oh, how strange life was. She would never have dreamed she would someday feel such sympathy for him.

"There were times when that book kept me from despair," Mr. Ravenel said. "It was one of the best things about my childhood." A self-mocking smile touched his lips. "Naturally, it was something I'd stolen. Henry left school for good before I could bring myself to return it. I've always felt badly about that."

Phoebe didn't want him to feel badly. Not anymore. "I gave Henry my copy after his went missing," she said. "He was able to read Stephen Armstrong's adventures whenever he wanted."

"That doesn't excuse what I did."

"You were a boy of nine or ten. Henry would understand now. He would forgive you, as I have."

Instead of reacting with gratitude, Mr. Ravenel seemed annoyed. "Don't waste forgiveness on me. I'm a lost cause. Believe me, compared to my other sins, this was a drop in the bucket. Just take the book and know that I'm sorry."

"I want you to keep it," Phoebe said earnestly. "As a gift from Henry and me."

"God, no."

"Please, you must take it back."

"I don't want it."

"Yes, you do."

"Phoebe . . . no . . . damn it . . ."

They had started to grapple, pushing the book back and forth, each trying to compel the other to accept it. The novel fell to the floor as Phoebe swayed off balance and staggered back a step. Mr. Ravenel snatched her reflexively and pulled her back, and momentum brought her against him.

Before she could draw breath, his mouth was on hers.

Chapter 13

$\mathcal{O}$NCE AS A CHILD, Phoebe had been caught outside in a summer storm, and had seen a butterfly knocked from the air by raindrops. It had fluttered and fallen to the ground, bombarded from every direction. The only choice had been to fold its wings, take shelter and wait.

This man was the storm and the shelter, pulling her into a deep, encompassing darkness where there was too much to feel—*hot soft firm sweet hungry rough silken tugging.* She strained helplessly in his arms, although she didn't know whether she was trying to escape or press closer.

She had craved this, the hardness and heat of his body against hers, the sensation familiar and yet not at all familiar.

She had feared this, a man with a will and power that matched her own, a man who would desire and possess every last part of her without mercy.

The storm ended as abruptly as it had begun. He tore his mouth away with a rough sound, his arms loosening. She wobbled, her legs threatening to fold like paper fans, and he reached out to steady her.

"That was an accident," Mr. Ravenel said over her head, breathing hard.

"Yes," Phoebe said dazedly, "I understand."

"The book was falling . . . I was reaching for it, and . . . your lips were in the way."

"Let's not speak of it again. We'll ignore it."

Mr. Ravenel seized on the suggestion. "It never happened."

"Yes—no, it was—forgettable—that is, I'll forget about it."

That seemed to clear his head rather quickly. His breathing slowed, and he drew back far enough to give her an affronted glance. "*Forgettable?*"

"No," Phoebe said hastily, "I meant I wouldn't think about it."

But he looked more disgruntled with each passing second. "That didn't count as a real kiss. I'd just started."

"I know. But all the same, it was very nice, so there's no need to—"

"*Nice?*"

"Yes." Phoebe wondered why he looked so insulted.

"If I have only one chance in a lifetime to kiss you," he said grimly, "I'll be damned if it's going to be second rate. A man has standards."

"I didn't say it was second rate," she protested. "I said it was nice!"

"The average man would rather be shot in the arse than have a woman call his lovemaking 'nice.'"

"Oh, come, you're making too much of this."

"Now I have to do it over."

"*What?*" An airless giggle broke from her, and she shrank back.

West reached out and hauled her against him easily. "If I don't, you'll always think that was the best I could do. I might as well be hanged for a sheep as a lamb."

"Mr. Ravenel—"

"Brace yourself."

Phoebe's jaw slackened in astonishment. He had to be teasing. He couldn't be serious . . . could he?

There was a gleam of laughter in his eyes as he saw her expression. But then one of his arms slid securely around her back. Oh, God, he meant it; he was really going to kiss her. A rush of confusion and excitement made her dizzy.

"Mr. Ravenel, I . . ."

"West."

"West," Phoebe repeated, looking up at him. She had to clear away the nervous catch in her throat before she could continue. "This is a mistake."

"No, the first kiss was a mistake. This one's going to fix it."

"But it won't," she said anxiously. "You see, I . . . I don't doubt your lovemaking skills, I doubt my own. For more than two years, I haven't kissed anyone over three and a half feet tall."

A breath of amusement fanned her cheek. "Then you should probably aim your gaze at least two and a half feet higher than usual." Gently he adjusted the angle of her chin. "Put your arms around me."

Inexplicably, the quiet command sent ripples of interest and excitement through her. Was she actually going to let him . . . ?

Yes, some reckless inner voice insisted. *Yes, don't stop him, don't think at all, just let it happen.*

The dreamlike stillness was disturbed only by the fitful pattern of her breathing. Her hands went to his sides and slid around to the powerful surface of his back. He cupped the back of her head securely, and in the next moment his mouth caught at hers, a light pressure that kept nudging and settling, as if he were trying to find the exact fit between them. Uncertain how to respond, she stood there with her face uplifted while his fingertips stroked her throat and jaw as tenderly as sunlight moving over her skin. She wouldn't have thought a man of his size could handle her with such gentleness. He deepened the pressure, urging her lips apart beneath his, and she felt the tip of his tongue enter her. The teasing lick felt so peculiar and sinuous, she stiffened and jerked back in surprise.

West kept her against him, his shaven masculine bristle rasping her soft skin. His cheek tautened as if he were smiling. Realizing her reaction had amused him, she frowned, but before she could say a word, his mouth had come to hers again. He explored her slowly, expertly, the intimacy shocking and yet . . . not unpleasant. Not at all. As the sweet, restless searching continued, delight resonated through her in thrills, like the parts of a harp that vibrated when certain notes were played. Tentatively she responded, her tongue darting shyly to meet his.

As she reached around his neck for support, she encountered the edge of his hair where it curled slightly against his nape. The dark locks were cool and lustrous as they slid through her languid fingers. His kiss roughened, his tongue sinking into her as he took what he wanted, and she was lost, drowning in a dark tide of sensation.

As a woman who'd been a wife, mother, and widow, she'd thought there was nothing left to learn. But West Ravenel was transforming every notion of what a kiss could be. He kissed like a man who had lived too fast, learned too late, and had finally found the thing he wanted. She couldn't help writhing in response, her body aching for deeper, closer contact. He reached down with one hand to anchor her hips against his, and it felt so good she could have swooned. She moaned and pressed as tightly as possible to the hard terrain of his body . . . so very hard. Even with the layers of clothing between them, she could feel how aroused he was, the shape of him thick and aggressive.

Trembling, Phoebe turned her mouth from his. Her body didn't seem to belong to her. She could hardly stand on her own. She couldn't think. Her forehead leaned on his shoulder as she waited for the wild pumping of her heart to subside.

West buried a quiet curse into the mass of her pinned-up hair. His arms relaxed gradually, one of his hands wandering over her slender back in an aimless, soothing pattern. When he'd managed to moderate his breathing, he said gruffly, "Don't say that was nice."

Phoebe pressed a crooked smile against his shoulder before she replied, "It wasn't." It had been extraordinary. A revelation. One of her hands crept up to his lean cheek and shaped to it gently. "And it must never happen again."

West was very still, considering that. He responded with a single nod of agreement and turned his lips to the center of her palm with urgent pressure.

Impulsively she stood on her toes and whispered in his ear, "There's nothing wicked about you, except your kisses." And she fled the room while she was still able.

Chapter 14

ᴇᴠɪᴇ, DUCHESS OF KINGSTON, had spent a perfectly wonderful afternoon picnicking with her three closest friends at Lord Westcliff's estate. Long ago she had met Annabelle, Lillian, and Daisy during her first London Season, when they had been a group of wallflowers sitting in chairs at the side of the ballroom. While becoming acquainted, it had occurred to them that instead of competing for gentlemen's attentions, they would do better to help each other, and so a life-long friendship had blossomed. In the past few years it had become a rare luxury for all of them to be together at once, especially since Daisy stayed in America with her husband, Matthew, for long periods of time. The trips were necessary for both of them: Matthew was a successful business entrepreneur, and Daisy was a successful novelist with a publisher in New York as well as London.

After a day filled with talking, laughing, reminiscing and making future plans, Evie had returned to Eversby Priory in high spirits. She was full of news to share with her husband . . . including the fact that the protagonist of Daisy's current novel in progress had been partly inspired by him.

"I had the idea when the subject of your husband came up at a dinner party a few months ago, Evie," Daisy had explained, dabbing at a tiny stain left by a strawberry that had fallen onto her bodice. "Someone remarked that Kingston was still the handsomest man in England, and how unfair it was that he never ages. And Lillian said he must be a vampire, and everyone laughed. It started me thinking about that old novel *The Vampyre,* published about fifty years ago. I decided to write something similar, only a romantic version."

Lillian had shaken her head at the notion. "I told Daisy no one would want to read about a vampire lover. Blood . . . teeth . . ." She grimaced and shivered.

"He enslaves women with his charismatic power," Daisy protested. "He's also a rich, handsome duke—just like Evie's husband."

Annabelle spoke then, her blue eyes twinkling. "In light of all that, one could forgive a bad habit or two."

Lillian gave her a skeptical glance. "Annabelle, could you really overlook a husband who went around sucking the life out of people?"

After pondering the question, Annabelle asked Daisy, "How rich *is* he?" She ducked with a smothered laugh as Lillian pelted her with a biscuit.

Laughing at her friends' antics, Evie had asked Daisy, "What's the title?"

"*The Duke's Deadly Embrace.*"

"I suggested *The Duke Was a Pain in the Neck,*" Lillian had said, "but Daisy thought it lacked romance."

When Evie had arrived back at the Ravenels' estate, she had found her oldest daughter waiting for her, eager to relate the events of the morning.

"Other than Mr. Ravenel," Phoebe had reassured her, "no one else was hurt. Justin was a bit shaken, but perfectly fine."

"And your father?"

"He was as cool as a cucumber about the whole thing, of course. He spent the afternoon playing billiards with the other gentlemen, and later went up to your room for a rest. But Mama, when he and I walked back to the house this morning, he said some very disagreeable things about Edward Larson—and about Henry!"

"Oh, dear." Evie had listened sympathetically to her daughter's account of the conversation and soothed her with a promise to speak to Sebastian and try to soften his views on Edward Larson.

Now Evie hurried upstairs in search of her husband as fast as possible without giving the appearance of haste. She reached their suite, a spacious and well-appointed bedroom with an attached dressing room and a tiny antechamber converted into a lavatory.

Upon entering the main room, Evie discovered her husband lounging in a large, old-fashioned slipper tub. Since the lavatory was too small to allow for a tub, a portable one had to be carried in by footmen and laboriously filled with large cans of hot water brought by housemaids.

Sebastian leaned back with one long leg propped at

the far end of the tub, a crystal glass of brandy clasped negligently in one hand. His once tawny amber hair was handsomely silvered at the sides and temples. The daily ritual of a morning swim had kept him fit and limber, his skin glowing as if he existed in perpetual summer. He might have been Apollo lazing on Olympus: a decadent golden sun god utterly lacking in modesty.

His lazy voice meandered through the veil of aromatic steam. "Ah, there you are, pet. Did you enjoy your outing?"

Evie smiled as she went to him. "I did." She knelt beside the tub so that their faces were level. "F-from what I've heard, it wasn't as eventful as yours." Since childhood, she had spoken with a stammer, which had lessened over the years but still attached itself to a syllable here or there.

His gaze caressed her face, while a forefinger traced a spray of freckles on her upper chest. "You heard about the incident in the paddock."

"And how you climbed in after Justin."

"I wasn't in a moment's danger. Ravenel was the one who held off a belligerent bull while I fetched the boy."

Evie closed her eyes briefly at the thought of it and reached for the crystal glass in his hand. She downed what little was left and set the glass on the floor. "You suffered no injuries?"

Two long, wet fingers hooked the top of her neckline and tugged her closer to the side of the bathtub.

Sebastian's eyes were pale, lucent blue, sparkling like winter starlight. "I may have enough of a sprain to require your services."

A smile curved her lips. "What services?"

"I need a bath maid." Catching one of her hands, he drew it down into the water. "For my hard-to-reach places."

Evie resisted with a throaty chuckle, tugging at her imprisoned wrist. "You can reach *that* by yourself."

"My sweet," he said, nuzzling into her neck, "I married you so I wouldn't have to do it myself. Now . . . tell me where you think my sprain is."

"Sebastian," she said, trying to sound severe as his wet hands roved over her bodice, "you're going to r-ruin my dress."

"Unless you remove it." He gave her an expectant glance.

Smiling wryly, Evie pulled away and stood to comply. He had always loved to have her undress for him, especially when the clothing was intricate with many fastenings. Her pink muslin summer dress had been topped with a matching vest fastened all down the front with pearl buttons . . . exactly the style of garment he fancied watching her remove.

"Tell me about the picnic," her husband said, sliding a bit lower in the water, his gaze moving over her intently.

"It was lovely. We were brought out in wagonettes to a green hill. The footmen spread cloths on the ground and set out picnic hampers and pails of ice . . .

and then we were left alone to feast and talk as much as we pleased." Evie worked diligently on the buttons, finding some of them difficult to unfasten. "Daisy told us about her latest trip to New York, and—you'll never guess—she's modeling a character in a gothic novel after you. A v-vampire!"

"Hmm. I'm not sure I like the idea of being a creature in a gothic novel. What exactly does he do?"

"He's a handsome, elegant fiend who bites his wife's neck every night."

His brow cleared. "Oh, that's all right, then."

"But he never drinks enough of her blood to kill her," Evie continued.

"I see. He keeps her conveniently on tap."

"Yes, but he loves her. You make her sound like a cask with a spigot. It's not as if he wants to do it, but he—did you just ask something?"

"I asked if you can undress any faster."

Evie huffed with a mixture of amusement and exasperation. "No, I can't. There are too many b-buttons, and they're very small."

"What a pity. Because in thirty seconds, I'm going to rip away whatever clothing you have left."

Evie knew full well not to take the threat lightly— he'd done it before, on more than one occasion. "Sebastian, *no.* I like this dress."

Her husband's eyes glinted with devilish humor as he watched her increasingly frantic efforts. "No dress is as beautiful as your naked skin. All those sweet freckles scattered over you, like a thousand tiny angel kisses . . . you have twenty seconds left, by the way."

"You don't even h-have a clock," she complained.

"I'm counting by heartbeats. You'd better hurry, love."

Evie glanced anxiously down at the row of pearl buttons, which seemed to have multiplied. With a defeated sigh, she dropped her arms to her sides. "Just go on and rip it off," she mumbled.

She heard his silky laugh, and a sluice of water. He stood with streams runneling over the sleek, muscled contours of his body, and Evie gasped as she was pulled into a steaming embrace.

His amused voice curled inside the sensitive shell of her ear. "My poor little put-upon wife. Let me help you. As you may recall, I have a way with buttons . . ."

LATER, AS EVIE lay beside him, deeply relaxed and still tingling in the aftermath of pleasure, she said drowsily, "Phoebe told me about your conversation during the walk back to the house."

Sebastian was slow to reply, his lips and hands still drifting over her gently. "What did she say?"

"She was unhappy about your opinion of Edward Larson."

"No more unhappy than I, when I learned he'd broached the subject of marriage with her. Did you know about that?"

"I thought he might have. I wasn't certain."

Propping himself up on one elbow, Sebastian looked

down at her with a frown. "God spare me from having to call another Larson 'son-in-law.'"

"But you cared very much for Henry," Evie said, surprised by the comment.

"Like a son," he agreed. "However, that never blinded me to the fact that he was far from Phoebe's ideal partner. There was no balance between them. His force of will never came close to matching hers. To Henry, Phoebe was as much a mother as a wife. I only consented to the match because Phoebe was too bull-headed to consider anyone else. For reasons I still don't fully understand, she would have Henry or no one."

Evie played with the light mat of his chest hair. "Whatever Henry's faults, Phoebe always knew he belonged to her alone. That was worth any sacrifice. She wanted a man whose capacity for love was unqualified."

"Does she claim to find the same capacity in that spineless prig Larson?"

"I don't believe so. But her purposes for marriage are different this time."

"Whatever her purposes, I won't have my grandsons raised by an invertebrate."

"Sebastian," she chided softly, although her lips quivered with amusement.

"I mean for her to partner with Weston Ravenel. A healthy young buck with sharp wits and a full supply of manly vigor. He'll do her much good."

"Let's allow Phoebe to decide if she wants him," Evie suggested.

"She had better decide soon, or Westcliff will snap him up for one of his daughters."

This was a side of Sebastian—high-handed to the verge of being autocratic—that almost inevitably developed in men of vast wealth and power. Evie had always been careful to curb such tendencies in her husband, occasionally reminding him that he was, after all, a mere mortal who had to respect other people's rights to make their own decisions. He would counter with something like, "Not when they're obviously wrong," and she would reply, "Even then," and eventually he would relent after making a great many caustic observations about the idiocy of people who dared to disagree with him. The fact that he was so often right made Evie's position difficult, but still, she never backed down.

"I like Mr. Ravenel too," Evie murmured, "but there's much about his background we don't know."

"Oh, I know everything about him," Sebastian said with casual arrogance.

Knowing her husband, Evie thought ruefully, he'd read detailed reports on every member of the Ravenel family. "It's not a given that he and Phoebe are attracted to each other."

"You didn't see them together this morning."

"Sebastian, please don't meddle."

"*I,* meddle?" His brows lifted, and he looked positively indignant. "Evie, what can you be thinking?"

Lowering her face to his chest, she nuzzled the glinting hair. "That you're meddling."

"From time to time, I may adjust a situation to achieve a desired outcome for the benefit of my children, but that's not meddling."

"What do you call it, then?"

"Parenting," he said smugly, and kissed her before she could reply.

Chapter 15

THE MORNING AFTER THE farm tour, a multitude of carriages and horses crowded the front drive of Eversby Priory as the majority of wedding guests finally departed. The Challons were staying on for another three days to deepen their acquaintance with the Ravenels.

"Darling," Merritt had entreated Phoebe during breakfast, "are you *very* sure you won't come to stay with us at Stony Cross Park? Mr. Sterling and I are going to spend at least a week there, and we would all love to see more of you and the children. Tell me how I can persuade you."

"Thank you, Merritt, but we're settled and comfortable here, and . . . I need some quiet time after the wedding and all the socializing."

A teasing light had appeared in Merritt's eyes. "It seems my powers of persuasion are no match for a certain blue-eyed charmer."

"No," Phoebe had said quickly. "It has nothing to do with him."

"A little flirtation will do you no harm," Merritt had pointed out reasonably.

"But it can lead to nothing."

"Flirtation doesn't have to lead anywhere. One can simply enjoy it. Think of it as practice for when you start mixing in society again."

After exchanging farewells with friends and acquaintances, Phoebe had decided to take her children and Nanny Bracegirdle for a morning walk before the heat of the day accumulated. Along the way, they would finally return the little black cat to the barn.

Although Phoebe had meant to take care of that particular errand yesterday, the plan had been derailed when Justin and Ernestine had taken the cat outside to one of the estate gardens to "answer nature's call." The creature had disappeared for the better part of the afternoon. Phoebe had joined in the search, but the fugitive was nowhere to be found. Toward evening, however, while changing for dinner, Phoebe had heard a scratching sound, and saw a pair of black paws swiping beneath the closed door. Somehow the cat had managed to slip back into the house.

Taking pity on her, Phoebe had sent for another plate of scraps from the kitchen. The cat had eaten voraciously, practically licking the glaze off the porcelain. Afterward she had stretched out on the carpet, purring with such contentment that Phoebe hadn't the heart to send her back. The cat had spent the night curled up in Ernestine's mending basket, and this morning had breakfasted on kippers.

"I don't think she wants to go back to the barn," Justin said, glancing up at Phoebe as she held the cat against her shoulder. Nanny walked beside them, pushing Stephen in a sturdy wicker pram with a white cambric parasol cover.

"The barn is her home," Phoebe replied, "and she's happy to be returning to her brothers and sisters."

"She doesn't look happy," Justin said.

"She is, though," Phoebe assured him. "She— *ouch!*—oh, galoshes—" The cat had climbed higher on her shoulder, its little claws perforating her muslin dress. "Nanny, I do wish you'd let me put her in the pram with Stephen. There's plenty of room for her to ride near his feet."

"The cat can't ride with Baby," came the adamant reply.

Unfortunately, Phoebe's plan to return the cat to its proper home was foiled soon after they reached the hay barn. She managed to pry the cat's claws from her dress and set her on the ground by the barn door. "There's one of your friends," Phoebe said, seeing a gray cat loitering near a tool shed. "Go, now . . . *shoo!* . . . Go and play."

The gray cat hissed balefully and slunk away. The black cat turned and made to follow Phoebe, her tail raised as if she were tipping a hat in hopeful greeting.

"No," Phoebe said firmly. "*Shoo.* You can't come with us."

But as they tried to walk away, the black cat followed.

Phoebe caught sight of a workman she recognized. "Good morning, Neddy."

He approached and touched the brim of his cap. "Milady."

"We seem to have borrowed one of the barn cats. We're trying to return her, but she keeps following. I don't suppose you have advice on how to make a cat stay?"

"If I could make a cat do that, it'd be a dog."

"Perhaps you might hold her long enough for us to escape?"

"I would, milady, but she'd shred my arms to ribbands."

Phoebe nodded ruefully and sighed. "You're probably right. We'll go on our walk. Hopefully she'll lose interest and return to the barn."

To Phoebe's dismay, the cat kept pace with them, and began to meow uneasily as the barn disappeared from sight. They proceeded along an ancient drove road, once used for taking cattle on foot between summer and winter pastures. Beech trees shaded the sunken path, which was bordered by hedges and earthen walls. As they neared a small wrought-iron footbridge arching across a stream, the cat's cries became plaintive.

Phoebe stopped with a groan. "So much for our peaceful stroll out in nature." She bent to pick up the little feline and winced as the cat dug its claws into her shoulder. Exasperated, she carried it to the pram. Before Nanny could object, she said, "I'll take charge of Stephen."

Nanny was expressionless. "You want me to push the cat in the pram, milady?"

"Yes, otherwise I'll be a sieve by the time we return to Eversby Priory."

Justin's face brightened. "Are we going to keep her, Mama?"

"Only until we can find someone else to take her back to the barn." Phoebe settled the cat on the white silk bedding of the pram. Stephen babbled with excited interest and reached for the furry creature, his little hands opening and closing like hungry starfish. With a laugh, Phoebe scooped him up before he could pull the cat's tail. "Oh, no you don't. Be gentle with kitty."

The cat flattened her ears and gave the toddler a baleful glance.

"Kitty!" Stephen exclaimed, leaning heavily in Phoebe's arms to reach the cat. "Kitty!"

Phoebe lowered him to the ground and kept one of his chubby hands in hers. "Let's walk beside the pram, darling."

Eagerly Stephen started forward in his spraddling gait. As Nanny pushed the vehicle along the path, the black cat poked its head over the pram's wicker edge, calmly viewing the passing scenery. For some reason, the sight of a cat riding in his pram struck the baby as uproariously funny, and he burst into giggles. Phoebe and Justin both chuckled, and even Nanny cracked a smile.

Before they crossed the bridge, they went down to have a look at the chalk stream, which was fringed with reeds, watercress, and yellow flag irises. The water flowing gently over the pebbled bed was gin clear, having been filtered through the Hampshire chalk hills.

"Mama, I want to put my feet in the water," Justin exclaimed.

Phoebe sent Nanny a questioning glance. "Shall we stop here for a few minutes?"

The older woman, who was never averse to the prospect of a rest, nodded at once.

"Lovely," Phoebe said. "Justin, do you need help with your shoes and stockings?"

"No, I can do it." But as the boy bent to unfasten the buttons of his kid leather shoes, an unexpected noise caught his attention. He stopped and looked for the source of the sound, which was coming from downstream.

Phoebe frowned as she saw a lone man walking along the bank of the stream, idly whistling a folk tune. A battered hat with a wide brim shaded his face. His build was rangy and athletic, the loose, confident stride curbed by the hint of a strut. Curiously, his loose shirt and cotton canvas trousers looked as if he'd gone swimming in them, the fabric clinging wetly to the hard lines of his body.

"Perhaps we shouldn't stop after all," Phoebe murmured, her instincts warning her to leave as quickly as possible. A pair of women and two young children were easy marks for a man that size. "Come with me, Justin."

To her astonishment, her son ignored the command

and ran toward the disreputable-looking stranger with a gleeful yelp.

The man's head lifted. A husky laugh sent a thrill of recognition along Phoebe's nerves.

"Oh," she said softly, watching as West Ravenel settled the battered hat on Justin's head, lifted him high against his side, and carried him back to her.

Chapter 16

PHOEBE HADN'T SEEN WEST since she'd visited his room yesterday. Since the unforgettable kiss she was supposed to forget. Except the sensations had somehow become woven into her skin, a subtle but constant stimulation she didn't know how to erase. Her lips still felt a little swollen, aching to be pressed and stroked and soothed—that was an illusion, she knew, but the feeling only grew stronger as he approached.

Justin was talking animatedly to him. ". . . but Galoshes wouldn't stay there. She followed us from the barn, and now she's riding in Stephen's pram."

"Galoshes? Why did you name her that?"

"It's what Mama says when the cat puts holes in her dress."

"Poor Mama." West's deep voice was edged with amusement. But his gaze was intent and searching as he looked at Phoebe.

She had already promised herself that when next they met, she would be composed and pleasant. Sophisticated. But that plan had already vanished like the fluff of a dandelion gone to seed, whisked away at the will of a breeze. She was filled with pleasure and excitement, momentarily too flustered to speak.

West turned to greet Nanny and grinned at the sight of the cat lounging in the pram. He set Justin down and slowly lowered to his haunches in front of Stephen.

"Hello, Stephen," he said in a gentle, vibrant tone. "What a handsome fellow you are. You have your mother's eyes."

The sturdy toddler half hid behind Phoebe's skirts and peeked at the engaging stranger while chewing on a finger. A shy grin split his face, revealing a row of little white teeth.

Phoebe noticed a dark bruise forming on West's forearm, which was exposed by a rolled-up shirtsleeve. "Mr. Ravenel," she asked in concern, "has some accident befallen you? What happened to your arm?"

He rose to his feet, his wet hair hanging over his brow in shiny dark ribbons. "It's sheep-washing day. One of them caught my arm with a hoof as she tried to turn over in the water."

"What about your stitches? Heaven knows what kind of filth your wound was absorbing while you stood in a sheep bath."

He seemed amused by her worry. "It's not bothering me in the slightest."

"It will bother you quite a bit if the wound turns sour!"

Justin was far more interested in the subject of sheep than hygiene. "How do you wash a sheep?"

"We created a temporary pool in the stream by damming it with a pair of old doors. Some of us stood waist-deep in the water while others handed over the sheep. My job was to help turn a sheep on its back and swish its wool in the water until it was clean. Most of them liked it, but every now and then one of them struggled to turn itself upright."

"How do you turn a sheep over?" Justin asked.

"You grasp a handful of fleece near its cheek, then take a hold of the opposite foreleg, and—" West paused, giving Justin a considering glance. "It would be easier to show you. Let's pretend you're a sheep." He lunged for the boy, who leaped back with a delighted yelp.

"I'm a sheep who likes to be dirty!" Justin cried, scampering away. "And you can't catch me."

"Oh, can't I?" Adroitly West dodged and pounced, snatching up the boy and making him squeal with laughter. "Now I'll show you how I wash a sheep."

"*Wait*," Phoebe said sharply, her heart thundering with anxiety. All her instincts stung in warning at the sight of her son being handled so roughly. "He'll catch a chill. He—"

West stopped and turned toward her with Justin clasped securely in his arms. He regarded Phoebe with a mocking lift of his brows, and she realized too late that he'd had no intention of throwing Justin into the stream. They had only been playing.

After setting Justin down with exaggerated care, West approached her, his eyes narrowing slightly. "Well, then. I'll have to demonstrate on you."

Before her mind had quite registered the words, Phoebe was stunned to find herself being seized and lifted off her feet. A shock went through her as she was hoisted high against a rock-hard chest, his wet shirt soaking the thin fabric of her bodice. "Don't you dare," she gasped, giggling and squirming. "Oh, God, you smell like a barnyard—put me down, you lout—" She was laughing uncontrollably in a way she hadn't done since childhood. Her arms clutched his neck. "If you drop me into that water," she managed to threaten, "I'll take you with me!"

"It's worth it," he said casually, carrying her toward the stream.

No one in Phoebe's adult life had dared to manhandle her like this. She pushed against him helplessly, but any effort to escape was futile. His arms were like steel bands.

"I'll never forgive you," Phoebe said, but ruined the effect with another burst of wild giggles. "I mean it!"

West's low laugh tickled her ear. "I suppose you're not big enough for a sheep-washing demonstration. You're only lamb size." He stopped, and for a few seconds he kept her like that, cradled and close against him. Phoebe held very still in that stolen embrace, while her mind conjured a stunning image of his body weighting hers to the ground, human warmth above and cool earth below. A shiver chased down her spine.

"Easy, now," West said gently. "I wasn't going to drop you." He cuddled her a little closer. "Poor lamb, did I give you a fright?" His voice was so dark and tender that it almost made her shiver again. With great care, he lowered her feet to the ground. But her arms didn't want to unlock from around his neck. A strange feeling had come over her, as if she were listening to the haunting prelude of a song that would never be written. Slowly she let go and stepped back.

Justin collided into her from behind, hugging her tightly and chuckling. A moment later, Stephen dove against her and clutched her skirts, grinning upward. The boys had loved seeing someone play rough-and-tumble with their mother.

Phoebe tried to sound casual as she told West, "We're going to play here for a few minutes. You're welcome to keep company with us."

He held her gaze. "Would you like me to?"

Phoebe might have thought the question was a mocking attempt to make her plead for his company. But there was a subtle note of uncertainty in his tone. He wasn't sure of her, she realized. He'd made no assumptions about her, or what she might want. The realization sent a flush of warmth through her.

"Yes . . . stay."

Before long, West was wading with Justin in the ankle-deep shallows, helping him collect interesting pebbles. Phoebe, who had discreetly removed her shoes and stockings, sat on a bank with Stephen, holding him while he dipped his feet and watched the minnows darting across the shallows. Nanny had spread a cloth on a patch of mossy ground and sat with her back against the trunk of a nearby willow tree, snoozing lightly.

Feeling a soft nudge against her side, Phoebe twisted

to discover that the black cat had jumped from the pram and was rubbing against her affectionately.

"Kitty!" Stephen exclaimed, clutching at the cat.

"Gently," Phoebe cautioned, and moved his little hand in a slow, stroking motion over the animal's back. "Oh, she likes that. Can you feel her purr?"

". . . the bands of white are chalk," West was saying a few yards away, bending to examine a pebble Justin held in his palm. "It's made out of the shells of creatures so tiny, you can only see them with a microscope."

"Where did the tiny creatures come from?"

"They formed on the ocean floor. All this land used to be covered with water."

"I know that story," Justin said brightly. "Noah and the ark."

"It was long before Noah."

"How long?"

"Millions of years."

Justin shrugged and said prosaically, "I don't know a million. I can only count to ten."

"Hmm." West pondered how to explain it. "Do you know how long a second is?"

"No."

"One. Two. Three. Four. Five." With each count, West snapped his fingers. "That was five seconds. Now, if I were to keep snapping like that without stopping for ten days, that would be almost a million seconds."

Although Justin didn't fully grasp the explanation, he clearly liked the snapping. He tried to imitate the sound, but his fingers couldn't quite manage it.

"Like this," West said, shaping the small hand in his, pressing the thumb and middle finger together. "Now try."

Frowning with concentration, Justin attempted another snap, but there was no sound.

"Keep practicing," West advised. "In the meantime, let's go to dry ground."

"But I need more pebbles," Justin protested.

West grinned. "You've filled your pockets with so many pebbles, you're about to lose your trousers. Come, let's show them to your mother."

The black cat retreated a few feet, watching warily, as Justin emptied the contents of his pockets onto a handkerchief Phoebe had spread on the ground.

Phoebe dutifully admired the many-colored pebbles and picked up a white-banded one. Glancing up at West, she asked, "How do you know so much about chalk formation, Mr. Ravenel?"

"It's because of the estate quarry. Before we started digging, I had to consult with mining experts, including a field geologist."

"What's a geologist?" Justin asked.

The question made West smile. "A scientist who studies rocks and drinks too much."

As Phoebe set down the pebble, Stephen grabbed it and tried to put it in his mouth. "No, darling," she said, taking it back, "that's not good for you." The baby whined irritably, reaching for the forbidden pebble. In a moment he began to squall, which awakened Nanny from her light nap. She rubbed her eyes and began to stand up.

"It's all right, Nanny," Phoebe said. "Justin, will you fetch a toy from the pram?"

Justin hurried to the vehicle, rummaged at the side of it, and brought back a little stuffed horse made of leather. Its legs had nearly worn down to nubs from the baby's teething. Stephen took the toy, regarded it disdainfully, and dropped it to the ground as he continued to fuss.

Instantly the cat darted forward, snatched the toy and hurried off with it.

West came forward, reached down to clasp Stephen around the ribs, and lifted him from Phoebe's lap. "What's all this racket?" he asked, settling the baby against his chest.

Stunned into silence, Stephen looked tearfully into the man's smiling blue eyes.

"Poor chap," West soothed. "How dare they offer you a toy when you had a perfectly good rock to play with? It's an outrage . . . yes, it is . . . an atrocity . . ."

To Phoebe's amazement, Stephen's temper subsided as the "stranger" continued to coddle him. He put his hand on West's cheek, exploring the bristly texture. In a moment, West lowered his face and blew a rude sound against the baby's tummy, making him convulse with giggles. He lifted him in the air and began to pitch him upward repeatedly, eliciting squeals of delight.

"Mr. Ravenel," Phoebe said, "I'd prefer you didn't toss my child about as if he were an old valise."

"He likes it," West replied, although he gentled the movement.

"He also likes chewing on discarded cigar butts," Phoebe said.

"We all have our bad habits," West told the baby kindly, lowering him back down to his chest. "Justin, come—we have work to do." He bent to pick up a stick the length of his forearm.

Phoebe's eyes widened. "What is that for?"

"We're clearing the area of crocodiles," West informed her, and handed the stick to Justin. "If one comes close, beat him off with this."

Justin squeaked in excitement and followed at his heels.

Although Phoebe was tempted to point out there were no crocodiles in England, she only laughed and watched as the three adventurers set off. Shaking her head, she went to sit beside Nanny.

"There's a lot of man in that one," the older woman remarked.

"There's *too much* man in that one," Phoebe said wryly.

They watched West stride off with the boys, still holding Stephen in one arm. Justin reached up with his free hand, and West took it without hesitation.

"They speak well of him in the servants' hall," Nanny ventured. "A good man, and a good master, who should have a household of his own. Well favored in looks, and the right age for fathering, too."

"Nanny," Phoebe said, giving her an amused, incredulous glance, "he's only half tame."

"Fie, milady . . . there's not a man alive who'd be too much for you to manage."

"I don't want a man I'd have to manage. I'd like a civilized one who can manage himself." Phoebe reached over to a patch of wild chamomile and plucked a blossom. Rubbing it between her thumb and forefinger, she inhaled the sweet apple-ish scent. Glancing sideways at the other woman, she added quietly, "Besides, you haven't forgotten what Henry asked of me."

"No, milady. Nor have I forgotten that he asked it when he was in his last fading. You'd have promised anything to ease his mind."

Phoebe felt comfortable discussing Henry with his old nanny, who had loved him from the first day of his life to the last. "Henry gave careful thought to my future," she said. "He saw the advantages of a match with Edward, who has a fine reputation and a gentlemanly nature, and will set a good example for the boys while they're growing up."

"A fine shoe often pinches the foot."

Phoebe gathered more blossoms to make a tiny bouquet. "I'd have thought you would approve of a match between me and Henry's cousin. Edward is so very like him."

"Is he, milady?"

"Yes, you've known him since he was a child. He's very much like Henry, only without the quirks."

Despite Edward's relatively young age, he was a gentleman of the old school, courtly and soft-spoken, a man who would never dream of making a scene. In all the years of their acquaintance, Phoebe had never once seen him lose his temper. She wouldn't have to worry that he would be unfaithful, or cold, or thoughtless: It simply wasn't in him.

It wasn't difficult to envision being content with Edward.

The difficult part was trying to imagine sleeping with him. Her mind couldn't seem to conjure it except in an unfocused way, like watching shadow puppets.

When it came to West Ravenel, however, the problem was exactly the reverse. The idea of sharing a bed with him made her mouth go dry and her pulse race with excitement.

Troubled by the direction of her thoughts, Phoebe wrapped a stem around the little chamomile bouquet and gave it to Nanny. "I should go see what Mr. Ravenel and the children are doing," she said lightly. "He probably has them playing with knives and sulfur matches by now."

She found West and the children on a low bank of the stream, all three of them muddy and disheveled. Stephen was perched in West's lap, his white linen smock positively filthy. They appeared to have made a project of stacking flat river stones into towers. Justin had used his stick to dig a channel in the sandy silt and was transferring water from the stream with his cupped hands.

Phoebe's brows flew upward. "I took a rock away from the baby," she asked West, "and you gave him a dozen more?"

"Shhh," West said without looking at her. A corner

of his mouth twitched as he continued, "Don't interrupt a man while he's working."

Stephen clutched a flat stone with both hands, guiding it to a stack with wobbly determination. He pressed it on top of the other stones and held it there while West gently adjusted its position.

"Well done," West said.

Justin offered Stephen another stone, and Stephen took it with a grunt of enthusiasm. His small face was comically serious as he maneuvered the stone to the top of the stack. Phoebe watched intently, struck by how excited and interested he was in the project.

Since the death of the father who'd never seen him, she had sheltered and coddled her youngest child as much as possible. She had filled his world with soft, pretty objects and endless comfort. It hadn't occurred to her that he might want—or need—to play with rocks, sticks, and mud.

"He's going to be a builder," West said. "Or an excavator."

"Lucky Stephen," Justin said, surprising Phoebe. "I wish I could have a job someday."

"Why can't you?" West asked.

"I'm a viscount. And they won't let you quit even if you want to."

"A viscount can have another job as well."

Justin paused in his digging to look up at him hopefully. "I can?"

"Perhaps if it's one of the honorable professions," Phoebe interceded gently, "such as diplomacy or the law."

West sent her a sardonic glance. "His grandfather has spent years running a gaming club in London. As I understand it, he is personally involved in its day-to-day management. Is that on your list of honorable professions?"

"Are you criticizing my father?" Phoebe asked, nettled.

"Just the opposite. Had the duke allowed himself to be hamstrung by the expectations of nobility, he probably wouldn't have a shilling to his name." He paused to adjust the pile of stones as Stephen stacked another one. "The point is, he runs the club, and ended up a duke all the same. Which means when Justin comes of age, he can choose any occupation he likes. Even a 'dishonorable' one."

"I want to be a geologist," Justin volunteered. "Or an elephant trainer."

Phoebe looked at West and asked indignantly, "And who will look after the Clare estate?"

"Perhaps Stephen. Or you." He grinned at her expression. "That reminds me: tomorrow I have to do some bookkeeping. Would you like to take a look at the estate account ledgers?"

Phoebe hesitated, torn between wanting to chide him for putting ideas in her son's head and wanting to accept the offer. It would be enormously helpful to learn the estate farm's accounting system, and she knew he could explain it in a way she could understand.

"Would we be alone?" she asked warily.

"I'm afraid so." West's voice lowered as if he were relating something scandalous. "Just the two of us in the study, poring over the lascivious details of income and expenditure estimates. Then we'll move on to the really salacious materials . . . inventory . . . crop rotation charts . . ."

The man never missed an opportunity to mock her.

"Yes," Phoebe said wryly, "I'll join you." She pulled two handkerchiefs from her pocket. "One for Stephen's hands," she said, giving them to him, "and one for Justin's."

"What about me?" West asked. "Don't you want my hands to be clean?"

Phoebe fished another handkerchief from her bodice and gave it to him.

"You're like a magician," he said.

She grinned and returned to Nanny, who was tidying the interior of the pram. "We'll go back to the house now," Phoebe said briskly. "Don't fuss when you see the boys: they're both filthy but they've had a splendid time. Did you happen to see where the cat went?"

"She's under the pram, milady."

Phoebe crouched to look beneath the vehicle and saw a pair of amber eyes gleaming in the shadows. The cat crept from beneath the pram with the toy horse in her mouth and came to drop it in her lap.

Phoebe was amused and a bit touched by the cat's obvious pride in the offering. The toy was no longer recognizable, the leather shredded and most of the stuffing removed. "Thank you, my dear. How very thoughtful." After tucking the toy in her pocket, she picked up the cat. For the first time, there were no needling claws as the creature settled in her arms. "I suppose we'll have to keep you until we leave Hampshire. But you're still not a house cat, and you can't go to Essex with us. My plans are fixed . . . and nothing will alter them."

C*hapter 17*

"T*HERE'S NOTHING WICKED ABOUT you, except your kisses."*

Ever since Phoebe's astonishing whisper in his ear, West had been in a most peculiar state. Happy. Miserable. Off balance, fidgety, hungry, hot. He woke repeatedly in the middle of the night, his blood clamoring for morning.

It reminded him of the days when he used to drink himself into a stupor and regain consciousness in a dark room, bewildered and groggy. Not knowing the day, the time, or even where he was. Remembering nothing, not even the pleasures of gross self-indulgence that had put him there.

He sat at the long table in the oak-lined study, with stacks of ledgers and document folios in front of him. It was one of his favorite rooms in the house, a compact rectangular space lined with bookshelves. The floor was thickly carpeted, the air agreeably scented of vellum, parchment and ink. Daylight poured through a large window filled with a multitude of glittering antique panes, each no bigger than his hand.

Usually he was happy to be sitting here. He liked

doing the accounting; it helped him understand how the estate was doing in every aspect. But at the moment his usual interest in the world around him—people, land, livestock, the house, the weather, even food—had narrowed down to Phoebe.

He needed to be either right next to her or very far away from her. Anything in between was torture. Knowing she was in the same house or somewhere on the estate, somewhere reachable, made every cell in his body ache to find her.

When West had seen her so unexpectedly yesterday morning, he'd been jolted with an intense feeling of happiness, pleasurable on the surface but painful several layers down. She had been so beautiful there by the stream, as flowerlike as the wild irises on the banks.

Of all the mistakes in his life, and God knew there had been many, the worst had been kissing her. He would never recover from it. He could still feel her head in his hands, and the softness of her lips against his. Twenty years from now, his fingers would still be able to shape the exact curves of her skull. Every sweet kiss she'd given had been like a promise, one hesitant leap of faith after another. He'd forced himself to be careful, gentle, when he was dying to crush and devour her. It had felt as if his body had been made for no other purpose than to pleasure her, his mouth to stroke her, his hardness to fill her.

As for what Phoebe might think or feel, West had no illusion that his desire was reciprocated. Not fully, anyway. If there was one thing he was good at, it was gauging the level of a woman's interest in him. There was liking and attraction on her side, but it didn't come close to matching his. Thank God. She had enough problems as it was—she didn't need to add him to the list.

"Here are the latest banking and investment statements," came his brother's voice. Devon walked into the room with a document folio and dropped it on the table in front of him with a smart *thwack*. "So far, Winterborne's advice has paid off well, especially concerning the railway shares and commodities." He pulled a chair back and sat with his legs stretched out before him. Contemplating the tips of his polished shoes, he commented, "The only blot on the portfolio, as usual, is the Norfolk estate. Still losing money."

A house and land in Norfolk had been among the various properties Devon had inherited along with the title. Unfortunately, the past three earls had neglected the maintenance of the estate, as they had done with everything else. Most of the fertile fields had gone to rough grass, and the elegant Georgian country house had been closed and abandoned. "There are only five tenant families left," Devon continued, "and we're paying more in annual taxes than we're taking in. We could sell the property, since it's not entailed. Or . . . you could do something with it."

West glanced at him quizzically. "What the devil would I do with it?"

"You could make it your home. The house is in

good condition, and the land is suited for the kind of experimental farm you said you'd like to start some-day. You could attract new tenants to bring in revenue. If you want it, it's yours."

A smile came to West's face. He would never cease to be grateful for his brother's generosity. Perhaps if Devon had been raised as a privileged heir, he would have behaved like an entitled jackass. Instead, he was unsparing with praise and rewards, recompensing West handsomely for his contributions to the estate's success.

"Are you trying to get rid of me?" West asked lightly.

"Never." Devon's gaze was warm and steady. For years, all they'd had was each other—their bond was unbreakable. "But it occurs to me that you may want your own life someday. The privacy of your own house. A wife and children."

"As much as I appreciate the gift of your tax liability . . ." West began dryly.

"I'll assume the tax burden until you start to turn a profit. Even after you hire an assistant manager to undertake your work here, you would continue earning a percentage of gross income in lieu of management fees. Obviously, we'll still need as much oversight as you can spare—"

"Devon. You don't owe me that."

"I owe you my life, in the most literal sense." Devon paused, his voice softening. "I want your life to be no less full than mine. You should have your own family."

West shook his head. "The day I decide to marry will be long in coming."

"What about Lady Clare?"

"I might have an affair with her in five or ten years," West said, "after her next husband starts to bore her. For now, however, she's not seasoned enough for my taste."

"Every time she enters the room, we can all hear your heart beating."

West felt his color heighten. "Bugger off."

Devon wore an expression of concern blended with a touch of exasperation. It was the same older-brother look he'd given West whenever he'd been caught bullying or cheating back in their school days. "For our entire lives, West, I've always taken your side. You've nothing to lose by telling me the truth."

Folding his arms on the table, West rested his chin on them and glowered at the bookshelves. "I think I'm in love with her. Either that, or I have a stomach disease with a side effect of uncontrollable sweating. But there's no doubt about one thing: I have no business marrying and reproducing. Somehow, you've managed to rise above our upbringing. You're a good husband, and by some miracle you're a good father. I won't tempt fate by trying to follow suit."

"What's stopping you? The fact that you used to be a rake?"

"*You* were a rake. I was a wreck. Two years of moderately decent behavior doesn't wipe away an entire personal history."

"It doesn't matter now."

"It will. Imagine Justin a few years from now, meeting another boy whose family was ruined because I once had an affair with his mother. Or when someone tells him about a formal party at which I turned up too drunk to walk straight. Or the charming fact that I was booted out of Oxford because I set fire to my room. Or how about this? Imagine the moment I have to tell him that his father hated me to his dying day for bullying him at boarding school."

"If his mother forgave you, don't you think he'll be able to?"

"Forgiveness be damned. It doesn't make any of it go away."

"I think you're missing the point of forgiveness."

Lifting his head, West said bleakly, "We have to stop talking about this; Phoebe will be here soon to look at the farm account ledgers." He sorely regretted inviting her. It had been a stupid impulse.

Sighing, Devon stood. "Before I leave, let me share a piece of hard-won wisdom about women."

"God, must you?"

"It's not all about what you want. It's also about what she wants. No matter what your intentions, most women don't like it when you make their decisions for them."

PHOEBE CAME TO the door of the study, which had been left partially ajar, and knocked on the doorjamb. It reminded her of when she'd walked into West's bed-

room and found him half naked, and she felt a pang
of nerves.

"Lady Clare." West appeared at the threshold, looking polished and handsome in a dark suit of clothes
and a conservative striped necktie. His hair was neatly
brushed back and his face clean-shaven. One would
never suspect what was beneath all those civilized layers, Phoebe thought, and blushed because she knew
there were stitches above his left hip, and a bruise left
by a sheep's hoof on his right forearm, and a tan line
below the waist, and a hairy chest that intrigued her
more every time she thought about it.

After welcoming her into the study, West seated her
at a table piled with books.

"What a refreshing change to see you fully dressed,"
Phoebe said lightly.

West turned and leaned back against the table, smiling down at her. "Are we going to start by flirting?"

"I wasn't flirting."

"Let's not deceive ourselves, madam: your allusion
to my clothing and my previous lack thereof was *definitely* flirting."

Phoebe laughed. There was something different in
his manner with her today, friendliness accompanied
by a slight distance. She was relieved; it would make
everything easier. "It was accidental flirting," she said.

"It could happen to anyone," he allowed graciously.

As Phoebe's gaze moved to a towering stack of ledgers, she winced. "My goodness."

"We keep a separate book for every department of

the estate. Household, crops, dairy and poultry, live-stock, pay list, inventory, and so forth." West gave her a questioning glance. "That's not how they do it at the Clare estate?"

"I've never looked inside the Clare account books," Phoebe admitted. "Only the household ledger, which the housekeeper and I used to oversee together. Edward Larson has handled the rest of the bookkeeping ever since Henry's health declined."

"Why didn't you have an estate manager handle it?"

"He was quite old and wanted to retire. It was a great relief when Edward offered to step in and manage things. Henry trusted him completely."

"They were first cousins?"

"Yes, but they were more like brothers. Henry didn't like to mix with people outside of his family or mine. He preferred to keep his world small and safe."

West's head tilted slightly, the light sliding over the rich chocolate luster of his hair. "And therefore, so was yours," he said in a neutral tone.

"I didn't mind."

He regarded her thoughtfully. "As much as I like the pace of life in the country, I'd go mad if I didn't occasionally visit friends in London and enjoy more sophisticated amusements than can be found here."

"There are things I miss about London," Phoebe said. "But now I'm obliged to stay away, especially during the Season. As a widow and the mother of an heir presumptive, I'll be the target of every fortune hunter in England."

"If it makes you feel better, I promise never to propose to you."

"Thank you," Phoebe said with a laugh.

Turning businesslike, West pulled a broad ledger from a stack and set it in front of her.

"When do you move to Essex?"

"In a fortnight."

"Once you're settled, ask for the general account books. One of them will contain yearly statements of the estate's profits and losses. You'll want to look at the past four or five years to—why are you frowning? It's too soon to be frowning."

Phoebe picked up a stray pencil and fiddled with it, tapping the blunt end against the edge of the ledger. "It's the idea of asking Edward for the account books. I know it will upset him. He'll take it as a sign that I don't trust him."

"It has nothing to do with trust. He should encourage your involvement."

"Most men wouldn't have that attitude."

"Any man with common sense would. No one will watch over Justin and Stephen's interests better than their mother."

"Thank you. I happen to agree." Her mouth twisted. "Unfortunately, Edward won't approve, and neither will Henry's mother. In fact, no one connected to the Clare estate will like it." Phoebe didn't realize she was clenching the pencil in a death grip until West gently extricated it from her fist.

"I know how intimidating it is to have to learn all

this," he said. "But it's nothing compared to what you've already faced." His warm hand slid over hers. "You have a backbone of steel. You went through months of hell looking after a small child, a dying husband and an entire household, with unholy patience. You missed meals and went without sleep, but you never forgot to read Justin a bedtime story and tuck him in at night. When you let yourself cry or fall apart, it was only in private, for a few minutes, and then you washed your face, put your broken heart back together, and went out with a cheerful expression and a half-dozen handkerchiefs in your pockets. And you did all of it while feeling queasy most of the time because you were expecting another child. You never failed the people who needed you. You're not going to fail them now."

Shocked down to her soul, Phoebe could only manage a whisper. "Who told you all that?"

"No one." The smile lines at the corners of his eyes deepened. "Phoebe . . . anyone who knows you, even a little, would know those things about you."

"PERUVIAN GUANO," PHOEBE read aloud from a list of expenditures. "You spent *one hundred pounds* on imported bat droppings?"

West grinned. "I would have bought more, had it been available."

They had spent hours in the study, but the time seemed to have flown by. West had answered Phoebe's questions in detail, without condescension. He had opened ledgers, spread maps of the estate and the tenant farms on the floor, and pulled books with titles such as *Agricultural Chemistry* and *Drainage Operations of Arable Land* from the shelves. Phoebe had expected it to be a dull session of tallying long columns of numbers and filling out forms. However, as it turned out, estate accounting was about far more than numbers. It was about people, animals, food, weather, science, markets . . . it was about the future. And the man explaining it to her was so articulate and keen on the subject, he could even make bookkeeping methods interesting.

The conversation was interrupted as a footman brought a tray of sandwiches and refreshments from the kitchen.

"Thank you," Phoebe said, accepting the glass of chilled wine West handed to her. "Are we allowed to drink wine while accounting?"

"I assure you, there's no way to face the inventory and valuation ledger without it." He lifted his glass in a toast. "God speed the plow."

"Is that a farmer's toast?"

"It's *the* farmer's toast."

"God speed the plow," Phoebe echoed, and took a sip of the tart, refreshing vintage. After the footman had left, closing the door behind him, she returned her attention to the list of fertilizers in front of her. "Why Peruvian guano?" she asked. "Don't British bats produce enough of it?"

"One would think so. However, Peruvian guano contains the most nitrogen, which is what clay soil needs." West turned a few pages and pointed to a column. "Look at these wheat yields."

"What do those numbers mean?"

"All totaled, that one hundred pounds of Peruvian guano helped us to grow nine hundred extra bushels of wheat."

Phoebe was electrified by the information. "I want all the Clare tenants to have that fertilizer."

West laughed at her enthusiasm. "Nitrogen won't work for every farm. Each plot of land has different soil and drainage issues. That's why an estate or land manager meets with each leaseholder at least twice a year to discuss the specifics of their situations."

"Oh." Phoebe's excitement dwindled rapidly, and she took refuge in a deep swallow of wine.

West stared at her alertly. "Larson doesn't meet with them regularly?"

Phoebe replied without keeping her gaze glued to the page in front of her. "The Larsons believe it's better not to become too familiar with their tenants. They say it encourages them to make too many demands, and ask for favors, and become lax in paying rent. According to Edward, tenant uprisings like the recent ones in Ireland could easily happen here. Some landowners have even been murdered by their own leaseholders."

"In every one of those cases," West said darkly, "the landowner was notorious for having abused and mistreated his tenants." He was silent for a moment. "So . . . Larson communicates with the tenants through a middleman?"

Phoebe nodded. "He sends an estate bailiff to collect rents, and if they—"

"He sends *a bailiff*?" West began to sound slightly less calm. "For God's sake, why? He could use a land agent or . . . my God, *anyone*. Is it really necessary to use local law enforcement to terrify the tenants twice a year?"

After draining her wine, Phoebe said defensively, "Things are done differently in Essex."

"No matter where you are, Phoebe, a manager's job usually involves having to bloody *manage* something. Is Larson so rarefied that he can't bring himself to have a conversation with a small farmer? Does he think poverty is bloody contagious?"

"No," Phoebe said earnestly. "Oh, I've made you dislike Edward by giving you the wrong impression. He's such a—"

"No, I already disliked him."

"—lovely man, always kind and caring—he spent so many hours at Henry's bedside, reading and comforting him—and comforting me, too. I leaned on Edward's shoulder and came to rely on him even at the darkest moments—"

"Actually, I detest him."

"—and he was very good with Justin, and Henry saw all that, which is why he asked for my promise to—" She broke off abruptly.

West stared at her without blinking. "Promise to what?"

Phoebe set aside her empty wine glass. "Nothing."

"What promise?"

"It's nothing."

"Holy hell," West said softly. She could feel his

eyes boring holes into her. "An insane thought just came into my head. But it can't be true."

Blindly Phoebe turned pages in the ledger. "I was wondering—how much is in a bushel?"

"Eight gallons. Tell me it's not true."

Feeling the need to escape, Phoebe pushed back from the table and went to the bookshelves. "How would I know what you're thinking?"

West's voice lashed out like the crack of a whip, making her start. "Tell me Henry didn't ask for your promise to marry his *blasted cousin!*"

"Will you be quiet?" Phoebe whispered sharply, whirling to face him. "I'd rather you didn't shout it to the entire household!"

"My God, he did." Inexplicably, West had flushed beneath his tan. "And you said yes. Why for the love of all that's holy did you say yes?"

"Henry was in an agony of worry for me and Justin, and the unborn baby. He wanted to know we would be loved and cared for. He wanted his estate and home to be safeguarded. Edward and I suit each other."

"He'll never be more than a counterfeit Henry to you."

"Edward is far more than a counterfeit Henry! How presumptuous of you, how—"

"There's not one damned spark of passion between you. If there were, he'd have bedded you by now."

She drew in a sharp breath. "I've been in mourning, you . . . you cretin!"

West didn't look the least bit apologetic. "It's been

two years. Were I in Larson's place, I'd at least have kissed you."

"I've been living in my parents' home. There's been no opportunity."

"Desire finds opportunity."

"I'm not some young girl hoping for a stolen kiss behind the potted palms. I have other priorities now. Edward would be a good father to my children, and . . ." Phoebe turned back to the bookshelves, neatening a line of volumes, rubbing away a trace of book dust from one of the ancient leather spines. "Physical relations aren't everything."

"Hang it all, Phoebe, they're not nothing, either."

Risking a glance at West, she saw that he'd dropped his head in his hands. "Women have different needs than men," she said.

His voice was muffled. "You're killing me."

One of the bookbindings had a torn edge. She stroked it with a fingertip, as if that would heal it. "The memories are enough," she said quietly.

Silence.

"Most of those feelings died with Henry," she added.

More silence.

Had West left the room? Baffled by his lack of response, Phoebe turned to glance at him again. She jerked in surprise as she found him right behind her.

Before she could say a word, he hauled her into his arms, and his mouth came down to hers.

Chapter 18

THE KISS WAS COOL and wine-sweet, swiftly gaining intensity. She felt the urgent stroke of his tongue, as if he were trying to gather as much of her taste as he could before she stopped him. He gathered her closer, and she couldn't help yielding, letting her head fall back against his supportive arm. This was the truth her body couldn't hide—she wanted this, his hunger, his heart pounding against hers.

West's mouth slid from hers and followed the line of her throat. Finding the throb of her pulse, he kissed and nuzzled it ardently. "You're not a possession," he said raggedly. "You can't be passed from one man to another like a painting or an antique vase."

Her voice was faint. "That's not how it is."

"Has he told you he wants you?"

"Not the way you mean. He . . . he's a gentleman . . ."

"I want you with my entire body." West dragged his mouth over hers, shaping her lips before settling in for a rough and ardent kiss. He hitched her up against him until her toes barely touched the floor. "You're all I think about. You're all I see. You're the center of a star, and the force of gravity keeps pulling me closer, and I don't give a damn that I'm about to be incinerated." He rested his forehead against hers, panting. "That's what he should tell you."

Somewhere in Phoebe's mind, there were practical thoughts, sensible words, but they were drowned in a tide of sensation as his mouth covered hers again. He kissed her with the fullness of a man's passion, slow and relentless, consuming her as if he were fire and she were oxygen. She opened for him, clung to him, her body melting into his. She was surrounded by arms so powerful he could have crushed her. Her blood raced at a speed that made her light-headed and weakened her knees.

West lowered her to the floor, easily controlling their descent. He knelt over her, stripped off his coat and tossed it aside, and roughly unknotted his necktie. She knew she could stop him with a word, but instead she lay there trembling with anticipation for things she couldn't even name. Reaching down, he pushed back the hem of her skirts a few inches to uncover her ankles. He removed her low-heeled slippers, his fingers curving gently beneath her heels, and then . . . he bent to press his lips over the silk of her stockings, kissing each foot in turn.

Phoebe could only stare at him, stunned by the tender, worshipful gesture.

He held her gaze, his eyes a shade of blue she'd seen only in dreams. He bent over her, the solid, exciting weight of him urging her legs apart beneath the skirts. One of his arms slid beneath her neck, and his mouth sought hers again. He was so careful, so assured, absorbed in her every response. His fingertips wandered over exposed skin wherever he could find it—her wrists, her throat, the shadowed places behind her ears.

The tender friction of his mouth sent fire dancing to the ends of her nerves, and she couldn't help squirming beneath him. She was beginning to understand temptation as she never had before, how it could unravel a well-behaved lifetime in a matter of minutes. The bodice of her dress was loose—he'd unfastened it before she'd even noticed. Her corset was partially boned and made with silk elastic, more flexible than the usual stiff contraption of steel and tough cotton coutil. After unhooking the top, he lifted her breasts free of the half cups. She felt the wet touch of his tongue, a line of heat painted across a tense nipple. His lips closed over her and tugged gently, sending shocks of pleasure down to her toes. Moving to the other breast, he drew the tender budded peak into his mouth, sucking and playing with it.

One of his hands reached down to grasp the front of her skirts, pulling up the fabric until the only layers between them were his trousers and the thin cotton voile of her drawers. He let her have more of his weight, hardness nudging against swelling softness, relieving the hot ache. She felt the slight roughness of his palm cupping beneath her breast, his thumb prodding and stroking the tip. No matter how she tried to stay still, pleasure stirred all through her . . . pulses, twitches, flutters, all begging to be gathered into a single chord of release. Her hips nudged upward in a rhythmic movement beyond her control. Later, she would be mortified at the memory of her wanton behavior, but for now the need was too overpowering.

A whimper rose in her throat as West rolled to his side, relieving her of his weight, and she tried to bring him back to her.

He was breathing in unsteady surges. "Phoebe—no, I'm so close, I can't—"

She interrupted him, her mouth locking onto his in a demanding kiss. He relented and pressed her back down into the chaotic ruffles of her dress. The loosened bodice pulled tight over her arms, making it difficult to move. He kissed her exposed breasts and licked the undersides, nuzzling the plush curves. Reaching beneath her skirts, he found the open slit of her drawers. His palm skimmed the tops of soft, dry curls in repeated passes, the sensation working down to the follicles and sending a quiver of awareness through her. Very gently he parted the curls and ran a fingertip along the private furrow.

Craving more pressure, more explicit contact, she pushed up against his hand, but his touch remained light and unhurried as he explored the intricate crevice. Oh, God, he knew what he was doing, coaxing her response by gradual degrees, making her wait in helpless anticipation. Softly, almost as if by accident, he teased deeper until his fingertip grazed the bud of her clitoris. Her entire body jerked.

A hungry shudder wracked her as his touch withdrew. "Oh, please . . ." she whispered through dry lips.

West looked down at her with a faint smile, his eyes smoldering-blue. His head lowered to her breast, his lips closing over the tip. For long minutes he suckled and licked, while his hand traversed her body in leisurely paths. She simmered and ached and moaned, forgetting everything but the pleasure of what he was doing to her. After torturous delays and detours, he finally reached between her thighs and touched the wet, vulnerable entrance of her body. Her hands gripped his shoulders, and she panted into the open neck of his shirt, her legs tensing. The blunt tip of a finger worked its way inward, the thickness of a knuckle stretching tender flesh. There was movement deep inside her . . . teasing strokes . . . a peculiar pressure that sent a shot of heat to the quick of her body.

Slowly he eased his finger out and toyed with the silky flanges of her inner lips as if they were petals before circling the taut peak of her sex. One wet fingertip moved easily over her swollen flesh, the slight abrasion of a callous rasping delicately, causing her toes to curl. Tension coiled inside her, so erotic and unbearable she would have done anything to relieve it.

"How sensitive you are," he whispered against her burning cheek. "It might be better for you . . . gentler . . . if I used my tongue. Would you like that?"

A breath stuck in her throat.

Amusement danced in the hot-blue depths of his eyes as he saw her reaction.

"Oh . . . I don't think . . ." was all she could manage to say.

His lips brushed lightly over hers. "My motto is, 'You'll never know unless you try it.'"

"That's the worst motto I've ever heard," she said faintly, and he grinned.

"Well, it makes life interesting." Those clever, wicked fingers tickled between her thighs as he whispered, "Let me kiss you here." At her hesitation, he urged, "Yes. Say yes."

"No, thank you," she said in rising worry, and he laughed softly. She felt pressure, and the helpless feeling of being invaded, and realized he was trying to slide two fingers inside her.

"Relax . . . You're so sweet, so soft . . . Phoebe . . . for the next ten thousand nights, I'm going to dream about your beautiful mouth, and the miraculous shape of you, and all these freckles that turn you into a work of art—"

"Don't tease," she said breathlessly, and bit her lip as her body yielded to the gentle intrusion, his fingers wriggling slightly as they filled her.

"You want proof of my sincerity?" Deliberately he pressed his aroused flesh against her thigh. "Feel that. Just the thought of you does this to me."

The man was shameless. Boasting about his male part as if it were something to be proud of! Although . . . one had to admit . . . it was impressively substantial. Phoebe struggled with nearly irresistible curiosity before letting her hand steal down to investigate. As her palm slid along the incredibly hard, heavy length of him, she blinked and said faintly, "Good heavens." She drew her hand back quickly, and he smiled down at her flushed face.

"Kiss me," he whispered. "As if we were in bed with the whole night ahead of us." His fingers eased deeper. "Kiss me as if I were inside you."

Phoebe obeyed blindly, butterflies swirling. He caressed and played with her, sometimes entering her with his fingers, sometimes withdrawing completely and toying with the damp curls between her thighs or gliding up to stroke her breasts. It was astonishing how much he seemed to know about her body, the places that were too sensitive to be touched directly, the steady rhythms that aroused her most.

She had never been filled with such acute sensation, every nerve lit and glowing. Whenever her excitement built to the point of release, he stopped and made her wait until the heat receded, and then he started again. She was trembling with the need to climax, but he ignored her pleas and protests, taking his time. His fingers filled her gently, and his other hand came to her mound, massaging on either side of her clitoris. Her intimate muscles clenched and released, over and over, in deep pulsations beyond her control.

Pleasure resonated through her at a clarion pitch, and this time he didn't stop, guiding her right into the feeling and through it. Her vision was flooded with brilliance, her muscles spasming, jerking. He took her low cry into his mouth and kissed her as hard and long as she wanted, and he didn't stop stroking and teasing until the shudders had eased to shivers, and the shivers had faded to quiet trembling. Very gradually, the long, flexing fingers eased out of her body. He held her, cradling her against him, while she gasped for air and slowly returned to herself.

Sorting through the exhausted muddle of her thoughts, Phoebe wondered what would happen next. From the way they were entangled, she could feel that he was still aroused—would he want satisfaction? What should she do for him, and how? Oh, God, her mind was all blurred and comfortable, and her body was as limp as a sack of crushed salt. She felt excruciatingly shy about what they'd just done, but also grateful and close to tears. Nothing had ever felt as good as this, being gathered in by his arms, every part of her safe and warm and replete.

Carefully West reached into the wild disorder of her clothes and began to pull garments into place, tying and fastening her clothes expertly. All she could seem to do was lie there like a discarded doll, dreading the return to reality.

He eased her up to a sitting position. When he spoke, his tone was dry and amused. "About those feelings you no longer have. You were saying . . . ?"

Phoebe glanced at him in surprise and stiffened as if he'd just thrown cold water in her face.

It wasn't what West said that shocked her, it was

his detached expression, and the way one corner of his mouth curled upward in an arrogant smile. The tender lover had vanished, leaving her with a sardonic stranger.

All the feelings of warmth and connection had been an illusion. He hadn't meant anything he'd said. All he had wanted was to prove that she still had physical needs, and he'd succeeded spectacularly, humiliating her in the process.

Her first intimacy with a man other than her husband . . . and it had been a game to him.

Oh, she felt so foolish.

"I hope we've learned our lesson," he mocked lightly, making it even worse.

Somehow Phoebe managed to cover her hurt and fury with a stony façade. "Indeed," she replied curtly, unable to look at him as she rose to her feet. "Although perhaps not the lesson you thought you were teaching." She yanked her bodice into place and straightened her skirts, and nearly leaped away like a startled doe as he moved to help her. "I require no more assistance."

West stepped back at once. He waited silently as she finished putting herself in order. "Phoebe—" he began, his voice softer than before.

"Thank you, Mr. Ravenel," she said, ignoring the weakness of her legs as she strode to the door. They were no longer on a first-name basis. As far as she was concerned, they never would be again. "The afternoon was most instructive." She let herself out of the study and closed the door with great care, even though she longed to slam it.

Chapter 19

ON THE SURFACE, DINNER that night—the last gathering before the Challons departed in the morning—was a sparkling and lighthearted affair. The wedding and subsequent visit had been a great success, deepening the acquaintance between the two families and paving the way for more interactions in the future.

For all the enjoyment West derived from the evening, he might as well have spent it in a medieval dungeon. The effort to appear normal was almost face-cracking. He couldn't help but marvel inwardly at Phoebe, who was perfectly composed and smiling. Her self-control was formidable. She was careful not to ignore him entirely, but she gave him no more than the minimum of attention necessary to keep from causing comment. Every now and then she glanced at him with a bland smile, or laughed politely at some quip he'd made, her gaze never quite meeting his.

It's for the best, West had told himself a thousand times since the torrid scene in the study. It had been the right decision to make her hate him. In the moments after her climax, as he'd cradled her in his arms and felt her beautiful body nestle trustingly against his, he'd been on the verge of pouring out everything he thought and felt for her. Even now, it terrified him to think of what he might have said. Instead he'd deliberately embarrassed her, and pretended he'd only been amusing himself with her.

Now there would be no expectations, no longing, no hope on either side. Now he didn't have to fear that he might go to her in a moment of weakness. She would leave tomorrow, and everything would go back to the way it was. He would find a way to forget her. The world was full of women.

Years would pass, while he and Phoebe led separate lives. She would marry and have more children. She would have the life she deserved.

Unfortunately, so would he.

After an abysmal night of broken sleep, West awakened with a lump of ice in his stomach. He felt as if someone had parked a traction engine on his chest. Slowly he went through the rituals that began every morning. He was too numb to feel the heat of the towel he used to soften his beard before shaving. As he passed the unmade bed, he was tempted to climb back into it, fully clothed.

Enough of this, he told himself grimly. It was unmanly, this moping and languishing. He would go about his day as usual, starting with breakfast. The sideboard would be laden with broiled chops, eggs, rashers of bacon and ham, potatoes hashed with herbs and fried in butter, bread puddings each in its own puddle of sauce, a platter of crisp radishes and pickles on ice, dishes of stewed fruit from the orchard topped with fresh cream—

The thought of food was nauseating.

West paced, sat, stood and paced some more, and finally stopped at the window with his forehead pressed against a cool pane of glass. His room afforded a view of the stables and carriage house, where vehicles and horses were being readied to take the Challons to the estate's private railway halt.

He couldn't let Phoebe leave like this, hating him, thinking the worst of him. He didn't know how things should be left between them, but not this way.

He thought of what Pandora had told him the day before the wedding, that she didn't feel she deserved to marry a man like Lord St. Vincent. *"There's nothing better than having something you don't deserve,"* he'd replied.

What a flippant ass he'd been. Now he understood the terrible risk and pain of wanting someone far above your reach.

West went downstairs to the study, where the books he had shown Phoebe yesterday had been arranged in stacks on the table. Sorting through the volumes, he found the one he wanted and pulled it out. He sat at the table and reached for a pen and inkwell.

Fifteen minutes later, he headed back upstairs with the book in hand. He didn't stop until he had reached the threshold of Phoebe's room. There were noises from within, drawers opening and closing, a trunk lid banging on the floor. He heard Phoebe's muffled voice as she spoke to her maid.

His heart was thrashing like a caged lark. Gingerly he knocked at the door. The sounds inside the room stopped.

Soon the door opened, and a lady's maid regarded him with raised brows. "Sir?"

West cleared his throat before saying gruffly, "I'd like to speak with Lady Clare—briefly—if I may." After a pause, he added, "I have something to give her."

"One moment, sir." The door closed.

Almost a full minute passed before the door opened again. This time it was Phoebe. She was dressed in traveling clothes, her hair drawn up tightly and pinned in an intricately braided coil high at the back of her head. She looked tense and tired, her complexion ghost pale except for the flags of bright pink at the crest of each cheek. The lack of color only served to emphasize the striking angles of her jaw and cheekbones. People would fall in love with that remarkable face before they even realized how much more there was to love beneath the façade.

"Mr. Ravenel," she said coolly, without quite meeting his gaze.

Feeling like an idiot, West extended the book to her. "For you to keep."

Phoebe took it and glanced down at the title. "*The Modern Handbook for Landed Proprietors*," she read in a monotone.

"It's full of good information."

"Thank you, how thoughtful," she said distantly. "If you'll excuse me, I must finish packing—"

"What happened yesterday—" West had to pause for an extra breath. His lungs felt half their usual size. "I misled you about why I did it. It wasn't to prove you still had those feelings. I wanted to prove you had those feelings for *me*. It was selfish and stupid. I shouldn't have taken liberties with you."

Frowning, Phoebe stepped out into the hallway, closed the door, and glanced at their surroundings to check for privacy. She looked directly at him then, her eyes light and piercing. "I wasn't offended by that," she said in a low, nettled tone. "It was the way you behaved afterward, so smug and—"

"I know."

"—so arrogant—"

"I was jealous."

Phoebe blinked, seemingly taken aback. "Of Edward?"

"Because you're going to marry him."

Her brows lowered. "I've made no decisions about that. With all I have to face when I move back to Clare Manor, marriage will hardly be at the forefront of my mind."

"But your promise to Henry . . ."

"I didn't agree to sacrifice my own judgment," she said curtly. "I promised to consider the idea because it was what Henry wanted. But I may never marry at all. Or I may marry someone other than Edward."

The idea of some unknown man courting Phoebe, making love to her, made West long to put his fist through the wall. "I hope you'll find someone worthy of you," he muttered. "To my regret, I have nothing to offer other than a relationship that would insult and lower you."

"Indeed? You seem marriageable enough to me."

"Not for you," he said without thinking, and immediately regretted it as he saw her face. "I didn't mean—"

"I see." Her voice could have sliced a green apple. "You desire me only as a mistress and not a wife. Is that it?"

The conversation was not going at all in the direction West had expected. "Neither," he said hastily. "I mean, *both*." He wasn't making sense. "Damn it!" After a hard swallow, he turned ruthlessly, painfully sincere. "Phoebe, you've always been sheltered from men like me. You've never had to face the consequences of someone else's sordid past. I wouldn't do that to you, or the boys. They need a father to live up to, not one they would have to live down. As for me—I'm not meant for marriage. And if I were, I'd never take a wife so far above me in every way. I'm aware of how small-minded that is, but even men with small minds know their limits."

"I'm not above you," Phoebe protested.

"You're too perfect to be entirely human. You belong to some higher order—not quite an angel, but close. No woman in my life, before or after you, will ever thrill me as you do. I don't know what to call this. But I do know you should be worshipped by a man who's earned the right—and that man is not me." He paused. "I'll take the cat now."

"Wh-what?" Phoebe asked dazedly.

"The cat. Put her in a basket and I'll take her back to the barn. Unless you want to keep her."

"No, I . . . thank you, no, but—"

"Go get her. I'll wait."

Seeming disoriented, Phoebe disappeared, leaving the door ajar. Soon she returned with a large, lidded basket, a few plaintive mewls slipping through the woven reeds.

West took it from her. "When you leave, I won't be there to see the carriage off. I can't. If I try to say good-bye, I'm sure to do something that would embarrass us both."

"Wait," Phoebe began, sounding breathless, "I need to ask—"

West didn't want to hear whatever it was. He couldn't bear it. Keeping the basket tucked in one arm, he reached out with his free hand, clasped the soft nape of her neck, and kissed her. He felt her lips tremble beneath his. The delicious warmth of her response stole through him, melting through the frozen despair. Finally, he could take a deep breath again. He savored her full, sweet mouth, pulling and teasing the silkiness, stealing as much of her taste as he could. He wanted to spend years kissing her. Instead he finished with a strong nudge and let go of her.

"Let's forget about that one too," he said, his voice slightly hoarse. And he left her while he was still able, carrying away the protesting cat in the basket.

"You can't go anywhere," Devon said, when West told him he was heading out to the barn. "The Challons will be leaving soon—you'll want to bid them farewell."

"No, I won't," West replied shortly, still holding the unhappy cat in the basket. "I'm going to stay away until I'm sure they're gone."

His older brother scowled. "I thought you might accompany them out to the railway halt."

"I'm accompanying this vicious cat back to the barn."

"What should I tell the duke if he remarks on your absence?"

"There are only three reasons anyone ever needs me around here," West said sourly, "when something is broken, overflowing, or mired in a bog. Use one of those. I guarantee the Challons won't give a damn whether I'm here or not."

"Did you quarrel with Lady Clare? Is that why you appeared to be sitting on a hedgehog all through dinner?"

West's lips twitched despite his bad mood. "Is that how it looked? I assure you, I wasn't nearly that comfortable."

Devon's frown eased. "You can't outrun your problems."

"Actually, I can," West said, walking away with the basket. "Look—I'm doing it right now."

"Have you tried being honest with her about your feelings?" came Devon's voice from behind him.

"Sweet mother of God, can you hear yourself?" West asked without turning around. "I'd get more manly advice from Kathleen."

He exited the back of the house and didn't stop

walking until he'd reached the group of farm buildings. The familiar sights and rhythms of the farm
helped to restore his balance and blunt the sharp edges
of misery. The coming days would be filled with no
end of hard physical work, which would hopefully exhaust him enough to let him sleep at night.

After reaching the hay barn, he gently set the basket on the ground, lifted the lid, and tipped out the little black cat, who hissed and gave him a baleful stare.

"Sorry, Galoshes," he said. "It's back to work for
both of us. Go catch some mice."

The cat slunk away.

West went to the blacksmith's shop, where Stub and
some of the men were busy repairing a broken axle.
They had raised a heavy cart with a set of differen-
tial pulley blocks to reach the broken parts beneath.
Although they didn't need his help, nor was there a
good reason for him to stay and watch, he lingered
as long as possible. Every few minutes he consulted
his pocket watch, which finally prompted Stub to ask
good-naturedly, "Are we not moving lively enough for
you, Mr. Ravenel?"

West smiled slightly and shook his head, replacing
the watch. "I want to make certain the guests have left
before I go back."

Neddy glanced at him with cheerful interest. "What
o' the red-haired widder and that little brush o' a lad?"
he dared to ask. "Didn't you wish to see 'em off, sir?"

"Lady Clare is a rare, fine woman," West replied
ruefully. "Too fine for me, unfortunately. With her, it

would be the cart before the horse, and I'm not a man to walk behind the cart."

There was a rumble of agreement among the men. But Neddy ventured, "Myself, I don't care if I'm at the tail of the cart, as long as my wife keeps us on the straight road." They all chuckled.

"Naither would I mind, if the wife was sweet to look upon," Stub declared. "And the widow Clare's a proven breeder: you'd get healthy kittlin' off such a good cat."

Although West knew the comment hadn't been meant disrespectfully, he gave Stub a warning glance to indicate the subject was closed. After the axle had been removed from the cart, West walked back to Eversby Priory. The morning had risen cool and blue. A good day for traveling.

He followed the graveled path around the side of the house to take a glance at the front drive. There were no carriages, no throng of busy servants; the Challons were definitely gone. Letting out a measured breath, he went in through the front entrance.

Despite his considerable list of tasks and chores, he found himself at a loss for what to do. He felt like a tree with a center of gravity offset from its base, liable to topple in an unpredictable direction. The household bustled quietly as servants cleaned the vacated rooms and stripped linens from the beds, while others cleared the breakfast room sideboard and removed plates and flatware. West glanced down at the empty mending basket in his hand. He wasn't sure what to do with it now.

He went to the room where Phoebe had stayed and set the mending basket near the threshold. The bed had been hastily made; the side where Phoebe had slept wasn't quite smooth. He couldn't resist drawing close enough to trail his fingers along the counterpane, remembering the slight, firm weight of her body, the feel of her breath on his cheek—

A plaintive drawn-out meow interrupted his thoughts.

"What the devil . . . ?" West muttered, walking around the bed. He was stunned to find the black cat there, dusty and irritable-looking. "How can you be here?" he demanded. "I just left you at the barn!"

Galoshes let out another disconsolate sound and wandered around the empty room. She must have raced to the house as soon as he'd set her free and had somehow found a way to slip inside. She jumped onto the bed and coiled at the corner of it.

After a moment, West sat on the side of the mattress. He reached for a pillow and hunted for any lingering trace of Phoebe. Discovering a faint soap-and-roses sweetness, he drew it in deeply. When his eyes opened, he found the cat staring at him, the golden eyes solemn and accusing.

"You don't belong in her life any more than I do," West said flatly. "You don't even belong in a house."

Galoshes showed no reaction, other than flicking the tip of her scraggly tail like someone impatiently drumming her fingers.

West wondered if she would keep coming back in search of Phoebe. It was impossible not to feel sorry for the skinny little creature. He let out an exasperated sigh. "If I did manage to help you reach her," he said, "I doubt she'd keep you. God knows what will become of you. Furthermore, do you really want to live in Essex? Does anyone?"

Flick. Flick. Flick.

West considered the cat for a long moment. "We might catch them at Alton Station," he mused. "But you'd have to go back into that mending basket, which you wouldn't like. And we'd have to go on horseback, which you especially wouldn't like." An involuntary grin crossed his face as he thought of how annoyed Phoebe would be. "She would kill me. I'm damned if I'll risk my life for a barn cat."

But the smile wouldn't go away.

Making the decision, West tossed aside the pillow and went to fetch the mending basket. "Choose your fate, cat. If you fight me over the basket, the adventure ends here. If you're willing to climb in . . . we'll see what can be done."

"Pat-a-cake, pat-a-cake, baker's man . . ." Evie chanted as she played with Stephen in the Challons' private railway carriage. They occupied one side of a deep upholstered settee, with Sebastian lounging in the other corner. The toddler clapped his tiny hands along with his grandmother, his rapt gaze fastened on her face. "Make me a cake as fast as you can . . ."

Phoebe and Seraphina sat on a settee directly opposite them, while Ivo and Justin stood at a window to watch the activity on the Alton Station platforms. Since the scheduled stop was short, the Challons remained in their carriage, which was paneled in gleaming bird's-eye maple and trimmed with blue velvet plush and gold-plated fittings. To keep the interior temperature pleasant, ice cooling trays had been set into the floor and covered with ornamental gridwork.

The nursery rhyme concluded, and Evie cheerfully began again. "Pat-a-cake, pat-a-cake—"

"My sweet," Sebastian interrupted, "we've been involved in the manufacture of cakes ever since we set foot on the train. For my sanity, I beg you to choose another game."

"Stephen," Evie asked her grandson, "do you want to play peekaboo?"

"No," came the baby's grave answer.

"Do you want to play 'beckoning the chickens'?"

"No."

Evie's impish gaze flickered to her husband before she asked the child, "Do you want to play horsie with Gramps?"

"*Yes!*"

Sebastian grinned ruefully and reached for the boy. "I knew I should have kept quiet." He sat Stephen on his knee and began to bounce him, making him squeal with delight.

Absently Phoebe returned her attention to the book in her lap.

"What novel are you reading?" Seraphina asked, looking up from a ladies' fashion periodical. "Is it any good?"

"It's not a novel, it was a gift from Mr. Ravenel."

Seraphina's blue eyes brightened with interest. "May I see?"

Phoebe handed it to her younger sister.

"*The Modern Handbook for Landed Proprietors?*" Seraphina asked, wrinkling her nose.

"It's full of information I'll need when I move back to the Clare estate."

Carefully Seraphina lifted the front cover and read the neatly handwritten lines inside.

My lady,
    When in difficulty, remember the words of our mutual friend Stephen Armstrong: "You can always swim out of quicksand as long as you don't panic."
    Or send for me, and I'll come throw you a rope.
                                                    —W. R.

Every time Phoebe had read those words—at least a dozen times since they'd left Eversby Priory—a giddy sensation rushed through her. It had hardly escaped her notice that West had marked sections of the book with x's, just as she had marked Henry's book so long ago. A sly bit of flirtation, those x's—she was welcome to interpret them as kisses, while he could still maintain deniability.

Infuriating, complicated man.

She wished he hadn't come to her door this morning. It would have been easier to leave Eversby Priory while she was still angry with him. Instead, he had undercut all her hurt and fury with searing honesty. He had laid bare his soul. He'd all but said he loved her.

This relationship with him—if that was what it was—had happened too fast. There had been no time to savor anything, no time to think. They had behaved as if they were in their teens, all passion and impulse, no common sense. She had never expected to feel this way again, young and hopeful and intensely desired. He'd made her feel as if there were untapped qualities in her waiting to be discovered.

"Will you send for him?" Seraphina asked softly, still looking down at the inscription.

Phoebe made certain their parents were still occupied with Stephen before she whispered, "I don't think so."

"He's very taken with you." Seraphina handed back the book. "Everyone could see it. And you like him, don't you?"

"I do. But there's too much I don't know about him. He has a disreputable past, and I have the children to think about." Phoebe hesitated, disliking the way that sounded, so prim and judgmental. Sighing, she added glumly, "He made it clear that marriage is out of the question."

Seraphina looked bewildered. "But everyone wants to marry you."

"Not quite everyone, apparently." Phoebe opened the book and touched the initials *W. R.* with her fingertip. "He says he's not suited for fatherhood, and . . . well, marriage isn't for every man."

"Someone with his looks should be required *by law* to marry," Seraphina said.

Phoebe gave a reluctant chuckle. "It does seem a waste."

A knock at the enameled door of the carriage alerted them to the presence of a porter and a platform inspector just outside.

Sebastian looked up and handed the baby back to Evie. He went to speak to the men. After a minute or two, he came back from the threshold with a basket. Looking perturbed and amused, he brought it to Phoebe. "This was delivered to the station for you."

"Just now?" Phoebe asked with a nonplussed laugh. "Why, I believe it's Ernestine's mending basket! Don't say the Ravenels went to the trouble of sending someone all the way to Alton to return it?"

"It's not empty," her father said. As he set the basket in her lap, it quivered and rustled, and a blood-curdling yowl emerged.

Astonished, Phoebe fumbled with the latch on the lid and opened it.

The black cat sprang out and crawled frantically up her front, clinging to her shoulder with such ferocity that nothing could have detached her claws.

"*Galoshes!*" Justin exclaimed, hurrying over to her.

"*Gosh-gosh!*" Stephen cried in excitement.

Phoebe stroked the frantic cat and tried to calm her. "Galoshes, how . . . why are you . . . oh, this is Mr. Ravenel's doing! I'm going to *murder* him. You poor little thing."

Justin came to stand beside her, running his hands

over the dusty, bedraggled feline. "Are we going to keep her now, Mama?"

"I don't think we have a choice," Phoebe said distractedly. "Ivo, will you go with Justin to the dining compartment, and fetch her some food and water?"

The two boys dashed off immediately.

"Why has he done this?" Phoebe fretted. "He probably couldn't make her stay at the barn, either. But she's not meant to be a pet. She's sure to run off as soon as we reach home."

Resuming his seat next to Evie, Sebastian said dryly, "Redbird, I doubt that creature will stray more than an arm's length from you."

Discovering a note in the mending basket, Phoebe plucked it out and unfolded it. She instantly recognized West's handwriting.

Unemployed Feline Seeking Household Position

To Whom It May Concern,

I hereby offer my services as an experienced mouser and personal companion. References from a reputable family to be provided upon request. Willing to accept room and board in lieu of pay. Indoor lodgings preferred.

Your servant,
Galoshes the Cat

Glancing up from the note, Phoebe found her parents' questioning gazes on her. "Job application," she explained sourly. "From the cat."

"How charming," Seraphina exclaimed, reading over her shoulder.

"'Personal companion,' my foot," Phoebe muttered. "This is a semi-feral animal who has lived in outbuildings and fed on vermin."

"I wonder," Seraphina said thoughtfully. "If she were truly feral, she wouldn't want any contact with humans. With time and patience, she might become domesticated."

Phoebe rolled her eyes. "It seems we'll find out."

The boys returned from the dining car with a bowl of water and a tray of refreshments. Galoshes descended to the floor long enough to devour a boiled egg, an anchovy canapé, and a spoonful of black caviar from a silver dish on ice. Licking her lips and purring, the cat jumped back into Phoebe's lap and curled up with a sigh.

"I'd say she's adjusting quite well," Seraphina commented with a grin, and elbowed Phoebe gently. "One never knows who might rise above their disreputable past."

Two strikes of the bell and a long whistle blast signaled the train's departure. As the locomotive began to pull away from Alton Station, Phoebe felt a hollowing sadness inside. There was something melancholy about a train whistle, the twin notes bracketing the air like an empty set of parentheses. Overcome by a longing that, for once, had nothing to do with Henry, she nudged aside the edge of a gold-fringed curtain to look at the platform.

Among the milling of passengers and porters, a lean, dark form stood with a shoulder casually propped against a support column.

West.

Their gazes met across the platform as the railway carriage passed. Phoebe stopped breathing, waves of alternating heat and chills leaving her shaken. It wasn't just physical desire—although that was certainly a considerable part of it. In the measure of a few days, a connection had formed between them. An inconvenient, painful connection that she hoped wouldn't last for long. She stared at him without blinking, trying to keep him in her vision every possible second.

With a faint curve of his mouth, West reached up to touch the low brim of his hat. Then he was out of sight.

Chapter 20

PHOEBE LOOKED UP FROM her writing desk as Edward Larson's tall, lanky form strode into the front parlor of Clare Manor. "Good morning," she said brightly. "I wasn't expecting you."

A warm smile crossed his lean face. "A pleasant surprise, I hope."

"Naturally."

As always, Edward was impeccably dressed and groomed, the perfect picture of a country gentleman. His medium brown hair was parted on the side and arranged in neatly trimmed waves. He was clean-shaven, but not by choice: he'd once tried to grow a pair of fashionable sideburns, but his facial hair had come in as sparse and patchy as a young lad's, forcing him to abandon the attempt.

"It looks different in here," Edward commented, glancing around the room. "What have you changed?"

"The curtains."

"These are new?" he asked, regarding the cream silk curtains.

Phoebe laughed. "Don't you remember the brown brocade ones that were there for the past thirty years?"

He shrugged, his brown eyes smiling. "Not really. In any case, I like these."

The curtains had been part of a redecorating project that Phoebe had undertaken as soon as she'd moved back to the Clare estate. She had been dismayed to discover that even after two years, the entire house still had the atmosphere of a sickroom. It had been quiet and musty, the rows of sash windows shrouded with heavy curtains, the walls and carpets dingy. Compared to her family's airy, light-filled home in Sussex, it had been appalling. If her children were to live here from now on, she had decided, it would have to be aired out and redecorated.

Using funds from her jointure, she had sent to London for books of wallpaper, fabric and paint samples. She had hired local painters to cover walls with cream paint, and craftsmen had sanded the floors and woodwork down to a natural finish. The ancient carpets had been replaced by hand-knotted rugs from Kidderminster with sage or cream backgrounds. Deep-buttoned chairs and sofas had been reupholstered in green velvet or floral chintz. Although Phoebe was far from finished, she was pleased by the results so far. The smells of mustiness and decay had been replaced by fresh paint, wood polish and newness. The house was alive again, emerging from its long spell of mourning.

"Shall I ring for tea?" Phoebe asked.

Edward shook his head and bent to kiss her cheek. "Not on my account. Regrettably, I can stay only for a few minutes. I have a bit of business to discuss with you."

"You've brought the account ledgers?" she asked hopefully.

Edward hung his head in a show of penitence.

Clearly, he hadn't.

His boyish charm did nothing to ease Phoebe's irritation, which stung in several places at once, as if she'd been surrounded by a swarm of bees.

For reasons she still didn't entirely understand, Edward had taken it upon himself to remove the entire mass of account books, including all the home farm and tenant ledgers, from the study at Clare Manor. He had transferred them to the private offices he and his father shared in the nearby market town. Not only did the Larsons manage their own property, they also superintended farmland for many well-to-do families in the county.

When Phoebe had discovered the Clare estate books were missing, Edward had apologized for having forgotten to tell her, and explained it was easier for him to manage the estate farms from his father's place of business. He had promised to return them as soon as possible, but every time Phoebe reminded him, he had a convenient excuse for delaying.

"Edward," Phoebe said reproachfully. "It's been three months since I first asked for those ledgers."

"I knew you were busy with the redecorating."

Somehow Phoebe managed to keep her voice calm, despite the crawling annoyance. "I'm capable of doing more than one thing at a time. I would like the account books returned as soon as possible. You've come to visit at least twice a week—happily for us—but on any of those occasions you could have brought them."

"It's not as easy as tossing them in a satchel," Edward pointed out. "It's an unwieldy load."

Phoebe's brows rushed down. "And yet you managed to cart them away," she said with an edge to her voice. "Can't you bring them back using the same method?"

"Phoebe, dear," Edward exclaimed, his tone changing. "I didn't realize how important it was to you. I just thought . . . it's not as if you're going to do anything with them."

"I want to look at them. I want to understand the state of affairs, especially where the tenants are concerned."

"The estate is doing well," Edward said earnestly. "The rents have come in like clockwork. There's nothing for you to worry about." He paused, looking wry. "I know the Ravenels have set you all atwitter about modernization, but it's in a landlord's interest to take a moderate approach. We don't want you to spend all your capital on impetuous schemes. My father recommends a slow and steady course of progress, and so do I."

"I'm not 'all atwitter,'" Phoebe protested, disliking the implication that she was being flighty or harebrained. "I intend to learn about my tenants' problems and concerns, and discuss reasonable options to help them."

A fleeting smile crossed his lips. "Any tenant you ask will have a long list of needs and wants. They'll do their best to wring every last shilling from you, especially if you're offering to buy machines to do their work for them."

"Surely it's not wrong of them to want their work to be less grueling. They could be more productive with less effort, and perhaps gain some leisure time in the bargain."

"What do they need leisure time for? What would they do with it? Read Plato? Take violin lessons? These are farm people, Phoebe."

"I'm not concerned with how they might spend their leisure time. The question is whether they have a right to it."

"Obviously you think they do." Edward smiled fondly at her. "That's evidence of a soft heart, and womanly sympathy, and I delight to find those qualities in you. Now, about the account books . . . if it will set your mind at ease, I'll return them as soon as possible. Although you won't be able to make heads or tails of them without me. The estate accounting system has its peculiarities."

"Then spend an afternoon here explaining accounting to me."

As soon as the words left her lips, Phoebe remembered the afternoon she'd spent with West . . . poring over books and maps, drinking wine, laughing at his silly quips about cows . . . and those searing minutes when she had ended up on the floor with him, half mad with excitement and pleasure. Oh, God, how she wished she could forget. West should have faded from her thoughts by now, but he hadn't.

In the past three months Edward had made careful advances, developing their friendship into an easy and undemanding courtship. There had been no declarations of wild passion, no smoldering glances or risqué comments. He was too much of a gentleman for that.

Edward's reply jerked her back to the present. "We'll make a day of it," he promised. "However, I won't have time for that until I return from my trip. That's the business I came to discuss."

"What trip?" Phoebe asked, gesturing for him to accompany her to the settee.

"It has to do with the dowager," Edward said. "She called at my parents' home yesterday morning."

"I didn't know about that." She shook her head in bemusement. "How is it that we live in the same house and she didn't see fit to mention it?"

Edward looked rueful. "I gather there's still friction between the two of you over the redecorating."

Phoebe groaned and leaned back into the corner of the settee, her gaze lifting heavenward. "I told her she couldn't turn the entire house into a shrine to Henry's memory. It was as dark as a morgue. I compromised by leaving most of the upstairs rooms untouched—I've even moved out of the master bedroom into a smaller one down the hall—but none of that seems to have satisfied her."

"She'll adjust in time," Edward said. "In the meantime, you'll be happy to learn she's found a resort where she wants to winter this year."

"Georgiana is leaving for the winter?" Phoebe asked blankly. "After badgering me for two years to move back here so she could see her grandchildren every day?"

"Are you looking a gift horse in the mouth?"

"*No*," Phoebe said quickly, making him laugh. "When is the gift horse leaving?"

"In two days."

"So quickly? Goodness gracious."

"There's a new resort in Bordighera, at the Italian Riviera, with furnished villas available at reasonable rates. However, there's a catch. The resort manager has reserved two villas for us to look at, but they can't be held for long, since they're in high demand. Georgiana asked me to escort her there and arrange for one of them and see to it that she's properly settled. I'm not sure how long I'll be gone. Possibly a fortnight. If Bordighera isn't suitable, I'll have to take Georgiana directly to Cannes or Nice and arrange for something there."

"It's a bit early to start wintering before autumn has begun, don't you think?"

"Gift horse," he reminded her.

"You're right." Phoebe sighed and smiled at him. "It's very kind of you to go to such trouble for her."

"No trouble at all. Henry asked me to take care of her, and of you, and so I will." Edward leaned over to press a brief, soft kiss to her lips, his breath scented pleasantly of cinnamon. "What would you like from Italy? Coral combs for your hair? A cut of glove leather?"

"Bring yourself back safe and sound."

"That I will do." He moved to kiss her again, but Phoebe drew back a few inches.

"*And* make sure to drop off the account ledgers before you leave."

"Obstinate lady," Edward whispered with amusement, and stole another kiss. "Incidentally, in all this discussion, Georgiana made an important point: After she leaves the Clare estate, my frequent visits here may cause some unflattering speculation."

"I'm not worried about scandal."

"I am," Edward said with a grin. "Think of *my* reputation, if not yours." He took her hand in a light clasp. "When I return, I'd like to bring my courtship of you out into the open. Will you consider that while I'm gone?"

Phoebe didn't like the idea at all. Once their courtship was made public, the clock would start ticking toward betrothal.

"Edward," she said carefully, "you should know that I'm in no hurry to marry again. Now that the fog of grief has cleared away, I intend to take responsibility for the estate, and help my sons learn what they need to know for the future."

"I can teach them what they need to know. As for the estate—you're already the lady of the manor—you don't need to be lord of the manor as well." He smiled at the idea. "The courtship can wait until you're ready. I've been patient this long, haven't I?"

"I haven't asked you to wait," Phoebe said with a frown.

"No, it's been my choice, as well as my privilege. However, I don't like to think of you going without a man's protection, or the boys without fatherly supervision. There are many ways I can make your life easier. After we marry, I can help manage Georgiana and serve as a buffer between you. She told me it would set her mind at ease to have a man about the house again, especially a family member she trusts." Lifting her hand to his lips, Edward feathered a kiss across the backs of her fingers. "I'll give you companionship. Security. We could have children—a sister for Justin and Stephen, perhaps a little boy of our own."

Phoebe gave Edward's hand a slight squeeze to convey affection before withdrawing her fingers gently. "My dear friend," she said carefully, "you deserve your own life, not the remnants of Henry's old one."

"I would hardly classify you and the children as 'remnants.'" Edward reached out and guided her face to his. "I've always been fond of you, Phoebe. But now it's turned into something more."

DON'T COMPARE, PHOEBE commanded herself as she went upstairs. *Don't.*

But she couldn't help it.

Edward had just given her several long and lingering kisses, and truth be told, it had been pleasurable. His lips had been soft and warm, stroking over hers repeatedly, his breath sweet as it mingled with hers.

But she had felt nothing close to the dizzying excitement of West Ravenel's mouth consuming hers, the rough urgency of his embrace. No matter how attractive she might find Edward, he would never leave her shaken with desire, never seduce her into some trembling and mindless version of herself.

It wasn't a fair comparison. Edward was a perfect gentleman, well-mannered and reserved by nature. West Ravenel, on the other hand, had been raised with few constraints, with the result that he spoke and acted more freely than another man of his class would. He was a full-blooded, unpredictable male: part hero, part scoundrel.

He was a mistake she couldn't afford to make.

Suffused with frustration and longing, Phoebe went to the tiny private parlor where her mother-in-law spent the greater part of each day. The door was ajar. After tapping gently on the jamb and receiving no response, she went inside.

The walls had been covered in deep plum paper, the furniture upholstered in heavy burgundies and browns. Thick brocade curtains had been drawn against the daylight, admitting just enough illumination to reveal Georgiana seated by the window.

The dowager was having tea at a miniature table. She was so still that she might have been a carved marble figure in a mausoleum. The only movement was a continuous curl of steam rising from the porcelain cup in front of her.

Georgiana's frame had shrunk to diminutive proportions since Henry's death. Grief had inscribed its history on her face like written lines on parchment. Dressed in twilled black silk with old-fashioned voluminous skirts piled around her, she resembled a finch huddled in its nest.

"Georgiana," Phoebe asked softly, almost remorsefully, "has my redecorating driven you out of the house? I've kept my promise not to touch the upstairs floors."

"I shouldn't have consented to any changes at all. It no longer resembles the home Henry grew up in."

"I'm sorry. But as I told you, it's not good for Justin and Stephen to be raised in dark rooms. They need light and air, and cheerful surroundings." *And so do you,* she thought, contemplating the elderly woman's chalky pallor with concern.

"They should stay in the nursery. The downstairs rooms are for adult company, not romping children."

"I can't confine the boys to the nursery. This is their home too."

"The child of bygone days was seldom seen and never heard. Now it seems a child must be seen and heard everywhere, and at all hours."

In Georgiana's opinion, children must be strictly managed and kept within controlled boundaries. To her frustration, she had never been able to corral her own son's irrepressible spirit or follow the twists and turns of his mind. One of Henry's first decisions after inheriting the estate had been to turn a formal courtyard into a topiary garden filled with animal shapes. It was undignified, she had complained, and far too expensive to maintain. "You turned an elegant courtyard into something perfectly outlandish," she had said for years afterward.

"*Perfectly* outlandish," Henry had always replied, with great satisfaction.

Phoebe knew the sight of Justin must stir up distant memories for the dowager. He was sturdier and more athletic than Henry had been, with none of the delicacy or shyness. But the impish gleam in his eyes and the sweetness of his smile were the same.

"They're too noisy, your boys," Georgiana said bitterly. "All this wild running about and shouting . . . the constant uproar hurts my ears. It *hurts*."

Realizing what was causing Georgiana such pain, Phoebe replied gently, "Perhaps staying in a mild seaside climate is a wise idea. All the sun and salt air . . . I think it will be a tonic. Edward said you're leaving quite soon. Is there something I can do to help?"

"You might start thinking about your sons' welfare. No man would be a better father to them than Edward. It would be best for everyone if you married him."

Phoebe blinked and stiffened. "I'm not convinced it would be best for me."

Georgiana made a flutter with one thin hand, as if waving away a gnat. "Don't be a child, Phoebe. You've reached the time in life when there is more to consider than your own feelings."

It was perhaps a good thing that Phoebe was temporarily speechless. As she reined in her temper with effort, she reminded herself that of the five children to whom Georgiana had given birth, Henry had been the only one to survive into adulthood, and now he too was gone.

"You needn't instruct me to think about my children's welfare," Phoebe said quietly. "I've always put them first, and always will. As for me being a child . . . I'm afraid I'm not nearly enough like one." A faint smile touched her lips. "Children are optimistic. They have a natural sense of adventure. To them, the world has no limitations, only possibilities. Henry was always a bit childlike in that way—he never became disenchanted with life. That was what I loved most about him."

"If you loved Henry, you will honor his wishes. He wanted Edward to have charge of his family and estate."

"Henry wanted to make sure our future would be in capable hands. But it already is."

"Yes. Edward's."

"No, *mine.* I'll learn everything I need to know about managing this estate. I'll hire people to help me if necessary. I'll have this place thriving. I don't need a husband to do it for me. If I marry again, it will be to a man of *my* choosing, in my own time. I can't promise it will be Edward. I've changed during the past two years, but so far, he doesn't see me for who I am, only who I was. For that matter, he doesn't see how the world has changed—he ignores the realities he doesn't like. How can I trust him with our future?"

Georgiana regarded her bitterly. "Edward is not the one who is ignoring reality. How can you imagine yourself capable of running this estate?"

"Why wouldn't I be?"

"Women aren't capable of leadership. Our intelligence is no less than men's, but it is shaped for the purpose of motherhood. We're clever enough to operate the sewing machine, but not to have invented it. If you asked the opinions of a thousand people whether they would trust you or Edward to make decisions for the estate, whom do you think they would choose?"

"I'm not going to ask a thousand people for their opinions," Phoebe said evenly. "Only one opinion is required, and it happens to be mine." She went to the doorway and paused, unable to resist adding, "That's leadership."

And she left the dowager fuming in silence.

Chapter 21

ON THE MORNING OF Georgiana's departure, Phoebe made certain her sons were dressed in their best clothes to see her off in style. Justin wore a pair of black serge short trousers and a linen shirt with a sailor collar, while Stephen was in a linen smock with a matching sailor collar. The three of them waited in the entrance hall with the dowager, while Edward directed a pair of footmen to load the last of the trunks and valises on the carriage waiting outside.

"Grandmother," Justin said, holding out a gift for her, "this is for you to read on the boat." It was a book of pictures he'd drawn and painted. Phoebe had stitched the pages together and helped him spell out words to accompany the illustrations. "Stephen can't draw yet," Justin continued, "but I traced his hand on one of the pages." He paused before adding helpfully, "It's sticky because of the strawberry jam on his fingers."

Georgiana took the gift and looked into the boy's sweetly earnest face for a long moment. "You may kiss me good-bye, child," she said, and bent to receive Justin's obliging peck on the cheek.

Although Phoebe tried to nudge Stephen forward, he resisted and clung to her skirts. She picked him up and held him on her hip. "I hope your journey abroad will be wonderful, Mother."

Georgiana gave her a wry glance. "Try not to paint the house pink in my absence."

Recognizing the attempt at humor as a peace overture, Phoebe smiled. "I won't."

She felt Edward's gentle touch at her elbow. "Goodbye, my dear."

Turning toward him, Phoebe gave him both her hands. "Safe and happy travels, Edward."

Lifting her hands, he kissed the backs of them gently. "Don't hesitate to call on my family if there's anything you need. They're anxious to be of service." He hesitated, looking sheepish. "I forgot the account ledgers again."

"No need to worry," Phoebe assured him blandly. "I knew you were busy with preparations for the trip." She didn't think it necessary to mention that as soon as he and Georgiana left, she was going to retrieve the books herself.

She took the children out to the front portico, while Edward helped Georgiana into the carriage. The dowager had to have her lap blanket arranged just so. The level of the window curtains had to be adjusted meticulously. An eternity seemed to pass until the team of matched bays finally drew the vehicle away, its iron-rimmed wheels crunching on the graveled drive. Phoebe and Justin waved cheerfully at the departing carriage, while Stephen waggled his fingers. At last, the vehicle passed a copse of trees and disappeared.

Filled with elation, Phoebe lowered Stephen to the ground and spread a flurry of kisses over his face, making him chortle.

Justin crowded against them and received the same treatment, giggling as the storm of kisses engulfed him. "Why are you so happy, Mama?"

"Because now we're free to do anything we want, with no one to complain or say we can't." It was such a relief to have both Edward and Georgiana gone. More than a relief. It was *glorious.*

"What are we going to do?" Justin asked.

Phoebe smiled into her children's expectant faces. "Shall we go on a picnic today?"

"Oh, yes, let's do that!" Justin enthused, and Stephen chimed in, "Mama, *picnic!*"

"I'll tell Cook to pack a nice big basket for us. We'll take Nanny and Ernestine, too. Now, let's go upstairs, so you can change out of these stiff clothes into your play suits. I have an errand in town to take care of, and after that we'll have our picnic lunch in your Papa's topiary garden."

To her surprise, Justin wrinkled his nose and asked, "Do we have to have it there?"

"No, but . . . don't you like the topiaries?"

Justin shook his head. "Nanny says they used to be shaped like animals. But now they all look like turnips."

"Oh, dear. I suppose they're overgrown. I'll speak

to the gardener." Phoebe stood and took their hands in hers. "Come, you two. A new day has begun."

After taking the children up to the nursery, Phoebe asked for her carriage to be brought around, and told the butler she would need two footmen to accompany her to town, as she would be returning with heavy parcels.

The day was pleasant and sunny, with flowering leafless crocus mantling the roadside on the way to town. However, Phoebe took little notice of the scenery during the ride to the Larson offices. Her mind was buzzing with thoughts. It would be a relief to have all the information she needed to start making accurate assessments of the home farm and all the leaseholds. But she also dreaded what the account books would reveal.

Despite Edward's reassurances, Phoebe didn't believe the tenants and leaseholds were doing nearly as well as he'd claimed. Every time she rode out in the company of a footman to take a look at the estate leaseholds, she saw a multitude of problems with her own eyes. Most of the steadings and structures on the tenant farms were badly in need of repair. The narrow, unfinished estate roads couldn't begin to accommodate the wheels of heavy agricultural machinery. She had seen pools of standing water in poorly drained fields, and sparse-looking crops. Even during haymaking season, one of the busiest times of the year, a listless, defeated feeling seemed to drift over the Clare lands.

The carriage passed picturesque greens, and streets lined with timber-framed shops and houses. After entering a square of symmetrical buildings faced with stucco and fronted with fluted columns, the vehicle stopped in front of the handsome brass-plated door of the Larson offices.

Once inside, Phoebe was obliged to wait only for a minute before Edward's father, Frederick, came out to greet her. He was tall and stout, his face square, the upper lip canopied by a handsome silver mustache with deftly waxed tips. As an established member of the Essex squirearchy, Frederick was a creature of habit who liked Sunday roast and his pipe after dinner, foxhunting in the winter, and croquet in the summer. At his insistence, traditions were maintained in the Larson household with the fervor of religious belief. Frederick hated anything intellectual or foreign, and he *especially* disliked newfangled inventions that had accelerated the pace of life, such as the telegraph or railway.

Phoebe had always gotten on well with the old gentleman, who was impressed by her father's title and connections. Since Frederick hoped to have her as a daughter-in-law someday, she was fairly certain he wouldn't risk antagonizing her by withholding the account ledgers.

"Uncle Frederick!" Phoebe exclaimed cheerfully. "I've surprised you, haven't I?"

"My dear niece! A most welcome surprise this is." He guided her into his private office, lined with black walnut cabinets and shelves, and sat her in a leather upholstered chair.

After Phoebe had explained the reason for her visit, Frederick seemed flummoxed by her desire to collect the Clare estate account books. "Phoebe, complex accounting is a strain to the female mind. If you tried to read one of those ledgers, you would soon have a headache."

"I keep the household account books and they don't give me headaches," she pointed out.

"Ah, but household expenses are in the feminine realm. Business accounting pertains to matters in the masculine realm, outside the home."

Phoebe had to bite her lip to keep from asking if the rules of mathematics changed when one ventured past the front door. Instead, she said, "Uncle, the empty shelves in the study at Clare Manor look so bereft. It seems only right and proper for the account ledgers to be kept there, as they always have been." She paused delicately. "One hates to break with decades, if not centuries, of tradition."

As she had hoped, that argument held more sway with him than anything else.

"Tradition is the thing," Frederick agreed heartily, and thought for a few moments. "I suppose it would do no harm to let the books reside on their old shelves at Clare Manor."

Seizing on a sudden inspiration, Phoebe said, "It would also oblige Edward to visit me more often, wouldn't it?"

"Indeed it would," he exclaimed. "My son could attend to the account books at Clare Manor, and enjoy your company at the same time. Two birds—I rather wonder that he hadn't thought of it yet. How slow-witted young men are nowadays! It's settled, then. Shall my clerks convey the ledgers out to your carriage?"

"My footmen can do it. Thank you, Uncle."

Eager to leave, Phoebe began to edge toward the door of his office. However, it appeared she would not escape without additional conversation.

"How are your young lads?" Frederick asked.

"Quite well. It will take some time for them to adjust fully to their new life in Essex."

"I expect so. I have concerns about what might become of growing boys with no paternal figure in the house. A father's influence cannot be too highly estimated."

"I'm concerned about that as well," Phoebe admitted. "However, I'm not yet ready to marry again."

"There are times in life, my dear, when one must set emotion aside and view the situation from a rational perspective."

"My reasons are quite rational—"

"As you know," he continued, "my Edward is every inch of him a gentleman. An ornament to his class. His qualities have often been remarked on. Many a marriage-minded young woman has set her cap for him—I wouldn't expect him to stay on the market forever."

"I wouldn't either."

"It would be a great pity for you to realize too late what a treasure you might have had in Edward. As the captain of your family's ship, he would steer a steady course. There would never be surprises with him. No arguments, no unconventional ideas. You would live in perfect serenity."

Yes, Phoebe thought, *that's exactly the problem.*

On the ride back to Clare Manor, Phoebe sorted through the cumbersome pile of ledgers on the seat beside her until she found one with yearly statements of the estate's profits and losses. After hefting it onto her lap, she began to page through it slowly.

To her dismay, the information was laid out very differently from the ledgers West Ravenel had shown her. A frown worked across her brow. Was the word "liability" used interchangeably with "debt," or did they mean different things in this system of book-keeping? Did "capital" refer only to property, or did it include cash? She didn't know how Henry or Edward had defined such terms, and to make matters worse, the pages were littered with acronyms.

"I need a Rosetta stone to translate all of this," Phoebe muttered. A sinking feeling came over her as she looked through another ledger, the crop book. Mystifyingly, some of the tenant farmers' yields had been reported four times, and each number was different.

As the carriage continued along the flint-graveled road, Phoebe considered what to do. She could ask the estate's land manager, Mr. Patch, to answer some of her questions, but he was quite old and infirm, and a conversation lasting more than a few minutes would exhaust him.

There was always the option of waiting for Edward to return, but she didn't want to do that, especially since he believed she shouldn't be bothering with accounting in the first place. And in light of the way she'd commandeered the estate ledgers and brought them home herself, Edward would probably be just a bit smug, and one could hardly blame him.

This would be a convenient excuse to send for West.

Holding an account ledger in her lap, Phoebe leaned back against the carriage seat and felt a pang of yearning so sharp, it hurt to breathe.

She wasn't at all certain West would come, but if he did . . .

How strange it would be to have him at Clare Manor: a collision of worlds, West Ravenel in Henry's house. It was scandalous for an unmarried man to stay in the home of a young widow, with no chaperone in sight. Edward would be appalled when he found out. Georgiana would have apoplexy on the spot.

Thinking back to that last morning with West, Phoebe recalled him saying something to the effect that he had nothing to offer except a relationship that would insult and lower her.

Love affairs were common among the upper class, who usually married for reasons of family interests and connections and sought personal fulfillment outside of wedlock. Phoebe had never imagined herself doing such a thing or having needs that might outweigh the risk of scandal. But neither she nor West was married; no vows would be broken. No one would be harmed . . . would they?

A shock went through her as she realized she was actually considering it. Oh, God, she was turning into a cliché—the love-starved widow seeking company for her empty bed. A particular figure of mockery, since women were supposed to be above the kind of base physical desire that was considered far more natural and explicable in men. She herself had liked to think so, until West had proved otherwise.

She wished she could talk to Merritt.

She tried to imagine how such a conversation might go:

"Merritt, I'm thinking about having an affair with West Ravenel. I know it's wrong . . . but how *wrong?"*

"Don't ask me," Merritt would probably say, her eyes laughing. *"As a moral relativist, I'm thoroughly unqualified to judge your decisions."*

"A fine help you are," Phoebe would retort. *"I want someone to give me permission."*

"No one can do that but you, dear."

"What if it turns out to be a mistake?"

"Then I suspect you'll have had a delightful time making it."

After the carriage had stopped at the front portico of Clare Manor, the footmen carried the stacks of account ledgers to the study. They placed the volumes on the empty bookshelves while Phoebe seated herself at the old oak desk. She smoothed a sheet of writing paper onto the desk's green leather inset, reached for a slim lacquered pen holder, and inserted a nib.

"Milady," said one of the footmen, "the books have been put away."

"Thank you, Oliver. You're free to go now. Arnold, if you'll wait a moment, I have another errand for you."

The younger footman, always eager to prove himself, brightened at the request. "Yes, milady." He waited at a respectful distance while she wrote a few lines.

Post Office Telegram
Mr. Weston Ravenel

Eversby Priory Hampshire

> *Knee-deep in quicksand. Need rope.*
> *Would you possibly have time to visit*
> *Essex?*
>
> — P. C.

After folding the paper and tucking it into an envelope, Phoebe turned in her chair. "Take this to the telegraph desk at the post office and make certain they dispatch it before you leave." She began to extend it to him, then hesitated as a tremor of mingled fear and craving ran through her.

"Milady?" Arnold asked softly.

Phoebe shook her head with a rueful smile and held out the envelope decisively. "Take it quickly, please, before I lose my nerve."

Chapter 22

"MAMA," JUSTIN SAID THE next morning, pausing in the middle of licking the drizzle of white icing on top of his breakfast bun. "Nanny said I'm going to have a governess."

"Yes, darling, I plan to start looking for one soon. Please eat the entire bun and not just the icing."

"I like to eat the icing first." As Justin saw the objection on her face, he pointed out reasonably, "It's all going to end up in my tummy, Mama."

"I suppose so, but still . . ." Her voice trailed away as she saw that Stephen had emptied his bowl of applesauce onto the tray of his high chair and was circling his hand through the puddle.

Looking very pleased with himself, the toddler squeezed applesauce through his fingers and licked at it. "Yummy apples," he told her.

"Oh, dear—Stephen, wait—" She used the napkin from her lap to mop at the mess, and called out to the footman who stood beside the sideboard. "Arnold, fetch the nursemaid. We need reinforcements."

The young footman dashed away immediately.

"You were doing so well with the spoon," Phoebe

told Stephen, catching his little wrist and wiping his dripping hand. "I rather wish you'd stayed with that method."

"Ivo didn't have a governess," Justin said.

"That was because Granny had time to help with his manners and all the other things a governess teaches."

"I already know all the manners," Justin said indignantly.

"Justin—" Phoebe broke off as Stephen smacked his free hand into the applesauce, sending splatters everywhere. "Goodness gracious!"

"It's in his hair now," Justin said, looking at his younger brother in the manner of a scientist observing a failed experiment.

The nursemaid, a wiry and energetic girl named Verity, charged into the room with a stack of nursery flannels. "Master Stephen," she scolded softly, "did you overturn your pudding again?"

"Applesauce this time," Phoebe said.

The toddler held up his empty bowl with a pair of sticky, glistening hands. "All gone," he told Verity brightly.

A snort of amusement escaped the nursemaid as she unlatched the tray from the chair. She shook her head as Phoebe reached out to help. "Stand back, if you please, milady—we can't have applesauce splashing on your dress."

Justin tugged at Phoebe's sleeve. "Mama, if I *must* have a governess, I want a pretty one."

Another snort from the nursemaid. "They start early, don't they?" she remarked in an aside.

"In my family, they do," Phoebe replied ruefully.

The applesauce was mopped up by the time the butler, Hodgson, brought the morning mail on a silver tray. It was far, *far* too soon to expect a reply from West— the telegram had been dispatched yesterday morning, for heaven's sake. Still, Phoebe's pulse turned brisk as she riffled through the stack.

She'd had more than a few second thoughts about having sent the telegram. If only she hadn't been so impulsive—she should have written a dignified letter. For her to have wired a message to West had probably appeared desperate, or worse, self-important. It was only that she had wanted him to come before Edward returned.

The more she thought about it, the more certain she was that he wouldn't. West must be very busy, especially since—according to *The Modern Handbook for Landed Proprietors*—September was the month to harrow and fertilize the fields for the sowing of winter wheat. Furthermore, both Kathleen and Pandora had mentioned in correspondence that West had gone to London at least twice during the summer in search of companionship and amusement. One of those visits had been to see Pandora after she'd undergone surgery for a shoulder injury. The operation had been performed by the only licensed female doctor in England, a charismatic woman whom the Ravenel family seemed to like excessively. "My sister Helen is determined to introduce Dr. Gibson to Cousin West," Pandora had written, "but I don't think it a likely match, since Dr. Gibson loves the city and hates cows."

But it was possible they had eventually been introduced and had been attracted to each other. Dr. Gibson may have decided that being wooed by a handsome specimen like West Ravenel was worth enduring the proximity of a few cows.

Phoebe forced her mind to turn to the plans for the day. First, she would go to the local bookshop and order manuals on accounting. She would also ask Mr. Patch to go over the crop book with her, and hopefully it wouldn't overtax him to explain some of it to her.

"Milady," came the footman's voice, and Phoebe glanced over her shoulder.

"Yes, Arnold?"

"A hired carriage from the station yard has just stopped on the front drive. Hodgson is speaking to a man at the door. He looks to be a gentleman."

Phoebe registered the information with a quick double blink and turned toward him. From the station yard? She couldn't think of anyone who would visit her by railway, except . . .

"Is he old or young?" she asked, distantly amazed at how calm she sounded.

Arnold had to lend the question serious thought. "Young to middlish, milady."

"Tall or short?"

"A big strapper." At her riveted expression, Arnold added helpfully, "With a beard."

"A *beard*?" Phoebe repeated, perplexed. "I'll go

see who it is." She rose to her feet, feeling weak-kneed and loose-jointed, like a marionette puppet held up by wires. As she straightened the skirts of her dress, a pale green poplin print, she discovered a few spots of applesauce on the bodice. Impatiently she dampened a napkin and dabbed at the stains. Hopefully they would be concealed by the pattern of tiny white-and-amber flowers.

By the time she reached the entrance hall, she was shaky with anticipation. *Oh, let it be him, let it be West* . . . but perversely, she was afraid to see him. What if the attraction was no longer there, and they turned out to be polite and awkward with each other? What if he'd only come out of a sense of honor, and not because he'd truly wanted to? What if—

The visitor stood at the threshold, tall and lean, his posture relaxed as he stood in the open doorway with a black leather Gladstone bag in hand. The sunlight was at his back, casting his face in shadow, but his silhouette, with those powerful shoulders filling up the door frame, was instantly recognizable. He was bigger than life, and outrageously masculine with a sunburnt glow and several days' heavy beard growth darkening his jaw.

The force of Phoebe's heartbeat resounded through her body as she drew closer.

West focused on her with a disarming stare, a slow smile curving his lips. "I hope you weren't asking for literal rope," he said casually, as if they were in the middle of a conversation.

"I didn't expect . . . you . . . you came in just one

day!" Phoebe stopped with an unsteady laugh as she heard how breathless she was. "I was waiting for your reply."

"This is my reply," West said simply, setting down the Gladstone bag.

Delight filled her until the sheer weight of the feeling almost set her off balance. She gave him her hand. He engulfed it in both of his, his grip warm and invigorating, and brought it to his lips.

For a moment Phoebe couldn't move or breathe. His nearness was too overwhelming. She felt light-headed, almost euphoric.

"How are you?" West asked quietly, retaining her hand longer than he should have.

"I'm well," Phoebe managed to say, "and so are the boys. But I think the estate is in trouble—I know it is—and I need help assessing how bad it is."

"We'll sort it out," he said with calm assurance.

"Is that your only luggage?"

"No, there's a trunk on the carriage."

Better and better . . . he had brought enough to stay more than a day or two. Trying to appear composed, Phoebe told the butler, "Hodgson, we'll need Mr. Ravenel's trunk brought to the guest cottage in back. Tell Mrs. Gurney to air out the rooms and make them ready."

"Yes, milady."

As the butler went to the bellpull, Phoebe turned her attention back to West. "You've caught me unprepared," she said apologetically.

"I could go," West offered, "and come back later."

Phoebe smiled up at him radiantly. "You're not going anywhere." Unable to resist, she reached up to his beard-roughened jaw. The new growth was thick and scratchy soft, like a blend of cut velvet and wool. "Why did you grow a beard?"

"It wasn't intentional," he said. "I had no time to shave during the last two weeks of haymaking. It took every man on the estate to help thatch the hayricks fast enough to keep pace with the harvest."

"All this after only a fortnight," she commented, still admiring the luxuriant beard. Poor Edward would have been incensed at the sight of it.

West shrugged modestly. "We each have a special talent. Some people can sing opera or learn foreign languages. I grow hair."

"It makes you look dashing," Phoebe said, "but a bit villainous."

The lines at the outer corners of his eyes deepened with amusement. "If the hero hasn't turned up, you may have to settle for the villain."

"If the villain's the one who turns up, he *is* the hero."

West laughed huskily, his teeth white against the inky darkness of the beard. "Whatever you choose to call me, I'm at your disposal."

He looked tremendously fit, but she noticed he was leaner than before, his well-tailored clothes draping a bit too loosely over the hard lines of his body.

"There's still breakfast on the sideboard," Phoebe said softly. "Are you hungry?"

"I'm always hungry."

"I should warn you in advance that Justin has licked the icing from all the breakfast buns, and there was a recent accident involving Stephen and a dish of apple-sauce."

"I'll take my chances," West said, picking up the Gladstone bag.

Phoebe led him toward the breakfast room, still finding it difficult to believe he was there with her. "Is everyone at Eversby Priory cross with me for stealing you away?" she asked.

"They're collectively weeping with gratitude. They could hardly wait to be rid of me." At her questioning glance, West added, "I've been short-tempered of late. No, that's not true—I've been a surly ass."

"Why?"

"Too much time in Hampshire, and no women. The lack of temptation has been demoralizing."

Phoebe tried to conceal how much that gratified her. Trying to sound offhand, she remarked, "I thought Lady Helen was going to introduce you to the lady doctor who treated Pandora's shoulder."

"Dr. Gibson? Yes, she's a marvelous woman. As a matter of fact, she came to visit Eversby Priory this summer."

All Phoebe's pleasant feelings abruptly turned disagreeable. "Surely not without a chaperone."

"Garrett Gibson doesn't bother with chaperones," West replied, his lips twitching as if at some private memory. "The usual rules don't apply to her. She brought a patient, Mr. Ethan Ransom, who was injured and needed to recuperate in peace and quiet."

Poisonous jealousy flooded Phoebe. The female doctor was an accomplished and unconventional woman— exactly the kind who would attract his interest. "You must have found her fascinating."

"Anyone would."

Averting her face to hide a scowl, Phoebe tried to sound nonchalant. "I suppose you became well acquainted during her visit?"

"More or less. Most of the time she was busy caring for Ransom. I stopped in London last night to see him. He's asked me to be his best man at their wedding."

"Their—*oh*. They're going to marry?" To her chagrin, Phoebe couldn't hide her relief.

She heard West's low laugh as he caught her elbow and stopped her. The contents of the leather bag rattled as he dropped it to the floor.

"Jealous?" he asked softly, drawing her to an alcove at the side of the corridor.

"A little," she admitted.

"What about Edward Larson? Aren't you betrothed?"

"No."

"*No?*" he echoed sardonically. "I assumed you'd have him hooked, booked, and cooked by now."

Phoebe frowned at the vulgar expression for courtship and marriage. "I'm not going to marry Edward. He'll always be a dear friend, but I . . . don't want him that way."

West's face was unreadable. "Have you told him?"

"Not yet. He's traveling in Italy for at least a fort-night."

To her dismay, West didn't seem especially pleased by the revelation. "Phoebe . . . I'm not here to take advantage of you. All I want is to help with the estate, in any way I can."

The words sent a little cold stab through her chest. Did he mean it? Was that *all* he wanted? Perhaps the feelings were all one-sided, just as she had feared. She forced herself to ask with difficulty, "The things you said to me that morning . . . is any of it still true?"

"Is any of it . . ." West repeated slowly, with a dumb-founded shake of his head. The question appeared to have set off a flare of impatience. Muttering beneath his breath, he paced away from her, swung around, and returned to her with heightened color and a scowl. "I'm haunted by you," he said brusquely. "I can't seem to stop looking for you everywhere I go. When I went to London, I tried to find a woman who could help me forget about you, even for one night. But no one has your eyes. No one interests me the way you do. I've cursed you a thousand times for what you've done to me. I'd rather be alone with a fantasy of you than have a flesh-and-blood woman in my arms."

"You don't have to settle for a fantasy," Phoebe said impulsively. "Just because you don't want forever with me doesn't mean we can't—"

"*No.*" West's breathing roughened despite his effort to moderate it. He held up a staying hand as she parted her lips, and the slight tremor in his fingers electrified her. "If you have any misguided thoughts about taking me into your bed, you would find it a vastly mediocre experience. I'd be on you like a crazed rabbit, and half a minute later the whole thing would be over. I used to be a proficient lover, but now I'm a burnt-out libertine whose only remaining pleasure is breakfast food. Speaking of which—"

Phoebe reached for him, brought herself up hard against him, and interrupted him with her mouth. West flinched as if scalded and held very still in the manner of a man trying to withstand torture. Undeterred, she wrapped her arms around his neck and kissed him as passionately as she could, touching her tongue to his stiff lips. The feel and taste of him was exhilarating. Suddenly he responded with a primitive grunt and his mouth clamped on hers, wringing sensation from her with demanding pressure. Forcing her lips apart, he searched her with his tongue the way she remembered, and it felt so good, she thought she might faint. A whimper rose from her throat, and he licked and bit gently at the sound, and sealed their mouths together in a deep, insatiable kiss that involved his lips, breath, hands, body, soul.

Whatever it might be like to go to bed with this man . . . it would be anything but mediocre.

Phoebe was so lost in the explosive sensuality of the moment, only one sound could have snatched her back to full alertness . . . her son's small voice.

"Mama?"

Jerking her head back with a gasp, Phoebe looked toward the sound, blinking in confusion.

Justin stood in the corridor, near the breakfast room, wide-eyed and uneasy at the sight of his mother in a stranger's arms.

"It's all right, darling," Phoebe said with an effort at composure, disentangling herself from West. She teetered on ramshackle legs, but West grabbed her reflexively and adjusted her balance. "It's Mr. Ravenel," she told Justin. "He looks a bit different because of his beard."

It surprised her to see the way her son's face lit up.

Justin charged forward, and West bent reflexively to catch and lift him in the air.

"Look at this big fellow," West exclaimed, holding the child against his chest. "My God, you're as heavy as a clamp of bricks."

"Guess how old I am now," Justin boasted, and held up a spread-fingered hand.

"Five? When did that happen?"

"Last week!"

"It was last month," Phoebe said.

"I had plum cake with icing," Justin continued eagerly, "and Mama let me eat some for breakfast the next morning."

"I'm sorry I missed it. Fortunately, I've brought presents for you and Stephen."

Justin squealed happily.

"I arrived in London late last night," West continued, "after Winterborne's department store was already closed for the evening. So Mr. Winterborne opened it

for me, and I had the entire toy department all to myself. After I found what I wanted, Winterborne wrapped
your toys personally."

Justin's eyes turned round with awe. In his mind, a
man who could have a department store opened just
for him must possess magical powers. "Where is my
present?"

"It's in that bag on the floor. We'll open it later,
when there's time to play."

Justin studied West intently, rubbing his palms over
his hair-roughened jaw. "I don't like your beard," he
announced. "It makes you look like an angry bear."

"Justin—" Phoebe reproved, but West was laughing.

"I *was* an angry bear, all summer."

"You have to shave it," Justin commanded, framing
the man's smiling mouth with his hands.

"*Justin*," Phoebe exclaimed.

The boy corrected himself with a grin. "Shave it
please."

"I will," West promised, "if your mother will provide a razor."

"Mama, will you?" Justin asked.

"First," Phoebe told her son, "we're going to let
Mr. Ravenel settle comfortably in the guest cottage.
He can decide later if he wants to keep his beard or
not. I for one rather like it."

"But it's tickly and scratchy," Justin complained.

West grinned and dove his face against the boy's
neck, causing him to yelp and squirm. "Let's go see
your brother."

Before they went to the breakfast room, however,

his gaze met Phoebe's for a searing moment. His expression left no doubt that their impulsive kiss was a mistake that would not be repeated.

Phoebe responded with a demure glance, giving no hint of her true thoughts.

If you won't promise me forever, West Ravenel . . . I'll take what I can have of you.

Chapter 23

ᏒAW-NERVED AND UNSETTLED, WEST went with Phoebe on a tour of the manor after breakfast. The majesty of the house, with its portico and classic white columns and banks of windows on all sides, couldn't have provided a greater contrast to the Jacobean clutter of Eversby Priory. It was as elegant as a Grecian temple, occupying a ridge overlooking landscaped parkland and gardens. Far too often a house seemed to have been placed carelessly upon a site as if by a giant hand, but Clare Manor inhabited the scenery as if it had grown there.

The interior was open and lofty, with high vaulted ceilings of cool white plasterwork and sweeping staircases. A vast collection of fine-grained marble statuary gave the house a museumlike air, but many of the rooms had been softened with thick fringed rugs, cozy groupings of upholstered furniture, and palms in glazed earthenware pots.

West said little as they went from room to room. He was feeling everything too deeply and struggling to hide it beneath the façade of a normal, reasonable person. It seemed as if his heart had just resumed beating after months of dormancy, forcing blood back into his veins until he ached in every limb.

It was clear to him now that he would never find a substitute for Phoebe. No one else would ever come close. It would always be her. The realization was beyond disaster . . . it was doom.

West was no less troubled by the fondness he felt for her children, both of them bright-eyed and heartbreakingly innocent as they sat with him at the breakfast table. He'd felt like a fraud, taking part in that wholesome scene, when not long ago he'd been a scoundrel other men wouldn't want anywhere near their families.

He thought back to the conversation he'd had with Ethan Ransom in London the night before, when they'd met for dinner at a west-side tavern. An easy friendship had struck up between them during Ransom's recuperation at Eversby Priory. On the surface, their backgrounds couldn't have been more different— West had been born into a blue-blooded family, and Ransom was an Irish prison guard's son. But they were similar in many ways, both of them deeply cynical and secretly sentimental, well aware of the darker sides of their own natures.

Now that Ransom had decided to discard his solitary ways to marry Dr. Garrett Gibson, West was both puzzled and envious of the other man's certainty.

"Won't you mind bedding only one woman for the rest of your life?" he'd asked Ransom as they'd talked over mugs of half-and-half, a drink of equal parts ale and porter.

"Not for a blessed minute," Ransom had replied in

his Irish brogue. "She's the delight of my soul. Also, I know better than to betray a woman with her own collection of scalpels."

West had grinned at that, but sobered as another thought occurred to him. "Will she want children?"

"She will."

"Will you?"

"The thought freezes my innards," Ransom admitted bluntly, and shrugged. "But Garrett saved my life. She can do whatever she likes with me now. If she decides to put a ring through my nose, I'll stand there docile as a lamb while she does it."

"First of all, you city toff, no one puts a nose ring on a lamb. Second . . ." West had paused and drained half his drink before he continued gruffly, "Your father used to beat you—buckle, strap and fist—just as mine did to me."

"Aye," Ransom said. "Rightsidin' me, he called it. But what has that to do with it?"

"You'll likely do the same to your own children."

Ransom's eyes had narrowed, but his voice remained even. "I will not."

"Who will stop you? Your wife?"

"*I'll* stop me damn self," Ransom had said, his brogue thickening. He frowned as he saw West's expression. "You don't believe me?"

"I don't believe it will be easy."

"Easy enough, if I want them to love me."

"They will anyway," West had said grimly. "It's something all violent men know: no matter what evil they commit, their children will still love them."

Ransom had stared at him speculatively while draining his own mug. "Ofttimes after my father gave me a black eye or a split lip, Mam would say, "Tis not his fault. 'Tis too strong a man he is, hard for himself to manage.' But I've come to realize Mam had it all wrong: the problem was never that Da was too strong—he wasn't strong enough. Only a weak man lowers himself to brutishness." He had paused to signal a tavern maid to pour them another round. "You may have a hasty temper, Ravenel, but you're not a brute. Neither am I. That's how I know my children will be safe from my raising. Now, as for your red-haired widow . . . what are you going to do about her?"

West had scowled. "I don't bloody know."

"You might as well marry her. There's no escaping women."

"I'm hardly going to throw myself on the sacrificial altar just because you did," West had retorted. "Our friendship doesn't mean that much to me."

Ransom had grinned and leaned back in his chair as the tavern maid approached the table with a foaming jug. "Take my advice, you daft block o' wood. Be happy while you're living—you'll be a long time dead."

West's thoughts were drawn back to the present as Phoebe led him to a spacious reception room with silk-paneled walls and a gilded ceiling. Above the marble fireplace hung a large three-quarter-length portrait of a young man. A slant of light from the windows caused his face to glow as if with its own illumination.

Fascinated, West drew closer to the portrait.

"Henry," he said with a faint, questioning lilt.

Phoebe nodded, coming to stand beside him.

The young man was clad in a loosely painted suit, shadows hollowing the fabric here and there. He posed next to a library table with a touch of self-conscious grace, one hand resting lightly on a stack of books. A handsome and touchingly vulnerable man, dark-eyed and chiseled, his complexion as fine as porcelain. Although his face had been rendered with precise edges, the borders of his coat and trousers were softly blurred, seeming to melt into the dark background. As if the portrait's subject had begun to disappear even as he was being painted.

Staring at the portrait with West, Phoebe said, "People always tend to idealize the departed. But I want the boys to understand their father was a wonderful, mortal man with flaws, not an unapproachable saint. Otherwise, they'll never really know him."

"What flaws?" West asked gently.

Her lips pursed as she considered the question thoughtfully. "He was often elusive. In the world, but not of it. Part of that was because of his illness, but he also didn't like unpleasantness. He avoided anything that was ugly or upsetting." She turned to face him. "Henry was so determined to think of me as perfect that it devastated him when I was petty or cross or careless. I wouldn't want—" Phoebe paused.

"What?" West prompted after a long moment.

"I wouldn't want to live with such expectations again. I'd rather not be worshipped, but accepted for all that I am, good and bad."

A wave of tenderness came over West as he looked into her upturned face. He longed to tell her how completely he accepted her, wanted her, how he adored her every strength and frailty. "I've never thought of you as perfect," he told her flatly, and she laughed. "Still," he continued, his tone gentling, "it would be hard not to worship you. I'm afraid you don't behave nearly badly enough to bring my feelings into proportion."

A hint of mischief glittered in Phoebe's light gray eyes. "If that's a challenge, I accept."

"It's not a challenge," he said quickly, but she didn't appear to hear as she led him from the room.

They went to a glass-and-stone corridor connecting the main block of the house to one of the side wings. Sunlight poured through the paned windows, warming the corridor agreeably.

"The guest cottage can be reached through the east wing," Phoebe said, "or by way of the winter garden."

"Winter garden?"

She smiled at his interest. "It's my favorite place in the house. Come, I'll show you."

The winter garden turned out to be a glass conservatory, two stories high and at least one hundred and twenty feet long. Lush ornamental trees, ferns, and palms filled the space, as well as artificial rock formations and a little streamlet stocked with goldfish. West's opinion of the house climbed even higher as he looked around the winter garden. Eversby Priory had a conservatory, but it wasn't half as large and lofty as this.

An odd little noise seized his attention. A series of noises, actually, like the squeaking of toy balloons releasing air. Bemused, he looked down at a trio of black-and-white kittens roaming around his feet.

Phoebe laughed at his expression. "This room is also the cats' favorite."

A wondering smile spread across West's face as he saw the sleek black feline arching against Phoebe's skirts. "Good Lord. Is that Galoshes?"

Phoebe bent to stroke the cat's lustrous fur. "It is. She loves to come here to terrorize the goldfish. We've had to cover the stream with mesh wire until the kittens are older."

"When I gave her to you——" West began slowly.

"Foisted," she corrected.

"Foisted," he agreed ruefully. "Was she already——"

"Yes," Phoebe said with a severe glance. "She was a Trojan cat."

West tried to look contrite. "I had no idea."

Her lips quirked. "You're forgiven. She turned out to be a lovely companion. And the boys have been delighted to have the kittens to play with."

After prying one of the kittens from his trousers as it tried to climb his leg, West set it down carefully.

"Shall we continue to the guest cottage?" Phoebe asked.

Knowing he couldn't trust himself with her if there was a bedroom in the vicinity, West suggested, "Let's stay here for a moment."

Obligingly Phoebe sat on the stone steps that formed

part of a bridge over the goldfish stream. She arranged her skirts to keep them from bunching beneath her and folded her hands in her lap.

West sat beside her, occupying a lower step so their faces were level. "Will you tell me what happened with Edward Larson?" he asked quietly.

Relief flashed across her face as if she were eager to unburden herself. "First," she said, "will you promise not to say anything insulting about him?"

West rolled his eyes. "Phoebe, I'm not that strong." But as she gave him a reproachful glance, he sighed and relented. "I promise."

Although Phoebe made an obvious effort to remain composed while she explained her difficulties with Edward Larson, tension strung through her quiet tone. "He won't talk to me about the estate's business. I've tried many times, but he doesn't want to discuss information, or plans, or ideas for improvement. He says it's too difficult for me to understand, and he doesn't want me to be burdened with the responsibility, and that everything is perfectly fine. But the more he tells me not to worry, the more worried and frustrated I become. I've started to wake up every night with a nagging feeling and a pounding heart."

West took one of her hands, warming her cool fingers in his. He wanted to kill Edward Larson for causing her even one minute of needless anxiety.

"It's hard for me to trust him now," Phoebe continued. "Especially after what he did with the account ledgers."

West glanced at her sharply. "What did he do with them?"

As Phoebe proceeded to explain how Larson had removed the account books from the estate without permission and had let three months go by without returning them, she became visibly agitated. ". . . but Edward kept forgetting to bring them back," she said without pausing for breath, "because he was very much occupied with work, and then he said they were too heavy, and finally after he left yesterday morning, I went to the offices in town to fetch them myself, and I know he won't like it at all when he finds out, even though I had every right to do so."

West stroked the back of her hand slowly, letting his fingertips delve into the valleys of her slim fingers. "When your instincts are trying to tell you something, don't ignore them."

"But my instincts must be wrong. Edward would *never* act against my interests. I've known him forever. Henry introduced us in childhood—"

"Phoebe. Let's not tiptoe around this. Larson's delay in bringing back the account books wasn't because he was too busy, or unable to lift them, or trying somehow to ease your burden. The fact is, he doesn't want you to see them. There's a reason for that, and it's probably not a pleasant one."

"Perhaps the estate farms aren't doing as well as he claimed."

"Perhaps. But it could be something more. Every man has his secret sins."

Phoebe looked skeptical. "You expect to find secret sins listed in a farm account ledger?"

"I expect to find discrepancies in the numbers. Sin is never free: there's either an up-front cost or an invoice to pay later. He may have reached into the wrong pot to settle a debt."

"But he's not that kind of man."

"I wouldn't make judgments about what kind of man he is until you find out the truth. If we uncover a problem, you can ask him about it. Sometimes people do the wrong thing for the right reasons. He deserves the chance to explain himself."

Phoebe glanced at him with a touch of surprise. "That's very fair-minded of you."

West's mouth twisted. "I know what his friendship means to you," he muttered. "And he's Henry's cousin. I would never try to poison you against him."

He went still with surprise as he felt Phoebe lean against him, her beautiful head coming to rest on his shoulder. "Thank you," she whispered.

The trusting and natural gesture felt better than anything he'd ever known. Gradually he turned his face until his lips touched the molten red gleam of her hair. All his life, he'd secretly yearned for this moment. For someone to turn to him for comfort.

"How long will you stay?" he heard her ask.

"How long do you want me?"

Phoebe made a sound of amusement. "At least until I'm out of trouble."

You're not the one in trouble, West thought, and closed his eyes in despair.

"WHAT DOES A COW say?" West asked Stephen that evening, as they sat on the parlor rug surrounded by carved wooden animals.

"Moo," the toddler replied matter-of-factly, taking the little cow from him and inspecting it.

West held up another animal. "What does a sheep say?"

Stephen reached for it. "Baa."

Phoebe smiled as she watched them from her chair by the hearth, a small embroidery hoop in her lap. After dinner, West had given Stephen a toy barn with a removable roof and a collection of carved and painted animals. There was even a miniature wooden two-wheeled cart for the horse to pull. Nearby, Justin played with his present from West. It was a Tivoli board, a game in which marbles were inserted at the top and clattered their way down through arrangements of pegs and chutes before dropping into numbered slots below.

Much earlier in the day, Phoebe had shown West to the guest cottage, a simple redbrick dwelling with sash windows and a white pediment over the door. He had changed from his traveling clothes and returned to the main house to have his first look at the account ledgers. "I see some of the difficulty," he'd said, scrutinizing the pages in front of him. "They're using a double-entry bookkeeping system."

"Is that bad?" Phoebe had asked apprehensively.

"No, it's superior to the single-entry system we use at Eversby Priory. However, being simpleminded in this area, I'll need a day or two to become familiar with it. Basically, each entry to an account requires an opposite entry to a corresponding account, and then one can check for errors with an equation." West had looked self-mocking. "To think of the courses I took in Greek history and German philosophy, when what I needed was an introduction to bookkeeping."

He had spent the afternoon in the study, shooing Phoebe out when she tried to join him, claiming her presence was too distracting for him to concentrate.

Later they'd had dinner alone, both of them seated near the end of the long mahogany dining table, in the wavering brilliance of candlelight. At first the conversation had charged at a headlong pace, partly fueled by nerves. It wasn't an ordinary situation for the two of them, dining with the intimacy of husband and wife. Phoebe had thought it felt a little like trying something on to see if it fit. They'd exchanged news and stories, debated silly questions and then serious ones . . . and after wine and dessert, they had finally relaxed and let down their guards. Yes, it fit, the two of them together. It was a different feeling, but a very good one. A new kind of happiness.

Phoebe knew West couldn't see beyond his own fears of being unworthy, of someday causing her unhappiness. But this high degree of concern was precisely what inclined her to trust him. One thing was clear: if she wanted him, she would have to be the pursuer.

West lounged on the floor between her two sons, a heavy forelock of dark hair falling over his forehead. "What does a chicken say?" he asked Stephen, holding up a wooden figure.

The toddler took it from him and answered, "*Rowwr!*"

West blinked in surprise and began to chuckle along with Justin. "By God, that is a fierce chicken."

Delighted by his effect on West, Stephen held up the chicken. "*Rowwr*," he growled again, and this time West and Justin collapsed in laughter. Quickly West reached out to the toddler's blond head, pulled him closer and crushed a brief kiss among the soft curls.

Had there been any doubts lingering in Phoebe's mind, they were demolished in that moment.

Oh, yes . . . I want this man.

Chapter 24

EARLY THE NEXT MORNING, Ernestine brought Phoebe her tea and helped to prop the pillows behind her.

"Milady, I have a message to relay from Hodgson, regarding Mr. Ravenel."

"Yes?" Phoebe asked, yawning and sitting up higher in bed.

"As Mr. Ravenel brought no valet with him, the under-butler would be pleased to offer his services in that capacity, should they be required. Also, my lady . . . the housemaid just came from tending the grate at the guest house. She says Mr. Ravenel asked for a razor and shaving soap to be sent over. Hodgson says he would be honored to loan his razor to the gentleman."

"Tell Hodgson his generosity is very much appreciated. However . . . I think I'll offer Mr. Ravenel the use of my late husband's razor."

Ernestine's eyes widened. "Lord Clare's razor?"

"Yes. In fact, I'll take it to him personally."

"Do you mean this morning, milady? Now?"

Phoebe hesitated. Her gaze went to the window, where the pale sky was rising through the darkness like a floating layer of cream. "It's my responsibility as hostess to take care of my guest, isn't it?"

"It would be hospitable," Ernestine agreed, although she looked a bit dubious.

Still considering the idea, Phoebe played nervously with a loose lock of her hair and took a fortifying gulp of hot tea. "I'm sure he'd like to have it soon."

"If you leave through the winter garden door at this hour," Ernestine said, "no one would notice. The housemaids don't start on the east wing 'til midmorning. I'll tell Hodgson not to send anyone out to the guest cottage."

"Thank you. Yes."

"And if you like, milady, I'll tell Nanny you'd prefer the children to have breakfast in the nursery this morning and join you for tea later."

Phoebe smiled. "I do appreciate, Ernestine, that your first instinct is not to prevent me from doing something scandalous, but to help me get away with it."

The lady's maid gave her a deliberately bland look. "You're only going out to take the morning air, milady. No scandal in going for a walk, last I heard."

By the time Phoebe exited the winter garden door and followed the crosswalk to the guest cottage, sunrise had started to gild the leaves and branches of the boxwood borders and spread a rosy glow across brackets of glittering windowpanes. She carried a lidded basket over one arm, walking as quickly as possible without giving the impression of haste.

As Phoebe reached the guest cottage, she gave the door two quick knocks and let herself in. "Good morning," she called out softly, closing the door behind her.

She had redecorated the cottage as well as the main

house. The front room, a parlor with sage green walls, fresh white plasterwork, and gilded accents, was perfumed by the vase of fresh flowers that occupied a satinwood console table beside the door.

In the silence of the cottage, West emerged from one of the bedrooms, his head tilting in perplexity to find her there. He was very tall in the low-ceilinged room, a potent masculine presence with his shirt left untucked and the sleeves rolled up to reveal hairy forearms. Phoebe's heart thudded heavily as she thought of what she wanted and feared might not happen. The idea of going the rest of her life without ever having been intimate with West Ravenel was starting to seem no less than tragic.

"I've brought shaving supplies," she said, gesturing with the basket.

West stayed where he was, his gaze slow and hot as it swept over her. She wore an "at home" garment that combined the appearance of a dress with the convenience of a robe, as it required no corset and fastened with a minimum of buttons. The scooped neck of the bodice was trimmed with spills of white Brussels lace.

"My thanks," he said. "I expected a footman or housemaid to bring them. Forgive me for putting you to trouble."

"It was no trouble. I . . . I wanted to find out if you'd slept comfortably last night."

He smiled slightly, appearing to debate the answer. "Well enough."

"Is the bed too soft?" Phoebe asked in concern. "Too firm? Are the pillows sufficient, or—"

"The surroundings are luxurious in every regard. I had unsettled dreams, that's all."

Tentatively Phoebe moved forward with the basket. "I brought Henry's razor," she blurted out. "I would be glad for you to have the use of it."

West stared at her, his lips parting with what seemed to be dismay. "Thank you, but I couldn't—"

"I want you to," she insisted. God, how awkward this was turning out to be. "It's a Swedish razor, made of the finest-grain steel. Sharper even than a Damascus blade. You'll need it, with a beard like yours."

Letting out a breath of amusement, West reached up to rub the brush-wire surface of his jaw. "How do you know so much about men's beards?"

"I shaved Henry quite often," Phoebe said matter-of-factly, "especially near the end. I was the only one he would allow to touch him."

Light angled across the upper half of his face, striking unearthly blue gleams in his eyes. "You were a good wife," came his soft comment.

"I became very proficient." A self-conscious smile tugged at her lips as she confided, "I love the sounds of shaving."

"What sounds?"

"The swoosh of the lather brush, and the scratchy-scraping of the blade cutting through whiskers. It sends a tingly feeling down the back of my neck."

West laughed suddenly. "It's never done that to me."

"But you understand what I mean, don't you?"

"I suppose."

"Isn't there a sound you find so pleasant that it seems to waken all your nerve endings?"

A long pause ensued before he said, "No."

"Yes, there is," Phoebe protested with a laugh. "You're just not telling me."

"You don't need to know it."

"I'll find out someday," she told him, and he shook his head, still smiling at her. Slowly she approached him with the lidded basket. "West . . . have you ever had a woman shave you?"

His smile faded at the edges, and he gave her an arrested stare.

"You haven't," she guessed.

West tensed as she drew closer.

"I dare you to let me," Phoebe said.

He had to clear his throat before saying in a rusty voice, "That's not a good idea."

"Yes, let me shave you." When he didn't respond, Phoebe asked softly, "Don't you trust me?" She was standing very close to him now, unable to fathom his expression. But she could almost feel his visceral response to her nearness, his powerful body radiating pleasure, like fire throwing off heat. "Are you afraid?" she dared to tease.

It was a challenge West couldn't resist. He set his jaw and backed away a step, staring at her with a mixture of resentment and helpless desire.

And then . . . he made a brief motion with his head for her to follow him into the bedroom.

Chapter 25

"How do I know that your tingles from the sounds of shaving implements won't cause you to accidentally butcher me?" West asked, seated in a wing chair beside the bedroom washstand.

"The sound doesn't send me into fits," Phoebe protested, pouring hot water into a white ceramic bowl on the washstand. "It's only that I find it satisfying."

"I'll be satisfied to have this scruff removed," West said, scratching his jaw. "It's starting to itch."

"It's just as well that you're not going to keep it." Phoebe went to set the small kettle back on the box stove at the hearth. "The fashion is for a long, flowing beard," she continued, "like Mr. Darwin's or Mr. Rossetti's. But I suspect yours would turn out curly."

"Like a prizewinning sheep," he agreed dryly.

Carefully Phoebe soaked a towel in the steaming water, wrung it out and folded it, and pressed it gently over the lower half of West's face. He slouched lower in the chair and tilted his head back.

Phoebe was still inwardly amazed that he'd agreed to let her shave him. The masculine ritual would undoubtedly be nerve-wracking if it weren't performed by a professional. By the time she had started shaving

Henry, he'd been too weak to do it for himself, and he'd already entrusted her with the countless intimacies involved in caring for a bedridden invalid. But this situation was very different.

She took a leather strop from the basket and tied it deftly to the top rail of the washstand. "I asked my father to show me how to do this," she said conversationally, "so I could take care of Henry. The first thing I learned was how to strop the blade properly." After she picked up the slender steel razor, she opened the embossed handle and began to strop with light, brisk strokes. "Who shaves you at Eversby Priory? Lord Trenear's valet?"

West tugged the hot towel away from his mouth as he replied. "Sutton? No, he complains more than enough about having to cut my hair every three weeks. I've shaved myself ever since the age of fourteen, when my brother taught me."

"But you've been to a London barber."

"No."

Setting down the razor, Phoebe turned to face him. "You've never let *anyone* shave you?" she asked faintly. "Ever?"

West shook his head.

"That's . . . unusual for a gentleman of your position," she managed to say.

West shrugged slightly, his gaze turning distant. "I suppose . . . when I was a boy . . . the sight of an adult man's hands always meant something bad for me. They only inflicted pain. I was thrashed by my father, my uncles, the school headmaster, teachers . . ." He paused and gave her a sardonic glance. "After that, the idea of letting a man hold a blade to my throat has never seemed all that relaxing."

Phoebe was stunned by the fact that he was willing to make himself vulnerable to her in a way he had with no one else. It was an enormous act of trust. As she held his gaze, she saw the chill of dread in his eyes . . . but still he sat there, voluntarily putting himself at her mercy. Carefully she reached out to take the damp towel.

"You deserve credit for living up to your motto," she said, her lips curving with the hint of a smile. "But I withdraw my dare."

A notch appeared between his dark brows. "I want you to do it," he eventually said.

"Are you trying to prove something to me," Phoebe asked softly, "or yourself?"

"Both."

His face was calm, but his hands gripped the upholstered arms of the wing chair like a man about to be tortured in a medieval dungeon.

Phoebe studied him, wondering how to make the situation easier for him. What had started as a lighthearted game to her had just become profoundly serious. It was only fair, she thought, to make herself vulnerable as well.

Jettisoning every last vestige of caution, she reached for the three buttons that fastened the front of her at-home dress and tugged the inner tie of the waist. The garment fell open and slid away from her shoulders, eliciting a shiver. Gooseflesh rose over her newly exposed skin. She shrugged out of the dress, draped it over her arm, and went to lay it on the bed.

West's voice sounded strangled. "Phoebe, what are you doing?"

She kicked off her slippers and returned to him in her stocking feet. Breathless and blushing from head to toe, she said, "I'm providing you with distractions."

"I don't . . . *Jesus.*" West's gaze devoured her. She was clad only in a white linen chemise and drawers, the fabric so fine and thin, it was translucent. "This is not going to end well," he said darkly.

Phoebe smiled, noticing that his fingers were no longer clenched around the chair arms but were tapping restlessly. After setting out the rest of the supplies from the basket, she shook a few drops of oil from a small flask into her hand. Spreading it evenly between her fingertips, she approached West. He drew in a swift breath as she came to stand between his open thighs.

"Head back," she murmured.

West complied, regarding her warily from beneath his lashes. "What is that?"

"Almond oil. To protect the skin and soften the beard." Gently she massaged the taut muscles of his cheeks, jaw, and throat with small, circular movements.

His eyes closed, and he began to relax, his breath turning slow and deep. "This part isn't so bad," he said grudgingly.

At this close distance, Phoebe was able to see fine

details of his face: the ink-black filaments of his eye-lashes, the subtle smudges of weariness beneath his eyes, the texture of a complexion that was silkier but tougher than her own, as only a man's could be. "You're too handsome to wear a beard," she informed him. "I might allow it someday if you need to conceal a sagging chin, but for now, it has to go."

"At the moment," West said with his eyes still closed, "nothing I have is sagging."

Phoebe glanced downward reflexively. From her vantage between his splayed legs, she had a perfect view of his lap, where the ridge of a rather magnificent erection strained the fabric of his trousers. Her mouth went dry, and she wavered between uneasiness and intense curiosity.

"That looks uncomfortable," she said.

"I can bear it."

"I meant for me."

The cheeks beneath her fingertips tautened as West tried—unsuccessfully—to hold back a grin. "If it makes you nervous, don't worry. It will disappear as soon as you pick up that damned razor." He paused before adding huskily, "But . . . it wouldn't be. Un-comfortable, I mean. If we were going to . . . I would make sure you were ready. I would never hurt you."

Phoebe shaped her fingers around his hard jaw. How surprising life was. Once she would never have considered this man for herself. And now it would be impossible to consider anyone else. She could no more stop herself from kissing him than she could keep from breathing. Her lips brushed tenderly over his before she whispered, "I'll never hurt you either, West Ravenel."

After she stirred up lather in a porcelain shaving cup, she worked it into his beard with a badger-hair brush. West remained with his head resting against the upholstered back of the chair as she moved around him.

He did stiffen, however, when Phoebe opened the gleaming razor and used her free hand to angle his face to the side. "It's me," she said gently. "Don't worry." She pulled the skin of his cheek taut with her thumb, held the razor in a practiced grip, and stroked downward with the blade at a perfect thirty-degree angle. After a few careful, neat scrapes—deliciously satisfying sounds—she wiped the blade on a shaving cloth draped over her arm. She didn't realize West had been holding his breath until he let it out in a controlled sigh.

Pausing, she looked down at him with her face directly over his. "Shall I stop?"

His mouth twisted. "Not if it's giving you tingles."

"Many," she assured him, and continued to shave, deftly stretching areas of his face and scraping them smooth. When it came time to work on his neck, she turned his face toward her and nudged his chin upward to expose his throat. As she saw his hands begin to tighten on the chair arms, she said, "I give you permission to look down my chemise."

He loosened his grip and regulated his breathing.

Phoebe shaved his neck with short and meticulous

strokes, revealing skin that gleamed like copper. She took special care with the strong angle of his jawbone, where there was no cushioning softness beneath the skin. "What a lovely jaw," she murmured, admiring the clean edge. "I've never properly appreciated it before."

West waited until the blade lifted from his skin before replying. "I was just thinking the same thing about your breasts."

Phoebe smiled. "Rogue," she accused softly, and moved around to his other side. After the rest of his neck and jaw was smooth, she put her face near his and covered her bottom teeth with her lower lip. "Do this."

He complied readily, and she shaved beneath his lip with delicate strokes. As she worked around his mouth intently, using featherlight pressure, she sensed that West had surrendered completely, his limbs relaxed and loose beneath her. Perhaps it was wrong, but she was enjoying the situation immensely, having his big, powerful body under her control. It hardly escaped her notice that he'd stayed hard all through the shave, his desire unflagging, and she enjoyed that too. Now and then she paused to look into his eyes to make certain he wasn't uncomfortable, and was reassured by the calm, almost drowsy softness of his gaze. As she checked for missed patches on his face, she found a residual bit of roughness near his jaw, and another on his left cheek. After daubing more frothy soap on those parts, she shaved against the grain to remove them.

She used a fresh hot towel to remove every last

trace of soap, and patted some rose-water tonic on his face with her fingertips. "All done," she said cheerfully, drawing back to look at him with satisfaction. His clean-shaven face was handsome enough to make her heart skip a beat. "And not a single nick."

Rubbing his smooth jaw, West went to the washstand to have a glance in the looking glass. "It's a better shave than I could give myself." He turned to face her with a brooding stare.

Wondering at his mood, Phoebe raised her brows questioningly.

Coming to her in two strides, he pulled her against him and took her mouth in a roughly fervent kiss. She began to smile at the demonstration of masculine relief and gratitude, but the pressure of his lips made it impossible. His hands slid over her body, stroking and gripping, molding her hips against his as the swollen length of his erection throbbed between them. He kissed and tasted his way along the side of her neck, his lips and cheek smooth against her skin. Her head tipped back as he kissed the hollow at the base of her throat and swirled his tongue there.

"Thank you," he whispered against the humid spot he'd left.

"Thank you for trusting me."

"I would trust you with my life." He reached higher, and she felt a gentle tugging at the combs that anchored her hair. The weight of the twisted locks fell and unraveled down to her hips. West took a step back, dropped the combs to the floor, and reached out to grasp a handful of the shining red hair. He brought a few of the ruddy locks to his face, stroking them over his cheeks and mouth, and kissed them. His face was grave, almost severe, as he stared at her with absolute concentration. "How can you be so beautiful?" Without waiting for an answer, he picked her up with an ease that caused her to gasp.

West settled her amid the dappled light and shadows of the bed, still rumpled from his sleep. He lay beside her, propped up on one elbow, his gaze following the path of his fingertips as he caressed the exposed skin of her upper chest. Reaching the edge of her neckline, he pulled gently to reveal a pale pink nipple. His thumb circled the tightening bud, stirring a sweet ache that caused her to arch and tremble. He lowered his head, his lips drifting back and forth across the sensitive peak, teasing lightly. The moist heat of his mouth closed over her, and he suckled gently, his tongue flickering and playing. Taking the stiff flesh between his teeth, he bit tenderly, sending a dart of heat to the pit of her stomach.

He lifted his head and stared down at the aroused nipple glowing a deeper shade of pink than before. "What am I going to do with you?" he asked softly.

Phoebe flushed so hard that her face prickled, and she had to duck her head against his neck before she could manage to reply. "I have ideas."

A huff of amusement filtered through her hair. She felt his weight leaning over her, his lips grazing her hot skin. "Tell me."

"That day at Eversby Priory . . . when we were in the study, and you . . ." She fidgeted, unable to find words for what he'd done.

"When I pleasured you over a pile of account ledgers?" West prompted, his hand sliding lazily over her back. "Do you want that again, love?"

"Yes," she said shyly, "but you offered . . . to use your tongue."

A quiet laugh tickled her ear. "You remembered that, did you?"

"I thought about it afterward," she admitted, amazed she was confessing something so shameless, "and . . . I wished I'd said yes."

West grinned and cuddled her close, his lips toying with the soft tendrils of hair around her ear. "Sweetheart," he whispered, "I would love above all else to do that for you. Is that all you want?"

"No, I . . ." Phoebe drew back enough to look at him earnestly. "I want you to make love to me. Please."

Their faces were so close, she felt as if she were floating in a deep blue ocean.

West's fingertips traced the fine edges of her face. "There's no future for us. We both have to agree on that."

Her chin dipped in a single nod. "But you'll be mine for as long as you stay at Clare Manor."

His voice was soft. "I'm already yours, love."

He sat up and began to undress her with deliberate slowness, untying the tiny silk ribbons of her chemise and pulling the garment over her head. But when she tugged at the hem of his shirt, her hands were gently pushed away.

"I want to take your clothes off too," she protested.

"Later." West unfastened her lace-trimmed drawers and eased them down over her hips.

"Why not now?"

She heard his unsteady laugh. "Because the briefest contact between any part of you and any part of me will end this in one flaming second." His eyes had turned heavy lidded as he gazed over her slender naked form, lingering at the sight of the red curls between her thighs. "I want you too badly, love. I want you the way dry earth soaks up rain. There may have been a time in my life when I could have seen you like this and still had some hope of self-control. Although I doubt it. I've never seen anything as beautiful as you." His hands trembled slightly as he removed her garters and stockings and cast them aside. Taking up one of her feet, he lifted it to his mouth and kissed the inner arch of her sole, making her leg twitch. "However," he said, playing with her toes, "if I do anything you don't like, you have only to tell me, and I'll stop. *That* much control I'll always have. Do you understand?"

Phoebe nodded, her hand stealing over the patch of private curls to conceal them.

Amused by her modesty, West asked, "What happened to the woman who just shaved me while dressed in nothing but her undergarments?"

"I can't just lie here spread out like a starfish,"

Phoebe protested, now wriggling to be free of him. "I'm not used to this!"

He pounced on her with a smothered laugh, pinning her arms to the sides and scattering kisses across her writhing torso. "You are the most adorable, *delicious* creature . . ." His mouth slid over her stomach, finding the ticklish hollow of her navel. But the warm, wet swirl of his tongue didn't make her laugh as she would have expected—it spread a peculiar molten feeling through her abdomen. "Delicious," he repeated in a different tone, low and vibrant. He traced the rim with the tip of his tongue before licking deep again. His lips rounded as he blew a cool light stream of air against the dampness. The muscles of her stomach tightened and quivered.

Transfixed, Phoebe lay passively beneath him as he settled between her thighs and pushed them wider. She was dimly aware of the abrupt reversal of their roles from earlier: now he was utterly in control and the surrender was all hers. Her gaze was filled with the brightness of the whitewashed ceiling. She'd never done anything like this in the daytime—it made her feel terribly exposed, and defenseless, and yet somehow that aroused her even more. West continued to play with her navel, kissing and nibbling, while his fingers sifted through the wispy curls covering her sex.

His mouth traveled down to the insides of her thighs, where he nuzzled and breathed against the thin skin, and she experienced a moment of misgiving, wondering what had possessed her to ask him for this. It was too much. Too intimate.

Before she could ask him to stop, a low hum resonated in his throat, a sound she'd heard him make when he especially enjoyed something, a glass of good wine, a taste of something sweet or succulent. A single fingertip slid along the plump crevice, finding the yielding, melting-soft entrance to her body. His fingertip pressed into the wetness for a dizzying moment, and then he reached up to her breast, rubbing the nipple with the touch of slickness as if anointing it with perfume.

Shocked, Phoebe began to wriggle away, but he pulled her back easily, his hands strong on her hips. A soundless laugh sank into the crisp curls, his tongue stirring through them slowly, wetting the skin of her mound. His palms pushed beneath her bottom and tilted her pelvis, propping her at a high, helpless angle.

She closed her eyes, all awareness focused on the sinuous strokes of his tongue as he explored the outer folds of her vulva, following the curves on each side, then tracing the delicate edges of the inner lips. His mouth slid to the small, grasping entrance of her body, the tip of his tongue drawing across it. She made an agitated sound as she felt the peculiar sinuous heat of his tongue slipping inside her. Unimaginable. Unspeakable.

The pit of her belly was hot and coiled. Another deep, deliberate lick . . . a teasing wriggle . . . a languid glide. She began to sweat and strain, biting her lip to keep from pleading. Her body no longer seemed to belong to her, becoming a thing made only for pleasure. The bud of her clitoris, bereft of his attentions, ached and twitched, and she shook with the need for him to touch her there. Just one brush of his finger, or the slightest friction from his lips, would send her into spasms of relief. She was making sounds she'd never made in her life, moans and sobs that came from the depths of her lungs.

When the hunger sharpened intolerably, her hand stole down to the triangle of damp curls to ease it herself. Her wrist was deftly caught and pulled aside, and she felt him chuckle against her throbbing flesh. She realized he'd been waiting for her to do that; he knew exactly how desperate she was. Frustrated beyond sanity, she gasped, "You're taking too long."

"Now you're the expert," West mocked gently, playing with the springy hair.

"I . . . I don't want to wait."

"But I want you to." Gently he pulled the hood of her sex back to expose the throbbing bud and blew cool air over it.

"Oh, *please* . . . West, I can't . . . please, please . . ."

His silky, remarkably agile tongue slid right where she needed it, circling and prodding, then flicking in a steady rhythm. He slid a finger inside her, giving the frantic muscles something to clench against. Heat flooded her, sensation wrenching every cell of her body. She was lost in him, feeling what he wanted her to feel, yielding every last part of herself.

The aftermath was like losing consciousness, her limbs too weak to move, her head giddy with sensation. Her face was wet with perspiration and perhaps tears, and she felt him wipe it gently with a corner of the sheet. She was gathered against a hard, furry chest, comforted by his soothing murmurs. He stroked her hair and traced aimless patterns over her back, and held her until her trembling eased.

He left the bed briefly and she rolled to her stomach, stretching like a cat and sighing. She had never felt so sated, so replete.

When West returned, he was completely naked. Phoebe began to turn over, but he straddled her hips and pressed her back lightly to keep her facedown. She lay quietly, aware of the textures of him, the muscles and coarse hair of his thighs, and the silky weight of an erection that felt as long and hard as a raffling pole. There was the sound of a glass stopper in a flask. His warm, strong hands descended to her back, rubbing and massaging, while the scent of almond oil drifted to her nostrils.

He squeezed the muscles of her shoulders and worked his way down on either side of her spine, releasing tension and sending ripples of pleasure through her. Phoebe moaned softly. No one had ever done this to her before; she would never have guessed it would feel so lovely. As his palms glided up to her shoulders, the length of his aroused flesh slid along the cleft of her bottom and partly up her back. Clearly he also took pleasure in the massage, making no effort to hide it. He kneaded her lower back and the full curves of her buttocks with increasing pressure until the clenched muscles relaxed.

One hand reached down between her thighs to cup the soft pleats of flesh, his fingertips riding tenderly on either side of the swollen, half-hidden nub. A few exquisitely light and indirect strokes, back and forth, caused her breath to catch. He touched the opening of her body, circling into the wetness before one of his fingers—no, two—entered in a gradual but insistent thrust.

Her body tried to close against the intrusion, but he was so gentle, his fingers undulating like the sway of water reeds in a slow current. Her legs spread a little, and soon she felt the need to push upward, to take more of him in. As she raised her hips, something inside her loosened and stretched to enclose him. He breathed her name raggedly, seeming to luxuriate in the feel of her, his fingers twisting and curling with protean grace. Keeping her crimson face pressed against the cool linen sheets, she squirmed and gasped and arched tightly.

As his fingers slid from her body, the opening felt oddly liquid, muscles clenching on emptiness. His weight lowered over her back, the hair of his chest tickling pleasantly as he bent to kiss and lick her shoulders and the nape of her neck. His lungs were expanding and contracting with full, heavy breaths. Her eyes opened wide as she felt an intimate nudge between her thighs, the shape of him broad and hard. He pushed, but despite her willingness, her flesh resisted.

"Wait," she gasped, flinching at a sharp ache. He stopped at once, lodged solidly but not quite penetrating. Panting with effort, she tried pressing back onto him, but hesitated as it began to hurt. "I can't, oh, I'm sorry, it's no use, I'm—"

"Darling," West interrupted, having the effrontery to smile against her ear, "before we admit defeat, let's try it another way." He rolled off her and coaxed her to leave the bed with him. After retrieving the small flask of oil, he led her to the upholstered wing chair.

Phoebe shook her head in bewilderment. "Surely you don't mean to . . . on a *chair*? . . ."

He sat and patted his knee.

She regarded him with amazement. "You great immodest creature," she exclaimed with a nervous giggle, "sitting there with a flagrant erection and showing not one hint of concern about it . . ."

"On the contrary, I'm very concerned about it. And since you're the cause, you should take some responsibility."

"I'll do my best," she said doubtfully, glancing at the upthrust length of him. "Although it's a bit more responsibility than one would wish for."

"Be grateful you don't have to live with it," he advised, pulling her onto his lap so she was facing him.

Seeming to enjoy her blushing discomfiture, West opened the almond oil, shook a few drops into one of her hands, and set the flask on the floor beside the chair. "Will you?" he asked softly.

"You . . . wish me to apply it?" she asked, thoroughly flustered to find herself sitting naked on a man's thighs in such an outlandish posture.

"Please."

Tentatively she rubbed the oil between her hands and reached for his face.

West caught her slim wrists, his blue eyes laughing at her. "Not there, sweetheart." Slowly he drew her hands down to the thick shaft straining between them.

"Oh." Mortified and amused, Phoebe stroked the length of him, covering the satiny, ruddy skin with a thin sheen of oil. His male part was large and well shaped, the rigid flesh alive with pulses and deep-secreted quivers. His breath became unsteady as she caressed him from base to tip and let her fingers slide back down to the heavy sack below.

"You're handsome even here," Phoebe murmured, gently grasping him with both hands.

"Thank you. I'm rather partial to it. However, I don't agree. Women's bodies are works of grace and form. Men's bodies are strictly for function."

"Women's bodies serve some rather important functions as well."

"Yes, but they're always beautiful." His fingertips went to her stomach, tracing the delicate crescent of a stretch mark gleaming silver in the daylight. "What was it like?" he asked quietly.

"Giving birth?" Phoebe glanced down ruefully at the faint lines low on her belly. "It wasn't as bad as I thought it would be. I was grateful to have the benefit of modern medicine." Her lips quirked as she watched his fingertips move from one mark to another. "They're not pretty, are they?"

His gaze met hers with surprise. "Everything about you is pretty. These are marks of a life well lived, and risks taken, and miracles you brought into the world. They're signs of having loved and been loved." He brought her closer, lifting her to her knees so he could kiss her throat and the upper curves of her breasts. "I'm sorry to say," he continued, his voice muffled in her cleavage, "my respect for the institution of motherhood doesn't affect in the least my desire to debauch you thoroughly."

Phoebe curled her arms around his neck and rubbed her cheek against the black-brown locks of his hair. Bringing her mouth close to his ear, she whispered, "I'm not sorry about that."

To her surprise, she felt a fine tremor go through him, like the vibrations of a piano wire. Drawing back, she stared into his flushed face, and smiled with a hint of triumph. "That's the sound, isn't it? . . . the one that gives you tingles. It's a woman's whisper."

Chapter 26

"$\mathcal{I}$ ADMIT NOTHING OF THE kind," West said, resuming his attentions to her breasts, cupping them together and kissing her nipples. Fastening his mouth on a stiff peak, he drew it deep and suckled. Gradually one of his hands smoothed over her stomach, down to her groin, idly fluffing the red curls. Despite his physical strength, he handled her with stunning gentleness, his caresses skillful and indirect, building anticipation.

His touch skimmed through delicately layered flesh, pressing her open like petals. The tip of his middle finger eased around the half-hidden nub, playing lightly. At the same time, his mouth moved to her other breast. Still straddling him on her knees, Phoebe felt her thighs quiver dangerously. She sank lower and jerked as she felt the taut head of his sex press against her.

"Don't stop," he said against her breast, one of his palms sliding over her bottom to guide her. At her hesitation, he lifted his head and read the uncertainty in her expression. "You've never done it this way?"

"Henry and I were both virgins. We only knew how to do it the one way."

West gave her a skeptical glance. "You never looked

at erotic postcards together? You would have discovered no end of ideas."

"Never," Phoebe exclaimed, more than a little shocked by the idea. "For one thing, Henry wouldn't have known where to find such materials—"

"The booksellers on Holywell Street and Drury Lane keep them behind the counters," he said helpfully.

"—and for another, he would never have shown anything like that to me."

West's eyes sparkled wickedly. "What would you have done if he had?"

Taken aback by the question, Phoebe opened her mouth to reply, then closed it. "I don't know," she admitted. "I suppose . . . I might have looked at one."

He laughed. "Only one?"

"Or two," Phoebe said, so embarrassed she half-expected to burst into flames. She leaned forward to hide her face on his shoulder. "Let's not talk about dirty postcards."

"You're having fun, you naughty girl," he said, one of his arms sliding around her. "Admit it."

Phoebe smiled against his shoulder. She loved how he teased her, the way no man would ever tease a duke's daughter or a respectable widow. "A little," she said.

The fragrance of his skin mingled with shaving soap and almond oil and a hint of some salty essence that she realized with a little shock might have come from her. Aroused by the thought of the intimacies she had already shared with this man, she turned her head and kissed his neck. She dragged her parted lips up to his cheek, and his mouth sought hers, kisses blooming within kisses like a field of poppies in endless summer. Those clever, inventive fingers played between the open bracket of her thighs, occasionally slipping into the snug sheath of her body and teasing the inner muscles into squeezing around them. His thumb brushed over her clitoris in flirting touches, drawing quivers from her and making it impossible to sit still. Reaching down to grip his shaft in her hand, she guided him into place, determined to take him inside.

"Easy," West said softly, cupping her bottom to control her descent.

Phoebe sank lower in his lap, and felt him adjust his position in the chair, altering the angle between them. Gasping with effort, she worked herself on him, easing farther each time. He held her carefully, watching her with rapt concentration, his breath turning choppy.

He was deep inside her now, impaling her to the point of discomfort, and yet she hadn't quite taken all of him. She paused, and he groaned softly, caressing her back and sides, muttering words of fervent approval and praise. Obeying the coaxing pressure of his hands, she eased downward, lifted and slid down again, enthralled by the sensation of being filled and caressed within.

"Like this?" she asked, wanting reassurance.

"God, yes, just like that, yes . . ." He reached for her head and pulled her in for a profoundly enthusiastic kiss.

Gaining confidence, she continued to move on him, discovering that when she arched and pushed her hips forward on each downward thrust, she could accommodate the entire length of him, her mound rubbing against delicious firmness. It caused a deep jabbing ache each time she did it, but the growing pleasure soon outweighed the pain. Overwhelmed with lust, she began to push harder, almost slamming on him, gulping for breath as an intense hot wave of fulfillment began to roll up her.

"Phoebe," she heard him gasp, "wait . . . easy, now . . . not so rough. You'll hurt yourself, sweet . . ."

She couldn't wait. The need was excruciating, and all her muscles were tightening and clenching in anticipation of relief.

A whimper escaped her as West brought it all to a sudden halt, clamping a forearm beneath her churning hips, easily lifting her away from his shaft.

She shuddered hungrily. "No, it felt good, please, I need—"

"It may satisfy you at the moment, but you'll be cursing me later when you're too sore to walk."

"I don't care. I don't care."

Phoebe continued to protest weakly as he lifted her up and carried her to the bed, her senses in a frenzy . . . He was saying something quietly, something about patience or . . . but she couldn't hear over the thunder in her ears. Her legs splayed wide as he dropped her onto the mattress, his big body settling between them, and she cried out as he slid back inside her, his hardness stretching her lusciously. He began to pump in a slow,

steady motion that wouldn't alter no matter how she
writhed and begged him to go harder, faster, deeper.

His mouth went to her breast, sucking at a nipple,
tugging sweetly in time to his thrusting. Her body
contracted every time he pushed inward, clasping him
hungrily, sensation building until a powerful climax
began, wringing every inch of her body with raw
force. She fell silent, her hips locked in a steep arch
against his weight. Still the measured rhythm went on,
extracting every last flicker of sensation. He was tire-
less, unhurried, using himself to satisfy her.

At last Phoebe collapsed down on the bed, shivering uncontrollably. West plunged into her . . . once,
twice, thrice . . . and pulled out to crush the thick wet
rod of his sex against her stomach. He buried a savage
growl in the bedclothes and clutched the mattress on
either side of her so hard she thought he might gouge
holes in it. As she felt the hot spill of his release, an
unfamiliar croon came from her throat, a sound of
primal satisfaction at having pleased her mate.

West began to roll off her, but she locked her arms
and legs around him to keep him there. He could have
broken her hold on him with laughable ease, but he
stayed obediently, striving to regain his breath. She
relished the feeling of being anchored by his weight,
the mat of hair on his chest teasing her breasts, the
fragrance of sweat and intimacy rising freshly to her
nostrils.

Eventually he brought his mouth to hers, kissing
her softly before he left the bed. He returned with a

damp cloth, wiping her in careful strokes, performing the lover's service with exquisite gentleness.

Dreamy and limp with relaxation, Phoebe turned to face him as he lay beside her again. West smoothed back stray locks of hair from her face and stared into her eyes. She felt as if they were still beyond the reach of the world, entangled even though their bodies were separate. He was part of her now, his name emblazoned on her skin with invisible but permanent ink. With a single fingertip, she traced the strong line of his nose and the edge of his upper lip. *What have we done?* she wondered, almost frightened by the connection between them, the unbreakable strength of it.

It seemed, however, that her companion's thoughts were focused on more immediate concerns.

"Will it be time for breakfast soon?" West asked hopefully.

"You poor man. Every day is an unending struggle to satisfy one or another of your appetites, isn't it?"

"It's exhausting," he agreed, kissing his way down her arm.

"I'll slip inside the house first, and you can follow a few minutes later. I'll make sure you're well-fed." Phoebe grinned and tugged her arm away. "We must keep up your strength for all that accounting work."

Chapter 27

As THE MIDDAY SUN slanted gently through the study windows, West leaned over a row of open ledgers on the oak table. He cross-checked entries and occasionally paused to rummage through folders of correspondence and legal documents. Phoebe sat quietly at the table, providing answers when she could and making notes for her own reference. She took pleasure in the sight of him, shirtsleeves rolled up over his muscled forearms, his trouser braces crossing over his broad back and down his front to his lean waist.

To her relief, West didn't seem at all glum or annoyed about having to spend a sunny day indoors. He liked having problems to solve. She sensed he wasn't the kind who would do well if he were set adrift for too long. He took a keen interest in the workings of everyday life, in practical matters. It was one of the qualities that made him very different from Henry, who had thought of leisure time as his real life, had hated being distracted by mundane subjects, and had *loathed* discussing money for any reason. Henry had preferred to look inward, and West to look outward, and in both cases, a little balance was needed.

Then there was poor Edward, who would have been far more like the high-minded Henry if he'd been able, but instead had been compelled by circumstances to earn a living. Henry's father had been a viscount, whereas Edward's father had been the second son. It certainly couldn't have escaped Edward that if he married Phoebe, he would finally be able to live as lord of the manor and acquire most of the power and privileges Henry had known. Then he would also be able to focus on the inner life and shrink from unpleasant realities.

Except that times were changing. The nobility could no longer live in lofty ivory towers from which they had no clear view of the people down below. West had made Phoebe more aware of that than ever before. If the estate went under, it would not be a slow submerging, like a leaky barge. It was a gradual approach to an unseen cliff. Hopefully she could change course before they reached the sudden plummet.

"Phoebe," West said, interrupting her thoughts. "Do you have any other financial files? Specifically one with a bank book and checks?"

Phoebe shook her head, watching as he sorted through a stack of folders on the table. "No, this is all we have."

"You may have missed one at the Larson offices, then."

She frowned. "Uncle Frederick assured me this was all the material they had pertaining to the estate. Why do you think something is missing?"

"What do you know about the loan that was arranged two and a half years ago from the Land Loan and Enfranchisement Company?"

"I'm afraid I know nothing about that. How much was it for?"

"Fifteen thousand pounds."

"*Fifteen* . . ." Phoebe began, her eyes flying open. "For what purpose?"

"Land improvements." West stared at her closely. "Larson never discussed it with you?"

"*No.*"

"The loan was charged against Justin's future inheritance."

"Are you sure?"

"Here's a copy of the loan agreement."

Phoebe shot up from her chair and hurried around the table to look at the document in his hand.

"This was tucked into a ledger," West continued, "but as far as I can tell, it was never entered properly into the books. Nor can I find any records from the loan account."

Dazedly she read the terms of the loan. "Seven percent interest to be repaid in twenty-five years . . ."

"The loan company was incorporated by a special act of Parliament," West said, "to help struggling estate owners." He sent the document a disparaging glance. "You could borrow at four and a half percent from a regular bank."

Phoebe examined a page bearing Henry's signature. "Henry signed this a week before he died." She put a hand to her stomach, feeling slightly nauseated.

"Phoebe," she heard West ask after a moment, "was he fully cognizant at that point? Would he have signed something like that without understanding what it was?"

"No. He slept a great deal, but when he was awake, he was quite sensible. Near the end, he was trying to settle his affairs, and there were so many visitors, including solicitors and managers. I was always trying to shoo them out, to let him rest. I don't know why he didn't mention the loan to me. He must have been trying to spare me from having to worry about it." Setting down the document, she passed a trembling hand over her forehead.

Seeing how upset she was, West turned her to face him. "Here, now," he said, his tone comforting, "it's not an unreasonable amount of money when it comes to making improvements on an estate of this size."

"It's not just the amount," Phoebe said distractedly. "It's a nasty surprise, leaping up like a troll from beneath a bridge. Henry knew I should have been made aware of something like this, if I were to manage the estate . . . but . . . he never expected me to manage it, did he? He expected me to leave everything in Edward's hands. And I did, for two years! I took no responsibility for anything. I'm furious with myself! How could I be so foolish and self-indulgent—"

"Hush. Don't blame yourself." Gently West took her jaw in his hand, steering her gaze to his. "You're taking responsibility now. Let's find out the facts, and then you can decide what to do. First we'll need access to the account information and records from the loan company."

"I'm not sure that's possible. Even though I'm Justin's legal guardian, Edward is executor of the will and administrator of his financial trust." Phoebe scowled. "And I doubt very much he'll want me to see those records."

West half sat on the desk, facing her. He uttered a quiet profanity. "Why is Larson executor of the will? Why not your father or brother?"

"Henry felt more comfortable prevailing on a member of his own family, who was familiar with the estate and its history. My father is next in line for the executorship, if something were to happen to Edward." The thought of Sebastian helped to calm Phoebe. With all his influence and connections, he would know what to do, whom to approach. "I'll write to my father," she said. "He knows people in Parliament and banking—he'll pull strings on my behalf."

Looking pensive, West took one of her hands and played lightly with her fingers. "I have another suggestion, if you're willing. I could ask Ethan Ransom to obtain the information for us. He'll accomplish it faster and more discreetly than anyone else could, even your father."

Phoebe stared at him in bewilderment. "The injured man who stayed at Eversby Priory? Why . . . how . . . ?"

"I neglected to explain earlier about how Ransom came by his injuries. He worked for the Home Office as . . . well, as an unauthorized agent."

"He was a spy?"

"Spying was one of the things he did. However, he

uncovered evidence of corruption by his superiors that extended to other branches of law enforcement, and then . . . he became a target. They nearly succeeded in killing him."

"And you gave him refuge," Phoebe said, realizing Ethan Ransom's summer visit to Eversby Priory had been about far more than needing a peaceful place to recuperate. "You were hiding him." Increasingly concerned, she drew closer to him and linked her arms around his neck. "Were you in any danger?"

"Not a bit," he said, a little too quickly.

"You were! Why would you do that for a stranger, and put the rest of the household at risk as well?"

One of his brows arched. "Are you going to scold?"

"Yes, you very much need scolding! I don't want anything to happen to you."

West smiled, his hands settling at her hips. "I took Ransom in when he needed help because he wasn't entirely a stranger. As it turns out, he's a relation on the Ravenel side. I'll explain more about that later. The point is, Ransom owes me a favor or two, and he could easily obtain the loan account records, since he's just been sworn in as the assistant commissioner of the Metropolitan Police. He's also been given the authority to organize and direct a small group of his own handpicked agents. I'm sure he'll regard this as a handy training exercise." He paused. "None of this is to be repeated, by the way."

"Of course not." Phoebe shook her head in bemusement. "Very well. If you'll write to him, I'll have the letter posted immediately."

"I'd prefer to send it by special courier. I want this done before Larson returns and I'm obliged to leave."

"Edward's return won't necessitate your leaving," Phoebe said, instantly annoyed. "He has no say over who stays in my house."

"I know, sweetheart." A shadow came over West's expression. "But you won't want both of us in the same vicinity for long, or the situation will turn into a powder keg."

"That doesn't worry me."

"It does me," he said quietly. "I've caused too many disgraceful scenes and left behind enough unhappy wreckage for a lifetime. I don't want reminders. Sometimes I fear . . ." He paused. "You don't understand how thin the veil is that separates me from what I used to be."

Phoebe did understand. Or rather, she understood that was what he believed. Staring at him compassionately, she laid her hands on either side of his face. With all his remarkable qualities, West also had his own vulnerabilities . . . fragile places that needed to be safeguarded. Very well—she would shield him from any ugly scenes involving herself and Edward.

"Regardless of how long you stay," she said, "I'm glad you're here now."

West's forehead lowered to hers, and the heat of his whisper caressed her lips. "God, so am I."

IN THE DAYS that followed, the decorum of Clare Manor was disrupted by the vigorous presence of

West Ravenel, and the sounds of his booted feet on the stairs, and his deep voice and rumbling laugh. He chased the children through the hallways and made them squeal, and took them out to romp outside, tracking dirt and pebbles on the carpet as they came back in. He investigated every corner of the house, learned the names of the servants, and asked innumerable questions of everyone. Charmed by his quick humor and affable manner, the staff obligingly paused in their labors to tell him anything he wanted to know. The old master gardener was delighted by West's ability to discuss the intricacies of weather and how best to defeat plant-destroying caterpillars. The cook was flattered by his hearty appetite. Nanny Bracegirdle enjoyed herself to no end lecturing him about having allowed Justin to jump in puddles after a rain shower and ruining his good shoes.

One afternoon, Phoebe went in search of West and discovered him reshaping the topiaries in the formal garden, which had gone untended since the old gardener's onset of rheumatism. Pausing at the threshold of a set of open French doors, she took in the scene with an absent smile. West had climbed an orchard ladder and was clipping the tree with shears at the direction of the old gardener who stood below.

"What do you think?" West called down to Justin, who was gathering twigs and branches into a pile as they fell.

The child viewed the topiary critically. "Still looks like a turnip."

"It's a perfectly recognizable duck," West protested. "There's the body, and this is the bill."

"It has no neck. A duck needs a neck, or he can't quack."

"I can't argue with that," West said ruefully, turning back to clip more leaves.

Laughing to herself, Phoebe withdrew back into the house. But the image of it stayed with her: West, tending Henry's beloved topiary trees, spending time with his son.

Thank God Georgiana was away for the winter: she would have been appalled by the way West's presence had dispelled any lingering sense that this was a house of mourning. Not that Henry was forgotten: far from it. But now the reminders of him were no longer anchored to gloom and sadness. His memory was being honored, while a breath of new life had swept into Clare Manor. He had not been replaced, but there was room for more love here. A heart could make as much room as love needed.

In the mornings, West liked to have a large, early breakfast, after which he would ride out to some of the tenant farms. Phoebe had gone with him the first day, but it had quickly become apparent that her presence unnerved the tenants, who were overawed and nervous around her. "Much as I love your company," West had told her, "you may have to let me approach them alone. After years of no direct interaction with any of the Larsons, the last thing they'll do is speak freely in front of the lady of the manor."

The next day, when he'd gone out on his own, the results were much better. West had met with three of the estate's largest leaseholders, who had shared a great deal of information and shed some light on a particular accounting mystery.

"Your estate has some interesting problems," West told Phoebe when he returned in the afternoon, finding her in the winter garden with the cats. He was in a buoyant mood, having been out riding and walking in the fields. He smelled like autumn air, sweat, soil, and horses, a pleasantly earthy mixture.

"I don't think I want interesting problems," Phoebe said, going to a tray table to pour a glass of water for him. "I'd rather have ordinary ones."

West took the water with a murmur of thanks and drained it thirstily, a few drops sliding down the front of his neck. Phoebe was briefly transfixed by the movements of that strong throat, remembering a moment the night before when he'd arched over her, his shoulders and back lifting as his muscles had bunched with pleasure.

"I saw some damned beautiful land today," he said, setting the empty glass on the tray table. "Now I understand why your crop yields are better than I would have expected, despite the primitive farming methods the tenants use. But there's no way to avoid it—you're going to have to invest in miles of field drainage and hire a steam-powered machine with rotary diggers to loosen up all that heavy clay. None of your fields have ever been cultivated deeper than a wineglass. The soil has been trodden by horses and compacted by its own weight for centuries, so it's a struggle for plants to sink their roots into it. The good news is, once the ground is loosened and aerated, that alone will likely double your production."

"Lovely," Phoebe exclaimed, pleased. "Is that the interesting problem?"

"No, I'm about to tell you that. Do you recall those puzzling entries in the crop book, in which some of the tenants give four different numbers for their crop yields?

"Yes."

"It's because many of your leaseholds are still laid out in an open-field system, the way they were back in medieval times."

"What does that mean?"

"It means a farm like Mr. Morton's, which I visited today, is divided into four strips, and they're scattered over an area of four square miles. He has to travel separately to farm each strip."

"But that's absurd!"

"It's impossible. Which is why most large landowners did away with the open-field system long ago. You're going to have to find a way to put all the acreage together and redistribute it so each tenant can have one good-sized plot of land. But that won't be as easy as it may sound."

"It doesn't sound easy at all," Phoebe said glumly. "The estate would have to renegotiate all the lease agreements."

"I'll find an experienced arbiter for you."

"Many of the tenants will refuse to take a plot that's inferior to someone else's."

"Persuade them to start raising livestock instead of corn growing. They would make higher profits than they're making now. Nowadays there's more money in milk and meat than grain."

Phoebe sighed, feeling anxious and irritable. "Obviously Edward and his father aren't the ones to handle any of this, since neither of them saw fit to bring it up to me in the first place." She made a face and looked up at him. "I wish you would do it. Couldn't I hire you? Indefinitely? How expensive are you?"

His mouth quirked, his eyes suddenly hard and humorless. "At face value, I'm cheap. But I come with hidden costs."

Drawing closer, Phoebe hugged herself to him and laid her head against his chest.

Eventually his arms lifted around her, and the pressure of his cheek came to her hair. "I'll help you," he said. "I'll make sure you have whatever you need."

You're what I need, she thought. She let her hands move over his spectacular body, so familiar to her now. Daringly she drew a hand down his front, her palm skimming over the fly of his trousers, where a firm bulge distended the soft woven fabric. His breathing changed. When she looked up at his face, she saw that his eyes had turned warm again, his features relaxed and lust-drowsed.

"I wish we didn't have to wait until tonight," she

said, a catch in her voice. In the evenings, after dinner, they relaxed with the children in the family parlor, playing games and reading until the boys were taken up to bed. Then West would retire to the guest house, where Phoebe would later join him under cover of darkness. In the single flame of an oil lamp, he would undress her beside the bed, his hands and mouth sweetly tormenting every inch of newly revealed flesh.

That would be hours from now.

"We don't have to wait," he said.

His head bent. His mouth came to hers, his tongue a gentle, exquisite invasion that caused a sympathetic quiver in a place lower down that also yearned to be invaded. But . . . here? In the winter garden in broad daylight? . . .

Yes. Anything he wanted. Anything.

Chapter 28

*J*N A FEW MINUTES, West had pinned Phoebe against a corner wall of the winter garden, in a sheltered space of stone and feathery leaves. He possessed her with passion-roughened kisses, almost eating at her mouth, greedily drawing in the honeysuckle taste of her. Her skin was milk-white with golden flecks, smoothness quivering at the stroke of his tongue. With one hand, he held the front of her skirts up at her waist, and with the other he reached inside her drawers, his fingers parting the soft lips. He played with her, flicking and stroking, his fingers sinking into her wet, gripping depths. It aroused him to see how hard she was trying to be quiet and couldn't quite manage it, strangled moans and gasps slipping out.

After unbuttoning his trousers and freeing his erection, West braced Phoebe up against the wall and entered her. She let out a cry of surprise at finding herself mounted on his hips, her legs dangling helplessly. Keeping her supported, he began to thrust, nudging against the bud of her sex with every upward plunge.

"Is this good?" he asked gruffly, even though he could feel her throbbing response.

"Yes."

"Too deep?"

"No. No. Keep doing that." She clutched at his shoulders, her pleasure rising rapidly toward climax.

But when West felt her clamping on him, her body tensing in readiness for completion, he forced himself to stop. Ignoring her groans and squirms, he waited until the need for release had subsided. Then he began the rhythm again, took her to the edge and retreated, and laughed softly as she whined and protested.

"West . . . I was just about to . . ." She paused, still too modest to say it aloud. He adored that.

"I know," West whispered. "I felt it. I felt you clenching on me." He rolled his hips, pumping slowly. He was barely aware of what he was saying, only let the words fall over her like a cascade of flower petals. "You're like silk. Every part of you is so fine . . . so sweet. I won't stop next time. I love to watch when you reach the peak . . . the look on your face . . . always a little surprised . . . as if it's something you've never felt before. You blush the color of a wild rose, everywhere . . . your little ears turn so hot, and your lips tremble . . . yes, just like that . . ."

He kissed her panting mouth, loving the damp, satiny insides of her lips, the little velvety tongue lapping at his. Every time he drew his cock partially out, her muscles worked frantically to close on him, tug him back inside. The delight was so intense, he was half afraid his essence was leaking from him, seeping into that lively, luscious channel. She was coming now, tightening, pulsing, milking his hard-swollen flesh, while he fought to keep every movement steady and controlled, to make it good for her. The weight of his bollocks drew up tight and heavy, his body primed for release. He held on, stroking hard and deep, making her ride the movement until she had stopped spasming.

Now it would be his turn. Except he hadn't exactly prepared for this. He had no sheath, nothing to contain his seed.

"Phoebe," he rasped, still thrusting. "Which pocket do you keep your handkerchiefs in?"

It took her a moment to reply. "This dress has no pockets," she said weakly.

West went still, gritting his teeth at the sharp, protesting twinges in his groin. "You don't have even *one* handkerchief?"

Looking apologetic, she shook her head.

He let out a guttural curse. Slowly he lowered her feet to the floor and eased his aching shaft out of her warm, succulent depths, his body aching in anguish.

"Why can't you . . ." Phoebe began, and then understanding dawned. "Oh."

Bracing his hands on the wall, West closed his eyes. "Give me a few minutes," he said curtly.

He heard the sounds of Phoebe straightening her clothes. After a moment, he heard her say, "I think I can help."

"There's nothing you can do."

Strangely, Phoebe's faintly amused voice seemed to come from below him. "I may never have seen any erotic postcards, but I'm sure there's *something* I can do."

West's eyes opened, and he froze in amazement as he saw her kneeling between his thighs. He couldn't make a single sound as she grasped his shaft in her hands, graceful and ladylike. Her head bent, and her beautiful mouth was on him, full lips parting carefully as she took him inside. Her tongue stroked and circled, painting wetness on the sensitive tip, and in a matter of seconds he cried out in ecstasy, delivered and overpowered by her . . . possessed by her. Owned for life.

PHOEBE YAWNED AS she came upstairs from the housekeeper's room, where they had spent the morning going over the monthly household inventory. There had been a discussion of missing dinner napkins—two had been scorched by an inexperienced housemaid and another was suspected to have blown off the line on a windy day. A concern over the new laundry-washing mixture had been broached—too high a proportion of soda was making the linens thin. The coal bill was acceptable. The grocer's bill had been a bit high.

The task of doing household inventory was always tedious, but it had been especially worse since Phoebe had had so little sleep the night before. West had made love to her for what had seemed to be hours, arranging her in one new position after another, exploring gently, patiently, until she'd been exhausted from too many wrenching climaxes and had begged him to stop.

Perhaps she should go up to her room for a short nap. The house was quiet. West was nowhere to be seen. He must have gone somewhere, or . . . no, he hadn't. She paused in the main hall as she caught a glimpse of his lean, powerful form in the front receiving room. He stood at one of the windows, looking out at the main drive with his head slightly tilted in that way he had. The sight of him made her feel warm all over and sent a quick flutter of happiness through her stomach.

Walking quietly in her thin-soled slippers, she stole into the receiving room and sneaked up behind him while he was still at the window. Standing on tiptoe, she pressed her breasts against his back and whispered near his ear, "Come with me, and we'll—"

The room spun around her with stunning force. Before she could even finish the sentence, she had been seized and pinned against the wall. One of his hands clasped her wrists over her head, while the other was drawn back as if he were about to strike her. Oddly, the sight of that lethal upraised fist didn't frighten her nearly as much as his eyes, hard and bright like the gleam of light on a knife blade.

Not West, her disoriented brain told her.

But this hostile stranger's physical similarities to West alarmed her even more.

A high-pitched yelp jolted from her as soon as her shoulders encountered the wall.

The man's face softened instantly, his fist dropping, all threat of violence disappearing. He released her wrists and gave her a remorseful glance. "I beg your pardon sincerely, my lady," he said in an Irish brogue. "Whenever someone approaches me from behind, I . . . a reflex action, is what they call it."

"I beg *your* pardon," Phoebe said breathlessly, inching away from him. "I thought you were s-someone else." His eyes were identical to West's, a singular shade of dark blue rimmed with black, surmounted by the same thick brows. But his complexion was fair-skinned, and his features were more narrow, and there was a thickness at the bridge of his nose where it had once been broken.

They both turned as West came into the room with swift, ground-eating strides, heading straight to Phoebe. He took her by the shoulders, his gaze raking over her. "Are you hurt?" he asked shortly.

The intense concern in his eyes and the familiar gentleness of his touch relaxed her immediately. "No, just startled. But it was my fault. I approached him from behind."

West eased her close and ran his hand up and down along her spine in slow, calming strokes. He glanced over his shoulder at the butler, who must have gone to inform him of the visitor's arrival. "That will be all, Hodgson." Turning back to the stranger, he spoke in a pleasant voice, his gaze murderous. "Is this how you introduce yourself to aristocratic ladies, Ransom? A word of advice: generally they prefer a polite bow and a 'how do you do' to being thrown about like a parcel post delivery."

Ethan Ransom spoke to Phoebe penitently. "A thousand apologies, my lady. On my honor, it won't happen again."

"It won't," West agreed, "or I'll come after you with a reaping hook."

Despite the lethal sincerity in West's tone, Ransom didn't seem at all cowed, only grinned and came forward for a handshake. "My nerves are still a bit dodgy after this summer."

"As usual," West said, gripping the other man's hand, "a visit from you is as soothing as a blister."

Phoebe was struck by the easy familiarity between the two, as if they had known each other for years instead of months. "Mr. Ransom," she said, "I do hope we'll have the pleasure of your company for dinner. You're welcome to stay the night, if you wish."

"I'm obliged, milady, but I have to be back on the next train for London." Ransom went to retrieve a small traveling bag that had been set beside a chair. "I've brought some materials for you to have a glance at. Make all the notes you like, but I have to take the original documents back with me and replace them before anyone notices they're missing."

West gave him an alert glance. "Did you find anything interesting in the account records?"

Ransom's mouth curved slightly, but his expression was deadly serious as he replied, "Aye."

Chapter 29

$\mathcal{A}$s PHOEBE LED THE way to the study, where they could speak in complete privacy, she noticed Ethan Ransom absorbing every detail of his surroundings. Not in the way of someone who appreciated interior décor, but rather like a surveyor examining distances and angles. He was pleasant and polite, with a guarded charm that almost made her forget the flash of ice-cold brutality in the first few moments of their disastrous meeting.

Even without having been told about Ransom's appointment with the Metropolitan Police, Phoebe would have known he held a position of responsibility in some potentially dangerous profession. There was something almost catlike about him—a quiet and lethal grace. She sensed that West's relaxed presence helped to make him far more approachable than he ordinarily would have been.

Once inside the study, Phoebe and West sat at the table, while Ransom stood on the opposite side and began to lay out documents. The review of the loan and initial expenses began predictably enough: there had been checks made out to brick and tile manufacturers for field drainage systems, and other checks for installation. There were also checks for land work such as hedge removal and leveling, and waste land reclamation. But soon they reached a run of checks written for less easily identifiable purposes.

"C. T. Hawkes and Associates," Phoebe read aloud, frowning as she saw a draft in the amount of five thousand eight hundred pounds. "What kind of work do they do?"

"It's a residential building company," Ransom replied.

"Why would Edward Larson pay such a large sum to a house builder? Do they also repair farm buildings?"

"I don't believe so, my lady."

Frowning, Phoebe scrutinized the next large entry. "James Prince Hayward of London. Who is that?"

"A coach builder," West said, his gaze moving farther down the list. "Here are expenses for a saddler and harness maker . . . a domestic employment agency . . . and more than a few charges at Winterborne's department store." He gave Ransom a sardonic glance, shaking his head slowly.

It vexed Phoebe that they both seemed to understand something she hadn't yet grasped. She mulled over the information. House . . . coach . . . horse furnishings . . . domestic servants . . . "Edward set up a household somewhere," she said in wonder. "With money he borrowed from my son's inheritance." A wobbly feeling came over her, and she needed ballast even though she was seated. She watched her slender white fingers creep over West's coat sleeve as if they belonged to someone else. The solid muscle beneath her hand was familiar and comforting. "Is there more you can tell me?"

West spoke in a flat, resigned tone. "Out with it, Ransom."

The other man nodded and leaned down to pull more papers from his bag. "Mr. Larson purchased a speculative house built not far from here, in Chipping Ongar. It has eight bedrooms, a conservatory and a veranda." Ransom set the floor plans and elevations in front of them. "There's also a walled garden and a small coach house occupied by a single-horse brougham." Ransom paused to glance at her with a faint frown of concern, as if to evaluate her emotional state before continuing. "It's been leased for the nominal sum of one pound a year to Mrs. Parrett, a woman of approximately twenty-two years of age."

"Why so large a house for only one person?" Phoebe asked.

"There seems to be a plan for the woman to turn it into a boardinghouse someday. Her true name is Ruth Parris. She's the unmarried daughter of a button maker who lives not far from here. The family is poor but respectable. About five years ago, Miss Parris left her family's home when it was discovered she was with child. She went to stay with a distant cousin, gave birth, and eventually returned to Essex to take up residence at the Chipping Ongar house with her son. A boy of four."

Almost Justin's age, Phoebe thought numbly. "What is his name?" she asked.

A long hesitation followed. "Henry."

Tears stung her eyes. She fumbled in her pocket for a handkerchief, pulled it out and blotted them.

"My lady," she heard Ransom ask, "is it possible your husband—"

"No," she said in a watery voice. "My husband and I were inseparable, and besides, he hadn't the health or opportunity to carry on an affair. There's no doubt he's Edward's." She struggled to fit this new idea of Edward in with what she knew about him. It was like trying to push her heel into a punishingly tight shoe.

West remained silent, staring fixedly at the floor plans without really seeing them.

"Even if Larson isn't the father," Ransom said, "you still have ample proof of negligence on his part. He abused his position as executor and trustee by using your son's inheritance as collateral for a loan and using the money to benefit himself. More to the latter, the loan company is at fault in failing to provide oversight, since the money was designated only for land improvement."

"Edward's executorship must end immediately," Phoebe said, her fist clenching around the handkerchief. "However, I want to proceed in a way that will cause the least amount of harm to Ruth and her child. They've suffered enough."

"They're living in an eight-bedroom house," West pointed out sardonically.

Phoebe turned to him, her hand smoothing his sleeve. "The poor girl has been made an object of shame. She couldn't have been more than seventeen years old when she and Edward . . . when their acquaintance began. Now she lives a half existence, unable to meet with her family openly. And little Henry has no father. They deserve our compassion."

West's mouth twisted. "You and your sons are the ones who've been wronged," he said flatly. "My compassion is all for you."

Ransom's face had gentled at Phoebe's words, his eyes now warm blue. "You've a rare, good heart, my lady. I wish I could have brought better news today."

"I appreciate your help more than I can express." Phoebe felt inadequate and overwhelmed, thinking of all the emotional and legal tangles ahead of her. So many difficult decisions.

After studying her for a moment, Ransom spoke with encouraging gentleness. "As my Mam always told me, 'If you can't get rid of your troubles, take them easy.'"

Ransom left Clare Manor as swiftly as he had appeared, taking the financial documents with him. For some reason, West's mood went rapidly downhill afterward. Turning grim and taciturn, he told Phoebe he needed some time to himself. He closed himself in the study for at least four hours.

Eventually Phoebe took it upon herself to see how he was. She knocked lightly on the door, let herself inside, and approached the table where West was writing. He had filled at least ten pages with lines of small, meticulous notes.

"What's all that?" she asked, coming to stand beside him.

Setting down the ink pen, West rubbed the back of his neck wearily. "A list of recommendations for the estate, including immediate needs and long-term goals. I want you to have a good idea of what the most pressing concerns are and what information you'll still need to find out. This plan will show you how to proceed after I'm gone."

"For heaven's sake, is your luggage already packed? You sound as though you're leaving tomorrow."

"Not tomorrow, but soon. I can't stay forever." He neatened the stack of pages and set a glass paperweight on top. "You'll need to hire a qualified assistant—I expect your father will know someone. Whoever he is, he'll have to build a relationship with your tenants and at least pretend to give a damn about their problems."

Phoebe stared at him quizzically. "Are you angry with me?"

"No, with myself."

"Why?"

A scowl darkened his expression. "Just a dash of habitual self-loathing. Don't worry about it."

This irritable melancholy was completely unlike him. "Come for a walk?" she suggested. "You've closed yourself in this room for too long."

He shook his head.

She dared to broach the subject that was preoccupying both of them. "West, if you were in Edward's place, would you have—"

"*Don't*," he said testily. "That's not fair to him or me."

"I wouldn't ask if I didn't need to hear the answer."

"You already know the answer," he growled. "The boy's welfare is the only thing that matters. He's the only one who didn't have a choice in any of this. After what I endured in my childhood, I would never cast my own son and his defenseless mother on the world's mercy. Yes, I would have married her."

"That's what I expected you to say," Phoebe murmured, loving him even more than before, if that were possible. "You have no illegitimate children, then."

"No. At least, I'm reasonably sure. But there's no ironclad guarantee. For a woman who doesn't like nasty surprises leaping up, you've a knack for choosing the wrong companions."

"I would hardly put you in the same category as Edward," Phoebe protested. "He borrowed money against my son's inheritance. You would never do anything to hurt Justin or Stephen."

"I already have. They just won't feel it until they're older."

"What on earth do you mean?"

"Too often in the past, I made a public spectacle of myself on the worst possible occasions, in front of the worst possible people. I was an absolute swine. Brawling at parties. Pissing in fountains and vomiting in potted plants. I've slept with other men's wives, I've ruined marriages. It takes years of dedicated effort to discredit one's own name as thoroughly as I did, but by God, I set the bar. There will always be rumors and ugly gossip, and I can't contradict most of it because I was always too drunk to know whether it happened or not. Someday your sons will hear some of it, and any affection they feel for me will turn to ashes. I won't let my shame become their shame."

Phoebe knew if she tried to argue with him point by point, it would only lead to frustration on her part and wallowing on his. She certainly couldn't deny that upper-class society was monstrously judgmental. Some people would perch ostentatiously on their moral pedestals, loudly accusing West while ignoring their own sins. Some people might overlook his blemished reputation if there was any advantage to them in doing so. None of that could be changed. But she would teach Justin and Stephen not to be influenced by hypocritical braying. Kindness and humanity—the values her mother had imparted—would guide them.

"Trust us," she said quietly. "Trust me and my sons to love you."

West was silent for so long that she thought he didn't intend to respond. But then he spoke without looking at her, in a flat and unemotional tone. "How could I ever count on anyone to do that?"

TO PHOEBE'S RELIEF, West's dark mood seemed to have been dispelled by that evening. He romped with the boys after dinner, tossing and wrestling and flipping them, eliciting squeals, grunts, shrieks, and end-less giggling. At one point, he was crawling on his hands and knees through the parlor like a tiger with both of them riding on his back. When they were all happily exhausted, they piled onto the settee.

Justin crawled into Phoebe's lap and leaned his head back against her shoulder as they sat in the light of a standing lamp with a yellow silk shade, while a small fire crackled in the hearth. Reading aloud from a copy of *Stephen Armstrong: Treasure Hunter*, she enjoyed Justin's spellbound interest as they neared the end of the chapter.

"'Stephen Armstrong watched as the sun's burning rays slanted over the temple ruins. According to the ancient scroll, at precisely three hours after midday, a telltale animal shadow would reveal the entrance to the treasure cave. As the minutes passed but slowly, the shape of a crocodile gradually appeared on one of the embedded stone slabs. Directly beneath Ste-phen Armstrong's feet, the treasure he had been seek-ing half his life lay in a deep, dark cavern.'" Phoebe closed the book, smiling at Justin's groan of protest. "Next chapter tomorrow," she said.

"More now?" Justin asked hopefully. "Please?"

"I'm afraid it's too late." Phoebe glanced at West, who was half reclining in the corner of the settee with Stephen against his chest. The two of them appeared to be slumbering soundly, with one of the toddler's chubby arms loosely clasped around West's neck.

Justin followed her gaze. "I think you should marry Uncle West," he commented, startling her.

Her voice came out breathless. "Why do you say that, darling?"

"Then you would always have someone to dance with. A lady can't dance by herself or she would fall over."

Out of the periphery of her vision, she saw West stretching and stirring. Holding Justin closely, she smoothed his dark hair and kissed his head. "Some gentlemen prefer not to marry."

"You should use some of Granny's perfume," Justin said.

Phoebe suppressed a laugh as she looked into his earnest face. "Justin, don't you like the way I smell?"

"Oh, I do, Mama, but Granny always smells like cake. If you smelled like cake, Uncle West would want to marry you."

Torn between amusement and dismay, Phoebe didn't dare look at West. "I'll consider your advice, dear." She gently eased Justin from her lap and stood.

West yawned audibly and sat up. Stephen was limp and heavy on his shoulder, still sleeping soundly.

Phoebe smiled and reached for the baby. "I'll take him." Carefully she gathered the toddler close and safe against her. "Come, Justin, let's go upstairs to bed."

The boy climbed off the settee and went to West, who was still sitting. "Good night," Justin said cheerfully, and leaned forward to kiss his cheek. It was the first time he'd ever made such a gesture toward West, who held very still and didn't seem to know how to respond.

Phoebe carried Stephen to the doorway but paused

as West stood and reached her at the threshold in a few long strides.

He spoke in her ear, too softly to be overheard. "It would be better if we stayed in our own beds tonight. We both need rest."

She absorbed that with a quick double blink, a chill running down her spine. Something was wrong. She had to find out what it was.

Chapter 30

LONG AFTER THE CHILDREN had been tucked into bed, Phoebe sat in her room with her knees drawn up and her arms wrapped around them. She argued silently with herself. Perhaps she should do as West had asked, and not go to the cottage. He was right, they both needed rest. But she wouldn't be able to sleep, nor did she think he would.

How quiet it was, this late at night. No movement anywhere, except for the anxious staccato of her own heart.

That odd, blank look on his face . . . What emotions had it concealed? What was he struggling with?

Abruptly she came to a decision. She would go to him but make no demands. She only wanted to know if he was all right.

She tied a heavy dressing robe over her nightgown, and nudged her feet into leather slippers.

Soon she was hurrying across the stretch of damp lawn between the winter garden and the guest cottage. The night air was cool, the ground alive with shadows and quiet blue shocks of moonlight. By the time she reached the cottage, she was breathing fast from anxiety and haste, and her slippers were sodden. *Don't let him be angry that I'm here,* she thought, her fingers trembling as she tapped softly on the door and let herself in.

It was dark in the cottage, except for thin silver gleams of moonlight stealing between curtains. Was West already sleeping? She would not wake him. Turning back to the door, she reached for the handle.

A gasp was torn from her throat as she became aware of movement behind her in the shadows. The door was firmly closed by a pair of large masculine hands. She froze in place with West's arms braced on either side of her. Warm breath fanned against the nape of her neck, rustling tiny wisps of hair. She dampened her dry lips. "I'm sorry if I—"

His fingers touched her mouth gently, silencing her. He wasn't interested in talking.

His hands reached around her to unfasten her robe, and he tossed it aside. She stepped out of her slippers, relieved to be rid of the clammy leather. As she began to turn toward him, he grasped her hipbones and compelled her to continue facing the door. His body pressed against hers long enough for her to realize he was naked and aroused.

He unbuttoned the nightgown from her throat to her navel, and let it whisper over her skin to the floor. Wordlessly he began to arrange her body, pushing her palms against the door. One of his bare feet came between hers, and he used his thigh to spread her legs until she stood in an exposed posture, her torso inclined forward. Remaining behind her, he let his hands slide over her body, cupping her breasts, catching the tips in gentle pinches and lightly swaying their weights. He stroked her hips, waist, bottom, one hand sliding between her thighs from the front and one from the back.

She made an agitated sound, quivering, as he opened and caressed her, fingering the soft outer lips, tugging at the inner ones, running his fingertips through moisture. She felt the cool air against the wetness of her sex, and the warmth of his fingers as he pressed the tender hood back from the stiffening bud. He teased and played slowly until her legs strained and she was weak with desire. Breathing fast, she leaned her weight more heavily on her hands, wishing desperately that he would take her to bed.

But he stepped closer to her, his hands adjusting the angle of her pelvis, and she let out a little sob of surprise as she felt him begin to enter her. He worked carefully inside her swollen depths, opening her with gradual advances and retreats. The hard shaft circled inside her, the sensation so good that her knees threatened to buckle. She heard his quiet huff of laughter, and he gripped her hipbones more firmly. When he was fully seated in her, he leaned over her and whispered, "Brace your legs."

"I can't," she whimpered. All her bones seemed to have softened into isinglass, and her muscles were trembling. The only strength she had left was deep in the core of her body, where she couldn't help clamping and kneading the rigid invasion.

"You're not even trying," he accused tenderly, his mouth curving against the back of her shoulder.

Somehow she willed enough strength back into her knees to satisfy him, and she moaned as he began to thrust more powerfully and deeply than ever before. Each inward drive was a sensuous jolt, lifting her heels from the floor. She breathed and sweated and pushed back at him, the feelings rising thickly to a crescendo. The repeated wet impacts of their flesh embarrassed and excited her, and there was nothing she could do about any of it; she had lost all hope of control. One of his hands slid to the triangle between her thighs, caressing her pulsing flesh, while the other went to her breast and clamped the nipple gently between his thumb and finger.

That was all she needed. She pressed her clenched fists against the door and cried out repeatedly, in ecstasy that sounded like anguish. Satisfaction rushed and ebbed, back and forth, in heavy waves that soon broke into shudders. She really couldn't stand then, her limbs quaking, and he picked her up and carried her into the bedroom.

Before her body had even settled completely on the bed, he was in her again, thrusting almost savagely, reaching beneath her hips to pull her up into each plunge. Still oversensitive from climax, she writhed uncomfortably at first, but soon the push-and-pull rhythm felt good, and then it turned into something she wanted, craved, had to have. She squirmed, her body taking him deeply, arching in counterpoint. The rhythm changed, his hips rolling against hers, and the awareness that he was about to climax sent her into another rush of spasms. He was going to withdraw just at the moment she wanted him to thrust even harder and deeper. Without thinking, she locked her legs around him.

"Don't pull out," she whispered, "not yet, not yet—"

"Phoebe, no, I have to, I'm going to—"

"Come inside me. I want you to. I want you—"

His hips froze, suspended in an agony of temptation. Somehow he withdrew in time, burying a vicious cry in the bed linens as his body jerked in release.

Panting and shivering, he rolled away from her. He sat at the edge of the bed, gripping his head in his hands.

"I'm sorry," Phoebe said sheepishly.

"I know." His voice was a scrape of sound. Then he was silent for a long minute.

Concerned, she moved to sit beside him, one of her hands resting on his thigh. "What's the matter?"

"I can't do this anymore," he said bleakly, keeping his face averted. "I thought I could, but it's going to kill me."

"What can I do?" she asked softly. "What do you want?"

"I have to leave tomorrow. For my own sanity, I can't stay with you any longer."

Chapter 31

ONE WEEK AFTER WEST had left the Clare estate, Edward Larson returned from Italy.

Phoebe had done her best to carry on as usual, maintaining a falsely cheerful façade for the children's sake and going through the motions of everyday life. She was good at that. She knew how to endure loss and had learned that it wouldn't break her. No matter how miserable she felt inside, she couldn't let herself go to pieces. There were too many responsibilities to face, especially those involving Edward and the fraud he'd committed as executor of the estate. Although she dreaded having to confront him, it was a relief when he finally came to Clare Manor.

As soon as Edward entered the parlor, Phoebe saw that he knew trouble had been brewing. Despite his smile and obvious affection, his face was strained and his gaze was sharp.

"*Ciao, mia cara,*" he exclaimed, and came forward to kiss her, the firm, dry pressure of his lips making something inside her cringe and recoil.

"Edward, you look well," Phoebe said, gesturing for him to sit with her. "Italy must have agreed with you."

"Italy was a marvel, as always. Georgiana is quite happily settled, and I will relate all the particulars of her situation. But first . . . I've been made aware of some concerning news, my dear, with some rather serious consequences on the horizon."

"Yes," Phoebe said gravely. "So have I."

"Rumors are flying about a houseguest you entertained during my absence. You are so charitable and generous in the way you treat other people that you doubtless expect them to treat you the same way. However, society—even out here in the country—is not half so kind as you." The touch of paternal beneficence in his tone irritated her.

"Mr. Ravenel came to stay for a few days," Phoebe acknowledged. "Our families are connected by marriage, and I requested his advice about the estate."

"That was a mistake. I don't wish to frighten you, Phoebe, but it was a grave mistake indeed. He is the worst kind of scoundrel. Any association with him is poisonous."

Phoebe took a calming breath. "I do not require a lecture on propriety, Edward." *Especially not from you*, she thought.

"His reputation is tarnished beyond redemption. He is a drunkard. A profligate."

"You know nothing about who he is," Phoebe said with a touch of weary exasperation, "or what he's made of himself. Let's not discuss him, Edward, there's something far more important for us to deal with."

"I saw him at a soirée once. His behavior was indecent. Staggering about drunkenly, fondling and flirting with married women. Insulting everyone around him. A more vulgar, sneering display I have never witnessed. The host and hostess were humiliated. Several guests, including myself, left the soirée early because of him."

"Edward, enough about this. He's gone now, and it's over. Please listen to me—"

"He may be gone, but the damage has been done. You are too naïve to understand, my innocent Phoebe, what jeopardy you've put yourself in by allowing him to stay here. People will have already begun to repeat the worst interpretations of the situation." He took her stiff hands in his. "You and I will have to marry without delay."

"Edward."

"It's the only way to contain the damage before you're ruined."

"*Edward*," she said sharply. "I know about Ruth Parris and little Henry."

His complexion turned bleach white as he looked at her.

"I know about the house," Phoebe continued, gently drawing her hands from his, "and how you used funds from the loan company to pay for it."

His eyes were dilated with the horror of someone whose darkest secret had been exposed, his protective veneer shattered. "How . . . who told you? Ravenel has something to do with this, doesn't he? He's trying to poison you against me. He wants you for himself!"

"This has nothing to do with Mr. Ravenel," she exclaimed. "This is about you and your . . . I don't know what to call her. Your mistress."

He shook his head helplessly, standing up from the settee and pacing in a tight circle. "If you only knew more about men, and the ways of the world. I will try to explain in a way you can understand."

She frowned, remaining seated as she watched his nervous movements. "I understand that you borrowed money on behalf of my son's estate to set up a young woman in a household."

"It wasn't stealing. I intended to pay back the funds."

Phoebe gave him a reproachful glance. "Unless you married me, in which case the money would have become yours anyway."

"You're insulting my character," he said, pain contorting his face. "You'll try to make me out to be a villain on the level of West Ravenel."

"Were you ever going to tell me, Edward, or did you plan to maintain Ruth Parris and her child in that house indefinitely?"

"I don't know what I planned."

"Did you consider marrying Ruth?"

"Never," he said without hesitation.

"But why not?"

"She would be the ruin of my future prospects. My father might disinherit me. I would be a laughingstock, marrying someone so lowborn. She has no education. No manners."

"Those things can be acquired."

"Nothing can change what Ruth is: an honest, sweet,

simple girl who is utterly wrong as a wife for a man of my position. She'll never be a society hostess, nor will she ever be capable of making clever conversation or telling the difference between the salad fork and the fish fork. She would be made miserable by requirements she could never satisfy. Any concern for her is unwarranted. I made no promises, and she loves me too well to make a wreck of my life."

"But what have you made of hers?" Phoebe demanded, outraged on the girl's behalf.

"Ruth is the one who insisted on keeping the child. She could have given him to someone else to raise and gone on with her life as before. All the choices that led to her current predicament were made by her—including the choice to lie with a man outside of marriage in the first place."

Phoebe's eyes widened. "Then the blame is all hers, and none of yours?"

"The risk of an affair is always greater for the woman. She understood that."

Could this really be the Edward she had known for so many years? Where was the highly moral, considerate man who had always shown such indelible respect for women? Had he changed somehow without her notice, or had this always been mortared in among the layers of his character?

"I genuinely loved her," he went on, "and in fact I still do. If it makes you feel any better, I'm deeply ashamed of my feelings for her, and of whatever coarseness in my nature led to a relationship with her. I'm suffering as much as anyone."

"Love is not born of coarseness," Phoebe said quietly. "The ability to love is the noblest quality a man can possess. You should honor it, Edward. Marry her and be happy with her and your son. The only thing to be ashamed of is the belief that she's not good enough for you. I hope you'll overcome it."

He seemed painfully bewildered as well as angry. "One cannot overcome facts, Phoebe! She is common. She would lower me. That opinion would be shared by everyone in our world. Everyone who matters would censure me. There would be so many places we wouldn't be welcomed, and blue-blooded children who wouldn't be allowed to associate with mine. Surely you understand that." His voice turned vehement. "God knows Henry did."

Now it was Phoebe's turn to fall silent. "He knew about Ruth? And her baby?"

"Yes, I told him. He forgave me before I could even ask. He knew it was the way of the world, that honorable men sometimes yield to temptation. He understood it had no bearing on my character, and he still thought it best for you and I to marry."

"And what was to become of Ruth and her child? What were his thoughts about that?"

"He knew I would do what I could for them." Edward returned to the place beside her, reaching out to cover her hands with his. "I know my own heart, Phoebe, and I know I'm a good man. I would be a faithful husband to you. I would be kind to your boys. You've never heard me raise my voice in anger, have you? You've never seen me inebriated or violent. We would have a clean, sweet, good life together. The kind of life we deserve. I love so many things about you, Phoebe. Your grace and beauty. Your devotion to Henry. It agonized him that he wouldn't be able to take care of you, but I swore to him I would never let harm come to you. I told him he would never have to worry about his children, either: I would raise them as if they were mine."

Phoebe tugged her hands away, her skin crawling at his touch. "I can't help but find it ironic that you're so willing to be a father to my sons, but not your own."

"Henry wanted us to be together."

"Edward, even before I knew about Ruth Parris and the loan money, I had already decided—"

"You must overlook her," he interrupted desperately, "just as I will overlook any indiscretions on your part. It can all be forgotten. I'll perform any penance you ask, but we *will* put this behind us. I'll have the boy sent abroad and raised there. We'll never see him. He'll be better off that way, and so will we."

"*No*, Edward. No one would be better off. You're not thinking clearly."

"Neither are you," he retorted.

Perhaps he was right: thoughts were colliding in her head. She didn't know whether to believe him about Henry. She had known Henry so well, his sweetness and forbearing, his concern for others. But he had also been a man of his class, raised to respect the boundaries between high and low, with a full understanding of the consequences should the order of things be disrupted. Had Henry really given his blessing to a future union between his cousin and wife, in full knowledge of poor Ruth Parris and her chance-born child?

Then, almost magically, the turmoil and distress subsided, and everything became clear.

She had loved and respected her husband and had always heeded his opinions. But from now on, she would trust her own sense of right and wrong. The sin was not love, but the lack of it. The thing to fear was not scandal, but the betrayal of one's own morality.

"You and I are not going to marry, Edward," she said, actually feeling a bit sorry for him, when he was so obviously making ruinous choices for himself. "There will be much for us to discuss in the coming days, including a tangle of legal matters. I want you to resign the executorship of the will, and step aside as trustee of the estate—and I beg you not to make the process difficult. For now, I would like you to leave."

He seemed aghast. "You're being irrational. You're going against what Henry wanted. I will take no action until you've calmed down."

"I'm perfectly calm. Do as you see fit. I'm going to seek the counsel of solicitors." She softened as she saw how distraught he was. "I'll always be fond of you, Edward. Nothing will erase all the kindness you've shown me in the past. I would never be vindictive, but I want any legal association between us terminated."

"I can't lose you," he said desperately. "My God, what is happening? Why can't you see reason?" He stared at her as if she were a stranger. "Were you intimate with Ravenel? Did he seduce you? Force you?"

Phoebe let out a short sigh of exasperation and left the settee, striding rapidly to the threshold. "Please leave, Edward."

"Something has happened to you. You're not yourself."

"Do you think so?" she asked. "Then you've never known me at all. I am wholly myself—and I will never marry a man who would want me to be any less than I am."

Chapter 32

"GOOD GOD, RAVENEL," TOM SEVERIN commented as West entered his carriage and took the seat opposite him. "I've seen better groomed whorehouse rats."

West responded with a surly glance. In the week since he'd left the Clare estate, primping and self-grooming had not been a high priority. He had shaved recently—a day or two ago—maybe three—and he was more or less clean, and his clothes were good quality even if they hadn't been pressed or starched. His shoes could use some polishing, and yes, his breath was a bit rank, as one would expect after days of drinking too much and eating too little. Admittedly, he wasn't a fashion plate.

West had been staying at the terrace apartment he'd maintained even after having taken up residence in Hampshire. Although he could have made use of Ravenel House, the family's London home, he'd always preferred to maintain his privacy. A cookmaid came once or twice a week to clean. She had been there yesterday, wrinkling her nose as she'd gone from room to room, picking up empty bottles and dirty glasses. She'd refused to leave until West had eaten part of a sandwich and some pickled carrot slices in front of her, and she had scowled when he'd insisted on washing it down with some fettled porter.

"You've a thirsty soul, Mr. Ravenel," she'd said darkly. He could have sworn she'd poured out the rest of the porter before she'd left—surely he couldn't have downed all of it in one afternoon. But maybe he had. It all felt wretchedly familiar, this churning in his gut, this endless poisonous craving that nothing would satisfy. As if he could drown in a lake of gin and still want more.

He'd been in reasonably good condition, that morning he'd left the Clare estate. He'd breakfasted with Phoebe and the children, smiling at the sight of Stephen's small hands grasping bits of fried bacon and mashing buttered toast into shapeless wads. Justin had asked more than once when he would return, and West had found himself responding in the way he'd always hated as a child when adults would say, *"Someday,"* or *"We'll see,"* or *"When the time is right."* Which everyone, even a child, knew meant *"No."*

Phoebe, damn her, had behaved in the cruelest way possible, by being calm and gentle and understanding. It would have been so much easier for him if she'd pouted or been spiteful.

She'd kissed him good-bye at the front door before he'd gone to the train station . . . clasping one side of his face with a slender hand, her soft mouth brushing his cheek, her fragrance sweet in his nostrils. He'd closed his eyes, feeling as if he were surrounded by flower petals.

And then she'd let him go.

It was at the station that the bad feeling had overcome him, a mixture of grayness, exhaustion, and powerful thirst. He'd planned to buy a ticket for Eversby Priory, and had instead found himself asking for Waterloo Station, with the vague intention of stopping in London for a night. That stop-over had turned into two days, then three, and then somehow he'd lost the wherewithal to make any decisions about anything. Something was wrong with him. He didn't want to go back to Hampshire. He didn't want to be anywhere.

It was as if he'd been taken over by some outside force that now controlled everything he did. Like demonic possession—he'd read about the condition in which one or more evil spirits would enter a man's body and take away his will. But in his case, there was no speaking in tongues, lunatic ravings, or doing violence to himself or others. If he was unwittingly hosting demons, they were very sad, lethargic ones who wanted him to take long naps.

Of all the people he knew in London, the only one West found himself reaching out to for companionship was Tom Severin. He hadn't wanted to be alone this evening, but he hadn't wanted to spend time with someone like Winterborne or Ransom, who would ask questions and offer unwanted opinions, and try to push him into doing something he didn't want to do. He wanted to keep company with a friend who didn't care about him or his problems. Conveniently, that was exactly what Severin wanted, and so they had agreed to meet for an evening of drinking and carousing in London.

"Let's stop off at my house first," Severin suggested, eyeing his scuffed shoes with disfavor, "and my valet can do something to spruce you up."

"I look well enough for our usual haunts," West said, staring at the passing scenery as the carriage lurched and rolled through the streets. "If you're too fastidious for me, let me out at the next corner."

"No, never mind. But we're not going to the usual places tonight. We're going to Jenner's."

West jerked at the name and stared at him incredulously. The very last place in London he wanted to go was the gentlemen's club owned by Phoebe's father. "The hell you say. Stop the bloody carriage, I'm getting out."

"What do you care where you do your drinking, so long as someone keeps pouring? Come, Ravenel, I don't want to go alone."

"Why do you assume they'll let you past the front door?"

"That's just it: I've been on the membership waiting list for five years, and last week I was finally allowed in. I thought I was going to have to have someone killed to clear a space, but thankfully some old codger passed away and spared me the trouble."

"Congratulations," West said acidly. "But I can't go in there. I don't want to risk crossing paths with Kingston. He visits now and then to keep his thumb on the business, and it would be my bloody luck for him to be there tonight."

Severin's eyes were bright with interest. "Why do you want to avoid him? What did you do?"

"It's nothing I'd care to discuss while sober."

"Onward, then. We'll find a quiet corner and I'll purchase the best liquor in the house—it will be worth it for a good story."

"In light of past experience," West said sourly, "I know better than to confide anything personal to you."

"You will anyway. People always tell me things, even knowing they shouldn't. I'm sure I don't know why."

To West's chagrin, Severin was right. Once they were settled in one of the club rooms at Jenner's, he found himself telling Severin far more than he'd intended. He blamed the surroundings. These rooms had been designed for comfort, with deep leather, button-back Chesterfield couches and chairs, tables laden with crystal decanters and glasses, crisply ironed newspapers and bronze cigar stands. The low, box-paneled ceilings and the thick Persian carpeting served to muffle noise and encourage private conversation. The main hall and the hazard room were more obviously extravagant, almost theatrical, with enough gold ornamentation to make a baroque church blush. They were places to socialize, gamble, and amuse oneself. In these rooms, however, powerful men conducted business and politics, sometimes altering the course of the Empire in ways the public would never know.

As they talked, West reflected privately that he knew exactly why people confided in Tom Severin, who

354 Lisa Kleypas

never muddled an issue with moralizing or judgments, and never tried to change your opinions or talk you out of wanting something. Severin was never shocked by anything. And although he could be frequently disloyal or dishonorable, he was never dishonest.

"I'll tell you what your problem is," Severin eventually said. "It's feelings."

West paused with a crystal glass of brandy close to his lips. "Do you mean that unlike you, I have them?"

"I have feelings too, but I never let them turn into obstacles. If I were in your situation, for example, I would marry the woman I wanted and not worry about what was best for her. And if the children you raise turn out badly, that's their business, isn't it? They'll decide for themselves whether or not they want to be good. Personally, I've always seen more advantage in being bad. Everyone knows the meek won't really inherit the earth. That's why I don't hire meek people."

"I hope you're never going to be a father," West said sincerely.

"Oh, I will," Severin said. "I have to leave my fortune to someone, after all. I'd rather it be my own offspring—it's the next best thing to leaving it to myself."

As Severin spoke, West noticed out of the periphery of his vision that someone walking through the club rooms had paused to stare in his direction. The man approached the table slowly. Setting down his glass, West gave him a cool, appraising glance.

A stranger. Young, well-dressed, pale and visibly

sweaty, as if he'd endured some great shock and needed a drink. West would have been tempted to pour him one, if not for the fact that he'd just pulled a small revolver from his pocket and was pointing it in West's direction. The nose of the short barrel was shaking.

Commotion erupted all around them as patrons became aware of the drawn pistol. Tables and chairs were vacated, and shouts could be heard among the growing uproar.

"You self-serving bastard," the stranger said unsteadily.

"That could be either of us," Severin remarked with a slight frown, setting down his drink. "Which one of us do you want to shoot?"

The man didn't seem to hear the question, his attention focused only on West. "You turned her against me, you lying, manipulative *snake*."

"It's you, apparently," Severin said to West. "Who is he? Did you sleep with his wife?"

"I don't know," West said sullenly, knowing he should be frightened of an unhinged man aiming a pistol at him. But it took too much energy to care. "You forgot to cock the hammer," he told the man, who immediately pulled it back.

"Don't encourage him, Ravenel," Severin said. "We don't know how good a shot he is. He might hit me by mistake." He left his chair and began to approach the man, who stood a few feet away. "Who are you?" he asked. When there was no reply, he persisted, "Pardon? Your name, please?"

"Edward Larson," the young man snapped. "Stay back. If I'm to be hanged for shooting one of you, I'll have nothing to lose by shooting both of you."

West stared at him intently. The devil knew how Larson had found him there, but clearly he was in a state. Probably in worse condition than anyone in the club except for West. He was clean-cut, boyishly handsome, and looked like he was probably very nice when he wasn't half-crazed. There could be no doubt as to what had made him so wretched—he knew his wrongdoings had been exposed, and that he'd lost any hope of a future with Phoebe. Poor bastard.

Picking up his glass, West muttered, "Go on and shoot."

Severin continued speaking to the distraught man. "My good fellow, no one could blame you for wanting to shoot Ravenel. Even I, his best friend, have been tempted to put an end to him on a multitude of occasions."

"You're not my best friend," West said, after taking a swallow of brandy. "You're not even my third best friend."

"However," Severin continued, his gaze trained on Larson's gleaming face, "the momentary satisfaction of killing a Ravenel—although considerable—wouldn't be worth prison and public hanging. It's far better to let him live and watch him suffer. Look how miserable he is right now. Doesn't that make you feel better about your own circumstances? I know it does me."

"Stop talking," Larson snapped.

As Severin had intended, Larson was distracted long enough for another man to come up behind him unnoticed. In a deft and well-practiced move, the man smoothly hooked an arm around Larson's neck, grasped his wrist, and pushed the hand with the gun toward the floor.

Even before West had a good look at the newcomer's face, he recognized the smooth, dry voice with its cut-crystal tones, so elegantly commanding it could have belonged to the devil himself. "Finger off the trigger, Larson. *Now.*"

It was Sebastian, the Duke of Kingston . . . Phoebe's father.

West lowered his forehead to the table and rested it there, while his inner demons all hastened to inform him they really would have preferred the bullet.

Chapter 33

WEST REMAINED SEATED AS night porters, table waiters and club members milled around the table. He felt trapped, and surrounded, and very alone. Severin, who liked nothing better than to be in a place where interesting things were happening, was having a grand time. He regarded Kingston with a touch of awe, which was understandable. The duke looked thoroughly at home in this legendary place, even a bit godlike, with that inhumanly perfect face and beautifully tailored clothes and that stunning self-possession.

Keeping hold of Larson as if he were a disobedient puppy, Kingston berated him quietly. "After the hours I just spent with you, providing excellent advice, *this* is the result? You decide to start shooting guests in my club? You, my boy, have been a dismal waste of an evening. Now you're going to cool your heels in a jail cell, and I'll decide in the morning what's to be done with you." He released Larson to the care of one of the hulking night porters, who ushered him away expediently. Turning to West, the duke surveyed him with a quicksilver glance, and shook his head. "You look as though you've been pulled backward through a hedgerow. Have you no standards, coming to my club dressed like that? For the wrinkles in your coat alone, I ought to have you thrown into a cell next to Larson's."

"I tried to have him spruced up," Severin volunteered, "but he wouldn't."

"A bit late for sprucing," Kingston commented, still looking at West. "At this point I would recommend fumigation." He turned to another night porter. "Escort Mr. Ravenel up to my private apartments, where it seems I'll be giving counsel to yet another of my daughter's tormented suitors. This must be a penance for my misspent youth."

"I don't want your counsel," West snapped.

"Then you should have gone to someone else's club."

West sent an accusing glare at Severin, who shrugged slightly.

Struggling up from his chair, West growled, "I'm leaving. And if anyone tries to stop me, I'll knock them flat."

Kingston seemed rather less than impressed. "Ravenel, I'm sure when you're sober, well-rested and well-nourished, you can give a good account of yourself. At the moment, however, you are none of those things. I have a dozen night porters working here tonight, all of whom have been trained in how to manage unruly patrons. Go upstairs, my lad. You could do worse than spend a few minutes basking in the sunshine of my accumulated wisdom." Stepping closer to the porter, the duke gave him a number of quiet instructions, one of them sounding suspiciously like, "Make sure he's clean before he's allowed on the furniture."

West decided to go with the porter, who identified himself as Niall. There wasn't really a choice, and he couldn't come up with an alternate plan. He felt slightly weak and foggy, and his head was filled with an on-and-off rushing noise, like the blasts of air that swept a train platform when a train was hurtling past. God, he was tired. He wouldn't mind listening to a long lecture from the duke, or anyone, as long as he could do it while sitting.

As they all began to leave the club room, Severin appeared somewhat forlorn. "What about me?" he asked. "Is everyone just going to leave me here?"

The duke turned to him, arching a brow. "It would seem so. Is there anything you need?"

Severin pondered the question with a frown. "No," he finally said, and heaved a sigh. "I have everything in the world."

West lifted his hand in a gesture of farewell and followed Niall. The porter was dressed in a uniform, some kind of rich matte cloth in a shade of blue so dark it looked black. No gilt or fancy trim, save for a thin, black, braided trim on the lapels of the coat, and on the collar and cuffs of the white shirt. Very discreet and simple, tailored for ease of movement. It looked like a uniform for killing people.

They went through an inconspicuous doorway and up a narrow, dark staircase. Niall opened a door at the top, and they went through some ornately decorated vestibule with a ceiling of painted angels and clouds. Another door opened into a set of beautiful serene rooms, gold and white, with pale blue water-silk paper on the walls, and carpets in soft, subdued colors.

West went to the nearest chair and sat heavily. The upholstery was soft and velvety. It was so quiet up here—how could it be this quiet with the clamor of nighttime London just outside the window, and a damned club downstairs?

Wordlessly Niall brought him a glass of water, which West didn't want at first. After he took a sip, however, a voracious thirst overcame him, and he gulped it down without stopping. Niall took the glass, went to refill it, and came back with a small powder packet. "Bicarbonate compound, sir?"

"Why not?" West muttered. He unfolded the packet, tilted his head back to dump the powder on the back of his tongue, and washed it down.

As he lifted his head, he saw a painting on the wall, in a carved and gilded frame. It was a luminous portrait of the Duchess with her children when they were still young. The group was arranged on the settee, with Ivo, still an infant, on his mother's lap. Gabriel, Raphael and Seraphina were seated on either side of her, while Phoebe leaned over the back of the settee. Her face was close to her mother's, her expression tender and slightly mischievous, as if she were about to tell her a secret or make her laugh. He had seen that look on her face, with her own children. And with him.

The longer West stared at the painting, the worse

he felt inside, inner demons jabbing at his heart with spears. He wanted to leave, yet he was no more capable of exiting that chair than if he'd been chained to it.

The duke's lean form came to the doorway, and he regarded West speculatively.

"Why was Larson here?" West asked hoarsely. "How is Phoebe?"

That caused Kingston's face to soften with something that resembled sympathy. "My daughter is well. Larson took it upon himself to come here in a panic and try to enlist my support in persuading Phoebe to marry him. He tried to present his situation in the best possible light, presuming I would be willing to overlook his relationship with Miss Parris because of my own profligate past. Needless to say, he was disappointed by my reaction."

"You'll be able to help Phoebe remove him as trustee?"

"Oh, without question. Breach of fiduciary duty by a trustee is a serious offense. I've never liked Larson's involvement in Phoebe's personal life or financial affairs, but I've held back to avoid accusations of meddling. Now that there's an opportunity, I'll meddle as much as possible before I'm put back on the leash."

West's haunted gaze returned to Phoebe's figure in the portrait. "I don't deserve her," he mumbled, without intending to.

"Of course you don't. Neither do I deserve my wife. It's an unfair fact of life that the worst men end up with the best women." Taking in the sight of West's drawn face and slouched figure, the duke seemed to come to a decision. "Nothing I say to you is going to sink in tonight. I won't send you out in this condition—there's no telling what trouble you'd find yourself in. You'll stay the night in this guest room, and we'll talk in the morning."

"No. I'm going back to my own apartment."

"Splendid. What, may I ask, is waiting for you there?"

"My clothes. A bottle of brandy. Half a jar of pickled carrots."

Kingston smiled. "I'd say you're sufficiently pickled already. Stay the night, Ravenel. I'll send Niall and my valet to draw a bath and set out some amenities for you—including a large quantity of soap."

WEST AWAKENED THE next day with only blurry recollections of the night before. He lifted his head from a soft goose down pillow and blinked at his luxurious surroundings in bewilderment. He was in a plush, remarkably comfortable bed with soft white linen sheets and fluffy blankets topped by a silk counterpane. Dimly he recalled the bath last night and staggering to bed with the help of Niall and the elderly valet.

After a good long stretch, he sat up and looked around the room for his clothes. All he could find was a gentleman's robe, draped over a nearby chair. He felt more rested than he had in a week, which was not to say that he felt well, or anything close to happy. But everything didn't look quite so gray. He put on the

Lisa Kleypas

robe and went to ring the service bell, and the valet appeared with startling promptness.

"Good afternoon, Mr. Ravenel."

"Afternoon?"

"Yes, sir. It's three o'clock."

West was astounded. "I slept until three o'clock in the afternoon?"

"You were somewhat the worse for wear, sir."

"Apparently so." Rubbing his face with both hands, West asked, "Would you bring my clothes? And coffee?"

"Yes, sir. May I also bring hot water and shaving supplies?"

"No, I don't have time for a shave. I have to go to . . . a place. To do things. Quite soon."

To West's dismay, Kingston came to the doorway just in time to overhear that last part. "Trying to dash off?" he asked pleasantly. "I'm afraid that jar of pickled carrots will have to wait, Ravenel. I intend to have a chat with you." He glanced at the elderly valet. "Bring the shaving supplies, Culpepper, and see to it that Mr. Ravenel has a hot meal. Send for me when he's fed and presentable."

For the next hour and a half, West submitted to a barrage of scrubbing, filing, trimming and clipping. On top of that, he was in enough of a fatalistic and dismal mood to actually let Culpepper shave him. Fine, let the old cheeser slit his throat, he didn't give a damn. It wasn't a pleasant process—his stomach was clenched, and he was twitchy with nerves the entire time. But the knotty, loose-skinned hands were amazingly steady,

the strokes of the razor light and skillful. By the time
Culpepper had finished, the shave was even closer than
the one Phoebe had given him. Although in a contest
between the two, the view down Phoebe's chemise still
put her far ahead.

His clothes had been miraculously washed, dried
and pressed, and his shoes cleaned and shined. After dressing, West sat down at a small table in an ad-
joining room, where he was served coffee with heavy
cream and a plate of coddled eggs and a thin, tender undercut of beef sirloin that had been fried on a
gridiron and dressed with salt and chopped parsley.
At first the very idea of chewing and swallowing revolted him. But he took a bite, and another, and then
his digestive system began to hum in gratitude, and he
consumed it all with indecent haste.

Near the end of the meal, Kingston came to join
him. Coffee was set at his place, and West's cup was
replenished.

"Still not back to form," the duke said, looking over
him critically, "but better."

"Sir," West began, and had to stop as the muscles
of his throat tightened. *Damn it.* He couldn't talk with
this man about anything personal. He would break.
He was as fragile as a blown glass bubble. He cleared
his throat twice before he could continue. "I think I
know what you want to discuss, and I can't."

"Excellent. I'd already planned to do most of the talking. I'll go to the point: I give my blessing to a marriage
between you and my daughter. Now, you will undoubt-

edly point out that you haven't asked for it, which will prompt me to ask why. Then you'll relate a few stories from your unsavory past and go through some tedious self-flagellation to make me aware of your unworthiness as a potential husband and father." The duke took a sip of coffee before adding, "I will not be impressed."

"You won't?" West asked warily.

"I've done worse things than you could imagine, and no, I'm not going to share any of my secrets as a sop to your conscience. However, I'll assure you from personal experience that a ruined reputation can be regilded, and gaseous society gossips will eventually seek new material with which to inflate themselves."

"That's not my worst concern." West rubbed the pad of his thumb across the dull edge of a butter knife, back and forth. He forced himself to go on. "I'll always have to wonder when my inner demons will lash out and drag anyone who loves me down to whatever circle happens to be propping up hell."

"Most men have inner demons," Kingston replied quietly. "God knows I do. So does a friend who's the finest and most genuinely moral man I've ever known."

"How do you get rid of them?"

"You don't. You learn to manage them."

"What if I can't?"

"Let's not go in circles, Ravenel. You're not perfect—we're both in agreement on that. But I've seen and heard enough to be assured you'll provide the kind of companionship my daughter wants and needs. You won't seclude her from the outer world. She and

Henry lived in that damned Greek temple on a hill like deities on Mount Olympus, breathing only rarefied air. You'll be the kind of father those boys need. You'll prepare them for a changing world and teach them empathy for the people who live on their land." His intent gaze met West's. "I understand you, Ravenel. I've been in your shoes. You're afraid, but you're not a coward. Stand up to this. Stop running. Go take up this matter with my daughter. If the two of you can't come to some satisfactory conclusion on your own, I'm sure you don't deserve to marry."

There was a discreet knock at the door.

"Come in," the duke said, the silvered locks at his temples glinting in the light as he turned his head.

A footman opened the door. "Your Grace," he said, and gave a decisive nod toward the window.

The duke rose from his chair and went to the window, glancing down at the street. "Ah. What perfect timing." He glanced back at the footman. "Proceed."

"Yes, Your Grace."

West was too consumed by his thoughts to pay attention to the exchange. In his life, he'd had more than his share of lectures, some brutal enough to leave permanent gouges in his soul. But no man had ever spoken to him quite like this—wry, honest, direct, bracing, and a bit high-handed in a way that felt oddly reassuring. Fatherly. Admittedly, the suggestion of cowardice had rankled, but West couldn't deny that Kingston was right—it was fear. He was afraid of too many damned things.

But the list was a bit shorter now. Shaving had just been crossed off. That proved something, didn't it?

Kingston had gone to the partially open door. He was speaking to someone on the other side of the threshold.

A muffled female voice, just the tone of it, awakened West's nerves like a handful of lucifer matches all lit at once. He stood so quickly, he nearly knocked the chair backward. As he moved closer to the door, his heart started beating fast and hard.

". . . brought the children," she was saying. "They're downstairs with Nanny."

Kingston laughed quietly. "Your mother will have a fit of temper when I tell her I had them all to myself here, while she was at Heron's Point." Becoming aware of West's approach, he stepped back and opened the door a bit wider.

Phoebe.

Joy filled West in a violent rush. Thunderstruck by the force of his feelings, he could only stare at her. In that moment, he knew that no matter what happened from then on, no matter what he had to do, he would never be able to leave her again.

"Father sent for me this morning," Phoebe said breathlessly. "I had to hurry to catch the train in time."

Clumsily West took a step back as she entered the room.

"I've done my part," the duke said. "Now I suppose I'll have to leave it to you two."

"Thank you, Father," Phoebe replied wryly. "We'll try to manage without you."

Kingston left, closing the door behind him.

West stayed exactly where he was as Phoebe turned to face him. Holy hell, it felt good to be near her. "I've been thinking," he said huskily.

A tremulous smile curved her lips. "About what?"

"Trust. When I told you I couldn't count on some-one loving me . . ."

"Yes, I remember."

"I realized that before I can have trust . . . actually feel it . . . I'll have to start doing it. Trusting blindly. I'll have to learn how. It's . . . difficult."

Her beautiful eyes shimmered. "I know, darling," she whispered.

"But if I'm ever going to try it with anyone, it has to be you."

Phoebe inched closer to him. Her eyes were so bright, they were like bottled lightning. "I've been thinking, too."

"About?"

"About surprises. You see, there was no way of knowing how much time Henry and I would have together before his decline started. As it turned out, it was even less time than we'd expected. But it was worth it. I would do it again. I wasn't afraid of his illness, and I'm not afraid of your past, or whatever might leap out at us. That's the chance everyone takes, isn't it? The only ironclad guarantee is that we'll love each other." Her voice thickened with emotion. "And I do, West. I love you so very much."

West's heart was thundering now, his entire life poised on the brink. "There is one problem," he said hoarsely. "I once promised never to propose to you. But I never said I wouldn't accept a proposal. I'm begging you, Phoebe . . . ask me. Because I love you and your children more than my heart can bear. Ask me as a mercy, because I can't live without you."

Her smile was blinding as she drew closer. "West Ravenel, will you marry me?"

"Oh, God, yes." He pulled her into his arms and kissed her passionately, too hard for pleasure, but she didn't seem to mind at all.

Now their story would begin, their futures instantly rewritten. Two futures joined into one. Light seemed to shimmer all around them, or perhaps that was just the effect of tears in his eyes. This, West thought in wonder, was far too great a portion of happiness for one man.

"Are you sure?" he asked in between kisses. "Somewhere out there, the perfect man you deserve is probably searching for you."

Phoebe laughed against his mouth. "Let's hurry, then—we can be married before he gets here."

Author's Note

THE PHRASE "GOD SPEED the plow" started in the 1400s. It relies on the original Middle English meaning of the word "speed": prosperity and success. Plowmen used to sing a song of this title on Plow Monday, the first Monday after Twelfth Night, when all the plowmen would go back to work hoping for a successful season.

According to the Oxford English Dictionary, the origin of using *x*'s in letters to represent kisses dates back to a letter written by British curate and naturalist Gilbert White in 1763. However, Stephen Goranson, a highly respected researcher and language specialist at Duke University, says the *x*'s in Gilbert White's letter were intended to mean blessings. Goranson found citations of the *definite* use of *x*'s as kisses from 1890 onward, including a letter from Winston Churchill to his mother in 1894: "Please excuse bad writing as I am in an awful hurry. (Many kisses.) xxx WSC."

As part of my research, I watched (along with my husband, Greg, who's a history buff) the BBC's British historical documentary *Victorian Farm* and the followup *Victorian Farm Christmas*. We were enthralled! The show recreates everyday life on a mid-1800s Shropshire farm by sending a team of three people—historian Ruth Goodman and archaeologists Alex Langlands and Peter Ginn—to live and work there for a year. We found it on YouTube—watch it, and you'll love it!

Thank you for your kindness and enthusiasm, my wonderful readers! I love sharing my work with you, and I'm grateful every day that you make it possible.

—L.K.

*West Ravenel's
Favorite Purée of Spring
Vegetable Soup*

THIS RECIPE, BASED ON many similar Victorian ones, is one we've used often. Not only is it easy, delicious and nourishing, it also makes use of those "odds and ends" vegetables that sometimes lurk forlornly in the refrigerator drawer. You can substitute or add any vegetables you like, including cabbage, cauliflower, parsnips, etc. Just add more broth if you need to make it more liquid for easy blending. Although the recipe calls for dried herbs, always use fresh if you have them. I like to use thyme and oregano, but any herbs you like will work beautifully.

Ingredients

   1 large (or two small) zucchinis
   1 large (or two small) yellow summer squash
   2 regular carrots, or a couple of handfuls of baby carrots

1 red or yellow bell pepper
2 tablespoons butter (or olive oil)
1 teaspoon minced garlic
1 yellow onion, chopped
1 quart chicken or vegetable broth
$1/4$ cup tomato paste
1 14-ounce can white beans, rinsed and drained
1 teaspoon salt
1 teaspoon ground black pepper
1 teaspoon dried thyme
1 teaspoon dried oregano
$1/2$ cup heavy cream or half-and-half

Directions

1. Chop vegetables into half-inch pieces. Don't worry about being terribly precise, since they're going to be blended, but you do want them to cook evenly.
2. Melt the butter in a large pot on medium high heat. Add the garlic, onion and other chopped vegetables and sauté for 10 to 15 minutes.
3. Add broth, tomato paste, beans, seasonings and herbs. Bring to a boil, then turn down to a simmer and cook for at least a half hour, or until everything is super tender and can be pierced easily with a fork.
4. Either blend with a hand immersion blender or a regular stand blender. If you use a regular blender, which is what I use, make sure to do it in batches—don't overfill!

   5.   Add the cream or half-and-half at the end, and add more salt and/or pepper if needed.

Serve with buttered croutons if desired, or if you want a really hearty meal, have it with a grilled cheese sandwich.

Do you love historical fiction?

Want the chance to hear news about your favourite
authors (and the chance to win free books)?

Mary Balogh
Lenora Bell
Charlotte Betts
Jessica Blair
Frances Brody
Grace Burrowes
Gaelen Foley
Pamela Hart
Elizabeth Hoyt
Eloisa James
Lisa Kleypas
Stephanie Laurens
Sarah MacLean
Amanda Quick
Julia Quinn

Then visit the Piatkus website
www.piatkusentice.co.uk

And follow us on Facebook and Twitter
www.facebook.com/piatkusfiction | @piatkusentice

piatkus